THE IRISH DEVIL

THE IRISH DEVIL

DIANE WHITESIDE

BRAVA

KENSINGTON PUBLISHING CORP.
http://www.kensingtonbooks.com

*My great-great grandparents, Thomas and Julia Graham,
left Waterford, Ireland, to help build America's
transcontinental railroad. When they finished,
they used their savings to buy a cotton plantation in
Alabama, where they founded a dynasty.
This book is dedicated to their memory and
to everyone else who ever crossed an ocean to
become Americans.*

Chapter One

William jolted awake as an orgasm roared through him. He rode it out, grinding his hips into the mattress as the pillow muffled his groans.

When the storm finally passed, he cautiously turned his head to one side and tried to catch his breath, still lying on his stomach. What in the name of Joseph, Mary, and all the saints had caused a wet dream like that?

The bedding was fine and the mattress soft so he was in a house, not sleeping under one of his wagons. Two women snored nearby, raising the question of how long they'd slept.

William warily opened his eyes. A hand-stitched motto greeted him, proclaiming the virtues of hard work. The flocked burgundy velvet wallpaper behind it told him he was in Rio Piedras's only parlor house, the most luxurious place a man could find willing women to slake his lust in this remote Arizona mining town.

William stretched, remembering more now. He'd come to Carrie Smith's establishment after ten days on the trail, eaten well, and accepted Pearl once again as his companion. Bloody hell, he'd even taken Fannie upstairs, too, just so he'd be sexually exhausted before he walked Rio Piedras's streets in daylight.

What the devil had he dreamed about?

Shrugging off the question, William slipped out of bed

stealthily and turned to check Pearl. She slept on undisturbed, her breath fluttering the embroidered pillowcase's hem. He cleaned up quickly and pulled on his clothes, mildly regretful that neither woman woke. He loved the smug sway of a woman's hips as she walked beside him, every step shouting, "I'm a beautiful woman who just had the best time of my life."

He slipped his family dirk up his sleeve, then quickly buckled on the weapons belt with his trusty bullwhip and Colt, a necessity in this rough mining town.

Still older habits made him check the walls one last time for peepholes. Carrie Smith was too good a businesswoman to anger a steady customer by exhibiting him to all comers. Even so, wariness learned first in a poorhouse and reinforced on Cobh's back alleys dictated caution.

He replaced the tin of condoms in his jacket pocket, always used whenever he rode a woman's pussy. Last night they'd protected him from the French disease and accusations of fatherhood. Paternity was an unlikely reproach, given he hadn't climaxed inside a woman's core since he'd first seen Viola Ross.

William cursed silently as he waited for his cock's usual reaction to any thought of her. Only a sluggish twitch in response, rather than the usual rapid lunge. He relaxed slightly; perhaps two women had been a good idea after all.

He tipped Pearl in the usual fashion after a dalliance with her and another girl: two gold coins beside her head and the same sum under the pillow. The other girl would know only of the monies in plain sight, the same way she'd be paid.

Pearl's brown lashes flickered and rose slowly. He straightened up and waited politely.

"Is it morning already?" She yawned and smiled at him.

"An hour past dawn," he answered as her fingers closed over the gold shining against the bed linen.

"You're a late riser today. Care to try another round? Cheaper when you stay two nights in a row," she invited, stretching languidly so her breasts came free of the sheet in a movement designed to distract him. She walked her fingers up his arm as her other hand delved under the pillow.

He shrugged, well aware of exactly what she was hunting for. "You must be tired after last night. Better if you rest before you leave town."

"I got plenty of time," she murmured, letting her palm glide down his torso. "And you were so fine, buckin' and poundin' like that. A girl could enjoy more rides on equipment like yours."

He caught her wrist well before she reached his fly. "Thank you but no."

She sighed. "Unusual to see you lose control in a bedroom. You're usually more commandin' than that, tellin' a girl what to do or drivin' her crazy with your mouth and hands 'til she'll do things she never thought possible."

"Pearl," he began.

"Oh, I like both sides of you, Donovan! Just would have enjoyed a longer acquaintance with the ragin' stud."

He stopped her chatter with a quick light kiss and a coin in her palm, only to have her start again when he moved away.

"You interested in Fannie, Donovan? Maybe another round of the three of us?"

"No."

Pearl raised an eyebrow at his tone and shrugged. "Not surprisin'. You like your women passionate and she wants her own parlor house more than she wants any man."

"Really? Then this should be a suitable farewell token." He set two gold coins beside Fannie where she slept on the daybed, still sprawled as her climax had left her.

"Good luck, Pearl." He paused to kiss her forehead as he left.

"Good-bye, Donovan," she whispered as the door closed.

He made for the stairs, both women forgotten before he took the first tread, while he considered the night's true surprise.

What the devil had he dreamed of? His oldest dream perhaps, a faerie queen spun of moonbeams and night, lithe and
strong and quick-witted . . . and so beautiful that an Irish lad
would count himself blessed to steal a single kiss from her
rosy lips? But no dream of that lady had ever shaken him so
deeply as last night's fancy.

He was still pondering the question when he reached Main
Street and a flash of silver-gilt caught his eye. He froze and
stared. Viola Ross was coming up the hill from the hut she
shared with Maggie Watson. Morgan had said she'd gone
into business with Maggie after Ross's death, but he hadn't
reminded William of her heart-stopping beauty.

Walking was too mundane a word for how she moved. She
glided like a faerie maiden, as if her feet and skirts floated
free of earth's heavy tug. She held her head high with a
queen's poise and balanced a heavy laundry basket on her
shoulder as if carrying it was a royal prerogative. A few
strands of silver-gilt hair escaped her faded blue sunbonnet. If
she came closer, he'd once again see eyes like the true blue of
spring's first bluebells, an indigo not yet purple. And hear a
voice whose faint huskiness only enhanced an aristocratic
clarity of speech.

The West offered a hard life to men and a harder one to
women with its unforgiving climate, continuous danger from
Indians, and isolation. It took a strong woman to survive it
and William readily honored those who did. Viola Ross had
done more than just survive in her five years on the frontier:
she'd founded and run a small business after her husband's
murder. All in all, she had a great deal of sand, as his teamsters would say.

A small girl ran out to her and she stooped quickly to answer. William sucked in his breath, immediately reminded of
how he'd first seen her almost a year ago. While peacefully
watering his horse Saladin, he'd heard shrieks of delight and
peeked through the cottonwoods to see the cause.

He'd discovered Viola splashing in the stream with two

small children. She'd been soaked to the skin, so wet the thin calico dress had clung to her womanly form, outlining her boldly upthrust breasts and nipples begging for a man's mouth. She had a waist so small he could wrap his hands around it, and hips made for cradling him when he settled into those dark shadows between her thighs. Her beauty was as clear to his enraptured eyes as if she'd slowly shed her clothes for him in a boudoir.

But she'd cared nothing for society's conventions as she enjoyed the children's company. Rather than shriek in horror or try to conceal herself, she'd laughed heartily as she chased the two imps. She'd been a faerie maiden come to life, who could captivate even a stream's guardian spirit.

Long minutes had passed before he'd been able to move away. He'd asked who she was, of course, hoping against hope she was unmarried and Irish. But no, her husband, the lucky fool, had been pointed out, as he staggered from a saloon.

Now William's cock swelled as strongly against his trousers' denim as it had for her the first time. He cursed vehemently and spun on his heel. He'd take another route to his compound and avoid seeing her again, the image of everything he hungered for and had always been rejected by.

Hell, he didn't have to dodge her for long. Once she married Lennox, she'd be gone in a New York minute, back to the high society that had formed her and barred him from being anything more than a well-trained servant. He needed to stop thinking about unattainable women and find himself a respectable Irish girl to marry, someone who'd tend his house and bear his children. And likely never wonder where his deepest desires were.

A half dozen strides down the boardwalk, his inner voice finally answered part of his earlier question. Last night's fantasy had involved the faerie queen; he'd dropped out of a tree and tangled her securely in his net. An old dream. So what in hell made this one so bloody strong?

His inner voice smirked and refused to answer, simply retreated into silence. Still cursing silently, William stomped down the street, eager to reassert control over his world.

Viola set little Jenny Browning down and watched her scamper back to her mother. She bent and picked up the laundry basket again, unconsciously balancing the weight as she had thousands of times during the past six months. The only difference today was she'd be delivering laundry to Mrs. Smith alone, rather than with Maggie.

They'd originally agreed it was best to do so together, rather than set tongues gossiping about two respectable widows entering the most infamous house of prostitution in Rio Piedras. But Mrs. Smith paid top dollar for fine laundry, providing the few profits that could pay off their inherited debts rather than just keep them alive.

Viola frowned slightly as she shifted the basket, careful not to snag her threadbare dress. Maggie had asked for privacy to bid farewell to her Colorado suitor, so Viola was delivering laundry alone. She shouldn't even take the time to enjoy any gossip as she did so, unlike her usual practice.

She reminded herself that Maggie had enough agony to bear on this mid-April day in 1871, the anniversary of her baby son's death. The usual rituals of death, like a visit to the cemetery or a walk to the chapel, could wait until later when Maggie was more composed. Perhaps then she'd be less angry and more inclined to remember her lost child.

Flinching from the thought of children, Viola forced her mind to other things, such as the possibility of a large tip and how it'd help remove their debts. If she worked hard enough and Rio Piedras's silver mines didn't play out too soon, she'd be able to pay off Edward's gambling losses and leave for San Francisco in another six years. And if she were truly lucky, she'd have enough money for a piano and could give lessons. Decades of listening to little girls massacre Beethoven sounded like heaven after a year in Rio Piedras.

Maggie had inherited fewer debts from her husband to worry about: she needed less than two years to become independent.

So Viola continued up the hill, easily carrying the heavy basket on her shoulder, as she whistled the "Minute Waltz." Her faded blue calico dress and sunbonnet were as immaculate as she could make them, silent advertisements of her skills as a laundress. Her pale hair was tidily pinned up under her bonnet, while her dress fitted her neatly from shoulders to waist in witness to Maggie's dressmaking talents. She lacked only her beloved brooch, left behind in Maggie's care, since the dress's calico was no longer strong enough to support the heavy gold.

Hopefully, she looked strong and capable, despite less than two hours of sleep the night before.

She moved quickly past the saloons and gambling halls Edward had once frequented in his endless search for luck and gold. On the streets behind them stood the brothels and cribs, where the middle and lower ranks of prostitutes labored.

She automatically averted her eyes from the Oriental Saloon, the most exclusive of all. Edward's one visit there had left him victim of a stab wound to the heart, a murder witnessed by no one who'd talk. The few coins in his pocket hadn't begun to pay off his mountainous debts.

"Good morning, Mr. Johnson." She nodded a polite response to Ted Johnson's tipped hat and was secretly glad that he didn't try to strike up a conversation. He hadn't asked her to marry him in the last two months but that didn't mean he wouldn't do so again, given a chance; nearly every other unmarried man who passed through Rio Piedras had. Amazing how many offers a girl could get from a man desperate for a home-cooked meal, however poorly prepared.

Now humming a sentimental Stephen Foster tune, she cautiously opened Mrs. Smith's back gate, watching for the guard dog. Jake bounded up to her silently and promptly sat at her feet, his beloved red ball in his mouth. Viola grinned and set the basket down, pleased that Jake was in the mood for play. That was much more enjoyable than facing his typical greeting to trespassers, which sent most of them screaming for the gate.

He dropped the ball into her outstretched hand and watched her eagerly. A few feinted tosses didn't fool him. Finally she threw it neatly between the outhouse and the garden shed. Jake barked happily and raced off in pursuit.

Viola grinned as she watched, remembering how her brother had taught her to play fetch with his dog, Horace. Her smile faded as she remembered the last time she'd seen Horace, the dreadful night when Hal ran away.

She returned to the business that had brought her here.

She quietly took the steps up to the back door of Mrs. Smith's immaculately painted house, easing the basket off her shoulder as she stepped onto the porch. Its cool quiet enfolded her as her mouth watered at the smells drifting outside. Her stomach grumbled once but thankfully stayed otherwise quiet.

Viola's head came up as women's voices reached her from the kitchen, hidden behind crisp gingham curtains unlike the heavy velvet drapes in the rest of the house. Eavesdropping was improper, of course, but it would be interesting to hear what Mrs. Smith's girls said when they thought no one else was around.

"So when do you think she'll wake up?" a girl asked.

"Put a dollar on six o'clock, Sally," Mrs. Smith's cook drawled, "and you should win the pool."

Viola bit her lip at the sum, which probably meant little to the women inside.

"Sleep fourteen or sixteen hours? After sharing one man with another girl? Not a chance," Sally objected.

"Ever spend a night with Donovan? No? Pearl often sleeps 'til midnight the next day. And no tellin' how long Fannie'll sleep. She ain't used to the likes of him," Lily Mae chuckled, her Texas drawl deepening and thickening.

William Donovan? Were they talking about the same man who owned Donovan & Sons, named for heirs he didn't have yet? The big freighting house that hauled supplies into Rio Piedras, coming through no matter what depredations the Apaches wreaked?

He had the heart-stopping masculine beauty of a Renaissance angel with his brilliant blue eyes, raven hair, and clean-shaven face, unusual among so many men who grew whiskers for fashion or convenience. Those attractions were combined with more than six feet of lean strength that could shred a rattler with his whip for threatening a child—after which he'd coax the little one into peals of laughter.

But beauty and money couldn't make a woman sleep for nearly a full day. So he must have some talents in the bedroom that brought sweet pleasure and ease to his partner.

Viola pondered what those skills could possibly be and came up blank. Edward had been drunk when they'd married and he'd consumed still more whisky after the ceremony. The wedding night hadn't occurred for another three days and had been marked by Edward's grunting, plus a great deal of blood on the sheets. She'd heard hints that some men did more during carnal encounters, but neither gossip nor her own imagination could account for Lily Mae's rich purr.

Perhaps he gave good massages. She smothered a chuckle at the ridiculous notion of a subservient William Donovan, humbly asking if madame would care for a little more attention to her knotted shoulders.

"Maybe you're right. I'll put a dollar on six o'clock," Sally said grudgingly.

Twelve hours or more after the man left? Viola's fingers had played pleasant games under the covers before sleeping. But she'd never overslept afterwards. She lifted her hand to knock but froze when Sally spoke again.

"Still, I don't know why he's never chosen me," Sally whined.

Lily Mae snorted rudely. "Honey, you lap up liquor like a fired cowhand. Donovan won't have anyone who indulges."

"Why, that's plumb crazy! Everyone drinks, gin or whisky or laudanum or—"

"He don't and he won't dally with those what do," Lily Mae said flatly. "If he's in town, Pearl's sober as a corpse 'til she's sure who's warmin' his bed."

If William Donovan only touched women who stayed sober then he couldn't have many liaisons, especially with so few women of easy virtue in this little town.

"Is that how she does it?" Sally mused.

"Yup. Donovan comes here four, maybe five times a week when he's in town."

Five times a week? Mother had compared men to volcanoes, prone to explode into orgies of adultery, rape, and physical violence. Or even homosexual embraces, unless granted regular sexual congress. But five times a week was more than Vesuvian; it was as impossible to imagine as washing laundry while staying totally dry. Still, Viola's ears stayed pricked for more gossip.

" 'Most always, she's the only girl who's sober. An' he's a damn fine tipper."

"How much?" Sally demanded, avarice sharpening her voice.

"Ten dollars a night, maybe more, 'sides what he pays Mrs. Smith. Depends on what he has in mind."

"Heard tell he has some strange ways . . ." Sally's voice trailed off, inviting confidences.

"He can be mighty odd. Likes to wear them French letters when he's ridin' a woman. Still, it's easy 'nough for Pearl to forgive him."

What on earth was a French letter? A piece of stationery wrapped around his privates? No, it couldn't be that; paper wouldn't last two seconds after a man started grunting and shoving, although a letter might provide something else for the woman to think about.

"For ten bucks, he could dress up as a Red Indian," Sally snorted.

"And Pearl always says a night with him is fine as dollar cotton." The purr was back in Lily Mae's voice. Viola shifted uncomfortably at the sound. The images it evoked caught her breath and sent a wet heat prowling through her core. Did Pearl truly find such frequent masculine attentions enjoyable, instead of boring?

Sally whistled. "Maybe I should take up temperance then."

Lily Mae snickered. "When pigs fly!"

Viola yanked her wits back from contemplating how much money William Donovan spent at Mrs. Smith's, how fast the same sum would release her to a new life—and just what he did with those girls in private.

She knocked loudly and waited. Inside Lily Mae and Sally fell silent before Lily Mae's ponderous steps sounded. She opened the door, her crisp white apron and scarlet turban as pristine as ever, and smiled at Viola. "Good morning, Mrs. Ross. Please come in."

"Thank you, Lily Mae," Viola accepted and stepped inside. The kitchen was brilliantly white with sun streaming in through the gingham curtains and across the embroidered tablecloth. It was a big kitchen with an immense iron stove, suitable for cooking the fanciest meal or feeding Mrs. Smith's half dozen "young ladies" every day.

Blond Sally smiled at Viola from the table, her flowered silk robes drooping over her plump body. A bruise was barely visible on the inside of one breast. She tightened the robe's sash and poured more coffee into her cup, masking the smell of whisky.

"Good morning, Sally." Viola nodded politely, settled the basket more comfortably on her hip, and turned back to Lily Mae.

"How's Mrs. Watson this morning?" Lily Mae asked.

"Saying good-bye to Mr. Jones. He leaves for Colorado today in that big wagon train Reverend Chambers is leading," Viola answered, keeping her eyes averted from the baker's rack and its burden of fresh-baked pies. At least one of them had to be apple and another one smelled like a chess pie, her childhood favorite. "I was able to remove the wine stain from the French corset," she remarked to stop herself from drooling.

"Splendid." Lily Mae beamed, her dusky face splitting into a grin. "Mrs. Smith will be mighty happy that she won't have to replace one of them fancy rigs. Just put that big basket down on that table over yonder."

Viola obeyed, trying not to sniff the mouth-watering aroma of biscuits and red-eye gravy from the stove. She turned around only to have Lily Mae place a cup in her hand.

"Have some coffee while I fetch last night's laundry."

"Thank you." Viola accepted it gratefully but stiffened when Lily Mae held out a scone. She'd never stooped to accepting charity and wouldn't start now.

"And tell me what you think of these fancy biscuits. I'm playing with candied ginger to match the raisins."

Viola hesitated. "Thank you, but I'm not hungry." Her stomach betrayed her with a growl. She flushed but kept her head high, daring anyone to say something about it.

Lily Mae smiled at her and put the plate directly into Viola's hand. "I'd sure appreciate your thoughts. It's a new recipe and I want to make sure they're suitable for fine company. Now you just sit down right here."

"Thank you." Viola accepted the face-saving excuse and joined Sally. She bit into the scone slowly, savoring its buttery richness as she tried not to gulp.

"You sure look all combed and curried in that blue dress, Mrs. Ross," Lily Mae offered as she returned with a basket of laundry and a small pouch of coins.

Yes, it almost gives me some curves. Viola's mouth twitched but she answered simply, "Thank you. Mrs. Watson took it in for me and wanted me to wear it this morning, given the fine weather."

"Any new proposals lately? I had two last night," asked Sally, one of the most notorious gossips in town. Word had it that she could retell any fight at any saloon before the sheriff managed to arrive.

"Six early last week, all from newcomers, and none since. Perhaps word is finally getting around that I won't remarry." The scone was really quite good.

"Or that you're still waitin' for mournin' to end so's you can wed the right fellow," Lily Mae drawled, adding a generous splash of cream to her coffee as she settled down at the sunny table.

"That's ridiculous! It's been six months since Mr. Ross died. Even my grandmother would have ended full mourning by now," Viola protested.

The other women shared a look before Lily Mae spoke in an altogether different tone. "Mighty powerful, mighty respectable man's been putting it about. Says you'll marry him when the time is right."

Viola's eyes narrowed. "Mr. Lennox is saying that?"

Sally nodded vehemently while Lily Mae answered, "Yes, ma'am. Been very insistent about it, too."

"So much so, other men don't question him," Viola said slowly.

Thunder crashed in her memory. It had been a dark night, some six months ago, lit only by lightning bolts from the coming storm. She'd been walking home from Maggie's hut and spotted Lennox washing in the water trough beside the livery stable. She shivered, remembering how he'd scrubbed at the dark stains on his white shirt, his face cold and intent in a flash of green light. She'd doubled back to avoid him, taking another route to her home.

"If Lennox crows, then it's daylight in Rio Piedras," Lily Mae said softly.

Viola's eyes flashed up and met Lily Mae's. She swallowed at the bitter knowledge and understanding there.

A deep breath brought enough composure to voice her decision. "It doesn't matter what the men here say or do, since I won't marry any of them. I've refused Paul Lennox two dozen times and I'll refuse him two hundred times more."

She took a swallow of coffee and concentrated on the scone. It tasted like dust now.

"Sure? Maybe you'll meet a man who's too good to refuse," suggested Sally.

Viola swirled her coffee for a moment before answering, watching the fine grounds chase each other on the surface. "I'll not marry any man in Rio Piedras, especially not one as consumed with gold fever as Paul Lennox."

"Not all men are like that," Sally protested.

"Name me one man in this town who doesn't see women as something to make hunting gold or silver easier," Viola flung back.

Sally opened her mouth, but closed it when Lily Mae lifted an eyebrow. Silence grew and stretched around the sunny room.

" 'Nother biscuit, Mrs. Ross?" Sally asked, her tone shifting the gathering into a ladies' tea rather than a bitter recital of men's shortcomings. "Would you believe Pearl actually asked to take the recipe with her when she leaves tomorrow?"

Viola fed the last crumbs of her scone to Jake as she left. Lily Mae's baking was excellent but this particular example hadn't regained its original attraction.

She weighed the pouch in her hand thoughtfully before slipping it into her pocket. It was heavier than the promised one dollar tip—perhaps it was two dollars? She sent up a quick prayer of thanks: now she could pay for groceries. And she'd give a few pennies to Padre Francisco, the only remaining man of God here, to help with his stray animals.

She danced a little quickstep of delight as she went down the stairs into the yard.

Sally's voice reached Viola just as she opened the gate. "Maybe if I only drank two glasses of wine, Donovan would choose me."

Lily Mae's laughter rang out and Viola closed the gate firmly, lifting the basket to her shoulder. Surely the two women were stretching the truth for their own amusement. Everything she knew from marriage said no one man's attentions could leave one woman, let alone two, sleeping for half a day. But five times a week did sound rather intriguing.

One last question teased her mind as she walked off, idly whistling a Mozart minuet. Could a woman have lusts as strong as a man's?

Chapter Two

William's razor moved smoothly over his cheek in the familiar ritual, a welcome relief after his rude awakening. Shaving always comforted him as it evoked memories of his family. His father had taught him the art in a shanty beside the Cobh of Cork, where hot water meant the room was warm enough for his father's work as a forger.

He'd removed all traces of his native Gaelic as a teenager, thus eliminating the easiest target of anti-Irish prejudice. He'd gained first an upper-crust English accent then a western drawl, both fluent enough to gain immediate acceptance. But he still remembered his origins every time he laid a razor against his cheek.

Abraham Chang waited behind him with a white towel draped over his arm, tall for a Chinese but just as impassive as folklore dictated for his race. He'd changed little in the fifteen years they'd known each other. The biggest differences now were the houseman's somber black suit and neatly trimmed hair he sported, in lieu of the tong enforcer's brilliant silks and long queue.

The familiar ritual soothed William until he slipped back into last night's dream. The faerie queen had featured in his earliest fantasies, always a nymph-like woman with blue eyes and moonbeam hair. His mouth quirked slightly as he recalled some of those dreams, in which an uncommonly brave and strong lad had found the lovely lady at his mercy in either an ancient oak forest or on a grassy knoll. This latest episode had been set amidst the woods wherein he'd captured her, thus setting her at his mercy.

He smiled slightly and tilted his head back to catch the underside of his jaw. Suddenly the dream's ending flashed back as he rhythmically scraped bristles.

His cock delved deep and hard and fast, urged on by her body's rhythmic pulses as she arched ecstatically under him. She cried out, her sweet curves half hidden beneath his net, as her climax tightened her around him. Her head flung back and her blue eyes, now almost purple with passion, flew open. They matched the pure indigo of a crocus flower, the color of the twilight sky above a mountain range.

Viola Ross lay under him, shuddering in pleasure from his attentions.

Fingers suddenly locked around his wrist like an iron vise. Abraham's eyes met his in the mirror for a moment, both pairs wide with shock as crimson welled up over the sharp blade and ran down William's throat. After a long moment, William carefully shifted the razor away from his skin until he could take first one free breath, then another.

Abraham released his hand and began to smoothly mop up the blood, face impassive once more.

He would have cut his own throat, if not for Abraham's speedy reaction.

But sweet singing Jesus, carnal relations with Viola?

William peeled out of his once white undervest, moving in short jerks. A dream of Viola Ross, by all the saints. A fancy less likely to come true could hardly be imagined. He wrenched his mind back to reality.

"Thank you for saving my life." His voice rasped against the stillness.

"An honor, sir, to repay at least part of the debt I owe." Abraham bowed deeply and William nodded, unwilling to start the old argument.

A silent but more watchful Abraham produced another undervest. William accepted it but refused the proffered crisp white summer shirt. "Red flannel, Abraham. We're loading Army wagons today."

"Excellent choice, sir."

William raised an eyebrow and Abraham elaborated.

"Red is the color of prosperity, good fortune, and wealth in my country."

"A noble sentiment, Abraham. But I'll wear it to remind myself of who I truly am: teamster, wagonmaster, and child of Ireland." And he'd continue to maintain his distance from aristocratic women who kept even their hems away from poor Irish lads.

"It takes a wise man to know himself so well," Abraham murmured. William chose to accept the phrase as a proverb, not a compliment.

He finally finished dressing, careful to keep his mind away from vagrant fantasies. Fortified by one of Sarah Chang's excellent omelets and eager for the distraction of hard work, he headed for his freight depot.

He passed a few blocks of shops, most with a warning sign in their windows: "Irish Need Not Apply." His mouth tightened briefly at the familiar sight. Even in this isolated town, where most of the miners were Irish, they still weren't welcome to hold jobs in more settled firms, such as a general store or bank.

Just before reaching the depot, a buckboard wagon rolled past, carrying a man and woman. The man lifted his hat to William, whose senses immediately came to full alert. Charlie Jones and Maggie Watson sat side by side, heading out of town.

Why wasn't Viola Ross chaperoning Maggie Watson, given Maggie's insistence on following all of society's rules?

"Good morning, Jones. Mrs. Watson," William greeted them.

The two nodded back, Jones beaming at him while Maggie

bobbed her head. "Good morning, Mr. Donovan," she trilled in her usual fluttery style.

"Hoped we'd see you, Donovan, so I could share the good news," Jones boomed. "Maggie became my wife this morning."

"Congratulations, Mr. and Mrs. Jones. Good fortune to both of you," William returned. What the devil was going on here? It was damned early in the day for a wedding. And why was Viola Ross delivering laundry, rather than celebrating with them? "May I ask who your supporters were at the happy occasion, that I might lift a glass with them? Mrs. Ross, perhaps?"

Maggie blinked rapidly and began to stutter. Jones spoke up quickly, his eyes sliding away from William's.

"Oh, no, no, Mrs. Ross went out on some business. We're traveling with Reverend Chambers's wagon train as far as Tucson, so we couldn't wait for her return. Can't waste time sitting around when there's Apaches to dodge."

William considered Maggie's nervousness and the strangely empty buckboard. Was it her usual discomfort around Irishmen or something else? The wagon was only lightly loaded, not what he'd expect of a woman who co-owned a small business.

"Do you need help shipping Mrs. Jones's belongings to Colorado?" William probed. "I could send one of my men over to pack them up."

"No, no!" Jones objected, glaring like a barnyard cat surrounded by hungry dogs. "Sold everything this morning so she'd have a fresh start. Washtub, washboard, all of it. A mouse wouldn't find anything at that hut."

"What about Mrs. Ross's belongings?" William demanded, going icy cold at the image. "Shouldn't they be guarded until she returns?"

Jones shifted slightly on the wagon seat in a move that could free up his gun. It also sent the old prefight stillness over William, who was well aware any of his weapons could kill Jones before the other's gun cleared leather. Maggie glanced apprehensively from one man to the other and finally uttered a coherent sentence.

"There's nothing left, Mr. Donovan. It took everything I could find to pay off Mr. Watson's debts. Besides"—she began to stammer under William's glare—"Viola had sold so much when Mr. Ross died that there wasn't hardly anything left. And she's going to marry Mr. Lennox anyway, so it doesn't much matter, don't you agree?"

William took a step toward her but brought himself to an abrupt halt. Maggie shrank back against Jones, shaking.

"Don't you dare look at my wife that way," Jones blustered, openly reaching for his Colt.

William simply looked at the other man, whose fingers quickly returned to the reins. The Irishman smiled mirthlessly then stepped back from the wagon.

"You'd best be moving on then, Jones. Wouldn't want the little woman to come to any harm."

Jones started to lift the reins but William spoke again.

"Our current deal runs out in June. It won't be renewed."

"What! But you're the only freighter who'll haul ore from my mine, high up as it is."

William shrugged.

"I'll double your pay."

"There's plenty of money to be made elsewhere with honorable men." He ignored the ghosts warning of cruel hunger coming to anyone who refused a profit.

"He'll be ruined!" Maggie gasped.

"You should have considered that before you stole a good woman's life and business. Good day." He touched his fingers to his hat in a mocking salute and walked on to his freight depot, the one place he could be sure of controlling matters.

The big depot was full of his men preparing to send out the next wagon train of military supplies. Sentries patrolled the rooftops against an Apache attack, backed by others in the compound's watchtowers. Some men loaded barrels, while others tied down tarpaulins over heavily laden wagons. The activity spilled out from the depot's yard and corrals onto the flat desert, where the supply train would assemble.

Men cleaned and oiled the heavy chains that would link wheels together, thus forming the wagons into an almost unbreakable barricade against attack. Every man had a rifle close at hand, of course.

Hammering rose from the wheelwright's and blacksmith's shops. Both shops contained the special equipment needed for dealing with the sixteen-foot Murphy wagons, like the special forge and crane to handle the seven-foot iron wheels.

Chickens clucked happily in their crates as they devoured their morning's grain. Quiet reigned in a side yard behind rough mud-brick walls and a railed gate, where two men carefully unloaded barrels of gunpowder.

The corrals were full of mules, twelve to twenty for every tandem hitch of two or three big Murphy wagons. A few had drifted to the rails to watch the teamsters' bustling busyness, while the rest drowsed or enjoyed the morning's first alfalfa.

Soon enough, William was happily planning next week's wagon train for the new fort. He checked the animals first, accompanied by his foreman.

"Glad you arrived early," Morgan Evans observed as they headed into the barn and its reassuring bustle of stock being groomed and prepared for the trail. "We'll need you and all the firm's best men to see Fort McMillan equipped. Even if we work Sundays."

"Mostly luck," William disclaimed. "Smooth steamship voyage out of San Francisco, plus we didn't sight a single Apache between here and Fort Yuma."

Morgan snorted. "Or Cochise didn't want to take you on again. Good reputation to carry on that road."

William glanced at the notoriously calm younger man. An Apache ambush seldom caused more than a yawn from this aristocratic veteran of Forrest's cavalry. So what was Morgan truly worried about?

He paused to greet Saladin, his big gray stallion, who'd poked his head over his stall's door. He needed to hear more of what had happened since his last trip to Rio Piedras seven months ago. "Quiet in town lately?"

"Cave-in last month killed six men." Morgan fed a carrot to his steady Indian pony as William crooned endearments to the fastest horse in the territory. "Tregarron resigned and took the last Cornish miners with him."

"Bloody damn. Lack of shoring?" The stallion's ears flicked toward William. He nudged his human's shoulder in an unmistakable demand.

"How'd you guess?"

"Lennox hasn't been paying as much for inbound freight. Timber's the heaviest cargo, now the stamp mill's running." William began to feed Saladin a handful of peppermints.

"Cheap bastard." Morgan's three syllables were an indictment. "Most of the old miners are gone now. It's too dangerous to mine their own claims and they won't work for Lennox."

"Cochise that busy?"

"Very. Killed Claiborne last week, not two miles out of town on the old road." In silent accord, the two men moved to look at the horses outside.

"Young fool must have been looking for the German's buried gold," William observed, searching for Tennessee, his most experienced lead mule.

"Probably. But an Apache bullet's a quicker death than drowning in a flash flood, as Mueller did." Morgan slipped into the corral and carefully brought a big chestnut forward for inspection.

William grunted agreement then turned to more important matters. "Tenn's better than I'd hoped from your description but we can't use him for the next train. It'll be eight days, maybe nine, before he's up to another run. We could hitch Blackie with Waffles instead."

"Or use another pair as leaders for the ammunition wagon,"

Morgan offered in his soft Mississippi voice, bringing Tennessee
to a halt before William.

"Who'd you have in mind?" William asked, just as a horse
and buggy turned into the yard from the street. The fancy
buggy and high-stepping mare were as out of place in the
depot as a dowager's diamond necklace in a saloon. Lennox
must have brought a new toy from back East.

"I'll hitch them so you can see them work together. Lennox
will want to talk to you, now that you're here," Morgan murmured and faded away. He avoided contact with Lennox as
much as possible, as did most war veterans. William lifted an
eyebrow but said nothing as he turned to meet his caller.

Paul Lennox pulled the buggy to a stop before the depot's
office. He quickly looped the mare's reins over the rail as he
looked around for William. A keg of beans thudded to the
ground in the yard beyond, making his horse toss up her
head in alarm. Lennox paid no attention to her fretfulness as
he headed toward his quarry, twirling his ever present walking stick.

Rio Piedras must be more restless than Morgan had mentioned, if Lennox was wearing a gun belt. Extravagantly or-
namented and holding a pair of pearl-handled guns, it was
still worn with the casual ease of someone all too familiar
with its weight.

"Donovan," Lennox hailed jovially.

William kept a polite smile on his face. He knew far too
well about men like Lennox, who were happy to do business
with him but would cut him dead if they met him at a private
party. "Good morning, Lennox. Handsome rig you've got
there."

"Thank you! You're very kind to say so. It commemorates
my acceptance into Pericles," Lennox purred, visibly preening. "Really, the club's even more magnificent than I'd heard.
Too bad you'll never see it."

"Congratulations," William bit out. The most elite private
men's club in New York, the Pericles Club was where much

of New York's banking business actually occurred. He had as much chance of entering its halls as he did of walking on the moon.

"Secretary of War Belknap, a very agreeable fellow, presided over my initiation," Lennox continued.

The most notoriously corrupt man in Grant's administration? He probably had been accommodating to someone with Lennox's money and connections.

"I've always found him and his staff to be quite effective," William agreed. Especially after a few bribes exchanged hands.

Lennox beamed. "Four generations of my family have celebrated acceptance there with a splendid equipage, such as this horse and buggy. Nothing else in the territory quite as fine, don't you think? And it should look magnificent when Mrs. Ross rides in it to our wedding."

William's jaw tightened. Lennox wasn't worthy of kissing her boot, much less putting a ring on her finger. A long-winded former Union cavalryman and New York real estate mogul, he'd never set foot west of the Mississippi until a year ago. She'd refused offers from far better men, but perhaps now she'd want the future he offered, since Mrs. Watson had absconded with the laundry's last funds.

"It certainly should be very impressive. What can I do for you on this fine spring morning?" William's voice was silky smooth, a perfect camouflage for his seething emotions. He stepped up to the colonnade that ringed the yard, drawing Lennox after him.

"Just wanted to exchange greetings and chat about the latest affairs in town." Lennox followed William and accepted the mug that Abraham produced, some magic telling the houseman when coffee would soothe William's business contacts.

William nodded politely and cradled the heavy stoneware in both hands. "I trust matters have been going well for you."

"Well enough now. You heard about the cave-in?"

"My condolences," William began but Lennox kept talking.

"Dreadful event. We lost at least a week's production over that."

And you're mourning lost revenue, not dead men. Hopefully, you'll take the offer from those San Francisco bankers and sell out.

"I had to take over management myself, now that expensive fool Tregarron's gone."

William kept his face expressionless at this dismissal of a great mining engineer. The stamp mill echoing through the town was Tregarron's masterpiece, a mechanical contraption that had more than quadrupled the Golconda's output.

"He used to handle problems in town for me, as well as at the Golconda. Now you and I both understand the need for our men to blow off steam, kick up their heels in a fashion that saloonkeepers don't always appreciate," Lennox murmured.

William's mouth twitched unwillingly. Even his handpicked teamsters occasionally raised a ruckus in town, and Lennox owned all of Rio Piedras's saloons, the most obvious target for such high spirits. The two men's eyes met in perfect understanding.

Lennox went on with barely a break in his voice. "Tregarron regularly explained to the saloonkeepers how business really works in Rio Piedras and then matters would settle down, a task I now have to perform. So until the new manager arrives, please feel free to call upon me if I can be of assistance in ironing out difficulties with any of the local business establishments."

"Thank you. I appreciate your consideration."

"My pleasure. I'm also bringing my best men out from New York to help keep the town orderly. Some of the miners have been a bit stubborn, but Conall O'Flaherty and his brothers should soon set them straight."

"Thank you for the warning." A thug named Conall O'Flaherty? No, surely he couldn't be the same man. It was twenty-four years and a different continent since that meeting. "I'll pass it on to Evans and my men."

"I'm sure it won't be an issue but I did want you to know the name."

William nodded acknowledgment and took a deep drink of coffee. Old memories swirled behind his eyes: his mother's arms wrapped around her swollen belly, Maeve and Caitlin sobbing against her skirts. His nose bloody from a futile attack on the men as he struggled against his father's tight grip. Their few possessions settling into the muddy road as the land agent urged his oldest son to throw a torch into the cow byre . . .

"Enough of business," Lennox said jovially. "Let's discuss gentlemen's interests, like this little mare I bought for forty dollars. She was a famous racehorse in Kentucky, so she should win next month's big race in Tucson."

William looked at the blood bay more closely. Excellent lines, very fast but delicately built. She'd be better suited to the grass racetracks of Kentucky, or perhaps California, than the cactus-marked sand and rock of southern Arizona. "How long has she been here in the desert?"

"Just over four weeks."

"Hardly enough time to learn how to run amidst cactus," William pointed out, an edge creeping into his voice.

"Exactly! The odds will be against her and I'll make more money when she wins."

More likely she'd go lame or break a leg, William thought acidly, assuming she settled down enough to race. The little mare was sweating heavily now as she sidled away from bursts of activity in the yard. Her nostrils flared and her eyes rolled back until the whites showed when a barrel of coffee was tossed up to a wagon.

Lennox turned back toward William, ignoring the restless

horse. "Once my mare races Taylor's gelding and wins . . ." He stared significantly at William as if to force agreement.

He nodded a response but didn't commit himself to abstaining from the coming meet. Taylor's gelding could run circles around every other horse south of Globe except Saladin.

"Then I'll have more than enough money to build the finest hotel in the territory. Right there!"

Lennox flung out his arm to indicate the chosen hilltop just as idle chance quieted the depot for a moment. His coffee mug flew out of his hand and crashed against a chest waiting to be loaded. The mug's destruction echoed like gunfire. Pottery shards and coffee lanced the air and found his mare.

The blood bay reared and screamed, laying her ears back flat against her head. The reins snapped, setting her free to wreak havoc. Lennox's eyes measured the distance from her to the gunpowder. He reached for his gun.

William dropped his mug and ran toward her.

The little mare kicked out, tearing chunks out of the buggy and breaking one of the traces. Her first panicky turn snapped the buggy against a wagon's iron wheel, turning Lennox's pride and joy into a shattered wreck careening around the yard to terrify other animals and trigger more destruction.

"Whoa!" William roared as Morgan and other men ran toward the disaster's center. A quick glance showed Abraham vaulting into the side yard to crouch in front of the gunpowder barrels, poised to block any charges.

Her wild lunges broke some barrels, pouring beans and coffee over the sand, and sent others rolling across the depot. Chickens squawked and flapped as a flour barrel crashed into their crate. The mare's panic infected even the normally stolid mules until they began to circle and stamp restlessly. One of them brayed anxiously and another half-reared to avoid being trapped in the milling throng.

William yelled again as he hurdled the buggy's fragments and reached the mare. His strong voice with its message of absolute command made her hesitate for a moment, giving him the chance to grab her headstall. He glimpsed Lennox leveling his big Colt at the terrified horse.

"Whoa!" William shouted again, shortening the word and deepening his voice to hold her attention. He put his full weight into stopping her next wild frenzy. Her four hooves hit the ground simultaneously but she still shuddered and tried to fight him. Her flanks heaved and foam dripped off as she fought for breath.

He crooned to her in the old language of the bards, soft gutturals that had calmed Irish horses for millennia, a tongue that instinct and urgency made him use. She bucked again halfheartedly but her ears pricked to catch his voice.

The men who'd come to help stopped and watched from a few paces away, letting him win her over.

He murmured to her about the delights of her stall, a good meal, sweet water, the beauty of her gait, the sheen of her coat . . . all a stream of love words calculated to seduce a restless female as his father and grandfather had taught him. Finally she leaned against him, trembling, and he petted her gently.

He'd need a bath when this was done, given the amount of horse sweat his clothes were soaking up.

Satisfied, his men backed away and began to cut her free from the buggy's remains. The debris quickly disappeared, while the corralled mules returned to their leisure. Abraham met William's eyes for a moment before he began to smoothly clean up the coffee mug's remains.

William hummed old lullabies to the mare until she nudged him, snuffling at the treats in his pocket. He chuckled as she eagerly accepted a peppermint stick.

"So you enjoy peppermints, little lady?" he laughed in English as he dug for another hard candy. Then he stiffened as a strident voice ripped into the depot's hard-won peace.

"The bitch shattered my new buggy." Lennox strode forward, his gun at the ready. "By God, I'll not have her near anything else of mine."

The mare neighed frantically and shied away, tugging at William's hold.

William blocked Lennox's path, his free hand reaching for his bullwhip. Eighteen feet of black leather, shot-loaded to increase its impact and with a cane shaft for accuracy, it should be enough to snatch Lennox's Colt from his hand.

"Out of my way, Donovan," Lennox ordered harshly.

William didn't move, as icy calm as ever in a fight. "She's a good horse, Lennox, but unaccustomed to a depot's hubbub," he remarked calmly. America was gone from his voice, replaced by more than a hint of the upper-crust accent he'd learned on the Anglo-Irish Ascendancy's great estates. He released the mare's reins in response to Morgan's hissed, "I have her, sir."

"Devil take her, Donovan, do you know how much that rig cost?" Lennox snarled. He took a few steps to his left then caught sight of the braided leather flowing restlessly beside William's leg. Lennox stopped abruptly as William flicked the whip casually.

"Actually, Lennox, I've always admired the look of your other buggy." William kept his tone calm and deep. *Use your voice first to cool matters*, Lady Irene had always said.

Lennox flushed angrily and cocked the revolver.

The bullwhip cracked gently. Lennox's hands froze. The mare neighed frantically from a few paces behind William. But neither man had eyes for her now.

"Its classical elegance reminds me of the rigs I've seen in London, on Rotten Row," William continued softly. *Soothe the man's pride as you build him a bolthole.*

"Do you really think so?" Lennox lowered the gun, all the while watching the whip with eyes as lethal as a caged tiger's.

"Indeed, yes. Your gelding matches it very well and his smooth gaits are calculated to win a lady's confidence." William's voice was as steady as his heartbeat.

A stiff smile slowly appeared on Lennox's face as he uncocked the Colt. "What do you suggest for the mare?"

The lady in question sidled further away from the Easterner's voice and Morgan quickly crooned to her.

"Perhaps she'd calm down if she were stabled with other horses, such as in my barn. I can give you forty dollars for her."

"She's worth a great deal more," Lennox protested half-heartedly.

"In gold, here and now."

Lennox stroked his muttonchops but wasn't fool enough to demand a larger sum. "Very well," he agreed finally. "After all, the gelding does match the other buggy so neatly."

Humming an Irish jig, Viola adjusted the laundry basket on her hip, now full of washing from three clients, and considered the treats tucked inside it. Perhaps the sugary cinnamon bread would divert Maggie's attention for a few minutes. They were one of Armistead the baker's better efforts, although not as good as Lily Mae's scones.

That thought brought her back to considering Mrs. Smith's house and how William Donovan carried on with the girls there. He was a fine figure of a man, which could account for some of their pleasure. His teamster's strength should give him stamina.

As for more intimate equipment, well, what made for excellence? The first time she'd seen naked men was when she was fifteen years old and hunting mushrooms in the woods. She'd happened on a handful of teenage boys enjoying a swimming hole's coolness on that hot day. She'd spied on them for a few minutes before running home ahead of a thunderstorm. Their privates had looked remarkably small and pasty white, hardly capable of causing trouble let alone bringing delight.

Edward had always insisted on proper decorum and respect in the marriage bed. Their marital encounters had been conducted in the dark, under the covers, and discreetly screened by both nightshirt and nightgown. The only time she'd seen him unclothed was when she'd laid him out for burial.

"Mrs. Ross, Mrs. Ross!" Little Jenny's piping voice reached Viola as she reached the cluster of shanties. "Come see, quick! We tried to stop 'em, honest we did. But they took everything!"

"Now, Jenny, calm down. I'm sure it can't be as bad as all that," Viola soothed automatically even as her skin prickled.

"Ma sent Eli for Pa but he couldn't do nothin', not with Mr. Lennox's men there. He tried talkin' to 'em but . . ."

All sound faded as Viola stared at Maggie's deserted hut, the song dead on her lips. No washtubs, no washboards beside the stream. No goat for the milk that Maggie claimed made coffee bearable.

The Golconda's stamping machines, usually strong enough to shake the fragile dwelling, now seemed distant and unimportant.

She broke into a run but stopped dead at the hut's threshold. It was completely empty, showing every inch of the dirt floor and papered-over mud-brick walls. Edward's photograph had vanished. In the far corner, Viola could clearly see an empty hole where her cashbox had been, containing her few funds and the mourning brooch for Grandfather Lindsay. Her heart stopped beating.

That piece of jewelry was the one item she'd kept from her childhood. She'd sold most of her jewelry and all of her good clothes early in her marriage to satisfy Edward's creditors. But somehow she had held onto the gold brooch, with its engraved frigate under full sail and her grandfather's lock of hair inside. Hal, like all of the Commodore's grandsons, had a matching watch. The brooch had more sentimental value than monetary, but now it, too, was gone.

Only a whisky bottle remained. It stood between the frayed curtains in the single window, filled with sprays of yellow roses from Edward's grave and weighted with sand to keep it steady. An envelope rested beside it like a communication from the dead. Viola dropped the basket on the floor and went unsteadily toward the missive.

"Come, Jenny. Let's leave Mrs. Ross alone for now."

Jenny's mother's voice came from a great distance and Viola didn't look back. She managed to pick up the envelope with only slightly shaking hands. The paper was crumpled but the address was clear enough: *Mrs. Edward Ross.* She hesitated for a moment then ripped it open. After all, bad news never improved with age.

> *My dearest, dearest Viola,*
> *I do not know how to break the news to you gracefully so I shall be quick about it instead. I have sold the house and all its contents to Mr. Paul Lennox. He was kind enough to pay an amount sufficient to remove Mr. Watson's debts and see Mr. Jones and me well started on our marriage.*
> *Please understand the necessity of my doing this. I simply cannot abide remaining in this barren waste for another day, especially when my beloved Mr. Jones is overdue to return to his mountain home.*
> *I am certain that you will manage well without my guidance. In fact, I know that all your possessions will swiftly rejoin you when you marry Mr. Lennox today. My only regret is that Mr. Jones and I cannot dance at your nuptials.*
> *Pray give Mabel an extra pat and some alfalfa for me.*
>
> > *Ever your most loyal friend,*
> > *Maggie*

Viola read the letter once and then twice without improving its meaning. Maggie had sold everything so she could run away. Then justified herself by saying that Viola would marry again, this time to a man heartily despised by most. Including Maggie, at least before she wrote this nonsense.

Viola balled the letter and hurled it against the wall. Dammit, Maggie was as weak as Edward had warned when she'd comforted the woman after her child's death.

When would she ever learn that people always chose money and power, never honor? First Mother, then Edward, and now Maggie. Would there ever be a man she could trust completely, someone to ride the river with, as the old saying went?

Somehow she had to rebuild her life without depending on anyone else.

She turned to stare out the window at the desert beyond and tried to think of something, anything, she could do to make a living with just the clothes on her back and a handful of change.

Restart the business? She laughed mirthlessly at that. She hadn't the means and no one here would loan it to her against Lennox's will. He owned the silver mine that kept this town alive and made sure that every man, woman, and child knew exactly whose money put food on their plates, clothes on their backs, and a roof over their heads.

Write her family? That was an even worse option. As he'd promised when she married Edward, her father had refused every letter she had sent thereafter. Even a telegram begging for forgiveness hadn't breached his legendary stubbornness.

As for remarriage . . . No! Even if there was a man she wanted to spend the rest of her life with, she had no offers to accept since Lennox had scared them off.

Unbidden, she remembered Lily Mae's purr as she spoke of Mr. Donovan, and snorted. As if a man like that would have anything to do with someone as scrawny as her.

"Your laughter falls on the air like rain in a desert, Mrs. Ross." A clipped New York accent broke into her thoughts.

Viola choked and whirled around, her hand automatically steadying her against the windowsill. Lennox, of course, dressed for a walk down Fifth Avenue and smirking like Alice in Wonderland's Cheshire Cat as he stroked his mutton-chops. He was a very impressive figure of a man, if you did-n't look too closely into his eyes or catch the reek of his pomade. At least he wasn't wearing his gunbelt.

He'd been back in town for almost a month; he'd pro-
posed and been rejected twice. What did he want now? "Mr.
Lennox. You startled me."

"My apologies, Mrs. Ross." He tipped his hat with a flourish. "May I come in?"

"As you will."

"My dear lady, you look magnificent in that dress." He
swept his hat off to bow over her hand. She retrieved it as
soon as possible, her skin prickling at his flattery. "You are a
vision of civilization, a reminder of a better world."

"You are very kind, Mr. Lennox," Viola murmured politely, and wished she hadn't seen him in a barbarian's blood-
stained clothing.

"Kind, Mrs. Ross? You are my dearest wish, the pinnacle
of everything I plan to gain from this barren desert."

Why did that particular statement ring true?

"Soon I will be the governor of New York and you will be
the envy of the world as my wife. We'll give parties for society's elite at my new mansion, next door to Roosevelt's estate. They will dine and dance with us all night long above
the Hudson, free from the stench of those Vanderbilt parvenus."

Ballrooms have pianos. Dear heaven, to play a piano
again . . .

"I shall be elegantly outfitted by London's best tailors,
while Paris will send its finest gowns to adorn you."

A Paris wardrobe again? For that and a piano, a woman
could consider marrying Lennox. Lost in the vision, Viola
barely noticed how close he now stood.

"Do you remember when we first met, in New York during
the recent unpleasantness? You were an enchanting young lady
from one of the finest families, while your mother was the
very picture of American beauty. Such a charming woman,"
he mused. "She could shop from sunrise to sundown then
sparkle brighter than the Northern Lights over dinner."

Viola stiffened. Wasn't that trip when Mother had bought the rifles?

"Marry me, Mrs. Ross," he continued, heedless of her silence, "and the world's merchants will be your devoted servants, as they were for your mother."

"No." The word was little more than a croak, uttered by a mouth dry with the ashes of lost dreams. "No, no, no," Viola said more strongly as her throat muscles worked to repudiate the nightmare. She would not, could not, be blackmailed into another marriage.

Lennox blinked, then cocked his head and crossed his hands on his walking stick, the image of a man who fully appreciated his own superiority. "My very dear Mrs. Ross, I'm afraid I didn't quite hear you. You must comprehend the advantages we bring each other."

She gathered herself together to speak in terms he might understand. "I'm afraid you misunderstand my circumstances, Mr. Lennox. Captain Lindsay disinherited me when I married Edward, so I can offer you neither grand associations nor a rich dowry."

His smile deepened as he wagged a finger at her. "My dear lady, Ross also objected to any rapprochement with your family. But I am convinced that when you arrive on Captain Lindsay's doorstep, properly contrite and with a well-bred husband at your side, forgiveness and riches will flow like the Niagara."

Roses brushed her arm as a phrase caught Viola's attention. "When did you speak to Mr. Ross about my father? He never mentioned such a conversation to me."

"At the Oriental Saloon, my dear. I happened to catch him just as he was departing."

Lightning flashed again in Viola's memory. "My husband only visited the Oriental once in his life," she said slowly, feeling her way through the implications.

"Indeed? He must have forgotten to mention it."

Edward's roses nudged her again. "Did you speak to him for long?" Instinctively, her hand crept toward the bottle.

She had to deal with this herself. Sheriff Lloyd would be of no use in any confrontation with Lennox. He was far more interested in pouring whisky down his throat than saying no to the man who paid his salary.

"I'm afraid so; he was a very stubborn man at times." Lennox came closer. "Come, my dear, we can discuss this later."

"Did you argue with him, Mr. Lennox?" She had to learn the truth.

"Gentlemen don't have arguments. We merely spoke with some emotion," he corrected.

"Did the discussion become heated? So hot you had to take action?"

"Mrs. Ross," he began, guilt creeping into his eyes.

"You killed him with your sword stick, the one you had to scrub. I saw you wash up at the livery stable's water trough." Edward's death wound had been too deep and narrow for a Bowie knife and Lennox had the only sword in town that night.

He fumbled for words. "He was inebriated, Mrs. Ross. We had words and he attacked me. I had to defend myself."

"You, who served four years in the Union cavalry, could do no better with your sword than kill a drunk in an alley?" Enraged at the murder and his lies, Viola took a half step toward him but kept her hand near the bottle. "Your actions speak of the gutter, sir, and render your offer unacceptable."

His eyes blazed at the insult and he tightened his grip on the swordstick's shaft. "I suggest you reconsider, Mrs. Ross."

"You can say nothing that would make me accept you."

"Consider your position, Mrs. Ross," Lennox snarled at her. "Where will you live? I can evict you from this hovel in five minutes."

Viola gritted her teeth and repeated stonily, "I will not marry you, Mr. Lennox."

He took a deep breath, visibly trying to collect himself. "Come, come, my offer needs more thought than that. You can have a glass of Riesling at my house and some biscuits while you reconsider. Perhaps you'd enjoy a matched string of pearls as your wedding present." He grabbed her elbow.

"No!" Viola yanked away from him. "No, no, no!"

Lennox glared at her and swept the sword stick up toward the canvas roof, ready to strike her.

Viola smashed the bottle against the windowsill and brought her newly formed weapon into position before her, business end toward her enemy as Edward had taught her on the long road west. A single spray of roses caught her cuff like reassurance and sunlight. "I think not, sir," she announced coldly, and swallowed hard.

He stared at the razor-sharp edge pointed at his privates. "You cannot be serious."

"Completely so, sir," Viola said brusquely, her pulse steady now as she faced him.

He brought the heavy cane down in a whistling arc aimed at simply knocking the bottle aside; Edward had always said most men discounted women in a fight. She countered as she'd been taught, aiming for Lennox's hand to disarm him. The broken bottle sliced through skin and muscle, setting off a gush of crimson.

He yelped as the cane fell to the floor. "Why, you vicious bitch!"

Viola waited, keeping her weapon ready to resume the fight. If she thought about what she'd done, she might faint. God must be smiling on her, to succeed with that move.

Blood ran down his hand. He wrapped a handkerchief around his wound, cursing continuously. "Devil take you, you'll pay for that."

He clenched his good hand but she quickly brought the bottle up to block him again. He bent down slowly and picked up the sword stick, watching her constantly.

"You're standing on my property, Mrs. Ross." Venom

lanced his voice. "You have an hour to compose yourself after the day's shocks. Then I'll return to escort you to my house, the only place you'll find shelter in this town."

"Get out." Her stomach felt like a rattlesnake's den, all twisting coils hidden from the light, but she held her ground.

He gripped his slim cane, started to rotate it, but stopped with a brief hiss of pain.

She turned the bottle so light glinted on the jagged glass as she stepped forward.

He backed up slowly, his eyes cold with fury, until he came to his old buggy. *What on earth had happened to the new horse and buggy that he'd been showing off around town yesterday?* The big gelding tossed its head at the unusual approach but steadied quickly as Lennox took the reins from Jenny's brother Eli.

"You have one hour to decide: starve or accept my offer. You'll marry me in the end, Viola Ross, so make it easy on yourself and come with me now." He swept their audience with a long glare, sending them back into their shelters like mice hiding from a rattler.

Viola kept her chin up, unwilling to let him see how his words affected her. Give him an hour and no one would dare offer her more than a drink of water. "I'd rather be an Apache's squaw," she said, and knew it for the truth.

"Don't be foolish, my dear. You know you're meant for me. We will meet again at noon." He had the audacity to bow, albeit mockingly, before he drove away.

Viola shivered and retreated back into the mud-brick hut, pushing aside the basket of dirty laundry just inside. She leaned against the wall, sliding slowly down to the dirt floor. She couldn't have taken another step if she tried, given how her legs were shaking. Her skin was cold as ice and her stomach wanted to rush up her throat.

What in heaven's name was she going to do now?

Chapter Three

Viola walked slowly back up the hill toward town, still trying to think of alternatives. Beg sanctuary from Padre Francisco? Lennox would torch the little church within hours; he'd bragged before of how he'd kept "Papist temples" away from his better properties in New York.

Send a telegram to her brother Hal? Even if she knew where he was currently piloting a riverboat, his objections to Edward had been louder than the Captain's. And her sister Juliet would never risk scandal by countering their father.

She could go to the Apaches if she could reach them before Lennox came after her. Cochise's band was known to watch Rio Piedras and attack any lonely travelers, a success rate unhindered by the new Army post. If she took the old road out of town, past the German's mine and up the canyon into the mountains, surely they'd find her quickly. After that, she would simply have to do her best to convince them she'd be a good, docile squaw.

Viola shuddered and came to a stop. Then she forced herself to start walking again. Starvation sounded better, although Apaches might be worth it. Especially if she could somehow see Lennox's face when he realized she truly did prefer becoming a squaw.

She was still smiling at that image when she opened Mrs. Smith's gate and fed Jake the bread she'd bought less than an hour ago. Just this one last bit of business to tidy up and then she could leave.

A quick knock brought Lily Mae to the door, her forehead creased in surprise. "Why, Mrs. Ross, I didn't 'spect to see you back here so soon!"

"I didn't anticipate it either," Viola agreed, balancing the laundry basket on her hip. "May I speak to Mrs. Smith?"

Lily Mae's frown deepened, but mercifully she didn't ask for an explanation. "If you'll come this way, ma'am, I'll see if she's in. Just put that down over here."

"Thank you." Viola deposited the basket on the same table she'd used earlier that morning and followed Lily Mae past an elegant music room with a new Steinway piano, and into a very small front parlor. She discreetly studied her first view of what the parlor house's clients saw, admiring the heavily carved rosewood and ebony furniture against silk wallpaper. It was a page from the fanciest illustrated ladies' magazine brought to life on the harsh frontier.

Yet despite the elegant decor, the air reeked with cigar smoke and other smells that she preferred not to guess at. Had anyone ever opened those velvet draperies and the windows beyond to air out the room?

A framed Currier & Ives lithograph reflected a lovely, well-dressed woman in the doorway watching her. Viola lifted her chin proudly, determined to show no embarrassment at her own shabby clothing, and took refuge in the proprieties drilled into her from childhood. "Good morning, Mrs. Smith."

"What a pleasure to see you here, Mrs. Ross. Would you care to sit down?"

"Thank you." Viola settled herself on the elegant rosewood chair indicated. She held her back straight and her chin high, as befitted a social caller and not a destitute widow.

Carrie Smith evinced no curiosity about the unexpected visit, instead taking the astonishing step of discussing the weather. Viola followed her lead, cloaking her shock at polite conversation in a brothel. Every time she shifted, the chair's horsehair stuffing rustled like a jury sitting in judgment.

There was a quiet knock before Lily Mae entered to set a silver tray down on the table in front of Viola. She left just as silently and the door shut with a soft, but distinct, click.

"Would you care to pour?" Mrs. Smith's soft soprano voice was more suited to the bedroom than to giving orders, even when phrased as a request.

Viola nodded and reached for the pot. Hopefully, her hand wouldn't shake enough to spill anything. The entire scene reminded her far too much of her mother's lessons in deportment, sessions which usually began and ended in a bitter attack from her mother on Viola's hoydenish conduct. "Cream? Sugar perhaps, Mrs. Smith?" she asked as if she was hosting the finest lady in town.

"Both, thank you." Mrs. Smith accepted the proffered cup and waited for Viola to serve herself.

"What superb coffee, Mrs. Smith," Viola complimented her hostess after a sip. "How do you manage fresh cream? It's such a marvel in this hot climate."

"One of my clients brings it every time he comes to call."

Viola flushed at the thought of what the man received in return.

"What brings you here, Mrs. Ross?" The madame's voice had a stronger edge now.

"I find that I must immediately leave the laundry business, Mrs. Smith. I have returned your property so that you can find someone else to accommodate you. Perhaps the small Chinese laundry on North Street would do. I understand they have superior expertise with fine fabrics." Uncomfortably aware she was prattling, Viola stopped talking.

"I will be very sorry to lose your services, Mrs. Ross. You have always performed to the highest standards." Mrs. Smith's voice was emphatic but softened as she went on. "Have you considered what you will do next?"

Viola's mouth tightened before she answered bluntly. "I

will not marry Mr. Lennox under any circumstances, Mrs. Smith. I am certain I can find another option." She sipped her coffee, trying not to picture that choice.

"May I suggest one possibility?"

Viola nodded warily, surprised by Mrs. Smith's hesitancy.

"Have you considered working for me? Or perhaps in another parlor house, if you choose not to remain where people have known you. I would be glad to loan you any funds necessary to free you from your obligations here."

Somehow Viola managed not to drop her cup into her lap. "Become a Cyprian? A . . . a *nymph du pave?*" A prostitute, her reeling brain clarified. "No, Mrs. Smith, I hadn't thought of that." She gulped a mouthful of cooling coffee.

"It should prove an excellent solution for your difficulties. The money is first-rate and the hours reasonable, far better than what most women of ill repute receive. And should you find one very special gentleman to be your protector, you could become quite wealthy."

Viola stared at her. Thoughts spun through her head like a kaleidoscope, rarely pausing to take coherent shape. A protector? He'd probably be a fat old drunkard with more money than wit, not an athletic young man.

She groped for a response, something polite to answer her hostess. "Mrs. Smith, I am flattered that you think so highly of my potential. But I cannot imagine that your clients would be interested in a woman of my few feminine charms."

"Mrs. Ross." Mrs. Smith shook her head, smiling. "You are a mistress of the conversational arts, even under the most difficult circumstances. Men value that a great deal, especially here on the frontier where their world is so very rough and ready."

Viola gaped at the compliment.

"And when the conversing is done by a woman of your unique coloring, who is most definitely female . . ." Mrs. Smith's eyes rested for a moment on Viola's bosom.

Viola closed her mouth and swallowed her disbelief at

having this discussion. Still, other women had chosen this route when hard pressed by circumstances. It did offer a few benefits, such as avoiding an Apache's attentions. But what did a courtesan do to make that much money? Probably very hard work, if Pearl could become so tired.

"Mrs. Smith, thank you for the offer, but your girls are famous for their, uh, proficiency in the boudoir. I'm afraid I lack those skills and would not be an asset to your business." That should be a sufficient reason to decline.

"Did you know everything necessary when you entered the laundry business?"

"No, of course not." Where was this leading?

"Were you willing to learn? Did you bend your every effort toward becoming the best laundry woman possible?"

"Certainly I did. How does that relate to your offer?"

"Carnal skills can be taught and learned like any other. It's only necessary that the student be willing."

An image of William Donovan soothing a stubborn mule flashed before Viola's eyes. It had become very complaisant under his beautiful hands and was now one of his most reliable leaders. Was it possible for women to learn intimate skills in a similar fashion?

"An adventurous spirit, which you have, my dear." Mrs. Smith leaned forward as she spoke earnestly to her guest. But Viola no longer heard her.

William Donovan was comfortably situated if Lily Mae thought him a good tipper. More to the point, his business depended on the Army and other mining towns, not on Lennox's goodwill. He might be willing to accept a woman who'd be more convenient than this house's denizens for slaking his lusts.

Could it work? Better to be his mistress than Lennox's wife or an Apache's squaw. She'd do her best to make him happy, performing any acts necessary. She was accustomed to hard work, after doing so much laundry and working Edward's small claim before that. Perhaps she could please him enough that he'd give her a fresh start somewhere else. Maybe she could make it to San Francisco and give piano lessons.

Viola became aware that Mrs. Smith was waiting for an answer. Still too caught up in thoughts of Donovan to prepare a pretty response, she stumbled into speech. "Mrs. Smith, I'm very sorry but I must decline. Frankly, I don't think I have the strength to welcome every man who seeks intimacy with me." She blushed at hearing herself speak so bluntly.

Mrs. Smith studied her for a long minute. "Are you certain? I know I sprung this offer on you. Would you care for more time to think?"

"No! I thank you, but no. I am deeply appreciative of your confidence in me but I cannot accept."

"Very well." The madame settled back in her chair with a sigh. Sincerity was emblazoned on her face. "Please consider yourself welcome to resume this conversation at any time."

"Thank you. I really must be going now; there is someone else I must see today."

"Then I will not delay you. Good luck, Mrs. Ross."

"The same to you, Mrs. Smith."

Viola escaped to the sunshine with a faint sense of optimism. If Mrs. Smith sought so strongly to employ her, then hopefully Mr. Donovan would at least consider hiring her.

The church bell sounded just as she reached the depot; only fifteen minutes remained before Lennox would come looking for her. Schubert's "Marche Militaire" faded from her lips.

Viola took a deep breath, wishing she had some idea of how to intrigue a man. Gracious, she didn't even know what Donovan liked to do with his women. Perhaps he stroked his women somehow, although that didn't sound sufficient to exhaust Pearl. At least his woman wouldn't need to wait up to see him stagger home drunk or brew strange concoctions the next morning to sober him up.

How on earth was she going to strike a deal with him? Beg, plead, grovel?

If necessary, answered a little voice. She shivered but kept her chin up. Better Donovan than Lennox or an Apache. She might even learn why Pearl said he was "fine as dollar cotton."

A different shiver rippled through her, setting off treacherous warmth between her legs. Perhaps he knew finger games, intimate play to bring pleasure and relaxation afterwards as she'd done for herself. What would his big hands feel like on her unprotected skin? Her breath caught as her nipples abruptly budded.

She bit her lip hard to break free of the fantasy. She licked away the resulting drop of blood and stepped briskly around the corner to approach the freight depot. Its mud-brick walls and buildings dated back to Rio Piedras's founding more than ten years ago beside a handful of natural springs, one of them now enclosed beyond the main corral.

Donovan & Sons was busier than usual, with men working hard to load a series of wagons. Viola's eyes passed over them quickly, seeking one particular fellow clad in a well-tailored suit. He could be found occasionally in a teamster's rough garb but only when driving a wagon. His clean-shaven face was always a strong contrast to every other man's abundant facial hair, such as Evans's mustache.

Her eyes lingered on a dark head above broad shoulders, tugging hard on a wagonload's embracing ropes. The right height and build, but red flannel? Then the man turned and Donovan's brilliant blue eyes locked with hers.

Viola gulped and nodded at him.

His eyebrows lifted for a moment, then he returned her silent greeting. He strode toward her, still gentlemanly despite his dust, after a quick word to Evans. She was barely aware of his men's curiosity.

"Mrs. Ross. It is an honor to see you here." Her grandmother would have approved of his handshake but not his appearance. His black hair was disheveled, his clothing was streaked with dust, his scent reeked of horses and sweat.

And his shoulders looked so much more masculine under the thin red flannel than they ever had in English broadcloth.

She swallowed and tried to think logically. She was here to gain his protection, no matter what distractions his appearance offered.

William smiled down at Viola, curious why she'd come to the depot. Probably for money to return back East.

"May I have a word with you in private, Mr. Donovan?"

Poor lady, she sounded so awkward and embarrassed. "Certainly. We can use the office," he soothed, and led the way across the yard. "Would you care for some fresh tea or coffee?"

"No, thank you. What I have to say should not take long."

She must want a seat on the next stagecoach out of town, if the conversation must be fast. Buy her that ticket and she'd be gone in a day. Bloody hell.

William ushered her into the small room, bare except for the minimum of furniture, all solid, scarred, and littered with paperwork. Morgan's numerous virtues didn't include pushing paper to the Army's satisfaction when his clerk was absent.

She accepted the indicated seat but was wretchedly nervous, almost fidgeting in her chair. He wanted to snatch her up and swear the world would never hurt her again, then hunt down Charlie Jones and his fool wife. William closed the wooden shutters on the single window, filtering out much of the light and noise from the bustling corrals, then settled into his big oak swivel chair.

"What can I do for you, Mrs. Ross?" He kept his voice gentle, his California drawl soft against the muffled noises from outside.

She took a deep breath, drew herself up straight and tall,

and launched into speech. "May I become your mistress, Mr. Donovan?"

"What?! What the devil are you talking about?" he choked, too stunned to watch his language. He knew his mouth was hanging open. "Are you making a joke, Mrs. Ross?"

"Hardly, Mr. Donovan." She met his eyes directly, pulse pounding in her throat. "You may not have heard, but my business partner sold everything to Mr. Lennox."

He nodded curtly. He must have been right before: she needed money. "I met Mr. and Mrs. Jones on their way out of town. I won't be doing business with them again," he added harshly.

"Quite so. But my only choices now are to marry Mr. Lennox or find another man to protect me. I'd rather be yours than an Apache's."

"Jesus, Mary and Joseph," William muttered as he stood and began to pace. *Think, boyo, think. She deserves better than being your woman.* Heat lanced from his heart down his spine at the thought of her in his arms every night. Marriage? No, she'd never agree to a Catholic ceremony. "There are other men, men who'd marry you," he pointed out hoarsely.

"I will not remarry. Besides, Mr. Lennox blocked all offers other than his."

"Son of a bitch." The bastard should be shot. "What about your family?"

"They disinherited me when I married Edward. Both families refused my letters informing them of his death."

How the devil could a parent abandon a child, no matter what the quarrel? His father had given everything to protect his children.

William's gut tightened at the thought. Condoms were helpful but not a guarantee. If she stayed in his bed long enough, the odds were good . . .

"You could become pregnant," he warned, his eyes returning to her face. Blessed Virgin, what he wouldn't do to see Viola proud and happy, holding his babe in her arms.

"I can't have children."

"The fault could be in the stallion, not the mare," William suggested, his drawl more pronounced. And this stallion would dearly love to prove his potency where another had failed, his cock caroled.

Breathe deep, boyo, let the lust fade, his brain warned. *You were trained by the best and you'll not leap upon a woman.*

Viola stared at him and firmly shook her head. "All of Edward's siblings have at least three children. No, the difficulty is entirely mine."

He considered her slender body thoughtfully as he remembered other fragile women who'd rarely, if ever, conceived. Viola could be correct about her infertility.

More to the point, she was stubborn enough to continue insisting on this madness of becoming his mistress, no matter what arguments he mustered. Perhaps if he took her, he could sate his hunger before her inevitable departure. His cock eagerly agreed with this reasoning.

He moved to the window before speaking again, trying desperately to think. She needed to be warned about what to expect if she stayed with him.

"I have strong demands and unique tastes." His voice was darker now. If she came to his bed, he'd play the games he loved, no doubt about it. But he'd never mastered a woman who hadn't consented and he never would.

"And I understand you pay Mrs. Smith's girls very well to satisfy them. I should think you would be glad to have a woman constantly available to you." A hot flush lit her cheekbones and her pulse pounded in her throat as she licked her lips. Blessed Virgin, she was aroused by this conversation, but did she know what he was talking about?

His fist hit the rough wall. "Mother of God, Mrs. Ross, do you have any idea of what I might do with you?"

She ignored his profanity. "No, but I'm willing to learn."

Dear God in heaven, the images those words evoked. Viola's moon-bright hair spilling across his thighs as she cherished his cock with her mouth. Viola, flung across silk sheets as she howled her pleasure under him. Viola's sweet ass, blazing red from his attentions, thrusting back against his cock as she begged for more . . .

What wouldn't she do as his mistress?

"Are you offering me carte blanche, Mrs. Ross, to act as I please in the bedroom?"

"Your horses love you and you whipped a man once for kicking a dog. I believe you'll treat me with at least as much consideration."

Did she mean it? Would she truly let him do what he wanted with her? His brain finally agreed with his cock on the need to grab her now, quickly, before she had time to reconsider. He gave voice to the bargain. "I give you my word on that. And I'll protect you from those who'd harm you as well."

"Such as Mr. Lennox?"

His jaw set. "Definitely against Lennox."

"Thank you." She smiled at him, then went on more briskly, "How much?"

William coughed at her businesslike words, which were a complete contrast to her nipples' eager thrust against the thin cloth. "What did you have in mind?"

"One hundred dollars a week. I believe you regularly spend more than that at Mrs. Smith's."

If he paid her by the week, she could leave after a few days' notice. Everything in him railed at the idea, desperate to keep her as long as possible.

William kept his expression shuttered as he answered, leaning back against the desk. "A weekly rate wouldn't suit me. It will take time to teach you my preferences."

"How long?"

His eyes hooded for a moment. What was the minimum stay for a student at Lyonsgate? "Three months."

She didn't blink. "One thousand dollars."

Bloody hell, she hadn't balked at the time he'd demanded. He summarized the deal clearly, needing her complete agreement before he acted. "And for that sum and my protection, you will live under my roof, be constantly at my disposal, and learn how best to please me."

"Yes, sir." She took a very deep breath, straining the blue calico over her slight breasts. A tremor ran up his spine. His balls were as taut as if this morning's relief had occurred weeks ago.

His eyes swept over her and she met them steadily. Then he stared out at the window shutters for a long time as he fought to think. Could he really do this? On the other hand, could he turn her down? He knew the answer to that: no.

He could hear one of his men whistling in the distance, against the steady thud of barrels being stacked in wagons.

"Very well," William said finally, his voice far too rough in his ears. "It will take a little time to gather that much cash together. Where would you care to wait?"

"No!"

He stared at her, caught by the first note of fear in her voice. Was she physically afraid of Lennox, not just annoyed by his attentions?

"I mean, we can commence now," Viola stammered. "I am sure you're good for the money."

Their eyes met and anger rose in William. The bastard had done something to her, probably threatened her. He deserved to be hung, even if he was Donovan & Sons' biggest client in this territory, other than the Army.

William bowed slightly to her. "Thank you for your confidence in me. Very well, we'll begin immediately." And give her one last chance to change her mind.

Viola shivered and blushed, looking delectable. He smiled, enjoying the anticipation drumming in his cock. He extended his hand to her and lifted her to her feet, his eyes searching hers for every hint of carnal interest. She trembled again.

William smiled as he kissed her hand, pleased at this assurance. He lingered a moment to savor her sweet, slightly musky scent. "Take off your bonnet, Viola."

"Yes, sir." She fumbled with the strings but finally managed to set it aside.

"Beautiful hair," he murmured as he tucked a stray lock behind her ears. "You'll wear it down for me often."

She blinked and nodded, clearly baffled by why he should want such behavior. She was still bemused when he glided his fingers over her throat, across her shoulders, and down her arms. Silken smooth, soft warmth under the skin. Strong muscle and bone from working Ross's claim. More exquisite than a dream.

His woman. For three months, his faerie queen would welcome only him. It had to be long enough.

He drew her hands up to his mouth and kissed them, fondling her fingers. "Pleasure me with these hands, Viola." His voice lingered over her name. "Ease me with your mouth before we leave."

"What?" she squeaked.

"Bring me to completion in your mouth, Viola."

"I don't know how," she whispered.

His blood raced with surprise, then hunger. By all the saints, he'd be the first to fill her mouth . . .

She blushed scarlet, in vivid contrast to her proper white collar, as she stared at him.

Easy now, boyo, don't frighten the innocent lady. He calmed his face and gentled his voice. "You'll find it easy enough to do, sweetheart. And I'll teach you everything you need to know."

"Very well." She swallowed hard, her pulse galloping in her throat. He kissed her trembling fingers before releasing them, then settled back into the big swivel chair.

"You can start by touching me. You'll need to undress me, too, at least somewhat."

"Of course." She came to him hesitantly, her eyes enormous. Had her fool husband mistreated her? Surely not: she hadn't seemed afraid during their negotiations. And she couldn't be untouched; she'd bargained too directly, unlike a skittish virgin. Besides, her husband must have taught her something during five years of marriage.

He trembled when she lightly touched his shoulders, and closed his eyes. She froze. Bloody hell, she didn't even know how to touch a man. He truly would have to guide her.

William took a deep breath, then another, easing his body's harsh urgency until he could take command. "Open my shirt, Viola. Bare skin to bare skin there first."

She carefully unbuttoned it and the soft white undervest below. Then she set her palm against him, brushing it lightly against his chest hair. She circled his nipple gently, then rubbed it.

If she was as ignorant as she seemed of men's pleasure, then she surely had a natural talent for building it, given a few hints.

"Oh yes, sweetheart." William kept his voice steady with an effort. "Kiss it for me. Use all of your mouth. Lips, tongue, teeth."

She nuzzled his nipple gently, awkwardly. Hesitated for a moment, until he nearly ordered her to get on with it, then she kissed it. Heaven on earth promptly appeared to him.

He groaned quietly at her lips' suppleness, so soon withdrawn from him. He needed more.

"Tongue and teeth, too, sweetheart." He'd build her obedience now, in little things that didn't threaten her.

She obeyed cautiously. The tentative damp flick set a fiery bolt lancing through his chest. Somehow he managed to stay silent, fighting for control of himself.

Her tongue circled his other nipple before she sucked. He growled, restlessly circling his hips against the chair. "Continue, but do so as you proceed down my chest and stomach, sweetheart."

He was ruefully proud of how steady his voice sounded. A

master, especially one as well trained as he, shouldn't want to howl over a few minutes' clumsy licking by a beautiful woman, no matter how often he'd dreamed of her. He distantly wondered what condition his brain would be in when his cockhead first felt her lips.

Viola nuzzled and licked the line of hair down his stomach, opening his shirt wider. He rewarded her with growls and shudders as she learned him, using his voice to lead her. "Ah yes, sweetheart. Very good. Linger a bit longer there. That's my girl."

She did so, sending a long shudder of delight through his gut and up his spine. His jaw clenched against the need to moan.

He urged her on as she experimented with various touches: hard or soft; push or circle; lips, tongue, or teeth. Blood raced through his veins, building in his cock and chest with the demand for more. He caressed her head, silently urging her closer. She leaned into his touch while continuing her attentions to his torso.

She jumped and stopped when the hot ridge under his trousers bumped her chin. His cock had just declared its objection to waiting for her.

"Open it, sweetheart."

"Mr. Donovan, are you really certain we should do this?" she stammered, her fingertips still making small circles against his stomach. He had little patience to set against his clamoring lust.

"You gave your word. Now open it." His harsh voice permitted no argument, all training gone from it until only a man's hunger remained.

She gulped and obeyed, her fingers fumbling so much it seemed deliberate torture. His cock leaped out of his trousers when the last button parted, as hot and red as if he hadn't ridden two women into exhaustion the night before.

Viola stared as if she'd never seen an aroused man before, but she didn't run even from equipment he knew to be larger than most men's. Her tongue ran over her lips and she swallowed, a hot flush sweeping across her cheeks. She stayed still, shaking a little.

Willing, he'd call her. Eager, too . . . but ignorant.

Could Viola be an unawakened sensualist? The blessed saints knew she'd obeyed him sweetly, like a woman ready to yield control, that irritating discipline of planning the next move—in return for the freedom to feel freely, without having to think. Perhaps she felt deference's complex pleasure, the joy of service mixed with the power of having a man's delight triggered by her touch.

Time to take her further. If she followed his lead eagerly, then the three months ahead could be better than any dream. William slowed his breathing until he forced his arousal back under control.

Then he lifted his hips. "Take my trousers and drawers off, sweetheart."

"Yes, sir." She took another deep breath and obeyed, slipping off his weapon belt and dusty high boots first, then placing the clothing on the desk. She settled onto her knees, waiting for his next instruction.

"Touch me again, sweetheart. Be certain to pay much attention to my cock."

"Cock?"

So he'd have the fun of teaching her a new vocabulary, as well. He grinned. He stroked the pole rising from his groin, the flesh rippling under his firm grasp. "Cock."

She blushed again. His nostrils flared as he caught the scent of a woman's rich musk in the air. She must be aroused under that respectable dress, thighs wet with her dew. Exultation roared in his veins, fired up by conquering a woman with only his voice and a few light touches.

She ran her hands lightly up his thighs, then explored another set of muscles and another, clearly enjoying the simple caresses. The last stroke found his pouch snug between her thumb and forefinger. She cupped it instinctively and William moaned. Triumph meant nothing to a man whose woman was fondling his balls.

The little hedonist kissed his cock.

He growled and his hips lifted, pushing himself against her mouth. If she didn't start sucking him soon, he'd explode in her face like a young fool.

Viola glanced up at him. He stared at her, his hand stroking his chest in a similar pattern to what she'd used on his thighs. "More, dammit," he snapped.

She smiled a purely feminine smile. Jesus, Mary, and Joseph, he'd succeeded: he'd taken her past the boundaries of ignorance until she'd had her first taste of a woman's power. Sherman could keep his march through Georgia; this Irish lad would rather know conquests like these.

"Yes, sir." She kissed his cock again and again, her mouth moving up and down the hard length while her fingers gently cradled his balls.

"Lick it for me, sweetheart," he rumbled. "And play with the tip. There's a point, just under the head, where . . . Ah!" Her tongue found the spot, and he arched against the chair, his heart skipping a beat. *She's here, she's ours, she's perfect,* his seed sang deep in his loins.

Viola's other hand crept behind his balls to bring them forward for more attention. He shuddered, wondering vaguely why they hadn't erupted yet. His head fell back, even as both hands stroked her braided hair. Next time, he'd have her sweep its silk over his groin.

The little temptress found the one irresistible touch, a circling lick on a single point, and he jerked. She tried it again and he growled. She purred against him, then set to work in earnest.

Would he survive her first lesson?

She licked him up and down his hard length, as his blood thundered under her increasingly sure strokes. Her hands played with him, while her tongue learned to swirl over him. Up, over, and down as he groaned and thrust himself at her for more.

Nothing mattered but this. If Morgan had shouted there was a fire in the powder wagon, he'd have stayed in his office just to feel Viola's fingers working his cock like a musical instrument.

Soon the only sounds he heard were his rasping growls and her wet slurping as she worked to attend to all of him.

Then she managed to take all of his cockhead into her mouth. He howled at finally being contained in her hot, wet cavern.

She froze, startled.

His hands tightened on her head as his seed, contained for so long, boiled out of his balls and raced through his cock. He saw stars as he poured himself into her, his climax shaking him to the bone.

How the hell would he be able to let her walk away after three months?

Viola swallowed. His essence tasted slightly salty and almost pleasant. Her body ached with frustration but she was proud of herself, content to be the one who put that look of boneless pleasure on his face.

Donovan's arms reached down. She squeaked as she allowed herself to be lifted and settled on his lap. Her head settled naturally against his shoulder.

"That's my girl," he praised softly. She blushed, acutely aware of his chest rubbing her. She wanted more, something to trigger her own satisfaction, but couldn't speak of it. Her pleasure wasn't part of the bargain, only his.

His strong fingers tilted her chin up. It was harder to meet his eyes, a man she'd just handled so intimately, than to ask to be his mistress.

"You did well, Viola. I'm very proud of you." He smiled at

her and her foolish heart leaped. He was still treating her as a person, not just a possession good only for sensual purposes.

Then Donovan kissed her. Relieved by his acceptance, she opened to him and found herself swept away. He took her mouth expertly, licking and nibbling and sucking, until all she could do was moan and hold on. His tongue played with hers, then moved deeper.

She realized he could taste both himself and her. That thought made the fire between her legs burst into raging life. She shuddered and clung to him, sobbing as he kissed her.

"Darling Viola," he murmured. "Are you hungry?"

His hand slid under her dress.

"You're wet, sweetheart. And aching. Open wider for me so I can feel you."

"Please, I shouldn't."

He cupped her breast. She almost shrieked at the jolt that lanced from her nipple to her core.

"Now, sweetheart." His voice was inflexible.

She whimpered as she spread her legs. His knowing fingers slid inside her drawers and she writhed, arching her back to move closer.

"Take your own pleasure, sweetheart. You've more than earned it."

He caressed her folds, evoking a gush of cream. Every bit of bone and flesh merged into a yearning for completion.

"I can't. I've never, not with anyone else. I mean . . ." Her head fell back against his shoulder as his hand became more demanding.

"Your body has the knack of it, sweetheart. Give yourself over. That's my sweet lady," he crooned.

Viola had no words, only animal sounds, to answer him as his voice and hands lured her on. At that moment, she cared not whether his mouth muffled her or not.

Then Donovan found the little bud only she'd known before. He pressed it hard and rapture shot through her veins.

She sobbed a stronger pleasure than she'd ever known before as she bucked and writhed against him.

Forever seemed to pass before she could think again, lying there in his arms with his cock hot and hard against her rump. Every muscle in her body was boneless with delight, like a praline still warm from the stove. Her lack of sleep caught up with her in pleasure's aftermath until movement seemed impossible.

Yawning, she wondered what else he enjoyed doing with women.

Chapter Four

William smoothed a vagrant strand of Viola's moonbeam hair off her brow. Damn, she had yielded sweetly. What to do next? His cock ached again as it clamored to fill her now, immediately. He bit the image back, willing himself back to discipline.

Viola mumbled something under her breath and shifted. Calico rubbed his groin as her delectable rump found another part of him to torment.

"Viola," he rumbled, his voice hardly more than a whisper. "Sweetheart, it's time to . . ."

A delicate snore glided into the room. Her head turned and came to rest against his shoulder, where her breath ruffled the soft flannel.

William began to laugh softly at himself. She was asleep. In all his fantasies, he'd never imagined this end to their first encounter. She must be exhausted since she'd probably worked late the night before.

He was flattered he'd overwhelmed her, pleased she trusted him this far, and frustrated beyond measure. His cock seemed a burning brand of desperation. William took one slow breath after another until he could think again.

Sweet Jesus, she'd been desperate. Penniless, homeless, bereft of her family.

The look on her face when she'd come to the depot, a thin

veil of polite determination over bone-deep agony, reminded him of his father's funeral when he, too, had been homeless and alone, desperate to find an alternative.

William stood by the graveside, barely aware of the pouring rain. His suit was fresh bought from a ragpicker, but so old that its cuffs were shiny from long use. His shoes pinched his feet and built more blisters atop the ones formed on the long walk from Cobh behind the coffin. The cap atop his head did little to keep his hair dry.

Mother, Maeve, and Caitlin slept in this churchyard. Da had spent hard cash to bring Baby Séamas's tiny corpse here from the field where he'd been born, died, and been buried. So here Da would rest, too, which had cost every penny of their meager savings, the money planned for a start in the New World.

Finally, the priest finished the ceremony and tossed mud clods over the coffin. William crossed himself and left quickly. Cobh was no place to set roots but it was better than this village.

He said a quick prayer when he passed his old playmates' cottage. Kevin, Donal, and their family lay dead inside, the cottage walled up by their father to provide privacy as they finally died of starvation. A few sheep lifted their heads as he passed, then returned to grazing on the quarter acre that had once provided for a family of nine. According to the law, people living on such a large farm wouldn't need public relief.

Three days later, after hard walking on muddy roads and sleeping in abandoned barns, William found himself outside Cobh's main train station, watching a bevy of well-dressed and well-fed English stream past.

A few paces away from William, one of Cobh's better known procuresses, Mrs. Mulligan, constantly scanned the young arrivals, looking for someone she could trick into becoming a prostitute. She'd approached William once, even though he was taller than most, but he'd promptly refused.

He'd never succeed in that trade, since he had no taste for other men.

He wished he, too, had passage out of town. He'd tickled trout once on the journey and eaten at soup kitchens twice. But his stomach still pressed against his backbone like a reminder of his chances without Da: none.

If Da hadn't swallowed his scruples after the girls died and turned to the family's old trade of forgery, they'd both have been six feet under the green sod five years ago. Instead they'd made their way here to Cobh and a pretense of life, in which Da forged and drank to escape the memories and William did his best to protect them both.

Now he needed money. He wasn't handy enough at forgery to earn a living. He was no hand at stealing and there were few legal jobs available, even for those with skills. Besides, Red Niall had made it very clear he wanted William as an enforcer. He'd allow no other role on his turf.

William had seen too many loved ones die, come too close himself to dying, for any illusions about the price of survival. Still, he'd linger as long as possible in the sunshine before he became a hired killer.

A flicker of movement caught his eye. Black Kevin driving a hansom cab and his brothers close at hand? Probably looking for a pigeon to pluck. Black Kevin, or Kevin Dubh in his native Gaelic, had earned that name for his heart, not his coloring, and had no known interest in honest work.

A fashionably dressed young brunette, with perhaps a score of years, came out of the station and hesitated, looking around. Mrs. Mulligan stepped forward hopefully, ready to spin her usual web of false concern.

Another woman, wearing the sober black of a prosperous shopkeeper's wife and followed by a tall manservant, raked Mrs. Mulligan with a glacial stare and brushed by her. No fool, Mrs. Mulligan retreated into a doorway's shadow.

The soberly dressed woman immediately approached the brunette and was recognized.

She seemed familiar to William and he studied her closely. Tall, golden-haired, strong nose and jaw. She had to be someone he'd known from his childhood. With that height, could she be Lady Irene, the mistress of Lyonsgate? But why would an aristocrat dress as a bourgeois or accost a woman at a train station?

The two women spoke, the younger one pretending reluctance for a few minutes before agreeing. Then the three left together, boarding a respectable carriage with two strong men on the box.

Black Kevin promptly whipped up his horse and followed them, his brothers leaping into the cab at the last moment.

William hesitated for an instant. It was none of his affair what Black Kevin did, and wise men avoided tangling with that spawn of Satan. But Lady Irene, who'd kept her tenants safe from the Famine, deserved help if anyone did.

He ran across the street, dodging traffic. "James, boyo, give me a ride in your cab!"

"And why would I be giving you anything?" James retorted, as the last travelers passed by his exceptionally shabby hansom.

"To spike Black Kevin's guns," William said softly.

James stared at him for an instant, then nodded. "Done."

William jumped aboard and they were off, barely managing to stay within sight of Black Kevin. The chase ended in a less than polite neighborhood near the docks, where the respectable carriage waited in front of a small, closed ship's chandlery.

James drove directly past the chandlery and William saw Black Kevin's hansom standing empty in the lane next door. No one in Cobh would be fool enough to harm it.

The narrow street turned sharply a few buildings later and James stopped as soon as they were out of sight.

"This is as much as I can do for you, boyo."

William jumped down and looked back up, with a quick touch to his cap. "My thanks to you."

"May the good saints protect you, boyo." And James was

off. Moments later, William was atop a roof, quietly working his way toward whatever mischief Black Kevin was brewing.

A woman screamed, "Help! Murder!" She was wasting her breath; no one in this district cared about another death.

He spotted the two grooms, lying unmoving inside the carriage, and guarded now by Mickey, Black Kevin's youngest brother. The men were probably still alive, since they were bound. No hope they'd be of help to him, though.

William slipped onto the shop's roof silently, ducked to avoid a broken window large enough for a bull, and found a very small, grimy window to look through. The scene inside on the second floor was as bad as he'd feared.

Black Kevin paced the room, gesticulating with his knife, as he issued orders in barely intelligible English. His brother Red Padraig leaned against the doorway, grinning as he listened and idly kicking the manservant trussed up at his feet.

The two women were bound to the bed's iron headboard, the young one dressed only in underclothes from the waist up. "I didn't ask for them," she bleated, indicating the two thugs. "This was supposed to be my fantasy!"

"Hush, child," Lady Irene soothed. "As for you, sir, you forget yourself. Release us immediately and you won't be arrested."

Black Kevin snorted derisively. "Who's going to arrest Padraig and me? Nobody'll give a damn about three more dead on this street."

The young woman wailed like a banshee at this.

"Silence, bitch. Or you'll be the one doing the bowing and scraping," he snarled, and sliced one of her chemise's shoulder straps. It flopped forward, barely preserving her modesty, and she cried louder.

The manservant tried to roll toward Black Kevin. Red Padraig kicked him back against the wall, where the man gasped for breath.

Black Kevin started to laugh as he tossed his knife from one hand to the other. "What shall I take next?"

A growl vibrated in William's throat. He slid back from his hiding place and silently headed toward the broken window. He'd have to rely on stealth and speed in the coming fight, given the difference in strength between himself and Black Kevin's kin.

Silently, he checked the dirk up his right sleeve, carried by his grandfather in the '97 Rising, and the cut-down saber under his coat, little bigger than one of the new American Bowie knives. Then he quietly slipped into the building.

He crossed the grimy sitting room and came up behind Red Padraig, whose attention was riveted on the hysterical women in the other room. William jumped the stout bully, throttling him with his forearm. A quick slash of his dirk opened the man's jugular.

Over Red Padraig's shoulder, William saw the young woman scream and kick as Black Kevin tossed up her skirts and began to unbutton his pants.

Lady Irene shouted "They'll hang you for this," and desperately tried to cover the other woman.

The blackguard roared with laughter, his attention totally focused on his female prey.

Somehow keeping himself from rushing, William slid the lifeless body to the floor outside the bedroom.

Some animal instinct must have finally warned Black Kevin of danger. He turned toward the door, snarling at the interruption. But the trussed manservant on the floor lashed out his feet and managed to trip the enemy.

William seized the heaven-sent opening and swept the saber through the villain's throat.

Black Kevin stayed upright for an endless moment as horrified realization dawned in his eyes, then crumpled into a disjointed heap on the floor. The servant jerked out of the way as Black Kevin's head came to rest against the wall.

The half-dressed woman fainted, her body sliding down the headboard. Lady Irene gasped and hid her face.

Silence finally filled the room.

William crossed himself automatically and yanked a curtain down to veil the corpse. Ladies weren't accustomed to a slum's everyday sights. He cut the manservant's bonds then went to rescue the young lady.

"Irene, my love," the man choked as he freed Lady Irene with Black Kevin's knife.

"Jocelyn, my darling," she sobbed. They clung together, shaking and kissing passionately.

William cleaned his weapons, then turned to leave. It was none of his affair if Lady Irene's lover was a servant. Rescuing those two grooms from Black Kevin's remaining brother was more important.

"Wait, lad. I'm coming with you."

William measured Jocelyn with his eyes, then nodded at Black Kevin's big knife clutched in the man's hand. "You know how to use that?"

"I've fenced with sabers in England and on the Continent."

"Right then. But be as silent as possible."

Just then, a call reached them from outside. "Kevin, can I come in now? You said I could have the tall one first."

Jocelyn growled almost soundlessly. William glanced at him, then indicated the stairs. They went down into the deserted shop, taking up positions on either side of the door.

The doorknob rattled. "Bloody hell, Padraig, if you're on her now, I'll crack your head in."

The door opened, and Mickey, a man close to William's age, marched in, still whining. "Kevin, you promised her to . . ."

Jocelyn sprang upon him before he finished the sentence. The following fight was savage but brief while William waited, ready to intervene if necessary. But the manservant was a better fighter than he'd expected. He easily blocked the other's first wild lunge and ran the big knife through the thug's heart. Mickey was dead in an instant.

Jocelyn stepped back carefully, his hand over his mouth,

then ran outside to retch. William's mouth twitched sympathetically. Killing a man was always hard and this was likely Jocelyn's first.

"Lad." Lady Irene stood at the foot of the stairs. She was pale and trembling, her hands clasped tightly. Still, she'd recovered her self-possession remarkably fast, as she always had in his father's tales.

"My lady." He took off his cap and bowed, as he'd learned in earliest childhood.

"My thanks, lad. You undoubtedly saved our virtue and our lives."

"I am honored to have been of service to you, my lady." Instinctively, William used the genteel English accent he'd mimicked as a child. "Is the other lady recovering?"

Lady Irene nodded absently but continued to scrutinize William. "Miss Whittington wished for some privacy while she used the facilities. Are there any remaining villains outside?"

"Not to my knowledge, my lady."

"Then let us free my two grooms while my companions compose themselves."

"As you wish, my lady."

The carriage was accompanied only by its horses and two grooms. William cut the unconscious men's bonds and Lady Irene checked their pulses. Satisfied by their condition, Lady Irene spoke again just as William turned to walk away.

"You're the true surprise, lad. Where did you learn to speak the Queen's English so well?"

So she hadn't recognized him. Not surprising: William had been barely eight when his parents were turned off, in his lordship's bid to save money after rent rolls collapsed during the Famine's first year. "My father was undergroom to Lord Charles Mitchell and my mother was nursery maid, God rest their souls."

Her eyes softened. "My condolences. Did you recognize me earlier, lad? My first husband was the Earl of Albany and we toured Bantry Bay often. We stayed with Lord Charles more than once."

"Yes, my lady. You own Lyonsgate."

She nodded, smiling. "I have that honor."

Jocelyn came up behind her quietly, having apparently recovered his composure, at least for the present. He produced some coins from his pocket, appropriate behavior for a servant escorting a gentlewoman, and held them out. Gold coins.

William hesitated, then took the chance. "If you please, my lady."

"Don't you want the money, lad?"

"If you please, my lady, I'd rather have a post at Lyonsgate."

"As boot boy?" she asked, raising one aristocratic eyebrow.

William gulped at the thought of regular meals, a roof over his head, and clothes on his back. But he held his ground. "I believe I would be more useful as a groom, my lady."

Her eyes widened with surprise, then narrowed. Jocelyn's eyes narrowed as well, but he remained silent. "How old are you, lad?"

"Seventeen in November, my lady."

"And you believe sixteen years of life qualifies you to tend my horses?"

"Yes, my lady," William said stubbornly. His jaw set hard. A few years of a groom's tips should be enough for passage to America. Even if his audacity cost him the money, he'd be no worse off than he'd been this morning.

She surveyed him for a long minute, a stare that might have quelled even the Lord Lieutenant of Ireland. Her lover was silent, watching her more than William.

Finally she looked over her shoulder at Jocelyn, who nodded slightly. Her gaze returned to William, bearing a hint of a smile.

"What's your name, lad?"

"William Donovan, my lady."

"Then you may be my fourth undergroom, William."

"Yes, my lady. Thank you, my lady. And you, sir."

"And here's my thanks for protecting my wife," the man added, finally dropping the coins into William's palm.

He was her husband? Then why was he dressed as a servant?

William bowed again. "Thank you, my lord."

"Mr. Fitzgerald to you, William."

"Yes, Mr. Fitzgerald."

"William."

"Yes, my lady?"

"How many men have you killed?" Her voice wavered for the first time on the last word.

"Do you truly want to know, my lady?"

"No need to say more, William. You have given me the answer."

He'd reached Lyonsgate, and a new life, within days. Lady Irene had also given James and his family a cottage on another estate. When William left in 1855 after three years' service, Lady Irene and Mr. Fitzgerald had given him the money and contacts needed to smooth his way in San Francisco.

William considered his time there, pondering what could be used in his present situation. What would Lady Irene, the daughter and widow of earls, expect to find for her comfort? Clothes, certainly, and good food. A maid. What else?

Viola shifted against him. William froze. She muttered something in her sleep, then relaxed again.

He exhaled slowly and kissed the top of her head. He hadn't known he was holding his breath.

What trinkets could aid his dalliance with Viola? He'd brought only a few gewgaws with him, preferring to keep his favorite trifles at home in San Francisco rather than use them to titillate courtesans. Now he wished he'd brought his entire collection with him, just to see Viola's face when she opened the first chest. Would her eyes widen in shock or close in rapture the first time he teased her with a bit of jade?

He choked as his cock jerked at the thought.

William carried Viola to the settee in the corner, mercifully free of the paperwork that cluttered every other surface. Her fingers slid down his arm as he stood up, evoking a frisson that ran all the way to his head and groin. He took a deep breath then moved away. There'd be time enough to savor her touch later.

He found Abraham sweeping the colonnade outside the office. Morgan was in the side yard, checking the fittings on the ammunition wagon, while all his other men were too distant from the office to have heard much. Unless of course, he'd shouted louder than he had thought.

"Yes, sir?" Abraham asked politely as he set aside the broom.

"There are a few matters needing your immediate attention, Abraham."

"Sir." Abraham came to full attention.

"Mrs. Ross will be my *chère amie* for the next three months. She will share my quarters and be under my protection at all times. Your first duty is to guard her as you would me."

The former enforcer bowed deeply. "My pleasure, sir."

"Mrs. Ross will also require a personal maid. Please ask Sarah to attend her. Ah Lum can cook for the household, as he did before our arrival. If necessary, ask China Mary to send additional help. Everything must flow as smoothly as possible."

"Certainly, sir. My wife and I will do our best to be worthy of your trust."

"There'll probably be trouble with Lennox and his thugs. Be careful, especially when Mrs. Ross is outside the compound or depot."

The other nodded. "She will be safe, sir. My life on it."

"Thank you," William said sincerely. Heaven forbid Abraham's phrase was a prophecy. He continued briskly, "Mrs. Ross will need clothes, as well. Ask China Mary for clothes the Chinese tailors can create quickly, items suitable for a lady of high fashion."

"Yes, sir."

"I'll also need some Chinese clothing for her, such as a very pampered concubine would wear."

"I will visit China Mary myself and select only the best for your woman, sir."

How had Abraham managed to change from implacable enforcer to suave man of the world without moving a muscle? "Good. We'll stay here at the depot till supper, which gives you some time to prepare."

Abraham bowed. "Until this evening, sir."

William smiled as he watched his houseman disappear up the street. Then he went to see how Morgan was faring with the ammunition wagon.

Lennox drove into the depot within the hour, his gaze sweeping across the busy confines. William finished the knot and left the wagon without a backward glance. Securing the colonel's furniture could wait until he'd dealt with the potential threat to Viola.

"Donovan," Lennox snapped, and yanked the gelding to a halt, causing the usually patient beast to toss its head in complaint. He smoothed his jacket back, disclosing a Colt's fancy handle. A bloody bandage was wrapped around his right hand.

William's eyes narrowed. "Lennox." He faced his visitor openly, hands away from his weapons in a show of peace. One of the sentries turned to watch and the depot's usual hubbub began to quiet as other men noticed.

Paul plastered a polite smile on his face as he waited for Donovan to approach. Damn all these arrogant Irishmen anyway. Why didn't they just crawl back into their hovels and die?

At least in New York he made money from them, selling them a few square feet in a tenement to rest their filthy bodies. But in this hellhole, he had to pay an Irishman if he wanted anything delivered. And to have his precious silver hauled out, the priceless ore that would give him back his proper position in society and crush that Vanderbilt scum.

Intolerable to be beholden like this.

Sunlight glinted from one of the sentries' rifles. Paul's eyes flickered around the depot quickly. Trust the Irishman to keep his stores well guarded, and by men who'd fought in the recent unpleasantness. He recognized a Union cavalryman he'd last seen fighting in the Wilderness, now standing beside a flour barrel with a very serviceable carbine in his hands.

Paul nodded an acknowledgment, which was curtly returned. Then he returned his attention to the big Irishman, careful to modulate his tone.

"What a pleasure to see you again, Donovan. Perhaps you can help me."

"Glad to do what I can, Lennox."

"I was told Mrs. Ross came here little more than an hour ago. Where did she go next?"

Donovan's face didn't change but Paul sensed immediately something had gone wrong. What could have happened? Had she run off to the Indians, as she'd threatened?

No, she mustn't die yet.

"Mrs. Ross is here with me," Donovan answered calmly.

Surely he'd misheard. "What do you mean, 'with you'? She's marrying me today."

Donovan shook his head. "Mrs. Ross will be living under my protection for the next three months."

Three months! Too damn long. Her brother could be here well before then to take her back to Ohio. Then he'd have to court her like anyone else, a ridiculous delay when he could have all that lovely money now. "The devil you say! You must be joking. She'd never tolerate the likes of you for five minutes."

Donovan's mouth tightened. "She asked for my aid, Lennox, and I gave my word on it."

"You cur, you've stolen her from me. Stand aside and let me through," Paul demanded, his voice rising, and reached for his revolver. His gelding sidled, clearly unsettled by the commotion.

A rifle was cocked up on the rooftops, then another, and a third only a few feet away.

Paul froze, recognizing the sound all too well. Slowly he removed his hand from his revolver, the cut complaining bitterly at the movement. Furious, he tightened the reins in order to quell his fretful horse, while he wondered how he could escape with his skin intact.

"No, she's resting and must not be disturbed," Donovan answered calmly. The arrogant prick had not even reached for a weapon, Paul realized. Not that he needed to, with so many of his men nearby. "My regrets for any misunderstanding that may have existed between us," Donovan added smoothly.

"Yes, a misunderstanding, of course." Irish scum. The other brutes were gathering now, their weapons blatantly ready, even without a signal from Donovan.

Paul gathered his last shreds of composure. The most important thing was to get out of here alive. After that he could decide how best to make Donovan regret his presumption, damn his dirty Irish hide. "Pray convey my compliments to Mrs. Ross. I shall hope to call upon her again when she is feeling recovered. Good day."

Donovan nodded in response. "Good day, Lennox."

Paul turned the buggy in a series of harsh jerks. Its wheels grazed more than one of the heavy wagons, scraping paint but not stopping him. Finally, he was free of the Irishman's mud-brick warren and on his own streets.

He cursed viciously as he drove. Losing Viola Ross like this was intolerable. He'd wed a toothpick if it brought him a quarter of a million dollars. But when an immense fortune was attached to a lady of the highest social standing? Such a bride would grind those Vanderbilt parvenus into the dust, along with the woman who'd dared to reject him then marry a Vanderbilt dependent.

Donovan had lied, of course, when he said Viola Ross came to him. Her parents came from the finest families in New York and Kentucky; she'd never sully herself with an Irishman. No, Donovan must have stolen her, hungry for a lady to assuage his animal lusts. Not because of her money or he'd have married her immediately.

An abortionist would have to flush her womb immediately after he regained her. No Lennox would ever rear or give his name to a bastard of that Irish devil.

He'd also need Donovan killed immediately. Paul stroked the reins slowly as he considered possibilities. Shot dead in the street perhaps. No, crippled and left for the Apaches would be better. He smiled at the thought, remembering the more lurid tales of their cruel creativity.

But who would run the freighting business then, and carry the silver out? It would probably be Evans, who wanted to raise the shipping rates into this hellhole. Paul cursed softly. He'd be better off dealing with Donovan, who was rarely in Rio Piedras and could probably be bamboozled by juggling numbers.

None of this solved the real problem: Viola's brother. Hal Lindsay, a first-class Missouri River pilot and Union Navy lieutenant during the war, was now searching for his sister somewhere in Colorado, possibly as close as Santa Fe. Lindsay was no man to be trifled with, especially with his formidable family's resources behind him.

No need, of course, to involve Nick back in New York. This matter should be solved in Arizona where it began.

The buggy climbed toward the mine offices, the gelding

trotting smoothly now. Paul barely noticed the men jumping out of his way.

He was glad he'd paid the hooligans in Santa Fe to attack Lindsay. That should buy him a little more time to obtain Mrs. Ross, even if Lindsay survived.

Perhaps money would loosen Donovan's grip on Mrs. Ross. If not, the O'Flahertys were very good at applying persuasion to stubborn fools. Donovan would be lucky to escape with his skin.

Paul chuckled at the thought of Donovan's face sliced open by one of Conall O'Flaherty's more inventive knife moves. His wounded hand lifted to fondle his muttonchops, causing a stab of pain.

Then he'd have the joy of punishing Mrs. Ross for cutting his hand with that bottle. Who would have thought a lady could pull off a veteran knife fighter's move like that? Ross must have taught her, of course. He'd been a cunning fighter in that last fight.

He'd had other ridiculous ideas as well. Imagine refusing to claim Mrs. Ross' inheritance after Paul informed him, saying he preferred to prove his capabilities by making his own fortune. Then he'd swaggered off to tell his wife the news. Paul hadn't believed for a moment Mrs. Ross would dismiss a fortune as quickly, so he'd run his sword stick through Ross, planning to marry her as soon as Ross was buried.

Then the stupid bitch had declined his offer over and over again.

She needed a lesson for humiliating him so often, with her refusals and then bloodying his hand. He'd mark her in return, someplace painful . . .

Paul smiled at the possibilities.

He tied off his buggy and headed into his office, happily fondling his muttonchops and ready to plan his grand mansion on the Hudson. The first blueprints had just arrived and the builder had promised to break ground by July if Paul approved.

Chapter Five

"**S**weetheart."

The baritone voice was a velvet rumble close by. Viola stirred reluctantly.

"Sweetheart, it's time to wake up."

Viola roused slowly. William Donovan was sitting beside her on the settee? How on earth could this have happened?

Memories flooded her, followed by a wave of heat. She closed her eyes in embarrassment.

Donovan kissed her hand. "It's time for dinner. I'll wait outside while you wash up. Then we can go uphill to the compound, if you're still willing to keep our bargain."

Viola nodded jerkily without opening her eyes.

He stood up and caressed her hair lightly. "Don't delay too long. I might have to come find you."

"I'll only be a moment," Viola managed. She was still trembling slightly when she joined him, every fold of her dress and hair on her head as tidy as she could make them.

Donovan's head came up at her entrance. His blue eyes traveled over her slowly, lingering on her hair. "You look as lovely as a rose garden in the moonlight, sweetheart."

She blinked at the unexpected compliment. Surely, he didn't need to pay homage when she'd already agreed to be his mistress. Still, it was very nice to be treated as a lady. She dropped a small curtsy to him. "Thank you, kind sir."

She accepted his proffered arm, feeling much more confident.

Donovan took her up the private path to the Donovan compound, instead of the more leisurely route through the public streets.

Rio Piedras's springs tumbled out of several points in the steep hills. One bubbled up at the big compound, which overlooked the depot from atop a sheer bluff. The location and year-round water made it the most defensible building in town, as well as one of the least convenient. Still, Viola well understood why Rio Piedras's original Mexican founders had built their first substantial dwelling on that rocky promontory.

She glanced over at Donovan as they climbed up the steep stairs. The setting sun highlighted the muscles in his wide shoulders. He must have carried her to the settee as easily as if she were a baby. How would he use that strength later?

Blushing, she sought something else to think about. A matron for more than five years and now a widow, she should be long past blushing like a schoolgirl over a handsome man. A boulder caught her attention, with its suggestion of silver ore. "Do any of the Golconda's galleries come near your compound, Mr. Donovan?"

"No, the closest one stops about ten yards away. Even if I agreed, they'd have to blast to come closer."

"Really? But silver is so easy to find everywhere else in town."

"Which makes the mine galleries so close to the surface that a heavy wagon can break through. Not by my operations, thank you."

Viola grinned at his emphatic refusal. Lennox must have been furious when Donovan denied him, something no one else would have dared to do.

The Donovan & Sons compound was a classic mud-brick structure built in the form of an irregular square, its thick walls providing protection from both Apaches and the sun.

Donovan took her in through a heavy wooden gate, scarred from past battles, and down a narrow passage into the great central courtyard, which swept in a series of terraces and steps up the hill.

She studied the compound eagerly, glad to finally see the inside of the largest residence in Rio Piedras. It was totally unlike Lennox's house, a very modern and quite ugly wooden structure.

They'd entered through the storeroom wing, the individual rooms marked by sturdy doors and few windows. The wing on its left held a small stable, with chickens, pigs, and goats penned outside. The other two wings were evidently living quarters, one holding the teamsters' dormitory and the entrance from the main street. The highest wing must contain living spaces for Donovan and Evans, plus the kitchen.

An arched colonnade ringed the courtyard, linking the different wings. Watchtowers stood at two diagonally opposite corners, occupied now by vigilant teamsters guarding the wagons and mules below. Viola could see them with their big telescopes through the watchtowers' enormous windows.

Yellow roses covered arbors in the courtyard, providing shade and an illusion of privacy. Water danced in a brilliantly hued tiled fountain in the courtyard's center, where the ancient spring brought life.

A small shrine, containing a statue of a woman, stood in one corner, and a graceful table holding candles, incense censers, and bowls of roses. Viola immediately hoped to examine the shrine more closely at another time. The statue looked Chinese, similar to one of Kuan Yin her grandmother owned, but held a small baby, as a Catholic's Madonna would.

She could hear balls caroming around a billiards table in the distance, but few other signs of Donovan's teamsters.

Viola nervously wondered how the main living quarters were furnished. Donovan wasn't here often but he was most considerate of his men's comfort, such as Evans who split his time between Rio Piedras and Tucson. Rumor said furniture and fancy goods had been delivered but no one knew what they consisted of.

Perhaps Donovan had a private parlor or even a private bedroom. She shivered at the thought and his hand tightened on her elbow.

"Are you well, Mrs. Ross?"

"Yes, thank you. Just a breeze from the valley, I think."

Donovan made a noncommittal sound but drew her closer. His hot male strength burned through the thin calico and his breath stirred her hair against her cheek. She wanted him to move away so she could remember how to breathe. At the same time, she longed for him to come closer so his knowing hands could touch her intimate flesh again.

She gulped at the thought.

Mercifully, they reached the main wing a few minutes later, after crossing the last terrace. His houseman waited there in front of the colonnade, face impassive when he bowed. "Good evening, sir."

"Good evening, Abraham," Donovan answered easily. "Mrs. Ross, this is Abraham Chang, my houseman, who I would trust with my life. I've asked him to guard you when I cannot."

Abraham bowed deeply. "Mrs. Ross."

Viola blinked, then smiled shyly at the big Chinaman. As the younger daughter and considered unlikely to marry, she'd never had a personal servant before, unlike her mother and older sister. "I'm very glad to meet you, Abraham."

Abraham bowed again. "It is my honor to serve you, Mrs. Ross."

"Is dinner ready, Abraham?" Donovan asked.

"Yes, sir." Abraham turned and led the way into a small parlor, prepared for a party of two. It was a man's room softened by bowls of yellow roses, with white candles rising tall and serene. Mouthwatering aromas rose from covered dishes on the elegant walnut table and sideboard. Rich Persian carpets covered the floor.

A magnificent, rosewood square grand piano fit neatly into the space by the far wall, unlike a modern curved grand piano which would have occupied most of the room.

Viola's fingers ached for it.

An exquisite Chinese woman, dressed in an upper servant's formal black, curtsied to Donovan. Viola's attention snapped back to the room's other occupants.

"Mrs. Ross, this is Sarah Chang, Abraham's wife. She will act as your personal maid, if that's agreeable with you. Nuns in China trained her as maidservant and cook."

A maid and a bodyguard? Dear heavens, Donovan was lavishing care on her. "I'm sure she will suit me very well, Mr. Donovan. I've never had a personal maid before. How do you do, Sarah?" Viola held out her hand and Sarah smiled as she shook it and dropped another curtsy.

Then Donovan's hand touched Viola's elbow again and coherent thought fled as they sat down, with her back to that alluring piano.

They talked a bit, mostly of trifles, although Viola couldn't have recounted the conversation later to save her life. She thought the food was delicious; she must have eaten some of it because Donovan didn't mention her lack of appetite. Abraham waited on them, silently anticipating their every want.

All the while, she could think only of Donovan and wonder what he meant to do.

He'd been gentle in his office, giving her pleasure when it added nothing to his comfort. Her breasts ached at the memory of how his voice and hand had worked together on her. Perhaps he really did know other things to increase a woman's passion.

"How's Tennessee?" Viola managed to ask, watching Donovan deftly peel an orange. Strong hands. Long fingers that had known her so intimately only a few hours ago. She wrenched her eyes away and fixed them on his face.

"Well enough. Give him a week's rest and he'll be leading

another ammunition wagon again." Donovan offered her a section of the rare fruit. She'd tasted one once before, a Christmas treat at her grandfather's Manhattan mansion.

Viola nodded acceptance, expecting him to pass it to her on a plate. Instead he lifted the delicacy up toward her, clearly expecting her to eat out of his hand.

Viola's jaw fell open in shock. He instantly popped the tidbit between her teeth. She helplessly closed her mouth and chewed, staring at his face. The fruit tasted delicious, tangy and sweet at the same time. She swallowed and another section was offered.

"Mr. Donovan," she managed to protest. "There's no need to feed me."

"But I enjoy doing so, sweetheart," he purred. His rich, hypnotic rumble made her heart skip a beat. "And you promised to serve my pleasure, did you not?"

He brushed the morsel over her lips, painting them with the tantalizing taste.

"Sweetheart," he urged. It was a command, for all that his voice was soft. What could it hurt, to obey him when the reward would be so sweet? Viola opened her mouth and accepted the second helping.

"There now, Viola, doesn't that taste good? Eat it leisurely so you can savor every morsel."

She obeyed him, baffled by how much attention he paid to feeding her.

"Here's another bite for you. Take your time," he coaxed. "Let its sweetness glide down your throat."

The fruit's exotic taste rolled over her tongue with every slow bite.

"Now shut your eyes and heed only the orange. Just chew and swallow. You've all the time in the world, sweetheart. Enjoy it," he purred.

Viola followed his voice's sweet persuasion, closing her eyes to better concentrate. The tangy juice brought new life to her mouth, so long accustomed to beans and cornbread.

Whenever she finished a bite, the next one waited for her. She was held in a world defined by his voice in her ears and his fruit wending its way through her mouth and deep into her belly.

She opened for the next morsel and his mouth captured hers. He played with her, as if the kiss was a game to explore her shapes and textures and taste. Caught off balance as she was, it felt completely natural to yield to his caress.

Viola moaned when his tongue first delved deep. Her hand came up to pull his head closer. She threaded her fingers into his hair's thick silk, fondling him. He growled softly and kissed her harder.

It seemed but an instant later when she came up for air and found herself lifted high in his arms. "Mr. Donovan," she protested, but it sounded rather more like a plea.

He glanced down at her. "Do you want to kiss me again, sweetheart?"

Viola gaped at him. "What did you say?"

"Like this." His mouth swooped down and she was lost again in a world of sweet sensation.

She blinked when he stopped, and slowly opened her eyes. She was in a small bathroom of very simple but modern design. Donovan stood directly in front of her, his big hands lightly caressing her shoulders. His touch sent quivers running through her skin and a hot flush up her throat.

"Be quick about it, sweetheart." He dropped a kiss on her hair and left. Viola shook herself for a few moments, trying to regain control, then obeyed him.

She came out shyly and found herself in a very elegant and simply equipped bedroom. The mahogany furnishings were sturdily built in a style suited to a gentleman of considerable means but discreet tastes. The walls wore a smooth white plaster coat and massive wooden beams supported the ceiling. Persian carpets flowed across the tile floor, while heavy cream brocade draperies covered the high windows. The linens were of the highest quality, with a silken coverlet draping the bed. The light, sweet scent of China roses and sage drifted in from the courtyard beyond.

But Viola paid very little attention to these elegancies. Instead her gaze was riveted upon the man himself. She'd been too nervous to consider his clean-limbed frame before. Now, the sight of him struck her like a thunderbolt. He had stripped off his shirt and was even now placing it on the campaign chest at the foot of the bed, revealing his bare back. Muscles rippled, bisected by the strong line of his spine until it vanished beneath his trousers. Oh happy woolen cloth, to envelop a firm masculine derrière such as his.

Her mouth went dry. She swallowed and tried to say something, anything.

"Sweetheart." He faced her with a single raised eyebrow. His chest was bare, except for a cross and two medals hanging from a gold chain around his neck. She stared, caught by strength as firmly defined as any sculptor's work.

Viola ran her tongue over her lips. "Mr. Donovan," she croaked.

"Sweetheart." His voice was deeper and closer to her. Those elegant brown nipples moved with every breath he took. She shook a little, unable to look away, while her own breasts heated.

He tilted her face up with one finger. "Sweetheart, do you want to kiss my chest again, so soon after this afternoon's dalliance?"

Her gaze shot up to his face. She quivered at the amused warmth in his eyes as he caressed her cheek with that callused finger.

"It sounds an amiable pastime to me," he drawled, and she swallowed hard. Heat glowed deep in her belly at the thought of touching him again.

"But for now I prefer the delight of fondling you," he finished. He swirled his tongue over her lips and she quivered, reminded of his gentle play with the orange. Donovan probed the seam between her lips and teased her teeth.

Viola yielded her mouth with a sigh. His hand slipped behind her head, supporting her while he took his pleasure, deep and long. Her senses shimmered, then focused only on what he was doing, here and now.

He lifted his head and smiled at her. "You're a tempting little filly and I would see more of you. Turn so I can unbutton you, sweetheart."

"Mr. Donovan," she began hesitantly. Surely he wouldn't expect her to undress in front of him, something even a husband didn't require. "Are you certain?"

Donovan's sapphire eyes narrowed. "Are you refusing me? Going back on your word so soon?"

"Certainly not!" Viola snapped, her spine stiffening in outrage. "Lindsays never break their word, Mr. Donovan." She spun around and presented him with the desired aspect of her body. *How dare he even suggest such a thing,* she fumed, tapping her toe.

She was still seething while he efficiently opened her dress down the back. Then he kissed the nape of her neck, nuzzling the sensitive point, and her affront vanished. Her brain skidded until she could barely remember he'd offended her.

Donovan slipped his hand inside the calico, and the corset beneath, until he cupped her breasts. His thumbs rubbed and plucked her nipples. He pulled her back against him so she straddled his leg. She twisted restlessly, unable to define what she wanted.

"Perfect," he murmured. She moaned when he licked the pulse point behind her ear. Her breasts were swollen and aching as his knowing hands incited her to madness.

He released her abruptly and pulled her dress down to the floor, pausing only to unbutton the cuffs. Another moment made quick work of her canvas corset. She barely had time to draw a few breaths before she stood in only her chemise and drawers, with her boots below.

Viola bowed her head, trying to regain mastery of her whirling thoughts.

Then he gripped her waist lightly, turned her around, and seated her on the bed. He dropped to his knees and began to rapidly unfasten her boots.

"Mr. Donovan," Viola stammered, looking down at the glossy black head so close to her loins. She could smell his scent now, all sandalwood and something uniquely him. Perhaps his musk. "Perhaps I should relieve you of that chore?"

"Did I say it was a chore?" He tossed one boot aside and went to work on the other.

"No, sir." Was she expected to believe that all men took their mistress's footgear off?

The second boot thudded against the wall next to the first. Viola's eyes were enormous as they scanned the untidy heap, which seemed so out of character for him.

Donovan stood up smoothly, close enough that she could feel his breath on her mouth. "Bend your head forward, sweetheart."

What on earth? "Yes, sir."

He plucked pins out with what felt like trembling fingers. Surely she was wrong about that: he must be skilled at undoing women's hair. He plunged his hands into the heavy strands with what sounded like a groan. Moments later, her pale locks rippled down to her waist.

"You are a very beautiful woman, sweetheart," he murmured, and kissed her again. She yielded gratefully, relieved to do something she understood at least partly. Heat strengthened in her gut and her skin was sensitive beyond all belief to his nearness.

His lips traveled over her face and down her throat until he reached her breasts. He lingered there, nuzzling and licking until her nipples glowed like cherries. He suckled and she groaned, her head falling back as sensations washed over her. She'd never thought anything could feel so sweet as the way his mouth's every pull tightened something deep inside her. Her fingers unconsciously threaded into his hair.

His warm hand cupped her mound through her drawers. Viola moaned. His finger teased her through the threadbare cloth as dew flowed in response. She tossed her head, sobbing and aching.

"Lean back, sweetheart." His voice was a dark ribbon of command. She obeyed instinctively and he removed her drawers.

A draft touched her knees as his tongue swirled through her intimate folds. Viola gasped in shock—and pleasure. Who'd have thought that such a simple thing could be so alluring? The first rhythmic pulse of ecstasy thudded deep in her loins.

Donovan licked her again and again, exploring her as if she were the road to El Dorado. Dew gushed and flowed, summoned by his caresses, until she twisted and moaned. Her legs wrapped around his head as she burned with need.

Then his finger explored her, circling the hidden entrance. His teeth tugged gently on her pearl and sent her hurtling into rapture, sobbing with shock as that single digit entered her.

She gasped when Donovan continued to drive her insane, denying her the time to catch her breath and return to the mundane world. His tongue danced over her skin to a rhythm she couldn't predict, yet excited her like nothing she'd encountered before. His rough, callused finger delved deeper into her tight sheath and teased unfamiliar nerves into life. Any comparison to what her own hand had evoked from her intimate flesh faded as ecstasy built once more.

"Mr. Donovan, please," she begged. "Must you do this again so soon?"

"Yes." He blew on her pearl. Viola gasped and climaxed helplessly.

More pinnacles followed as his knowing hands and mouth turned her into a being of liquid fire, every nerve responsive to his lightest whim. He worked a second digit into her, and a third. Her heated folds stretched to accommodate his insistence and the accompanying pleasure. If she twisted and sobbed, it was only so her hips could rub her yearning flesh against him.

Did she have two more climaxes? Or three? Perhaps there were four.

Finally a pause enabled her to open her eyes. She found Donovan leaning over her, watching her with half-shuttered eyes and face gleaming with her carnal juices. Her chemise had vanished at some prior moment, as evidenced by his big hand slowly fondling her bare, and eagerly upthrust, breasts.

More shockingly, his trousers had also departed. Now his hips were snug against hers so his crisp hairs teased her intimately. His cock pressed against her feminine folds like a burning iron brand.

A slow wave of heat mounted to her cheeks. "Mr. Donovan, please," she begged, but couldn't have said for what.

"You're hot and wet and yielding, sweetheart. Are you ready for me?" He rubbed himself against her. She closed her eyes at another gush of dew from her loins. She needed more, whatever happened.

"Please," she groaned. "Mr. Donovan, please take me." Shyly, her hand stroked his arm, savoring the hard muscles and the surprisingly delicate veins.

"Ah, sweetheart, you've a way of expressing yourself that any man would find irresistible." A faint brogue softened his deep voice. He moved away from her and she glimpsed his cock: immense, brilliantly crimson, throbbing. She quivered with fear and anticipation.

Then he opened a tin with a small click and extracted something from it. A moment later, he deftly slipped a sheath, made of a very thin membrane, over his cock and tied it in place with a ribbon. "Is that a French letter?" she asked without thinking, then blushed scarlet.

His eyes twinkled. "Indeed it is, sweetheart. But I prefer its older name of condom. And you will use that name, as well."

Viola gulped and nodded as Donovan returned to his previous position between her legs, rubbing himself against her and fondling her tender breasts until she thought she'd go mad. "Mr. Donovan, why must you tease me so? Please, I beg of you, do something."

He chuckled, more a strained groan than a laugh. His cock nudged her then slowly entered, restrained only by his discipline. Her body burned with the pain of accommodating him. Yet it felt right to do so.

She lay there with him and her breathing gradually steadied. Her deep internal muscles slowly adapted to the differing widths of his cock's head and shaft.

A callused finger toyed with her nipple. Slowly her body's ache changed from the agony of accepting him to the torment of needing more. Her sheath pulsed pleadingly and her womb clenched in hunger.

"Mr. Donovan, please . . ."

"Easy, sweetheart, easy," he soothed her. "Don't be ruining a fine moment with your impetuosity." The Irish accent was definitely stronger now but Viola didn't care. She wanted satisfaction, not self-control, from him.

"Donovan, dammit, hurry up." She grabbed his shoulders, digging her nails into him.

"Sweetheart, I'd no idea your mouth could shape vulgarities," he drawled as another inch of his heated shaft sank into her.

Viola wrapped her legs around his hips and heard him groan. She sighed with relief as he entered her further and further, urged on by her throbbing loins and shuddering groans.

He stopped too soon, with a light breath of air against her intimate folds rather than his hot skin. She was stuffed full of his masculinity, her channel spread wider than she'd ever imagined. Every sense was engorged by him, the scent of his musk, the sound of his seductive voice, the feel of his hands gripping her . . .

But it wasn't enough. She wanted all of this man, burned

to contain every inch of his shaft. She wanted nothing between then, not even the hint of a breeze. Her hips circled and arched in a desperate bid for completion. Suddenly, something deep inside shifted and opened for him.

And Donovan's cock settled its last inch in her as easily as a knife into hot custard. He choked out a word in a language she'd never heard before. His arms slipped around her as she happily took his full weight.

"Oh yes," Viola moaned, and nuzzled his shoulder. Her channel flexed around him, eager for his next move. "Oh yes, Donovan."

Then he began to move. His cock glided out of her until only its head linked them. He slowly filled her again and repeated the cycle.

Viola tightened herself around him when he withdrew the second time. He growled at that but kept to his desired tempo, gradually building up speed until he was slamming into her with a force that made the bed shake.

"More, Donovan, more! Please," Viola sobbed. She wrapped her arms and legs around him so that her limbs clung to his torso as strongly as her folds kissed his cock. Sweat dripped from both of them as their flesh slapped against each other.

Still he rode her, hard and long, while his sapphire eyes watched her. He varied the angle and depth of his strokes as if exploring even the most hidden parts of her. He slowed whenever she approached a climax, then returned to shafting her when her breathing eased.

"Please, please," she begged, but he continued to push them both further. Rapture built in every fiber of Viola's body. She was agonizingly aware of him and desperate for the release only he could give.

"That's my sweetheart," he praised her after one particularly anguishing pause. She could only moan in response, having lost the ability to form words under the pressure of her sensual agony.

His speed increased again and again until she was sliding back and forth across the bed's silken coverlet with every stroke. Drums built deep within her core, gathering together in a demanding choir.

Suddenly he froze and threw his head back with a shout. His cock pulsed and erupted deep inside her. Freed by his pleasure, waves of rapture thundered up through her core.

Viola sobbed her pleasure to the universe as she climaxed.

She drifted back to consciousness slowly and found herself curled amidst the sheets, the silken coverlet now tossed onto the floor. Viola blinked at the disarray next to the bed, which didn't match any memory of something she'd done. The only light came from a single small lamp near the bed.

Then a cool washcloth stroked the inside of her thighs, soothing her tender skin. She purred as her legs automatically fell further open.

"Good girl," a dark voice rumbled.

She squeaked and stared up for the first time at the cloth's wielder. "Mr. Donovan, what are you doing?"

"Preparing you for our next ride, sweetheart." He rinsed the cloth in a basin and gently cleaned her intimate folds.

"Next ride? When?"

"As soon as you're refreshed and ready, sweetheart."

"Tonight?"

"Of course." He dipped the washcloth into the cool water again. "You're an exciting filly and I'll enjoy you every chance I have. Did you expect something different?"

Viola gulped. "No, sir." No wonder he spent so much money at Mrs. Smith's if his appetites were this strong. Still, his first possession of her *had* been as fine as dollar cotton.

She smiled at the recollection and shot a quick glance at his groin. His cock rested against his thigh, rich with color but not yet rampant with eagerness.

Donovan dropped the cloth into the basin finally and returned both to the bathroom. She rolled to her side to watch him and fumbled for a sheet when he returned.

"Sweetheart," he warned. "Did I tell you to hide yourself from me?"

Her hand stilled guiltily. "No, sir."

Donovan drew the fine linen away from her, making her tremble. He sat down next to her and thumbed her nipple casually as he watched. It promptly remembered its adventures earlier that evening and hardened in anticipation.

"Your breasts are too rich a treasure to be hidden, sweetheart," he mused.

Viola couldn't think of a word to say. She'd always considered herself scrawny, hardly the sort of female a man would like to watch. Her pulse pounded and dew built between her legs again.

"You'll only cover yourself with what I give you, sweetheart. Do you understand?" Donovan looked up at her face, his hand still doing miraculous things to her eager flesh.

She blinked. Was there a hidden meaning to his command? It seemed innocuous enough. It was so hard to think when his fingers moved like that. "Yes, sir, I understand."

"Good filly," he praised, and dropped his mouth to her. She gasped and arched up against him.

And Donovan savored her breasts as if he'd only just encountered them . . .

William lay quietly in the bed with Viola, listening to her sleep. Her delectable rump was tucked neatly against him, a warm pillow for his cock. Moonlight slipped around the curtains and painted her in shimmering silver.

He stroked her slowly, savoring the contrast between satin skin and strong, lithe muscles. She'd actually managed to lock her heels in the small of his back, the adorable little hedonist. He'd be able to explore some very obscure positions with her, perhaps some he'd only heard of.

Or maybe he'd just spend weeks teaching her the simplest

methods. Take her so often she'd always remember him, and how he felt inside her, no matter whom she married.

He cursed silently, the Gaelic phrases summing up his jealousy of that unknown man. His hand slipped up and cupped her breast, kneading it. His, dammit, his.

She firmed under his touch and her hips pushed back against him.

"My Viola." He bared his teeth in a smile that was almost a snarl. He kissed her neck, lapping at that most sensitive point.

She gasped and moaned, "Mr. Donovan."

He snatched a condom from the tin on the night table, reared up, and applied it hastily. His breath caught as he stared at her beautiful rump, gleaming in the moonlight.

"My filly, the sweetest ride in the world." He lifted her hips up and shoved a pillow underneath. He was in her before she could say another word, cock settling into her velvet sheath like homecoming.

"Donovan," she moaned again as her head drooped, baring her exquisite nape for him.

"Mine, all mine," he growled as he rocked his hips against her.

He shafted her hard and fast, years of discipline swept away by the thought of her with another man. He'd never before handled a woman with the desperate frenzy she evoked, making him more beast than man. She was his, at least for now.

She reached her climax within minutes. He bellowed his triumph as he followed her into orgasm, her muscles drawing his seed from its deepest roots. Rapture pounded up his spine and out through his cock, battering him like nothing he'd ever felt before.

Afterwards, she muttered something then slept. He had barely enough sense to slide off her before he too slept, an arm and a leg thrown possessively over her.

Tomorrow he'd consider how to control himself around her.

Chapter Six

A sleepy blue eye peered at William over the coverlet. "You're awake, Mr. Donovan."

Viola started to struggle upright. William restrained her with a gentle hand. "Relax, sweetheart, and go back to sleep."

"Are you certain?" She blinked up at him, looking adorably tousled with her swollen mouth and silver-gilt curls tumbling over one bare shoulder. His trousers tightened as his cock signaled its strong appreciation of the sight. *Down, boyo—you've three months to enjoy her delights.*

"Quite sure," he answered firmly. "You can do as you please until I return."

"Thank you. God give you good day, Mr. Donovan." She was asleep again before he reached the door.

William strode down Main Street to the depot, feeling at peace with all the world. A smirk threatened but he fought it back, opting for the sober mien of a prosperous businessman.

He paused to watch the weekly stage's arrival. On time, praise the saints, so perhaps they hadn't encountered any Apaches on this run. Three men climbed down and William froze.

Conall O'Flaherty was a grown man now . . . and an exact copy of his father, the land agent who'd evicted William's family. Pig's eyes, thick-bodied with a boar's strength, so he seemed every bit the paid thug he was. All three brothers bore a strong family resemblance, varying only in the sheen of their bald pates and the whiskery forests sprouting from their chins.

The dirk pressed against his arm, from where a twitch of his hand could launch it. His mother had died in childbirth, an agony of tears and blood sheltered only by a ruined cottage. Baby Séamas had followed her to heaven without drawing a single breath in this world. They'd have survived except for these scoundrels and their torches, which had destroyed his father's world after being turned off by Lord Charles.

Now those brutes had come to the New World to serve a man with money and no scruples, just as their father had done in Ireland.

Jesus, Mary, and Joseph, he wanted to kill them. Slowly and with fire, the way the Apaches tortured their enemies. But he couldn't. So far, they'd done nothing wrong in Rio Piedras. Damn.

His revolver nudged his leg as if pleading for use. His fingers twitched. He recovered himself with an effort that left him sweating and turned toward his depot.

"Donovan!" An all too familiar voice snapped his head around.

"Lennox," he responded warily. The man had his sword stick but no apparent guns.

"Allow me to present my men, the O'Flaherty brothers."

"Mr. Donovan," the three murmured, their hard eyes measuring him before giving respectful nods.

"Boys." William nodded curtly. He was grimly amused by how polite they were to him, behaving very much as hired help toward neighboring gentry. They obviously didn't recognize him, which was fair enough: he'd inherited his height from his mother's family. "Is there anything else, Lennox?"

"Just one matter." The O'Flahertys drew back at Lennox's glare. Their master lowered his voice confidentially. "I understand you've encountered some difficulties handling freight here."

William murmured something noncommittal and waited.

"Perhaps a one-time payment might alleviate your difficulties. Say, five thousand dollars?"

William frowned. Why was Lennox, the cheapest bastard in the territory, offering money? "Five thousand dollars, Lennox? You feel the road hazards have strengthened that much?"

"Not road hazards, Donovan. But a peril lurking within your compound, that of an unmarried woman."

"Mrs. Ross." William was quite calm now. His senses heightened until he could see the pulse in Lennox's temple.

"Exactly. If I paid five thousand dollars or even ten thousand—a significant sum, sir!—would you release her into my custody? Then I'd marry her immediately and propriety would be satisfied. I have the funds waiting in my office."

William's fist moved before Lennox finished speaking, and set the arrogant fool sprawling in the dust. Passersby halted to stare. Even the stage driver stopped his bustle of activity.

The O'Flahertys started forward but Lennox rejected their help. He stood up and dusted himself off, glaring at William.

William waited, hoping for a fight. Feet pounded up the street as his teamsters swarmed to the scene. Lennox cast them a single, fulminating stare.

"I said nothing disrespectful of Mrs. Ross, Donovan," the slimy bastard snapped. "Any interpretation you put on a sharp business offer is your own. I'll not make such an offer again. Good day."

"Lennox." He'd have to watch that snake but he'd done business before with worse. Given the Army contract, Donovan & Sons would be in Rio Piedras for months to come.

And he must consider how best to deal with the O'Flahertys.

Viola buried her nose deeper in the mug and savored the deep, rich aroma of real coffee. A small wriggle situated her more comfortably in the bed. She was tender and sore in places she'd not thought possible. She shrugged off the aches as simply the aftermath of strenuous exertion.

The rich, buttery scent of brioche floated up to her from the tray across her lap. Her father always insisted on having exactly this meal every morning. Now its presence wrapped around her like homecoming, even on an Arizona late afternoon.

The family tradition had started as her great-grandfather's first meal in France after escaping from a British prison ship during the Revolution. The taste of civilization and freedom, he'd called it. Even Hal had inherited a weakness for coffee and brioche, despite his abhorrence of anything their father liked. He'd sworn to have this meal as often as possible once he became a first-class Missouri River pilot.

Viola leaned back against the cushions and smiled as she remembered her brother. Hal was two years older, but they'd been inseparable as children. She'd tagged along with him on more than one expedition to go horseback riding, ride the river, or explore the woods. He'd written her every week for four years, no matter where he was on the wild Missouri, after he ran away from home.

When he'd returned at age twenty, she'd gone with him while he enlisted in the Union Navy.

Viola had hurried home afterwards to tell their mother.

"Mother, Hal's joined the Navy!"

Silence answered her. Juliet had married her New York beau a month earlier, which left Mother alone in the house except for the servants. But why didn't she answer?

"Mother?" Viola ran into the front parlor, barely remembering to be careful of its intricately carved rosewood furniture and innumerable objets d'art collected by the Lindsay family during decades in the China Trade. "Isn't it marvelous? Now he'll be a naval hero just like Grandfather and Great-Grandfather. And Father, too, of course, now that he, too, is serving in the Union Navy."

Desdemona Lindsay was looking out of the front window, her small fist pounding a tattoo on the frame. She swung around and glared at Viola, so similar in coloring but not in build. Viola was flat as a board but more than one man had written odes to her mother's rich curves. "Naval hero? Nonsense!" she spat.

Viola came to a halt at yet another round of maternal disappointment. She tried to soothe her parent. "He'll be well, Mother, truly. Father and Hal will be home in six weeks after they win the war and Jefferson Davis goes back to Mississippi."

The older woman snatched up a priceless Ming vase and hurled it into the fireplace. It broke with a loud crash and Viola flinched as shards flew across the Aubusson carpet.

"Mother?" Viola stammered, startled by the uncharacteristic destruction of property.

"Those fools, those arrogant fools! They're fighting for the wrong side and we'll lose everything. My father was right when he said I shouldn't marry a Yankee."

Viola's mouth hung open. "Grandfather said that?"

Her mother charged across the room and shook her by the shoulders. "Don't you see, Viola? You're the last one left to me and you must understand, as I learned from my father. One day there will be a great Southern empire stretching from California to Virginia and as far south as Venezuela. The world will crawl to us for our cotton, gold, and horses."

Viola gaped. She remembered Grandfather Davies saying something of the sort during family gatherings at Fair Oaks, his big plantation outside Louisville. She even recalled how heated her uncles became when expounding on the subject to Father. Hal always laughed at the idea, saying the true empire lay to the west and not the south. She tried again to defuse the storm. "Are you sure, Mother?"

The Kentucky-born aristocrat began pacing again. "Of course I am! This war will destroy us. Your father will lose everything: his fleet of steamboats, his money, this magnificent new house. All our valuables will be gone forever if he supports the Union."

"Perhaps he considers his country worth the cost," Viola ventured. "After all, the British put a price on Great-Grandfather Lindsay's head and burned his home."

Richard Lindsay's wife shuddered. "Intolerable. I have never understood how a man could destroy his wife and family's future in such a fashion."

"He stood by his word, Mother, as a man of honor must."

"And men are fools to be bound by frivolities like that, my dear. The South is going to win. I know it as clearly as I can see your face. You and I must make sure our family survives and prospers."

Chills ran across Viola's skin. She licked her lips nervously. She hoped her face didn't show her thoughts. "What are you thinking of, Mother?"

"Assisting our Southern brethren every way we can, Viola."

"How?" Viola stammered, hoping her mother meant something innocent, such as sending letters to the relatives at Fair Oaks.

"There are a great many avenues we can explore, my dear. Taking messages will be easy, of course; no one would dare stop us. More useful will be obtaining interesting tidbits of information from loose-lipped Yankees, for transfer to the right parties in the South. You could be very helpful if you'd just learn to flirt."

"Spying?" Viola's voice cracked. The next words emerged in a whisper. "But that's treason."

For the first time in her life, Viola thought her mother truly looked at her.

The older woman hesitated for a moment and her mouth tightened. Then she laughed, a girlish peal that had captivated more than one man, but never a woman. "My dear child, criminal behavior is out of the question. Don't be absurd."

Viola wanted to believe her more than she'd wanted anything in her life. But she needed to be certain. "Truly, Mother?"

Mrs. Richard Lindsay patted her daughter's cheek. "You have my word on it, Viola. I will never commit treason."

Viola closed her eyes in relief.

* * *

Chills chased across Viola's skin at the memory.

She'd forgotten on that 1861 morning that treason was a crime defined by the victors, making it irrelevant to the deeds of those on the winning side. But Mother had reminded her more than once of that truth during the next four years, as she single-mindedly pursued a Confederate victory.

Viola took another mouthful of coffee.

She'd always wanted someone to trust completely and now she had exactly that: herself. She didn't need anyone else to honorably win her free of this town. Her bargain with William Donovan would pay off Edward's debts and provide a fresh start in San Francisco. And surely Mr. Lennox would stay away, now she was living with another man.

Honor also demanded she give Donovan her best work. Viola had never imagined she'd labor in the bedroom, and truly, yesterday's activities hadn't felt like drudgery. She smiled, memories circling of Donovan's handling, his mouth's skillful play over her skin, and his big cock stretching her from within.

Warmth blossomed in private places at the memories. She took another sip of coffee.

Best of all had been the last time, when he'd bent her over the bed and ridden her hard. No hint of self-control had colored his actions then. He'd been all man and she'd been the woman at the center of his universe.

Viola smiled again as Sarah Chang knocked on the door. She would happily perform such labors whenever Donovan asked.

"Mrs. Ross? Are you ready now?"

"Yes, thank you." She rose cautiously and made her way to the bathroom on rather unsteady legs.

Amazing how a night of Mr. Donovan's attentions could exhaust one. And make one sleep remarkably late. She silently apologized to Sally and Lily Mae for ever doubting their account of William's prowess.

A long hot bath, followed by an expert massage, restored

her. She declined the proffered cheese straws and coffee, still replete from the earlier brioche. Sarah worked exotic oils into her skin until even Viola's calluses started to soften. She was a puddle of relaxation stretched across the bed, but curiosity insisted on satisfaction.

"How long have you worked for Mr. Donovan, Sarah?"

"Almost twelve years, Mrs. Ross."

"So long? How did you start?"

"He took both Abraham and me into his household after Abraham left the tong to marry me."

"What? What do you mean?" Viola flushed at her rudeness and apologized. "I'm sorry. It's none of my business to ask about your private life."

"Oh no, Mrs. Ross, I am glad to tell you since it brings much credit to Mr. Donovan. But I am not accustomed to speaking of these things in English so please forgive my clumsiness."

Viola's ears pricked. She smiled and nodded, indicating her willingness to hear anything Sarah wanted to say.

Sarah hesitated for a moment then spoke, clearly searching for words. "I was a rich man's concubine in San Francisco. He found me ugly, since my feet are too big, and did not visit me. I spent much time sitting in the courtyard. Abraham spied me there and came to see me more and more often. Gradually, we began to talk through the grille and became friends. He started to save money to buy me."

Viola twisted her head around. Sarah was smiling softly, her gaze turned to the past. "Did you find him handsome?"

"He was a tall northerner, not like anyone I'd known, and a *boo how doy,* or fighting man. But yes, I found him most attractive." Sarah's English was more fluent now as she moved further into her story. "One day, my master died. Ming Long declared I belonged to him, as inheritance from my master. Abraham announced that our attraction was of long standing and he had the right to buy me, if he could do so in a reasonable time. Ming Long disagreed violently."

"What happened?" Viola asked, hanging on Sarah's every word. She rolled over to pay more attention and Sarah draped a cotton quilt over her, forgoing the massage in favor of the story.

"Ming Long expressed himself in a very insolent manner. Abraham's tong took offense, since an insult to one is an insult to all. The other tong swore neither Abraham nor his tong would have me. The two tongs fought bloodily."

"Like Romeo and Juliet," Viola breathed.

"A little, perhaps. Neither tong could win and both were furious at the other. Many worried the war would consume Chinatown."

"And then?"

"Mr. Donovan was Abraham's friend from the gold fields. He offered to buy me from the other tong's supreme council. It would be good business and no insult to sell me to an outsider like him. He also asked to hire Abraham from his tong for the rest of his life. Both offers were accepted."

"And?" Viola sat up on the bed.

"Mr. Donovan gave me away at our wedding. We took new names for our new start. Abraham also cut his queue, in honor of his new life."

"How lucky you both are," Viola breathed.

"Thank you. We light a candle every day for Mr. Donovan, in hopes he, too, may find domestic harmony."

Viola stiffened. She changed the subject. "Thank you, Sarah, for sharing your story. You said something earlier about clothing?"

Sarah's eyes twinkled for a moment and Viola realized guiltily just how obvious she'd been. Then Sarah smoothly resumed her previous role of perfectly behaved maidservant. "Yes, Mrs. Ross. Your new clothes are on the trunk."

She returned with a dazzling array of brilliantly hued silks. But there wasn't enough cloth for a respectable woman's wardrobe, certainly not the yards and yards needed for a skirt.

Viola shook her head instinctively, rejecting the idea she might don such garments.

"Mr. Donovan chose these himself," Sarah said emphatically and shook out the garments. A Chinese tunic and pants were revealed to Viola's disbelieving eyes. Made of the finest pale gold silk and embroidered in gold, they were nothing a respectable American woman would consider wearing.

"I'm supposed to wear that?" Viola's voice cracked on the last word.

"And you'll look beautiful in it, sweetheart."

Viola jumped. Donovan was leaning in the doorway, neatly dressed in a prosperous businessman's suit. He tilted his hat back with a casual finger as he drawled, "I'll enjoy watching you."

"You expect me to clothe myself like this? Without a respectable corset or chemise? In trousers?" She came to her feet, still clutching the cotton quilt. Sitting on the bed seemed too vulnerable a setting for this conversation.

"Yes."

"But it's scandalous attire."

Sarah set the clothing on the trunk and slipped out, silently dropping a curtsy to Donovan as she went. He nodded politely to her but his eyes remained on Viola as he stepped forward into the room and closed the door.

"Because I told you to do so and you promised to cover yourself only with what I gave you. Remember?"

Viola recognized the trap. Still, such attire was hardly decent. "Yes, but this isn't proper! A respectable woman would never be seen without her corset, for one thing. And as for wearing trousers . . ."

She shuddered. She'd worn men's clothing to work Edward's mine, but that had been a matter of necessity. A woman's skirts could not survive wriggling through small cracks and crevices. But she'd always been careful never to be seen by anyone else when wearing such garb.

"Are you saying no, sweetheart?"

Viola gulped but stood her ground. "I cannot wear these clothes, Mr. Donovan. What if someone else saw me?" she pleaded, hoping he'd understand and relent.

"If you refuse, then you must be punished for your disobedience."

In one smooth move, Donovan snatched her up, sat down on the bed, and stretched her facedown across his lap.

Viola squeaked as a big, warm hand smoothed her behind. She was entirely naked under the quilt and overwhelmingly conscious of his thighs' iron strength beneath her and his body's heat beside hers. She struggled to sit up but he cuffed her hands in one of his big paws, trapping them firmly behind her back. "Mr. Donovan, what are you doing?"

He smoothed the quilt over her behind with his free hand. Viola gasped, agonizingly aware of how vulnerable she was to him. "Mr. Donovan, I am certain we can reach an amicable compromise if you will just let me sit up."

"There's no need for a compromise, sweetheart. Did you honestly think I'd humiliate you in front of other men?"

Viola closed her eyes and spoke the truth. "Yes, sir."

"Does such behavior sound like protection?"

"No, sir." Her voice was husky.

"Do you deserve retribution for your lack of trust?"

"Yes, sir." She swallowed hard. She doubted his idea of punishment would be anything like what she'd experienced before. Still, she had insulted him and his honor had to be satisfied.

"Thank you for your honesty and sense of fairness, Viola. I swear I won't abuse you."

"Oh, I never thought you would do that, Mr. Donovan!"

"Thank you." He smoothed the quilt down again, then rested his hand over her behind. She could have described exactly where every finger and his palm molded her. Breathing was suddenly difficult.

He patted her lightly through the cloth. "Mr. Donovan, are you sure you want to do this?"

"Quite sure. Especially when your voice becomes husky like that. It reminds me of how you pleaded last night, sweetheart."

Viola choked.

He patted her again on the other side, then rubbed her behind. His touch, whether the staccato pulse of a pat or a lingering caress, felt delicious.

Viola blushed at the idea a spanking could be pleasurable.

"Where shall I punish you next?" he continued. "The curve of your sweet rump? Or shall it be the underside?"

Donovan swatted her again, caressed her, then swatted her. The quilt might not have been there for all the protection it offered.

"Your rump is turning quite pink, sweetheart. Are you melting as fast on the inside as on the outside?" he purred, then went on without waiting for an intelligible answer from her.

He varied the rhythm, whether fast or slow. Sometimes the pats came close together, sometimes he paid more attention to fondling her.

"Mr. Donovan!" Viola gasped after one particularly solid swat made her jump. "Must you make me feel so unlike myself?"

Donovan chuckled. "And your musk smells delicious, sweetheart."

Viola found herself moaning.

"Does a harder touch excite you, sweetheart? Then perhaps I should try something gentler," Donovan mused, and fondled her under the quilt.

"Mr. Donovan, please." Viola shifted restlessly, hungry for more.

He traced the crease between her leg and buttock, then followed the crevice upward between her thighs.

"Open your legs, sweetheart," he murmured. She obeyed eagerly.

His finger outlined her folds, evoking a gush of her heated dew. Viola tossed her head and tried to move closer.

He swatted her behind. Somehow the harder blow exacted more dew from her aching flesh.

Viola sobbed and squirmed against his leg. "Mr. Donovan, what are you doing?"

Donovan slid the quilt aside and set to work in earnest with his hand, always varying the rhythm and strength. His cock was a hard ridge against her arm but he ignored it.

Oftentimes his hand returned to her hidden secrets. He teased her pearl into a throbbing center of lust, while denying orgasm to her. "Such a responsive filly you are, sweetheart. Shall I touch you again?"

"Please." She shuddered. "Anything."

He took the quilt entirely away from her backside then.

She was helpless against his hand's strength but all she wanted was more. Viola gasped and shrieked occasionally at the harder blows. She writhed harder and harder against him. She was a blaze of desperation, centered wherever his hand lingered.

"Mr. Donovan," she whimpered as a finger swirled inside her. "Mr. Donovan, please."

A second finger entered her swollen flesh, the calluses rough and exciting against her slick inner surfaces. "I'm touching your pussy, sweetheart. Say the word for me."

She choked, unable to form that most improper word.

His two fingers pumped her slowly. Viola groaned and yielded. The need to climax was agony. Nothing mattered except that. "Pussy," she sighed.

"Very good, sweetheart," he purred. His fingers thrust into her again, exciting her but still not permitting rapture.

When she thought she could bear it no longer, his thumb pressed her pearl in the stroke he'd used in his office. Viola keened with relief as every muscle and sinew burst into rapture.

She drifted back to awareness and found him lightly spreading a soothing liquid over her flaming derrière. She blushed at the realization he was painting her with her own dew. She hid her face, but something deep inside throbbed at the act's casual intimacy.

"Do you trust me now?" His hand stopped moving.

Viola fumbled to think. "Yes. Yes, I do," she said more strongly. He could have taken a belt to her or worse, instead of this sensual spanking.

In truth, she feared that if he spanked her again, she'd likely melt in eager anticipation.

Chapter Seven

"Lindsay!"

Hal spun on his heel and grinned as he recognized the speaker. "Rogers, you reprobate!"

The cavalry officer waved as he ran across the Plaza in Santa Fe. Hal met him halfway and the two men shook hands eagerly. "Good to see you, you old so-and-so. Last time we met, you were heading off to join Sherman at Chattanooga."

"And you had just been given command of your own gunboat." Rogers slapped Hal on the arm.

"Care for a drink for old times' sake?"

"Glad to. Powell runs a saloon over in Burro Alley and should have something for you to drink."

They found a table in Powell's saloon a few blocks away. A jovial reunion was followed by a long discussion before Hal selected a brand of whisky.

Rogers leaned back in his chair, chuckling. "Still drinking only the best, I see."

"Why not?" Hal cocked an eyebrow at their old joke.

"Because Missouri pilots are paid more than Army officers. What is it now, ten thousand a season?" There was only laughter, not envy, in his words. "Might be worth it, to escape the petticoat brigade on shore."

Hal poured for both of them. "Are you suggesting you'd leave your wife and daughter to serve on a mountainboat?"

"Daughters. Five of 'em."

Hal choked then lifted his glass. "Here's to the Rogers young ladies: may they be as beautiful, loving, and kind as their mother."

"Hear, hear." The two men drank solemnly. Formalities satisfied, they grinned at each other and settled back.

"Stayed in, I see."

"Army life suits me better than civilian boredom. Mercifully, Caroline seems to thrive on it, as do the girls. And you? You come from a family of females, as I remember."

"Two sisters, both married."

Perceptive as always, Rogers caught the betraying flatness in Hal's voice. "Don't like either of your brothers-in-law?"

"Townsend's what I expected Juliet would choose: prominent family, rich, stupid enough to be led around by the nose. He bought a substitute to fight for him, of course."

Rogers shrugged that off. Most monied men had paid their way out of the draft. "And the other one? What was her name?"

Hal studied the light passing through his whisky. "Viola married Edward Ross in '65."

"What? That drunken malingerer married your favorite sister?"

Hal nodded and drained his glass.

"The devil you say." Rogers took a healthy swallow in sympathy before speaking again. "She could have chosen worse. He stood his ground that first day at Shiloh, you know, and served those big siege guns that saved us."

"Perhaps. At least that's what I keep telling myself." Hal refilled the glasses.

"You never can tell whom a woman will fall for. Caroline's family still doesn't understand what she sees in me."

"That's the strange part: Viola never mentioned love, just announced she was going to marry him. Nothing I said could convince her to break the engagement."

"Big fight, huh?"

"The worst. I swore I'd never speak to her again if she held to that man."

Rogers grunted, a world of understanding in the sound. "I gather she won the battle."

"You could say that. She married him and I haven't seen her since. Neither has anyone else in the family."

"Sorry to hear that."

The whisky levels sank somewhat during the succeeding silence. Finally, Rogers spoke again.

"So what brings a river pilot to the New Mexico desert?"

"I'm looking for Viola. I promised Grandmother before she died that I'd bring my youngest sister home."

"And you think you'll find her in New Mexico?"

"She and Ross went west after the marriage to make their fortune in the gold fields. I went to California first and now I'm working my way through the Rockies."

"Any luck?"

"I've hunted her from Virginia City, Montana, to Leadville, Colorado. Heard a lot of stories about a drunken fool and his petite blond wife. Found Viola's pearl necklace in Denver, that she'd pawned years ago, but no sign of her. Next stop is Silver City."

He'd have been happier if he'd found the mourning brooch for the Commodore, which held great meaning for Viola. Sighting it would mean she was probably close by.

"What about Arizona?" Rogers asked.

"Few whites but many Apaches," Hal reminded his friend. It seemed the least likely place to find Viola.

Rogers shrugged. "There's gold out there, and silver. Folks have been moving in steadily since the war ended. Rio Piedras has a fair-sized mine, for example."

"Rio Piedras?"

"The Golconda silver mine. Mostly a company town, with maybe a thousand people, but still has some small claims. It's a day south of Tucson by stage."

"Could be possible. Thanks for the tip."

"If you head that way, keep an eye out for Paul Lennox, who owns Rio Piedras."

Hal's mouth tightened, remembering an old fight. "Met a banker in New York named Nicholas Lennox once. But they're probably not related."

"Could be. He likes to brag about his fine old New York family." Rogers took a slow swallow before continuing. "Lennox served in a cavalry regiment during the war and spent considerable time in the Shenandoah Valley. A number of civilians, including babies, died 'accidentally' when he seized provisions from their farms. He's not welcome at Army reunions and I heard his fiancée broke off with him."

"Son of a bitch." Sounded like the same kind of weasel as Nick Lennox. "Thanks for the warning."

Rogers shrugged. "It's the least I can do. You saved my neck on the Tennessee."

"Hey, you were just a soldier boy ruining my clean deck with your blood," Hal teased, lightening the moment.

Rogers met his eyes for a long minute then grinned. "Navy puke!"

The two men burst into laughter.

Hal and Rogers were still chuckling when they stood up to leave the saloon hours later, full of good food, good whisky, and good companionship. Hal's present state of sobriety wouldn't have withstood close inspection by his father. On the other hand, the Captain was a thousand miles away and nothing his son did had ever pleased the old autocrat. Except for enlisting in the Union Navy, of course.

Rogers paused to say good-bye to Powell, while Hal walked ahead onto the boardwalk. Moonlight and lamplight escaping from the neighboring saloons and dance halls were Burro Alley's only sources of light. Like any other frontier town, the shadows whispered of possibilities, most of them violent.

The cool night air acted poorly on his whisky-sodden reflexes. He caught himself on a pole supporting the board-walk's roof, just as someone yelled, "That's him! Get 'im, boys!"

A thick cudgel lashed downwards toward the back of his head. Hal used his grip on the pole to push himself away from the attack, but it still dealt him a nasty blow. He whipped backwards, using the pole as a pivot, and drove his elbow back into the unknown assailant behind him. An agonized grunt told him of the move's success.

Hal grabbed the thug's arm and flipped him neatly over his shoulder. A quick stomp on the wrist freed the cudgel, which he promptly kicked away as he drew his Colt. He looked around for the attacker's fellows and spotted two men running away.

"Jesus, Hal, I can't even turn my back on you for a minute before you find trouble," Rogers drawled. The sparse light glinted on his Colt as he aimed it at Hal's prisoner. "Recognize him?"

The thug sprawled in the dust was notable only for his anonymity: medium height, medium build, dark hair. And the Colt strapped to his waist that he hadn't bothered to draw.

Hal started to shake his head but stopped, wincing. He put up his hand to his head and it came away covered with blood. "Never seen him before in my life."

"What are you talking about?" the fellow whined and started to get up.

Rogers put a bullet between the thug's feet as Powell burst through the saloon's doors, shotgun in hand. He assessed the situation with a single glance, then took up a position between the thug and the alley beyond. No one else came outside, although Hal caught a flicker of movement at a dance hall's doors.

The thug fell back and stared up at them. "Whaddya want to know, sir?"

"Why did you attack me?" Hal demanded. He swayed

slightly but pulled himself steady with an effort, his Colt still firmly in hand.

The thug squirmed away from the shotgun until he was brought up short by Hal's boot. "I was offered five dollars to mug you," he stammered, glancing nervously between the two revolvers and the shotgun trained on him.

"By who?" Rogers asked.

"Mickey Clark."

"Who's he?" Hal asked.

"Local hoodlum," Powell snorted. "Did Clark say why?"

"Some man named Lennox didn't want you visiting him in Arizona."

Rogers looked over at Hal. "Ring true?"

"Yup. Let him go."

The thug scrambled up and froze when Powell prodded him with his shotgun. "If I see you again anywhere near my saloon," Powell growled, "I'll kill you for having troubled my friend."

"Yes, sir!" The thug vanished into the shadows.

Rogers stepped up behind Hal and inspected his head in the poor light. Powell picked up Hal's hat and dusted it off.

"Looks like you'll need stitches for that," Rogers observed.

Hal winced away from the probing fingers. "When's the next stage to Tucson?" he responded. He had the devil of a headache, which would only get worse.

"Tomorrow morning."

"Then we'd better find a doctor who likes to work in a hurry."

"Maybe you should wait a few days until your head heals," Rogers suggested.

"Not if my sister's anywhere near Lennox. Let's go find that doctor."

Viola accepted the chair Abraham held for her, careful to keep her eyes from the piano. She hissed slightly as her derrière made contact with the seat. Thin Chinese silk was no defense for her sensitized skin against the rough wool upholstery. She quickly recovered and plastered a smile on her face as she looked across the table at Donovan.

"You are very beautiful tonight, sweetheart," he remarked as he inclined his head to her. His eyes drifted over her hair and still lower, expressing his appreciation and anticipation.

Viola blushed and almost squirmed at his open admiration. Her abortive movement rubbed her intimate parts against the wool, promptly reminding her of how high he'd built her lusts when he'd spanked her a few minutes earlier.

She gasped. Then she promised herself she'd stay quite still no matter what he said or did during the rest of the evening.

Donovan's mouth quirked. "Would you care for some soup? And perhaps after dinner you can play a melody or two on the piano, the one you're so careful not to look at."

"Oh, thank you, Mr. Donovan! I cannot imagine anything I would enjoy more." She realized her words could be taken as an insult to him and blushed. She started to stammer an apology but he held up a hand.

"I understood perfectly, sweetheart, and took no offense. Some piano music would be very enjoyable for both of us on an evening like this."

Viola smiled at him gratefully. "Why did you obtain a piano? Does Mr. Evans play?"

"Not to my knowledge. The Oriental's manager ordered it but found bringing it here too much for his budget. In the end, Lennox refused the bill so Morgan kept the piano in lieu of payment."

"It looks magnificent."

"And it has a beautiful sound."

The meal passed quickly after that. The food was excellent, comparable to that provided in a first-class New York hotel. Donovan's table manners were excellent, as smooth and polished as any she'd met. Viola suspected the conversation was less successful, since she spent much of her time either eyeing the piano, wiggling as the chair's brocade scratched her through the thin Chinese silk, or remembering just why her intimate folds were so sensitive.

Finally, Abraham produced fresh coffee and a plate of ginger cookies before disappearing. Viola reached for the pot but Donovan's hand closed gently around her wrist. Her eyes flew to his.

"Go meet your plaything, sweetheart. I can pour my own coffee."

"Are you sure?" Viola hesitated, worried she'd be rude if she ignored him in favor of the piano.

"Go." He pushed her gently.

She rose before he could change his mind and sat down before the glorious rosewood instrument like an acolyte before the high altar, her aches forgotten. She'd only played the piano twice, for a total of less than an hour, in the six years since she'd left her parents' house. Both of those pianos had been small and forgettable, while this instrument looked perfectly suited for a concert hall.

Viola touched middle C lightly. The answering tone was perfect. Her fingers ran an octave, then two octaves. Equally perfect. She flexed her fingers, praying some of her old skill remained, and struck the opening chords of Chopin's "Military Polonaise."

The heroic dance filled the room, reminding her of Poland's gallant past. It swept her into that world of great music, where she'd so often found comfort before. The notes flowed out of her bones and she performed them with skill, the one feminine accomplishment she'd gained while growing up.

The polonaise led to a waltz, again by Chopin, then one of Beethoven's sonatas. She played "Für Elise," the song so often performed by young piano students, with a private smile at the memories it evoked.

Stephen Foster's "The Voice of Bygone Days" brought back memories of Juliet, flirting as she sang. William sang a snatch of the chorus under his breath in a fine baritone, but fell silent when she returned to the verse.

Matters were going so well that Viola embarked on Chopin's Polonaise in A flat major. She'd always loved the brilliant piece and worked for months to master it during the war. Her fingers stumbled on the first chromatic run and the notes stuttered to a halt.

She rested her hands in her lap. Then she tried again more slowly. But she couldn't perform it any better this time, even though she was well warmed up. Her hands were simply too stiff, their old dexterity rusted away from years of disuse.

Viola bowed her head and fought back the lump in her throat. She set her right hand to the keys again and played a beginner's exercise, designed to increase the performer's fluidity. She would use every possible minute of her three months with Donovan to rebuild her friendship with the piano.

"Sweetheart." She sensed his warmth and clean scent from directly behind her.

"Mr. Donovan." She started to turn around but he scooped her up in his arms. "What on earth are you doing?"

"Settling down." He did exactly that: sat down in the sitting room's big armchair with the air of a man making himself at home.

Viola stared up at him. Would he ever stop surprising her?

He pressed a kiss to her hair. Viola gradually relaxed against him.

"Does the piano need to be tuned, sweetheart?"

"No, it's perfect right now," Viola assured him.

"Good. Still, we'll have the tuner visit at least weekly. He's one of the independent miners and can use the extra money."

"Thank you." Viola snuggled contentedly against him and considered pieces she could play, thankful she'd memorized so many. Rio Piedras lacked any sort of music store.

Donovan kissed her hair again, and her forehead. His breath was warm and soft against her skin. She stirred and tilted her head to provide him more access. He rumbled something deep in his throat and nuzzled her. She purred and enjoyed his gentle attentions.

"Mr. Donovan," she sighed when he kissed her cheek.

"William." He nuzzled her again.

Viola blinked. "William? Do you want me to call you by your first name, sir?"

"When we are alone, sweetheart." He kissed her mouth.

She stared at him when he lifted his head, then surrendered at the quiet determination in his eyes. "William," she agreed.

"Good girl."

He returned to enticing her. He explored her ear delicately until he'd worked his way to her lobe. He licked it and the warm pulse points behind it until she shivered and sighed his name.

He sucked her earlobe in a regular rhythm that made her womb clench and release. A slow fire built inside her, bringing dew between her legs. His hand stroked the inside of her thighs, as hot against her skin as if the silk trousers weren't present. "Open your legs, sweetheart."

She obeyed without thinking, more interested in the effect his kisses had on the curve of her neck. Then his fingers found her through a slit in the silk and she dripped for him.

"That's my sweetheart," he encouraged her, stroking her folds as he nipped her neck.

"Oh, William," she gasped as the harsher sensation quickened her senses. Her entire being focused on his touch, on the ravishing effect he had on her woman's body. She was hot, flushed, unable to stay still. She twisted on his lap, uncaring of how his trousers' wool rubbed her behind. Her skin was so sensitive, she thought it might burst asunder.

"Oh dear heavens, what are you doing to me? Oh my goodness," she groaned as his finger probed her entrance.

He worked another finger into her, then began to pump her in rhythm with his mouth's workings on her neck. The two sensations combined to stretch her like a bowstring, rhythmic contractions wracking her in time with his movements. Viola sobbed and writhed on his fingers, eager to move closer.

His hand thrust deep as he bit her neck just hard enough to draw blood. She shattered with a cry of rapture.

Viola recovered consciousness to find herself sitting astride him. The Chinese silk trousers were nowhere to be seen. She blinked, trying to decipher the meaning of her situation.

"Ah, William," she ventured. "What are we doing now?"

Laughter rumbled in his chest but his voice was perfectly decorous when he answered. "Where is my cock, sweetheart?"

Viola blushed scarlet and hid her face against his chest, her arms lightly resting on his.

"Answer me, Viola."

"Inside me," she managed before she hid her face again. In fact, he was in her to the hilt. She knew exactly where his cock's head and shaft rested and how her folds greeted his warm, furry pouch.

"To be precise, it's inside your grotto, sweetheart. But I doubt you've heard that term before."

Viola shook her head without looking at him.

"Now it's time for you to learn a new exercise."

"What do you mean?"

"You're an excellent pianist, sweetheart. How long did you practice to achieve such prowess?"

"Years," she admitted honestly.

"Carnal skills also need diligent practice, sweetheart."

"Mrs. Smith said as much," Viola observed, tilting her head back to look at him.

"She was correct. As your fingers needed training to become a better musician, so do your internal muscles."

"What good will that do, William?"

"Increase your stamina, for one thing. You can also use them to caress me when I'm inside you."

"Caress you?" She could feel an occasional pulse from his cock, setting off an answering flutter in her channel.

"Precisely. Tighten yourself around me now."

"What? How?"

"As if you needed to relieve yourself but couldn't do so yet. Do it, Viola."

Viola obeyed him, certain her face was scarlet. The action intensified her awareness of the different shapes of him: the fatter head, the long shaft, his balls. Her pearl throbbed. She desisted with a gasp, startled at how eagerly she'd grown wet again.

"Now do that again but hold it for a count of three."

"Must I?"

"Obey me, sweetheart."

She did as commanded. Her body ached for him, from her deepest cavern to her folds resting against his crisp private hairs. Now that she knew what joy could be found in his arms, she wanted an orgasm, not this waiting game.

"William, please, can't you just take me?" she begged. The tunic's silk rubbed her peaked nipples until she wanted to scream.

"No, you do better when you clench around a hard object. And this way, I know when you're exercising correctly. Now clench and hold again."

"William," Viola groaned as she tightened herself around him again. Dear heavens, she wanted more of him than this. Anticipation built. She shivered when a breath of air danced across her flushed cheek.

The worst part was that they were both fully clothed from the waist up, except for her naked loins clasping his waist. It was improper, scandalous and unbearably arousing. She slid her arms around his neck, enjoying how his wool jacket brushed her skin through the silk. She quivered again.

"What if someone sees us?" Viola whispered.

"No one will come into the sitting room, bedroom, or bathroom if the door is closed, unless they're invited. Clench and hold again, Viola. You've done three and must do it seven times more."

"Seven?" Viola wailed. "Seven? I cannot possibly wait that long."

William swatted her rump. She gasped, jerked, then did as she was told.

"Again." His voice was implacable. "And count them."

"That was four," Viola gasped, her head falling back. "And five."

His cock pulsed inside her. How could she wait a moment longer for the climax?

"You're torturing me, William, do you hear? Torturing me, you devil!"

"The sooner you finish, the sooner you'll get what you deserve, sweetheart."

Viola cursed but obeyed. She was burning up, consumed by need for him and the pleasure only he could provide. Waves, but not the longed-for crest of sensation, rocked through her muscles and veins. Even her breasts ached for him.

"Six." His cock pulsed inside her but his hips didn't move.

"Damn you, seven," Viola snarled. "What did I ever do to deserve this torment?"

"Again, sweetheart. Three times more." His voice was implacable, although she could feel the tremors running through him where they were joined. She knew he would do exactly as he said, no matter what his body wanted.

"Torture," she muttered. "Eight. Oh, my heavens," she sobbed. Her pearl throbbed. "Nine. Ten, dammit!"

William grabbed her hips and slammed her down upon him as he surged up into her. Viola gasped as the waves now moved faster and faster through her.

"More, please, William!" She bit his jacket's lapel to muffle her cries.

His fingers bit into her as he set the pace, hard and demanding like the blood roaring through her veins. Then he froze, shuddered and roared as he spent himself inside her, blasting her into rapture like a miner touching off dynamite.

"You'll have to practice those exercises regularly, sweetheart," William remarked a few minutes later while unbuttoning her silk tunic.

"Yes, William." Viola nodded, but paid more attention to the contrast between his tanned fingers and her white breast.

"Ten times in a set, three sets a day. Without me inside you." He stroked his thumb along one vein. Viola sighed happily before she caught his meaning.

"Without you? But that won't be enjoyable at all."

"Was practicing the piano always fun?"

"No, of course not." Her nipple budded under his hand and Viola moaned.

"You'll start tomorrow, sweetheart."

"Yes, William. But you must have had either a wicked teacher or natural-born talent to think of such torments."

William laughed.

Chapter Eight

William led the pony around the ring one more time, watching for any sign of injury as he cracked his long whip behind her encouragingly. Like every other horse at Lyonsgate, Daisy was well fed and usually more than pleased with her lot.

But two of Lyonsgate's female students had raced their pony carts back from the village yesterday and overturned one cart. So far, the ponies were doing better than their drivers: Lady Irene had immediately dismissed one silly female for disobeying the rules and confined the other to her room for a week. If this pony had suffered, then that student would also be sent home.

William smiled at Daisy's smooth gait. He, too, had prospered during his year at Lyonsgate. He'd grown and filled out so he was no longer a gangly boy but hopefully a young man. His savings had also increased, to the point where he now had more than enough for a boat ticket.

And yet he still lingered here. He'd been curious from the beginning about the curriculum. Now that he had a better idea what it entailed, he wanted desperately to be a student, which was impossible.

Europe's finest families sent their young men and women here for grooming. Some of the longtime servants here had assisted in that training, but always as animated props: they collected silks as they were cut from a student's evening dress, hoisted a bound and giggling female till she swayed from the ceiling, or presented a collection of paddles for a gentleman to choose from.

William wanted more than that. He wanted to cut the dress, bind the woman, paddle her behind until she climaxed. He was now rated as accomplished with a whip for a groom, but he wanted to be expert at using one to invoke pleasure from a woman. And other things, too, matters that he heard whispered and moaned from behind closed doors while he stood at attention just outside. The activities that he wondered about late at night, while his hand worked his cock until he came.

Oh, he'd enjoyed women here, too, for the first time in his life. He'd always been very wary of the whores found in Cobh's back alleys, with their avarice and diseases. But Lyonsgate's atmosphere encouraged sensual pleasures and he'd taken full advantage, once he'd had access to condoms.

The servants were welcome to enjoy each other as they chose, provided the men always used the condoms which Lady Irene generously provided. He'd explored the maid's pleasures and his own, but it hadn't been nearly enough.

He didn't want to leave until he, too, knew how to take a woman to the edge of her femininity and convince her, in a torrent of pleasure and pain, that she was a goddess.

He just hadn't figured out yet how to persuade Lady Irene to provide him with that training.

"Donovan."

William turned and bowed. "Yes, my lady?"

"Do you know where O'Connell is?" Lady Irene was wearing a walking dress so she'd probably just returned from an excursion to the waterfall, one of her favorite retreats.

"He's down at the pavilion, my lady, with Lord Philip and Lady Aurelia." William didn't add that Lord Philip was a nervous fool, barely tolerated by the horses. Or that the ponies always turned good-natured around Lady Aurelia.

Lady Irene pursed her lips and considered William closely before speaking again. "Run down and send him here to me immediately. You can remain at the pavilion in his stead."

"Yes, my lady."

"One more item, Donovan."

"My lady?"

"Do you think little Daisy here will recover?"

"Yes, my lady. She took a bit of a fright yesterday, nothing more."

"Good. Well, hurry up then, Donovan."

William bowed. He handed Daisy to one of the other grooms and headed off at a run down the hill. Lady Irene tolerated no slackness from anyone carrying out her orders.

The pavilion was a gaudy place, the size of a very large gazebo and intended to imitate a Turkish pasha's tent. It had been designed and built decades earlier by the same architect who created the Prince of Wales's pleasure palace at Brighton. Its comforts included steam heat from a coal-fired boiler until the occupants could fancy themselves in an Arabian desert, rather than the Irish countryside. William had never seen its interior.

William found O'Connell pacing well within earshot of the pavilion. Lyonsgate protocol dictated that one servant had to be available at all times for the guests' comfort and safety. They exchanged a few words, then O'Connell ran toward the main house while William took his place.

Lord Philip and Lady Aurelia must be well into their dalliance, given the very loud slurping sounds coming from within the pavilion. William's pulse quickened as he imagined the possible causes and he stood close to the front door.

"Uh, what do you call me, you obstinate slave girl?" Lord Philip's voice came from inside the pavilion, sounding uncertain.

"Sahib, if it pleases you," Lady Aurelia replied confidently.

The wet noises redoubled and Lord Philip moaned. "Deeper, woman. Take me further into your throat."

William's trousers seemed a prison for his aching cock. He clasped his hands behind his back to avoid fondling himself.

"Ah, ah . . ." Lord Philip was gasping faster now, matching the rhythm of Lady Aurelia's sucking. "Hell and damnation," he cried, his voice breaking on the last syllable.

William fought back the need to climax at the same time.

"What have I done?" Lord Philip wailed a long minute later. "She's striped and bruised, and may even bleed."

William's head came up, ears pricked.

"How can I ever forgive myself for hurting her?" Lord Philip choked back a sob.

"Sahib, have I done something to displease you?" Lady Aurelia seemed uncertain for the first time.

"I used a riding crop on you," Lord Philip answered, crying loudly now.

William frowned. Lady Aurelia had sounded more than content. What was happening in there?

"But Sahib, I begged you to punish me," she whimpered. "What did I do wrong?"

William reached for the door just as Lord Philip stumbled out, buttoning up his trousers. To his shock, Lord Philip fell into his arms, sobbing like a baby.

"Lord Philip?"

The only answer he received was another loud wail from Lord Philip and a small sob from Lady Aurelia.

William tried again. "My lord, what of Lady Aurelia?"

Lord Philip shuddered convulsively. "Take me away," he begged. "Take me away from this hellhole, where I disgraced myself."

William made up his mind. He put two fingers into his mouth and whistled, the piercing call that summoned any servant within earshot. Jack, an under-gardener, arrived on the run within a minute.

"Here," William commanded, nodding down at Lord Philip, who was now a hysterical weight on his arm. "Take him to the main house and find Lady Irene. Tell her I'll do my best to comfort Lady Aurelia until she arrives."

"Right." A big man of few words at any time, Jack supported Lord Philip up the hill. William took a deep breath to compose himself and entered the pavilion.

A scene out of an Arabian fantasy met his eyes. The room was ringed with spectacular silk tapestries, while layers of silk rugs cushioned the floor. The center was occupied by an immense bed, really an enormous platform, covered by still more silks and pillows.

Lady Aurelia lay spread-eagled across this divan, held down by gilded chains which vanished into the silk. She was utterly naked, except for her gilded aureoles and pussy . . . which also highlighted how swollen and flushed they were. A few pale lines traced across her thighs where a riding crop had touched her. Delicate beads of her dew gleamed like diamonds on her dark thatch.

William shuddered and found it hard to breathe.

Lady Aurelia's enormous dark eyes found him and widened. She licked her lips. "Warrior," she whispered.

"Yes?" William rasped, all training in how to address his betters gone.

"Warrior, if I may ask you, why did Sahib leave?" Her breasts rose and fell, while her nipples hardened.

William frowned; Lady Aurelia must still be under the fantasy's spell. He tried to answer in terms from the same imaginary world. "The Sahib was called away on important business, woman."

"Oh," she breathed. Her eyes flicked over his body then lingered at his crotch. William's cock promptly tented his trousers.

"Did he send you to have your way with me, warrior? Have I been so wicked that I must serve you, too?" She licked her lips, still staring at his crotch.

William's disbelieving eyes saw her nipples harden into

stiff peaks. She must be excited by the thought of playing out this fantasy with him.

"*Kadin*. Pearl of the harem." William tried to find a way to refuse, difficult when his lower parts wanted to do the thinking.

"Please, warrior, now that Sahib is gone"—her voice sharpened briefly then returned to its rich plea—"there is no master except yourself to grant me release. I beg of you, warrior, let me finish my tasks with you."

William swallowed. Lyonsgate protocol allowed a servant to enact fantasies but only at the guest's request.

Then he drew himself up, like a general inspecting his troops. He paced around the divan and scrutinized Lady Aurelia from every angle.

She trembled. "Warrior, what do you want of me?"

He stroked her hair and ran his fingers lightly over her face until he found the sensitive point below her ear. He stroked her neck, a caress he'd learned the maids enjoyed, and cupped her mound of Venus.

"Your musk perfumes the tent, *kadin*." Without conscious volition, William's voice had deepened.

She sighed and turned her head to kiss his hand. "Warrior," she whispered, "I pray you, use me as you will."

His heart stopped beating. For the first time in his life, a woman had just utterly yielded to him. He'd reward her as best he could for that.

William fondled her full breasts, teasing her until she sobbed and wriggled. He stroked her belly and chuckled when she arched to follow his touch. He traced the muscles in her thighs upward to her pussy. All the while, he watched her closely, judging her arousal.

She rocked her hips, trying to follow his light touch. "Warrior," she moaned, "please lick my pussy."

William fondled her nether lips again. Lady Aurelia sobbed. "Please, warrior, please taste my pussy."

"Are you ordering me, *kadin?*" He managed to make his voice stern.

"Oh no, warrior, never that. But you overwhelm my senses until I can say only what my body desires," she quavered.

He kept his gaze stern somehow, and his fingers unmoving on her pussy.

Lady Aurelia whimpered. "Your touch is a temptation, warrior. Please do with me as you will."

William smiled. He dropped to his knees and licked her belly. She moaned again, long and low.

Her anticipation was as keen in his throat as if it were his own. He swirled his tongue lower and lower, until it delved into her thatch and circled her clit. Her body arched up, pressing her pussy against his mouth. Her hunger couldn't have been clearer if she'd shouted it from the rooftops.

William licked her, trying a variety of strokes as he watched every expression that crossed her face. Her legs tightened on the fifth pattern, as she tried to come closer to his face. He purred silently and repeated the same stroke over and over again.

She gasped and moaned broken sentences. Her increased pulse and tension came clearly through her clit and into his mouth. He could taste her anticipation, an even finer delicacy than her musk.

"Warrior, please, put your finger into me."

William deliberately stroked her again with his tongue, while his hands held her thighs.

Lady Aurelia groaned, shuddering under his caresses.

He slipped a single joint of his index finger into her.

Her eyes were dark and pleading, her breasts flushed. He fondled one nipple and she moaned again, her eyelids slipping down.

William slid his finger all the way into her, still licking her clit. Her sheath clamped around it eagerly. She was hot and wet, roomier than any of the serving girls under the same caress. He pumped her, slowly at first. Her sheath tightened greedily as her hips lifted toward him.

He read her reaction clearly but kept the same steady pace. She wanted more, but he'd make her ask and build her excitement while she waited.

William could feel his own self-control now, an elegant shield that her ecstasy could trust and his lust couldn't breach. It was far more satisfying than any quick tumble with a chambermaid.

She begged for faster, then for a second finger. He gave her two fingers, using the same deliberate rhythm as with only one.

She writhed and sobbed, "Rougher, rougher, please. Oh, warrior, what must I do?"

He speeded up the tempo, enjoying how frantically she humped his hand. She was so beautiful to him as she lusted for his touch.

William considered his next move. A third finger? He'd never had more than two inside a serving girl. He shoved the third finger into her without breaking his rhythm.

"Oh yes, warrior!" she groaned and clamped down.

William smiled triumphantly. He was the one who'd brought her to this, not the weak Lord Philip. His balls were heavy and full, but not desperate for relief.

He studied Lady Aurelia again. Was she as excited as he could make her? His fingertips drummed against the sensitive spot deep inside her grotto.

Lady Aurelia almost came off the bed at that stroke. Her muscles clenched around his hand rhythmically and her eyes stared sightlessly at the ceiling. Her gasps and groans accented the wet music of her pussy welcoming him.

William rubbed her clit hard, determined she'd reach the peak at a time of his choosing. She launched into climax, sobbing, as her channel clamped around his fingers. Her body convulsed as wave after wave rippled through her.

Finally she collapsed, gasping for breath. He caressed her hair and covered her with a silk coverlet.

"Thank you, warrior," she whispered, and kissed his hand. "I am fortunate indeed to have served you."

A moment later she began to snore, and William straightened up.

"Well done, Donovan." Lady Irene's voice was soft.

"My lady." William bowed, startled she'd been able to approach him unawares. She handed him a towel and indicated they should leave the room.

Once outside, they stood in silence for a minute as he wiped his face and hands.

"Thank you for dealing so well with Lord Philip. He was quite complimentary about your discretion, once he recovered enough to talk sense."

William bowed again but said nothing.

"So it seems I am once again in your debt and must ponder how best to express my thanks."

William waited, watching her warily.

"I have been watching you closely, Donovan. You have a knack for appearing on the edge of many fantasies and also when students are being educated. How much do those activities interest you?"

His heart leapt but he kept his voice level. "A great deal, my lady."

"Have you ever thought of entering my school here?"

William's lips tightened. Students always began as colts or fillies, the yielding partners in a fantasy. That role held no appeal for him. "My lady," he began.

Lady Irene laughed. "Donovan, your expression is priceless. You'll have to manage it better if you're to succeed. Were you thinking you'd have to become a colt?"

"Yes," William gritted.

She chuckled. "All masters must spend at least three months as a colt or a filly, in order to better understand that side of the reins."

William shuddered. Still, if it was the fastest way to graduate to the true curriculum, it could be worth it. He swallowed hard before answering. "Very well."

"Are you sure?"

"Will you school me if I don't agree to yield?"

"Certainly not."

"Then I'll do it." And he'd probably puke after every lesson.

"You're a brave man, Donovan. Educating you will be an adventure for both of us."

Lady Irene had been quite correct: learning to be a master had taken two years of very hard work. But it had been worth every minute.

The question now was how best to use those lessons to explore Viola's fantasies and pleasures? He had three months with her and, sweet singing Jesus, he meant to make the most of every minute.

William crossed his arms behind his head and began to plan in earnest, while his faerie maiden slept beside him in the big bed. Tomorrow he'd do his best to free up more time with her.

Morgan Evans knocked once at the office door and waited.

"Enter," William answered, calm as always. The men now laid bets on which tune he'd whistle during an Indian fight.

Morgan obeyed, shutting the door behind him as he tossed his hat onto the rack. William nodded a welcome then returned to the column of figures he was summing up.

"Sorry about the missing clerk," Morgan offered.

"Don't be a fool. You couldn't stop Crampton from breaking an arm any more than you could persuade someone else to clerk here for a few months."

"I did find one fellow who would."

William glanced up from the litter of paper scattered across the desk. "Then why isn't he here?"

"Wanted miner's wages to do so."

William laughed. "Four dollars a day? No wonder you left him in Tucson. Have some coffee and sit down, Morgan. I'll be with you as soon as I finish checking the munitions tally."

Morgan poured himself a cup of coffee and added a generous dollop of milk, from one of Donovan & Sons' local milk cows, before taking the chair across from the desk. When he'd ordered the furniture for the depot and the big compound from Missouri, he'd made sure it was large enough for either himself or William. Now he settled into the expansive upholstery with a sigh of relief: it was so much more comfortable than a wagon's wooden seat.

He watched William unobtrusively as he sipped. Morgan had come a long way from the ragged scarecrow whom the big Irishman had hired so calmly in Memphis. But he was still learning from the man, even as he gradually built his own empire.

He followed William's hiring practices easily now. Any man who could do the job was welcome, no matter what the color of their skin. The majority were Confederate veterans, as most teamsters in Arizona were. But there were also Union veterans, Irish, Negroes, even a pair of Cheyenne Indians working for Donovan & Sons.

Of course, doing the job meant no drinking on the trail and no starting fights, whether with Indians or other Donovan & Sons employees. There were also the other rules typical of top freighting houses: punctuality, honesty, and so on. Break any of William's rules and he'd fire you immediately.

But if you did a good job for William, then he paid you very well indeed. Hell, William even paid your family a pension if you died while working for him. He made sure his men were fed and rested as much as possible on the trail. He was fair, generous, and better at the job than most of his employees.

Morgan considered William the brother he'd never had

and the only man, other than Bedford Forrest, whom Morgan would ride through hell for.

"Did you manage to find all the chickens?" William asked.

Morgan laughed, eyes crinkling as he recalled the search. "Yes, finally. Including the ones who'd taken up housekeeping in the barn. So they're all going to join the Army, whether they want to or not."

William laughed with him as he finished the tally with a flourish. "Maybe they'll like it better at the fort than in Rio Piedras."

"Probably. William, how long before the Golconda plays out?" Morgan finally asked the question that had been burning his tongue for months. William had seen every major strike since 1855. He'd hauled freight for the fabulous Comstock Lode in Nevada when they'd first struck silver there. He'd know the answer if anyone would.

William shrugged. "Ore's still the same quality as at the beginning. Mine's been around over a year, so it probably struck a rich vein, not a glory hole. My guess is Lennox will have water problems before he runs out of silver ore."

"Bad enough to shut down?"

"Maybe; there's enough water in these rocks. Even the Comstock has been nearly closed by flooding. The big pumps, which saved them, can only be hauled by railroads, not wagons."

"How long?"

"No way to tell. But last month's cave-in could mean they're closer to underground springs than they'd like."

Morgan whistled. "When that happens, it'll be time to move on to the next strike."

William sorted the papers into neat piles, then began to file them into the appropriate cubbyholes. "For you and me and the miners, but not as easily for Lennox. There's always money to be made, hauling supplies. The risky bet is owning a mine."

"Big profit for the mine owner."

"Sometimes. But nothing at all when the mine is gone."

"Steadier money in hauling freight or selling supplies."

"People always have to eat," William agreed.

Morgan set down his empty cup of coffee and stretched. Now to keep William away from Lennox for a bit longer. He disliked Lennox, as did anyone who'd heard of his brutish deeds in the Shenandoah Valley. But better he spend an hour listening to Lennox's complaints than see William shot in the back by that murdering bastard.

"If you'd like, I'll walk Lennox's latest invoice up to his office now."

"You sure? I planned to take it."

Morgan shrugged. "I'm the one who usually discusses payment with him. I also need to talk to him about the extra dynamite he wants hauled. At a discount."

William snorted and handed over an envelope. "Damn fool. In that case, you have my permission to talk to him. Maybe this time you'll persuade him dynamite just can't be treated like beans."

Morgan rose and bowed with an exaggerated flourish, as if in his grandmother's drawing room. "I will do my best, sir."

William laughed again and saluted Morgan in return.

Following Lennox's rat-faced clerk, Morgan found the mine owner poring over blueprints, apparently of a house. His office was as ornately furnished as if it stood on Wall Street, down to the ornate glass lampshades that danced to the stamp mill's beat.

The clerk coughed. "Mr. Evans is here to see you, sir. From Donovan & Sons," he added, hissing the final word.

Lennox's head came up. For a moment, his expression was as viciously cold as any rattler lurking in the rocks. Then it wiped clear, to be replaced by the appearance of warm-hearted friendship.

The house shuddered and the lampshades tinkled as the stamp mill pounded rocks into dust for refining.

The hair pricked on Morgan's neck. What the hell was going on? Lennox had never been more than grudgingly polite to him. At least the man wasn't wearing a gun and his sword stick rested in a stand by the door.

"Evans, my dear fellow!" Lennox offered his left hand in greeting.

"Lennox." Morgan shook it politely and retrieved his own as soon as possible. What had caused Lennox to bandage his right hand?

"Would you care to join me for a drink? Something civilized, to remind us of our families back east." Lennox almost shouted to be heard over the stamp mill.

"Thank you," Morgan accepted, the unexpected offer making him still more wary. Lennox providing refreshments, something he'd never done before, was like an Apache asking a cavalryman to drink from Apache Spring.

"Sherry? Or chilled Riesling from the well house, perhaps?" Morgan tensed. The last time he'd drunk sherry was with Jessamyn Tyler in 1863, while spying for Bedford Forrest. He'd sworn never to have it again until she was tied up in his bed, as he'd been tied up in hers. His voice was a little hoarse when he answered, "Riesling, thank you."

"Ah yes, a cool drink to take away the heat." Lennox returned with two tall crystal goblets, their sides sweating lightly in the room's warmth.

Morgan accepted his with thanks and sipped cautiously. This was no time to get drunk.

Lennox sat down in a chair next to Morgan's, rather than behind his big desk. An almost companionable silence followed before Morgan stirred.

"I brought your latest invoice," he began.

Lennox waved the envelope aside. "Let's not worry about shopkeepers' trifles like that. Just leave it on the desk and I'll send payment over tomorrow."

"Very well." Lennox accepting an invoice without a word of complaint? If he'd still been riding for Bedford Forrest, Morgan would have had every gun cocked and loaded by now.

"Have you ever thought of owning a great estate, Evans? A magnificent home and acres of cotton, such as your family held before the war?" Lennox's voice was almost, but not quite, idle.

"Often," Morgan answered honestly. He'd redeemed Longacres, the Evans family cotton plantation in Mississippi, four years ago by paying off back taxes with savings from his job. His cousin David ran it now and sent Morgan regular reports.

"A beautiful vision, is it not? The fields humming with your workers making money for your future, the mansion aglow with light beyond the driveway, and the wife eager to charm you and your guests as you build alliances. The gracious lady who comes from a family as old and noble as your own, a woman who will bear you sons."

"A spectacular dream," Morgan agreed, and shoved away the vision of Jessamyn Tyler doing exactly that. He took another sip of Riesling as he tried to guess Lennox's goal in this conversation.

"I'm sure, as a gentleman born and bred, you'll understand how terrible it is to see a lady living in surroundings unworthy of her."

"What are you talking about?" Morgan set down his glass.

"Mrs. Ross, of course. To see her living in that Irishman's house is an affront. I'd marry her in an instant if she were under my roof."

"Quite so," Morgan murmured noncommittally. He had no idea why Lennox was so set on marrying Mrs. Ross. There weren't any other women around from Lennox's class, but Morgan had always thought Lennox would look for a wife in New York, the city he always bragged of. The man's repeated proposals to Mrs. Ross smacked more of obsession than love, especially since the fellow showed no signs of being besotted with her.

"So you'll help me, then. Splendid! If you can get her out of the Donovan compound and bring her to me, let's say to-morrow—"

"What the devil are you talking about?" Morgan came to his feet in a smooth lunge.

"Why, removing Mrs. Ross from Donovan's grasp, of course. There'll be good money in it for you, to help you gain a home and family of your own. Say, five thousand dollars?"

Morgan threw his wine into Lennox's face.

Lennox sat stock still for a moment, Riesling dripping off his chin. His eyes blazed like a rattler's considering the best strike. Then he forced a smile. "I gather that's a refusal."

"You're damn right it is, you coward." Morgan waited hopefully to hear the demand for a duel.

Lennox's glare would have stopped a basilisk but he stayed still with a visible effort. All the while, the stamping machines pounded their inhuman beat of destruction.

"You'll pay for that," Lennox hissed and finally took a deep breath. "But you're only a hired hand and not worth fighting. You may leave now."

"Donovan will destroy you."

Lennox laughed, a spine-chilling sound. "He can try. Do you mean to stay and debate it?"

Morgan's fists clenched, then he turned for the door.

Two steps later, he caught a reflection on the lampshade of Lennox pulling a revolver from the desk drawer. Morgan whirled, drawing his own, just as Lennox pointed and cocked his. It was the fastest he'd ever drawn.

Each man now stared down the barrel of the other's gun.

"If you shoot," Lennox growled between clenched teeth, "you'll be tried for murder."

"And if you shoot first, you'll be dead before I hit your Brussels carpet. Mexican standoff, Lennox."

Lennox snarled but didn't lower his Colt. "Get out."

"My pleasure." Morgan reached for the doorknob behind him.

"Don't bother to come back, little man. Lennox Mining will do no further business with Donovan & Sons after this month."

Morgan nodded curtly. "As you wish. Donovan & Sons can do without Lennox Mining, but how long can Lennox Mining live without a freighting house?"

"We'll manage very well. Lennox Mining will be a power long after Donovan & Sons is forgotten," Lennox sneered.

Morgan snorted and stepped out of Lennox's office, careful to keep his eyes on the blackguard. He didn't allow himself to relax until he reached the street.

He'd have to warn William, of course.

William quietly crossed the courtyard, enjoying the music coming from the main wing. Even the eternal billiards game had stopped so the men could listen. He'd last heard that Schubert art song in Dublin, performed by an excellent soprano and pianist. Viola played it superbly, but as an accompanist rather than a soloist, leaving space for the absent singer to provide the melody.

She finished the song just as he reached the sitting room and paused. She slowly played the opening chords of Foster's "Beautiful Dreamer."

William smiled. He strolled into the room, singing.

Viola's head snapped around. She stared at him, then her eyes lit up like sunlight on the ocean waves. She continued to play the lovely song, adapting it smoothly to his voice and phrasing, until they became a single performer.

He leaned on the piano and smiled at her when they finished. "Bravo! You're the best accompanist I've had the pleasure of performing with, Viola."

She blushed, her fingers still caressing the black and white keys. "Thank you. You have a wonderful baritone, William."

He bowed his head in silent thanks for her compliment. "Another song, perhaps?"

" 'Camptown Races'?" She struck the opening notes and he laughed.

"Doo-dah, doo-dah!" he agreed, and they joined in the rollicking tune. It was far better to frolic innocently with Viola than worry about Lennox's villainy.

Chapter Nine

Viola shifted uncomfortably on the piano bench's upholstery, reminded yet again of just how passionate William had been the previous night. Singing their favorite songs, then dinner, then the bedroom where they'd . . .

She blushed.

She'd been glad when he went to Mass that morning with Abraham and Sarah. At least now, she could focus on her music without thinking of him.

She began another popular song, stringing the songs together in a pattern similar to the way she'd played them at musicales during the fighting. Her mother greatly enjoyed those evenings, where she could roam the audience while Viola accompanied the other performers. She remembered one evening during September 1863, when she'd accompanied some young gunboat officers at just such a musicale.

Viola finished the final notes of "The Vacant Chair," holding them a little longer than necessary to allow Ensign Johnston time to recover from his tears. He had a superb tenor and always sang on key, making him a pleasure to accompany. But he'd just returned from Vicksburg, where his gunboat had suffered heavy casualties.

He forced the betraying vibrato out of his voice and nodded at her. She let the last note die out. Their audience was most appreciative but quickly started to take their leave.

Viola searched the crowd with her eyes, while automatically responding to Johnston. "Yes, I'd be delighted to accompany you at church this Sunday."

"Perhaps we can meet before then to practice? And you can tell me more stories of your famous grandfather, Commodore Lindsay." His voice had lowered, as if wrapping them in something private. He was well-bred, well off, and her father strongly approved of him.

Viola ignored the ensign's advantages as she finally found her mother. Dear heavens, she was flirting with Captain Peterson. He held an important post at the shipyards and could always be relied on to talk at great length to any woman who seemed interested.

Viola flinched.

"Shall I see you on Saturday then?" Johnston asked hopefully.

"I'm sorry but I really can't make any plans at the moment. I must see if my mother is well. Good evening, Ensign." She nodded to him and slipped away through the crowd without waiting for an answer.

She could hear Peterson talking about how to armor the ships from halfway across the room. Viola popped up next to her mother's elbow and plastered a smile on her face. "Thank you for waiting, Mother," she said mendaciously. "I'm ready to leave now."

From this close, she could see Desdemona Lindsay clench her teeth briefly. But the woman recovered quickly and smiled charmingly at Peterson. "Please forgive me, Captain, but my daughter needs me. I would greatly enjoy hearing the remainder of your fascinating discourse. Perhaps tomorrow at the Floyds' dinner?"

Peterson bowed. "My pleasure, dear lady."

Viola made a mental note not to let her mother out of

earshot at that dinner party. She hadn't planned to attend, but the presence of an adult daughter seemed to be an excellent conversational damper, especially for attempted flirtations with men who possessed information related to the war effort.

She sighed inwardly but kept her face straight. She didn't eat when she was guarding her mother, not that food seemed appetizing anymore.

Desdemona Lindsay glared at her daughter as they boarded the carriage. She sank into the luxurious velvet upholstery and seethed for the entire drive. Viola settled into the smallest space possible, carefully avoiding her mother's ornate dress, and kept her mouth shut. Silence had become their usual custom when they were alone together, once Desdemona had realized no amount of tantrums would shake Viola's determination to keep her from gaining information useful to the South.

At the Lindsay mansion, Desdemona went straight upstairs, where her old maid waited to undress her, ignoring the Irish maids who had waited up for them.

Viola sighed privately, but greeted Molly and Brigid warmly. Thankfully, neither showed any inclination to chatter. Molly helped Viola undress, while Brigid fetched a cup of mint tea to settle Viola's stomach. They disappeared quickly afterwards and Viola was left alone with her books in her sanctuary.

Dumas, Sir Walter Scott, James Fenimore Cooper looked back at her from her bookcase: *The Three Musketeers, Ivanhoe, The Last of the Mohicans.* Her best-loved books, although the shelves were full to overflowing. D'Artagnan, the country bumpkin and great swordsman, was her favorite hero. She had a weakness for Athos's bitter past but D'Artagnan held her heart.

Viola stretched, then idly fondled her breasts. The only advantage of their small size was that her slender hands could easily hold and rub them. She sighed as she imagined D'Artagnan in his rough country clothes, all raw masculinity as he strode through the marketplace.

She moaned softly as her breasts firmed and swelled in her hands, her nipples peaking against her fingers.

She blew out the lamp and settled against her pillows to fantasize. It had rained earlier that evening and the air was gentle and cool as it whispered through the room. Her embroidered white lawn nightdress was soft and sheer, the perfect weight for a late summer evening. It was also exactly what a young lady would have worn while chained in the cardinal's prison.

Viola plucked her nipples, enjoying the sharp stab that ran through her body as she considered the dungeon. *It would be dark, of course, with only a few torches to give light. The guards would be in the guardroom playing cards, not close enough to hear her.*

She drew her nightdress higher up on her thighs as she fantasized.

She'd be chained to the wall with her hands high and her legs wide, helpless to resist any man who chanced by. But no one would have come yet.

Her fingers slipped under her nightdress and stroked her intimate folds with the ease of long practice. She knew just the motions that would sharpen her pulse and she employed them now. Dew flowed, dampening her fingers and her nightdress underneath her legs.

D'Artagnan would appear suddenly out of the darkness, tall and strong with a face like an angel. His sword would be ready in his hand.

Her hips twisted at the thought and dew gushed forth. She moaned and fondled her bud where it hid between her legs. It throbbed in response. Viola closed her eyes, enjoying the sensations. Yes, oh yes . . .

"Mademoiselle, you are beautiful," he would say, his eyes devouring her. "My senses are ravished by the sight of you."

Viola moaned. Her body arched as her pulse pounded. Her fingers delved deeper. A single fingertip actually entered her body and moved rhythmically in and out. In and out . . .

"One kiss for your rescuer before we depart," D'Artagnan would say. His mouth would close over hers. Sweet-tasting, of course. His lips would be firm and his tongue would sweep between her teeth . . .

She rubbed her bud rapidly. Her body arched again as the soft pulse of rapture flowed sweetly through her veins.

Lovely. She smiled, and rolled over as she settled herself to sleep.

Viola shook her head, remembering that young girl's innocence. To climax, simply by dreaming of a kiss.

Now she slept with a man whose kisses were an enticement to carnal delights she still didn't have words for. He was everything and more Sally had spoken of, as her sore body could attest.

She squirmed on the bench, remembering just how her thighs had come to be so tender. Then she determinedly started to play the piano, choosing a piece that wouldn't remind her of a young girl's innocence. A Chopin etude stormed from her fingers as she fought not to think of what William might want to do next.

Morgan took another sip of coffee as he read David's latest report on Longacres, while Mrs. Ross played the piano inside. He was happy to guard her while William, Abraham, and Sarah attended Mass. He'd be happier when he finally killed that scoundrel, Lennox.

Mrs. Ross was a gutsy little lady with a good many friends. She was always helping folks out, no matter who they were. Pretty enough, although not as beautiful as Jessamyn Tyler.

He'd seen her often enough, thanks to that so-called friend of hers, Maggie Watson, who had constantly tried to gain his attention. He'd finally told her, in no uncertain terms, that he had no interest in her as a wife. She'd married Jones a week later and left town. For good, he hoped.

The music stopped and Mrs. Ross wandered outside, stretching. He stood up politely. "Ma'am."

Mrs. Ross's head snapped around. Her jaw dropped and she turned flaming red when she saw him. Clearly William hadn't warned her who'd be guarding her this morning. Pity swept over him at her embarrassment. He kept his tone gentle. "You're a very fine piano player, Mrs. Ross. Chopin, wasn't it?"

She visibly pulled herself together. "Thank you," she stammered. "You're very kind. Yes, that was the Étude in C minor."

Evans nodded. "Thought I recognized it. My mother also enjoyed playing the piano and tried to teach me. But I'm afraid I defeated her best efforts. Would you care for a cup of coffee, ma'am?"

"Thank you." She turned to the fountain as he went inside, and was adding an extra rose to Abraham and Sarah's shrine when he returned. After that, she strolled the herb garden with her coffee until William returned.

Viola stole another glance at Evans, still embarrassed at meeting him in public. He'd treated her with every courtesy, but everything about him, from his face to his clothes to his voice, told of his good breeding. Although not as attractive as William to her eyes, Evans was a very handsome man with his chestnut hair and gray eyes. His cavalry mustache was neatly groomed, as was his beautifully tailored suit and the immaculate linens that covered his long-limbed frame. His skin was darkened by the sun, but his long fingers were elegant and deft as he dined. He ate his eggs au gratin and ham—how had Sarah provided ham in Rio Piedras?—with every appearance of enjoyment.

He insisted on treating her as William's hostess, giving her all the respect she'd had before accepting William's protection. Of course, then she'd been watching Maggie chase

Evans like a housewife at breakfast time with only one chicken in the yard: intent and frantic. He must have finally said something very blunt to Maggie. Viola didn't know precisely what, just that Maggie had been furious. The next week, Maggie was married to Charlie Jones and gone from Rio Piedras.

She dipped into her own eggs au gratin and caught William eating a spoonful of oatmeal. Viola stared. He'd wrapped his lips around her breast in exactly the same fashion, little more than an hour ago. He'd used his teeth in the same way, too: slow, steady, gentle bites that had set her moaning in anticipation of his next move.

Viola blushed and looked down quickly. She needed to stop thinking about him, which was impossible in this compound. Every room in this wing held memories of his lovemaking.

Even the clothing she wore reminded her of sensual games. At the moment, she was dressed in a very fashionable royal blue walking dress, whose numerous folds cushioned her from the chair's brocade seat. But she'd have to change to its Chinese counterpart, a sinfully smooth blue tunic and pants, before he returned from the depot that evening.

Just so she'd be ready for his return, he'd ordered as he'd laced her into her low-cut French corset this morning. Then he'd suckled her breasts till they hardened and ached, and kissed her silly while his hand played wicked games through the slit in her drawers. She'd shattered in pleasure, gripping his shoulders till her fingers turned white.

Where could she go that wouldn't make her dream of such things? Another look at Evans gave her the answer.

"Mr. Donovan, may I help you at the depot today? I am sure you must be rushing to prepare for the supply train's departure. Surely there's a great deal to do, even on a Sunday, with Mr. Crampton nursing a broken arm back in Tucson."

The two men shot a look at each other. "No," snapped Evans.

"Do you feel trapped here at the compound?" William asked simultaneously.

Viola hesitated, then nodded. It was true enough, although she'd been caged before. The long years of the war had felt like decades, while she watched her mother and fretted, always worried just how far her mother would go to support the South.

The two men looked at each other again. Viola saw worry on Evans's face. Donovan was harder to read; he seemed to be weighing his options, rather than fearful. She held her breath.

"We'd be glad of your company, Mrs. Ross, and there's plenty to do. But you'd have to stay within the depot at all times, so you might feel confined there, too."

Viola brightened. "I'm sure I will be very comfortable." And surely she wouldn't have to practice those exercises of his, if she was working in the depot.

William smiled at her, a slow intimate smile that set her pulse skittering. "You'll adorn my office, Mrs. Ross."

Viola smiled back at him. "Why, Mr. Donovan, you do say the sweetest things," she managed, uttering the first flirtatious gambit of her life.

William inclined his head in acknowledgment, eyes dancing. "Always a pleasure to be around a lady, Mrs. Ross."

Viola blushed at the possibilities his deep voice evoked.

An hour later, William and Evans escorted Viola through the depot. The men who saw them paused to touch their hats to her, then returned to their duties. They behaved exactly as they had before she started sleeping with William, as if it was nothing unusual to see her leave an unmarried man's house in the early morning. Something inside Viola relaxed almost imperceptibly at their easy acceptance of her.

Everything else was a pleasant bustle: the wagons custom-made by Murphy & Sons of St. Louis to meet Donovan & Sons' famously high expectations, the mules bred for Donovan

& Sons' demand for speed and stamina, even the teamsters joking as they returned from their regular target practice. She'd heard gossip for years about the firm's high requirements and the almost military demand for discipline. Meeting those standards was what kept Donovan & Sons in business, delivering freight to even the riskiest parts of the West.

"Mr. Donovan." Lowell, one of the teamsters, appeared beside them. He touched his hat to Viola but his attention was entirely on William. "Can you settle a wager for me?"

"Another bet, Lowell? What is it this time?" William's voice was indulgent and patient.

Viola's mouth twitched. Lowell's interest in betting on anything was famous, even here on the frontier where everyone, both men and women, gambled.

"How many strokes with a whip would you need to cut a newspaper into pieces? I said six, but Harrison said four."

"Do you want me to demonstrate here and now?"

"Yes, sir." Lowell had the appearance of a puppy about to wag its tail.

"With your help, of course. Very well."

Lowell took a deep breath, then nodded. "Yes, sir." He stepped into the middle of the yard and shook out a single sheet of newspaper, his movements only slightly rushed. The other men gathered around, staying well back from Lowell.

"Wait for me on the porch, would you, Mrs. Ross?"

Viola nodded and moved to the better vantage point. She'd heard gossip of William's skill before, that he could take a fly off a horse's ear and similar feats. But she'd never seen him in action.

William shook out his whip casually. Viola's knees weakened at the elegance of the movement, the restrained power of the whip in his strong hand. It was a deadly weapon but none of the men seemed afraid of it.

He flicked it several times, keeping it close to the ground. "Will you count, Evans?"

"My pleasure." Evans stepped up next to Viola.

Lowell faced William, the newspaper stretched between his hands. William took a step forward, cracking the whip as he did so, but the teamster didn't flinch. The newspaper split cleanly in half.

The sound of the whip ran through Viola's bones.

"One." Evans's voice was slightly bored.

Lowell held a remaining half sheet between his hands. Another crack and another piece of newspaper fell. Viola gripped the rail harder as arousal shimmered within her.

"Two."

"Three." Lowell was completely calm, his breathing unhurried, as he stretched smaller and smaller pieces between his hands.

"Four."

William was as calm as when he'd returned from Mass.

"Five."

Her breasts were as swollen and aching as if William had been suckling them.

"Six."

The only sound in the depot was Harrison's faint muttering.

"Seven."

Lowell glanced at William, who nodded. His confidence in the man with the whip couldn't have been more obvious, even though the remaining piece was less than an inch long.

Viola held her breath, ignoring the fiery lances jolting her breasts and womb.

"Eight."

Lowell let the last shred of newspaper fall. Cheers went up and money exchanged hands. Lowell strutted like a rooster.

William stretched a bit and smiled quietly as he coiled his bullwhip.

Viola wondered if a whip could be used in carnal play.

Evans disappeared with a murmured farewell, leaving William and Viola to enter the office alone. He settled her at the clerk's smaller desk, now covered by neat stacks of tally sheets. It was fairly self-explanatory work, but he gave her a solid explanation while she waited patiently.

"Crampton's gear should suit you," William murmured, and opened a drawer.

Viola blinked. What sort of things could that finicky little man possibly have to interest her? She laughed when William produced a leather apron, an eyeshade, and cuff protectors. "Is that how he does it?" she exclaimed.

"Be so incredibly clean all the time? Oh yes, and he fights Apaches the same way."

Viola considered the results of wearing Crampton's protective gear in the window's reflection, and chuckled again. Her mother or Juliet would swoon in horror before appearing in public like this. On the other hand, her beautiful new dress should stay quite presentable. "Sarah's cleanliness standards should be satisfied, if not her fashion sense," she remarked. "She has very strict standards, you know."

"We'll make sure she doesn't see you then. Her disapproval is something best avoided."

Viola cocked an eye at him but didn't ask how he'd learned that. Perhaps they'd be friendly enough to exchange such confidences in the three months they had left together.

Soon she was up to her elbows in paperwork, humming the Stephen Foster tune about the Swanee River while William worked at the other desk. Emboldened by the comfortable silence, she raised a popular conversational topic.

"William, do you think about railroads often?"

"As much as anyone else, I reckon. Why?"

"Do you worry they'll take your business away from you?"

"No, never that."

Viola blinked in surprise. Most teamsters, even riverboat captains, were convinced railroads would take over everything. "Why not?"

"Railroads can't, and won't, go everywhere. There'll always be business hauling freight to everyplace else."

Viola nodded, understanding the strategy. It'd work for a teamster, although it might not for a riverboat. Railroads satisfied more predictable schedules than a river allowed. They also served the same large settlements as riverboats, making them more of a threat.

"Also, there will always be a business hauling high-risk cargo," William continued, in his slightly guttural California drawl. "Donovan & Sons regularly escorts special freight on railroads, for example."

"And the higher the risk, the higher the profit," Viola said slowly.

"Exactly." William finished writing and came over to her. "Here you are, sweetheart. These are receipts for payment of Ross's debts, plus a letter of credit drawn on my bank in San Francisco. It's good anywhere in North America and most of Europe. Plus some coins to jingle in your pocket."

Viola nodded silently, staring at the slips of paper in her hand as William placed a handful of money on the blotter. He'd written the letter of credit for the full thousand dollars, rather than the fraction left after paying Edward's bills. Freedom and a new life lay before her.

She sprang up and hugged him, tears sparking her eyes. "Thank you," she choked out. "You didn't have to do this, not pay me the full sum in the beginning."

He held her close and kissed the top of her head. "My pleasure, sweetheart."

They remained like that for a long minute before she sniffled. He released her immediately and handed her a handkerchief.

"Are you always this generous in business?" Viola asked as she wiped her eyes.

William snorted. "Not often called generous, sweetheart. Honest, yes. But sometimes worse."

"No wonder your men love you," Viola went on, disregarding his modesty. She'd heard too much about him in this small town that he and Lennox dominated.

He spluttered. "Love? Sweetheart, who the devil are you speaking of? Teamsters don't love their boss."

She was still laughing at the look on his face when a knock sounded. "Mr. Donovan?"

William shrugged and went to the door. "What is it, Lowell?"

"Begging your pardon, sir. Ma'am. We're having some difficulty lashing down the colonel's personal effects. Could you please take a look?"

"Five minutes, Lowell." He shut the door and leaned against it, studying Viola. She looked back at him quizzically.

"Ever considered playing games in the office, sweetheart? Carnal games?"

"What?!" Viola squeaked. With a guilty glance at the window, she lowered her voice. "William, what on earth makes you think such a thing would be possible? It would be entirely outside the normal course of behavior in a business setting."

"Ever meet an impertinent clerk? Perhaps she receives her just desserts from her manager in a sensual fashion. All just for play, of course, like a pageant."

Viola was speechless. Carnal punishment? In the office? Her breasts heated at the thought.

"Have you ever been in a pageant, sweetheart?"

"Yes," Viola whispered, her nipples hard and aching now.

William's eyes rested on her for an appreciative moment. "Good. Then think on it while I'm gone."

He clapped on his hat and departed with a quick salute to Viola. It was a few minutes before she could return to adding up gunpowder barrels.

Shortly, another polite knock followed by a diffident, and very deep, voice interrupted her. "Mrs. Ross?"

"Come in." She smiled tentatively as Hank Carson, the blacksmith, entered. He was a very respectable man, with a wife and children back in Santa Fe and a legendary knack for finding a church wherever he went. What would this Methodist deacon think of her liaison with William Donovan?

"I fixed the big desk lamp, Mrs. Ross." He produced an elegant student lamp, gleaming bright in the filtered sunlight. "There was a hole in the stem, right here, that I mended. Perhaps you can use it while you're down here."

"Thank you, Mr. Carson. That's very kind of you."

He set the lamp on her desk, careful to align it with the stretch of leather blotter. Then he stepped back and looked her in the eyes. Viola's pulse thudded in her throat.

"I've been elected by the boys to talk to you, Mrs. Ross."

"Yes?" Viola held her breath.

"You're a member of the Donovan family now, Mrs. Ross, and we take that very seriously. If there's ever anything one of us can do for you, you just holler and we'll all come running."

Whatever she'd expected, it wasn't this. "Thank you, Mr. Carson. Please extend my sincerest appreciation to the other men, as well. I cannot begin to express how safe you've made me feel."

Carson nodded. "I'll do that, ma'am. There is one other matter, if you don't mind. If anyone in this town should treat you with less than the proper respect due a lady of quality, you just let me know. I'll be glad to give them a lesson in manners straightaway."

Joy bubbled up in Viola, so bright and vivid it came out as tears. She blinked hard and managed a smile. "Thank you, Mr. Carson. I will keep your offer in mind. But Mr. Donovan does show me every courtesy."

"Mr. Donovan is a gentleman, even if he is Irish born and bred." He nodded again to her. "Good day, Mrs. Ross."

"Good day to you, Mr. Carson."

Viola returned to adding up the number of gunpowder barrels with a considerably lighter heart. At least someone in the community accepted her actions.

And Donovan & Sons were notoriously loyal to their own, closer than blood ties could be. Her mother, for example, had set little stock in blood ties.

Viola hummed an old Latin Christmas carol as she and the other two women walked up to the house's back door. She always used the servants' entrance whenever she went out with Molly and Brigid O'Byrne. Christmas morning Mass, her first Catholic church service, had been just as beautiful as the two Irish girls had promised. She'd enjoyed the lavish service and had even understood some of the priest's sonorous phrases, thanks to studying Latin with Hal all those years ago.

She gave thanks yet again that Hal and Father were well, on this fourth Christmas of the war. Her mother had never been arrested either, despite her occasional trips into Kentucky and her lavish hospitality for Union military men.

Viola couldn't count the number of times she'd headed the conversation away from military matters at one of her mother's dinner parties. She'd always been ignored at social functions before, when all the attention focused on her mother or Juliet. But when she'd caught her mother coaxing detail after detail about the gunboats' overhaul from Mr. Pook, the shipyards' foreman, she'd promptly interrupted. After that terrifying dinner party in 1861, she'd made sure to be present whenever her mother was around Union military men.

But now with Grant's army surrounding Richmond and Sherman's capture of Savannah, surely the war was almost over. She could relax without worrying about her mother's loyalties. Father and Hal would come home soon and they'd be a family again.

A flash of light caught her eye from the mud beside the path. Viola stooped to pick it up. An officer's button. She cleaned it as best she could with her mittened hands and studied it in the thin winter sunlight.

"What is it, Miss Viola?"

"Are you cold, Miss Viola? You're looking a bit wan. Come in and we'll make you a nice hot cup of tea," Brigid's twin sister Molly urged.

Viola's hand closed around the button. A Confederate officer's button. Dear God in heaven, what had Mother done?

Her heart plummeted into her stomach but she managed a smile for the girls.

Somehow Viola had become friends with them since she'd hired them a year ago. They'd matched her in age, if not education or family background. She'd taught them how to read and write, while they'd taught her how to do laundry, including the oddities of cleaning the most fragile fabrics. She knew they also protected her from some of her mother's worst vagaries, but no one acknowledged that.

"Tea would be lovely, thank you." Viola tucked the incriminating button away in her pocket as they went inside to the kitchen.

"Viola! Viola, where are you?" Desdemona Lindsay's voice floated down the back stairs.

Molly and Brigid shared a long look before smiling at Viola. "We'll put the water on to boil now, Miss Viola. Your tea will be ready whenever you want it."

"Thank you." Viola headed for the hallway, stripping off her coat and mittens. She had no eyes for the vibrant Persian carpet, the highly polished wooden floors, or the oil paintings of Empress Josephine's roses.

"Viola!" Her mother ran down the stairs, eyes sparkling and little spots of color high on her cheekbones. She looked stunning, like a woman just returned from a ball, with a spectacular string of pearls gleaming against her dress's cobalt blue wool. But Desdemona had excused herself from any invitations for the night before, pleading a headache.

"Yes, Mother?" Viola's stomach was churning like a paddlewheel steamer's wake. She heard the door into the kitchen swing shut.

"Have you seen my sealskin muff? I'm calling on Beatrice Johnson and I must look my best."

Viola held out her hand, the officer's button displayed on her palm like an accusing eye. Muffled sounds of cast iron banging together came from the kitchen as Molly and Brigid started to prepare breakfast.

Desdemona stopped short, her eyes fixed on the button, and her hand flew to her throat. She started to speak, caught Viola's eye, and stopped.

"What is this button doing at our house?" Viola demanded. She was colder than she ever remembered being, despite her heavy woolen clothing.

"How dare you talk to me in that fashion! I'll have you know I did nothing to disgrace my wedding vows. General Bryant was here only a few minutes."

"Joseph Bryant, the rebel cavalryman? He's been in prison for months. What did you do?"

"My duty as a Southerner, of course. By now, General Bryant should be safely across the Ohio and back in Kentucky. In a few weeks, you'll be reading about him again in the newspapers as he wins another glorious victory."

"Victory? He'll kill Union soldiers!"

Desdemona harrumphed scornfully. "Conscripts, not true believers in a cause. But our Southern boys can truly fight, especially with the rifles I sent them."

"Rifles?" Viola choked. Visions crowded in on her, of Father clutching his shoulder as blood spurted between his fingers. Of Hal, pale in death as he sprawled across his quarterdeck, a single bullet wound in his temple. "Mother, what if one of those guns shoots Hal or Father?"

Desdemona hesitated for the first time, but quickly recovered. "Impossible. I bought those rifles last summer in New York and had them delivered directly to the right people in Richmond."

Viola flinched. All the time they'd been in New York, she'd

thought Desdemona was thinking about her new grandson, not killing people.

"Besides," Desdemona continued, "Richard and Hal understand the risks. We simply fight on opposite sides. Someone in this family must ensure we come out on the winning side and keep our property."

Viola shuddered and buried her face in her hands. Tears welled up until they overflowed down her cheeks. "How could you do this?" she choked. "What will happen if Hal and Father discover you betrayed them?"

"They will never know because neither of us will ever tell them."

Viola cast an incredulous glance at her mother. "You're mad."

"Am I wrong? Will you speak of this to them?"

"No," Viola whispered, acknowledging the brutal truth. Father's sanity might survive his wife's betrayal, but Hal? How could she tell him their own mother had risked his life?

The front doorbell rang, startling them both. Viola's heart stopped beating, while Desdemona turned white.

Molly tapped lightly on the kitchen door, then came through into the hallway.

"Shall I say you're at home to callers, Mrs. Lindsay?" she asked calmly, ignoring Viola's tear-stained face.

"I am not at home but my daughter is. I'll be in my room." Desdemona ran upstairs faster than she'd come down.

A man pounded heavily on the door. Viola's stomach dived for her boots. She gripped a baluster, willing the dizziness to recede.

"Are you sure you're feeling well enough for callers, Miss Viola?" Molly questioned in a much warmer tone than she'd used for the senior lady of the house.

Viola nodded and released the wooden prop to wipe her eyes with the back of her hand. "Yes, of course."

Molly walked slowly to the front door and opened it deliberately, catching the Union officer with his fist raised to knock again. Captain Edward Ross, with a half dozen soldiers behind him. Viola shook and fought to compose herself.

"I've come to speak to Miss Lindsay," he announced, looking past Molly. Five and a half feet of stolidity, he'd done well at Shiloh. Since then, he'd occupied himself, so to speak, commanding the guards at the big shipyards. He came from a poor family in Pittsburgh and reeked of whisky at any time of day. Viola had always avoided him, despite his frequent attempts to court her and flatter her mother.

"Yes, Captain, I am here. What can we do for you?"

"May I speak to you privately, Miss Lindsay?"

Viola gulped but nodded. "In the library."

Leaving the other soldiers outside the house, Ross shut the library door with an ominous thud, turned to Viola, and held out his hand. A single button gleamed in the center.

Viola's knees went weak. She held herself upright by sheer force of will.

Ross's eyes never left her face. He smiled slowly, like a lion surveying an injured gazelle.

Viola wished she'd eaten something, anything, before going to Christmas Mass. Perhaps nausea wouldn't be so strong if she had a full stomach.

"I see you recognize it."

"What do you want?" Viola disdained beating around the bush. She'd rather get this over with as fast as possible.

"Mrs. Lindsay's the one who got him out, isn't she?"

"I cannot answer that."

"You're no hand at lying. I can see the truth in your eyes."

"What do you want?"

He ignored her question as he smirked down at her. "I can cover it up. Nobody will ever know that fancy reb general was here."

"How?"

Ross laughed, the sound a mockery of honor and duty to his country. "How doesn't matter."

"What if the authorities suspect?"

"They can suspect all they like, but nobody will touch Captain Richard Lindsay's son-in-law."

"No!"

"Oh yes. You're going to marry me and we're going to have a real fine life together, thanks to your money."

"What if there's no dowry? You must know Captain Lindsay is not fond of you," Viola stammered. Her father had cut Ross dead at church the one time they'd met.

"He'll come around. No man's going to cast off his little daughter. I've already picked out where we'll build our house."

"He is not known for letting sentimentality guide him," Viola insisted desperately, hoping for a way to escape Ross's blackmail.

"He'll give us the money because you'll make sure of it. Otherwise, I'll tell him about his wife's treason."

"Dear God Almighty," Viola breathed.

"I'm glad you finally see the inevitability of our union, my dear."

The next four months had been a long series of fights, both in writing and in person, whenever a Lindsay male visited Cincinnati. Viola had insisted on marrying Ross but she'd never said why. She simply couldn't bring herself to claim love for Ross, or even a pretense of infatuation.

Finally Ross had set a wedding date, confident her father would change his mind once they were married. He'd been wrong: Father had disinherited her on the same day, swearing he'd never speak to Captain or Mrs. Ross. Hal had done the same, cutting off all contact with her.

Ross had been furious. He'd sworn he'd be richer than her father was, even if he had to dig gold out of the ground to do it. Viola's decision to marry Ross was privately reinforced by

Lincoln's assassination and the public anger toward all traitors. Her only consolation in the following years was that Hal didn't know of their mother's treachery.

After tasting the fruit of her mother's lies, Viola could hold to William Donovan's honesty for three months. She turned her attention back to adding up the tally sheets and deliberately lost herself in contemplation of how many barrels of beans were currently in the depot.

She refused to consider the invoices and letters awaiting filing on the shelf next to her desk. They came from nearly every state and territory in the Union, damning evidence of how widespread Donovan & Sons' connections were. And just how much William sought money.

"Mrs. Ross?" William's broad shoulders blocked sight of the corrals beyond the doorway as he stepped into the office. "Are you daydreaming?"

"Of course not," Viola answered automatically. "I've almost finished accounting for the gunpowder barrels."

"Are you sure about that?" He shut the door behind him. He'd shed his jacket and his sleeves were rolled up. He was dusty and sweaty and completely masculine, far more interesting than any proper businessman. A single finger pushed his hat back on his head. His eyes were very intent on her. "You look like an impertinent clerk to me."

Something clenched deep inside her core at the look in his eyes. She remembered his words about playing games, in a manner similar to a pageant. This must be what he wanted now. Viola tried to think of what an uppity employee might do.

"Mr. Donovan," she began, as superciliously as possible, "your account books are intolerable."

His eyes heated while his mouth twitched, then firmed. Encouraged, Viola went on.

"You, sir, must take immediate steps to correct this situation, before I am forced to count barrels myself." She tilted her nose in the air.

"I must do something?" he drawled. "I am your employer and you are the one who must do as I say."

"Impossible, Mr. Donovan." Viola sniffed and cast a hopeful glance at his trousers. The ridge behind his fly was most pronounced. "You are the one who must act and should do so immediately."

William vaulted the desk. He grabbed Viola's hands and held them over her head. She was intensely aware of his strength and yet she felt free to enjoy herself. She was suddenly glad she'd practiced those exercises earlier.

"You are most definitely an impertinent clerk," he drawled, more casually than the tight grip of his hand around her wrists indicated. "What should I do with you? I warn you, further insolence would warrant a heavier punishment."

Viola's ears pricked up. "Why, you . . . you brute," she tried a phrase as she twisted away halfheartedly. He leaned against her a bit closer, bracing his free hand on the other side of her head. His wonderful scent enveloped her and her breasts promptly firmed in response.

"Such resistance to my will," he clucked, and circled his hips against her. Somehow the ridge inside his trousers seemed larger than before. "Mrs. Ross, have you any idea of how foul language could add to your punishment?"

Her eyes widened. In six years around miners and teamsters, she'd heard a great many words unworthy of a church hall. Perhaps he wanted to hear some of those.

She fought him, kicking his shins and cursing him in the foulest terms she knew, even inventing a few phrases. Her struggles didn't harm him, of course, especially when muffled by her skirts. Finally, he pressed her hard against the wall and bracketed her with his big body.

She could feel every inch of him, from the hard muscle in his chest and thighs, to the fierce erection pressed against her belly.

Words failed her. Her pussy was wet and aching, desperate for him.

He pushed his hips against her. "You are an uppity female, Mrs. Ross. Your behavior demands retribution."

"No," she gasped, forcing her eyes to stay open. She needed a kiss so badly. Dew slipped down her thigh.

"Little liar. Your nipples are begging for my touch." His free hand stroked up her side and teased her breast.

Viola moaned at the echoing pulse in her loins. "Yes, Mr. Donovan."

"Say my name, as I taught you."

"William."

He took the final syllable from her with a kiss, his mouth plundering hers like Stuart's cavalry. She met him fiercely, angry at him for delaying the passion he evoked so effortlessly. He kneaded her breast until she arched against him, groaning.

William pulled his head back and yanked her skirts up, watching her with a feral stare that burned her veins. She shuddered. Slowly, deliberately, he thrust his leg between hers. The rough wool of his trousers rubbed her aching folds through her fine linen drawers, evoking more dew.

"Are you sorry for your behavior, little clerk?"

"No." And indeed she was not. She'd speak a few pretty phrases again if he wished, just to reap this reward.

He rocked her hips against him, sensitizing her everywhere but not satisfying her. Heat lanced from her breasts to her womb. Her body craved rapture from this man, immediately.

Viola moaned, her eyelids drooping shut.

"Apologize," he repeated. "Speak the words or you'll get nothing further from me."

"Mr. Donovan, please." Viola knew that if he'd just shift his leg a bit, he'd rub her clit and she'd gain that tantalizing orgasm.

"Say it!"

"I regret . . ." She never uttered the final word, *nothing*. She'd do this again as soon as she had the chance.

His cock slammed into her, finding her through the slit in

her drawers. He rode her hard, slamming her against the wall.

Viola sobbed with pleasure, uncaring of any listeners. Her channel gripped and released his cock, using the muscles he'd trained. And all the while, he watched her, sapphire eyes intent and glittering as he grunted with exertion. Their agonized breathing and the wet, solid slaps of their bodies were the only sounds in the small room.

Climax approached. She bit his shoulder hard, like a wildcat being covered by her mate. Her teeth tightened on his clothing's wool and linen and clenched around his shoulder's hard muscle.

He stiffened in surprise. Then he threw his head back and growled like a cougar as he climaxed. Answering rapture shook her body to the bone.

Afterwards, Viola hid her face against his shoulder while he cuddled her in his big chair.

Somehow he'd managed to don a condom without her knowledge. She wondered drowsily, in satisfaction's lazy aftermath, what it would be like to feel his seed flooding her womb or to carry his child under her heart.

She closed her eyes at the thought and didn't speak.

Chapter Ten

Viola finished tying her bonnet strings and smiled at William. Much as she enjoyed being near William and his men, she also hated the continual reminders of just how big Donovan & Sons' empire was. "Yes, I'm ready to leave, Mr. Donovan."

She'd been very busy for all of the two days she'd worked with him. She hadn't had a chance to slip off to the stables to see his famous stallion, Saladin. Mules worked very well for heavy freighting, but there was nothing like a really good horse. She'd enjoy seeing Saladin close enough to compare him to her grandfather's prized Kentucky Thoroughbreds. If she had time alone with him, she might whisper a few words about her beloved Muffin, the mare she'd left behind in Cincinnati when she married.

Lost in thoughts of Muffin, it was several minutes before she realized they were walking up Main Street. Her hand tightened convulsively on William's arm. He patted it and glanced down at her. "Relax, Mrs. Ross, and trust me."

She gulped, then nodded. No matter what social penalties she encountered, she had to believe he'd protect her. She did hope they didn't encounter any of the respectable ladies; masculine techniques might not work well against the darts thrown by those women.

Then she realized something else. "Mr. Donovan, we're walking on the south side of the street. Shouldn't we be on the north side?"

"Certainly not." His voice was firm, as were his footsteps and the thud of Evans' boots behind them.

"But I'm a . . ." she fumbled for words but couldn't find one to express what she'd become. "I'm not a respectable woman," she managed. "I should only appear on the north side."

"No. You're a woman who deserves every possible courtesy. You'll stay on this side if I have to carry you."

"Mr. Donovan, that would be disgraceful," Viola exclaimed.

"Then don't make me do it."

Viola opened and closed her mouth several times without thinking of a counterargument. Finally she set her jaw and sailed up the street beside him, trying to pretend she was doing nothing remarkable.

A man walked out into the street ahead of them and waited there, squinting against the setting sun. Three other men followed him but remained on the boardwalk. Lennox and his three hoodlums from New York, the ones he'd sworn would keep Rio Piedras's saloons quiet.

"Bloody hell," muttered William. "Where are the lads, Evans?"

"A few steps back," answered Evans as he stepped up on the other side of Viola. "What is the cur up to now?"

"Looks like we'll find out."

They stopped abreast of Lennox, facing him from the boardwalk, and a few paces away from his thugs. "Lennox," William acknowledged.

"Donovan. Mrs. Ross." He bowed to Viola, who nodded coldly. The atmosphere was as chilly as if they stood at Hudson Bay, rather than in the desert. "May I have the favor of a few words with you, Mrs. Ross?"

She hesitated, but surely there was nothing he could do to her in the middle of a public street. "One minute then, Mr. Lennox."

She walked into Main Street, careful to stay out of Lennox's reach. He was carrying neither sword stick or Colt. Still, she didn't trust him. He could have a pocket gun or intend to snatch her.

Lennox produced a bouquet of red roses from behind his back and offered it to Viola. She shook her head and stepped back, wary of being lured closer. "What do you want, Mr. Lennox?"

His face flushed scarlet at her refusal, but his voice was civil, too much so, when he spoke. "Mrs. Ross, would you do me the honor of becoming my wife? I am prepared to overlook your dalliance with that peasant and give you the protection of my name."

"As I have said before on numerous occasions, I will never marry you. Do you have anything else to discuss?"

"You little bitch, don't you understand I'm offering to rescue you?" he hissed, his eyes sliding behind her. "You should be grateful I've condescended to offer the Lennox name to a slut like yourself."

"Then keep it for someone else who'll appreciate it as you do," Viola snapped back at him. "I myself would rather be dead than your wife."

"Very well then, go hide behind your Irish scum for now. You'll learn to mind your manners when you're my bride."

Viola snorted. "When pigs fly. Good day, Mr. Lennox." She marched back to the men waiting on the boardwalk. She didn't consider his threats to be idle ones, but she'd never let that murderer know she was frightened of him.

"Mr. Donovan, shall we continue on our way?"

"Certainly, ma'am."

She accepted William's arm and he nodded to Lennox, still standing in the street holding the red roses. Lennox's face flushed darker as his chin came up. He made no other move, but his three thugs stepped off the boardwalk, leaving it clear for Viola and her escort.

Viola was still shivering when they reached the compound, shaken by the venom and determination in Lennox's voice. She'd hoped becoming a woman of ill repute would eliminate Lennox's interest in her, given his obsessive family pride. Why on earth was he so set on marrying her?

William hugged her tight as they entered his bedroom. She clung to him, gratefully absorbing his warmth and strength. "You were very brave, sweetheart, facing him like that."

"I wasn't brave," Viola denied. "He couldn't harm me with you and all your men around."

"He could have shot you with a hidden gun."

"He wouldn't do that, not when he wants to marry me," she shrugged. "I was safe. And very, very glad you were there." She burrowed closer.

He kissed the top of her head. "Your courage deserves a reward, sweetheart. You can tell me what you want after we eat."

"Reward?"

"Reward. Make a request and I'll honor it, as best I can. Now I'll leave you with Sarah to prepare for dinner."

Viola nodded, dumbfounded. She could name something she wanted and he'd do it. She considered the possibilities as she undressed and slipped into the hot bath, one of William's more surprising quirks. The gossip at Mrs. Smith's hadn't mentioned his liking for a very clean companion.

What could she request? New clothes would be silly, since he already had provided so many. Food? No, she had more than enough now and Sarah did tend to hover over her. Obtaining sheet music would require days of travel.

Something enjoyable. Something carnal perhaps? Ask William Donovan to do something for her amorous pleasure? What a turnaround that would be. Still, it should be something enjoyable for both of them. Carnal delights were so much better when shared.

Warmth budded deep inside her, far from the hot water lapping at her skin. Viola purred and slid down, running ideas through her mind.

"Some cheese and crackers, Mrs. Ross? Or a glass of milk?"

Viola blinked and opened her eyes reluctantly. Sarah, with still more food. She was always offering Viola something to eat. "You're very kind, Sarah, but I think I should wait until dinner."

"Perhaps just a nibble. The smoked cheese is particularly delicious," Sarah coaxed, offering a plate at eye level.

They did look tempting. "Well, just one."

Sarah immediately fed one to Viola, looking as pleased as if her child was taking its first steps. Viola waved a second cracker away.

"Sarah, why are you always trying to feed me?"

Sarah hesitated for a moment before answering. "So you can gain weight."

"You think I'm skinny."

"Too thin to conceive a child, yes."

"What?!" Viola all but erupted from the bath, splashing water across the plate and into the glass. When they finally settled down from cleaning up the mess, Viola was ensconced in a heavy silk robe in the bedroom and Sarah sat on the chair facing her.

"Sarah, please explain. Do you mean that if I was heavier, I could become pregnant?"

"Yes, Mrs. Ross. Women's wisdom in China teaches that just as a duck must be well fed, so a woman must have curves if she is to produce babies. You are thin and very strong, like one of our gymnasts. I believe that if you weighed just a little more, you could conceive a child. Not much, Mrs. Ross, perhaps five or six pounds."

Viola's hand flew to her mouth. "Dear Lord, could this be true?"

"I have seen it work before, Mrs. Ross. Such a little change, not enough to disturb the shape Mr. Donovan delights in. But so much joy afterwards."

A child. She could have a child, if she just gained a little weight. It seemed logical since she was thinner and stronger than almost any woman she knew. The only ones she'd met who were skinnier also had few children.

She, too, could be a woman with her child on her hip.

Viola wrapped her arms around herself and rocked back and forth on the bed. Her eyes blurred and she choked back tears of joy. Sarah hugged her and Viola cried in earnest, while the other woman comforted her.

William studied Viola in the sitting room's lamplight. She seemed calmer than before, more secure, if that was possible. Perhaps facing Lennox had settled her nerves, although she was a gallant little filly at any time.

Bloody hell, Lennox deserved death. But it was almost worth letting him live, just for the look on his face when Viola refused him. He'd be twice as dangerous now that she'd humiliated him so publicly. Still, there were men who'd travel thousands of miles to see Lennox look the fool.

"Have you thought about your reward, sweetheart?" William asked quietly, letting his voice flow into the lamplit room. To his delight, Viola immediately blushed and sat up straighter.

"Yes, I have, William." She studied her hands before looking up at him again.

"What do you want?" he prompted, enjoying her anticipation. His blood began a slow drumbeat of interest.

She hesitated.

"Speak up, sweetheart, else you'll lose your reward."

His heart stopped at her wistful look. It'd be damned hard if he ever needed to discipline her, given the way his body responded to her slightest distress.

"I tried to think of something you'd enjoy," she said softly.

Blessed Virgin, she'd thought of his pleasure when considering her treat. For that alone, he'd give her the stars. Still, he managed to keep his voice fairly stern.

"What is it?"

She gulped but spoke. "I enjoyed it yesterday when you held my wrists in your hands while we, we"—she blushed but continued bravely—"had carnal relations. I'd like you to do something like that, confine me in some fashion, the next time."

William stared at her, his blood boiling through his veins and his cock. She met his gaze, hot color in her cheeks. "Can you tell me why you fancy that, sweetheart?"

"I've always dreamed of being the princess tied to a stake, until freed by a knight. I suppose this is as close as I can ever come to that."

William smiled slowly. He didn't care if he looked like a lion surveying a gazelle. Joseph, Mary, and all the saints, she truly wanted a bit of bondage. He'd give her that and more if she had a true partiality.

His cock was full and hard behind his fly, yet he'd never been calmer. He would give his faerie maiden a very sweet reward that evening.

Viola's tongue swept nervously over her lips. What if he thought she was insane or a hussy for asking him this? She started to speak again, to take her words back, but stopped. She would be gone in three months, so how much did it truly matter what he thought of her desires? She had survived more than five years with Edward; three months with anyone else seemed no more than a passing fling.

Then William smiled and her heart skipped a beat. She knew that look after four days in his bed. It promised carnal delights that could make a woman's head spin.

"But it's such a simple reward. Don't you want something more?" he purred. "Something sensual or exotic or lavish, perhaps?"

Viola swallowed hard and shook her head. How could she think when he sounded like that, all black velvet and lamplight? "Just that, if you please."

"Very well then." He rose to his feet and glided toward her. Viola shivered, her pulse thudding in her veins as her breasts firmed and ached under the gleaming black silk.

"Place your hands on the chair arms, sweetheart. Keep them there while I fetch a few items."

"Yes, sir," Viola whispered, and obeyed. The carved walnut lions' heads seemed made to hold her fingers comfortably. She worried only slightly about how he'd tie her. Hal had practiced tying her in knots when they were children and he'd still planned to follow their father into the Navy. She'd learned very early how to escape from any bonds he put on her. Surely she could be certain that William, who was so protective, wouldn't tie her any more tightly than Hal had.

She drummed her fingers and tried some different ways to position her feet. She was flushed and achy, and as fretful as if he were running his hands over her. She'd be more comfortable if she weren't wearing one of his Chinese outfits. And of course, if her dew stopped heating and surging out of her.

William returned to the sitting room with a bevy of red silk scarves draped over a small wooden box.

Incredibly, a flash of fire burned from her breasts to her pussy at the sight. Viola gulped.

"Did you move your hands while I was gone, sweetheart?"

"Of course not," Viola snapped, offended by the suggestion she'd disobey an order.

"Good girl. That was your first lesson: you were held as strongly in your chair by my command, and your obedience, as if I'd fastened iron manacles around your wrists."

Viola's eyes widened as she considered the implications.

"Questions?" William asked softly.

"No, William."

"Now I will wrap these scarves around your wrists. You'll

be able to free yourself at any time, if you dislike what transpires."

"What are you going to do?"

"Feed on your sweet pussy, sweetheart."

Viola choked at his matter-of-fact response. Dear heavens, her body thought his plan was excellent, given how hard her nipples were.

William's mouth twitched. "A warning, sweetheart. If you lift your hands at any time, I'll understand it as a signal to stop immediately."

"What do you mean? Of course, I'll keep my hands on the chair."

"But suppose you placed them on my head. Since you had removed your hands from the chair, I'd immediately stop licking you."

"That's wicked," Viola gasped. He'd set a pretty trap for her. He knew she enjoyed the feel of his thick black locks, especially when his mouth was busy on her.

He shrugged. "Your choice, sweetheart, not mine."

"Do your worst, William. I will continue to grip the chair, no matter what," Viola vowed.

William bowed, his eyes glinting with laughter. He twisted a scarf around each of her wrists and the carved wood underneath, then draped the ends down to the floor.

Viola flexed her hands cautiously. She could free herself with a single yank if she chose, but why would she want to? Her blood was pounding in her veins and her skin was as flushed as if he'd been kissing her for minutes.

"Comfortable, sweetheart?"

She smiled up at him. "Very, William. And I feel somehow freer than before."

"Excellent, sweet Viola. Now I intend to enjoy myself immensely." He kissed her mouth, hot and sweet, until she moaned and arched toward him. Then he quickly unpinned her hair and combed it with his fingers until it fell loose over her shoulders.

"Why did you do that?" she queried, perplexed by why he'd undo her hair if he meant to attend to her private parts.

"Because I enjoy the look of you. No more questions, sweetheart. Just think about your reward."

He dropped to his knees before her.

"Now slide your hips forward, sweetheart. A little further until you're balanced on the very edge." His big hands guided her, warm and strong through the silk. "That's my filly. Perfect."

He slipped a towel under her derrière then draped her knees over his shoulders.

Viola stared at him, kneeling between her legs as if it was the most ordinary activity in the world. Her nipples promptly hardened in anticipation.

"You have the most amazing breasts, sweetheart. They're already eager for your reward," he remarked, cupping her breasts with his hands.

She shuddered when he fondled them, his touch burning through the silk and unhindered by any underthings. His fingers played with her nipples until she gasped at the pain and the pleasure lancing through her.

Then he stroked her mound through the silk, playing with her until the fabric was no protection against the flood of dew he evoked. She wiggled, desperate to touch him. "Ah, William, how can I stay still?"

"Just pay attention to my hands, sweetheart," he crooned to her as his wicked fingers encouraged her. She tossed her head and twisted, following his hand's movements. She tightened her grip on the carved lions with a silent prayer that she could hold on and not reach for the heavy silk of his hair.

"Sweet filly, enjoy this." His finger slipped through the trousers' slit and played with her. Her breasts began to throb in the same rhythm as his fingers.

"Lovely," she moaned shamelessly at the familiar delight, and lifted her hips toward him.

He rumbled something not in English and finally laid his mouth to her burning pussy.

"Merciful heavens," she moaned as her fingernails scraped desperately over the chair's wood. Her breathing was harsh as she fought not to touch him.

He savored her leisurely, tracing every fold with tongue and lips and fingers as if he'd never touched them before. Her body arched and lifted for him, until everything but her hands followed his touch.

She moaned as she climaxed for the first time, simply from his tongue circling her pearl without touching it directly.

But he didn't permit her to relax, to calm down and reestablish her grip on the chair. His tongue continued to lave her in the same rhythm. Her hips arched upwards and she howled when his teeth gently scraped her folds.

And she climaxed under long strokes of his tongue, laid on like a lash of fiery delight against her folds, as she sobbed his name.

She climaxed a third time as his fingers pumped her while he suckled at her clit, her hands aching from their fierce grip on the lions' heads.

She floated back to sanity very slowly. Something was different inside her. Something quite pleasurable in an odd way, and in an unexpected place.

"Do you sense the dildo, sweetheart?" he asked gently, still kneeling before her. "It's inside your backside, where I've fondled you before. A small dildo, no larger than my finger."

Viola gave an experimental wiggle and gasped when the dildo moved. A throb of pleasure danced from her backside to her pussy at the changed pressure. "Oh," she moaned without opening her eyes. She couldn't find words to express how it made her feel.

"Enjoyed it when the dildo shifted, did you?" He stroked her thighs lightly.

"Yes. Oh my, it's delicious." She circled her hips cautiously and moaned again. He chuckled softly.

Air caressed her breasts and she looked down, blinking until she could focus. Her trousers were gone, banished to someplace she couldn't see. Her tunic had been folded back until all of her body was uncovered except her shoulders and arms. Her chest was still flushed with passion, her nipples red as rubies. Her mound gleamed where his tongue had painted it.

She tossed her head back, feeling her hair brush against the chair. "You have freed me of everything except the scarves."

He nodded, his eyes bright and fierce as he studied her. "Clever girl. Yes, I've done exactly as I wished."

The intensity of his gaze burned her like the sun in high summer. She knew she was the center of his world at this moment. She could see it so very clearly, without polite society's veils of words and prescribed manners. He wasn't the Donovan of Donovan & Sons. He was simply a man watching a woman. And in a moment, he'd act and they'd both reach rapture because of his deeds.

Viola smiled, as full of anticipation as any cat watching a saucer of cream approach.

"Questions?"

"Just one. Where did you learn to kneel for so long?"

William chuckled. "Ah, sweetheart, you are full of surprises when you ask questions like that. A friend taught me when I first learned my way around a woman's body. Kneeling is a very useful posture and I still practice it."

"Clever friend," Viola murmured. "I'd like to thank her."

He went still for a moment before answering. "Perhaps you will one day. Now," he went on more briskly, "the dildo has some useful properties. It stretches you, which increases your sensitivity. It also limits your channel's freedom to expand."

"You're going to do something wicked. Inside my channel," Viola added, feeling a rush of dew at the thought.

"Not immediately, sweetheart. Perhaps in a minute or two." He lifted her breasts and squeezed them. "Or perhaps another hour."

His callused fingers rubbed her nipples, making her gasp

with pleasure. Her head fell back helplessly as she arched up toward him.

William was entirely correct about the dildo's effect. She felt every touch of his hands against her folds as if it were the first time that evening. She moaned and sobbed his name when his tongue lapped at her. He laved her pussy and nipped her delicately until she begged for release. Her skin was so hot and tight, she thought she'd explode.

Still he denied her. He slowed his touch, removed his intimate kiss, until she could breathe again. Then he returned to stoke her passion yet again.

Viola's language descended into the gutter as she implored him for an orgasm. He chuckled, he paused, then began again.

She could hear his breathing, harsh and fast. But he kept to the pace he'd chosen and she clutched the chair desperately.

Finally, when nothing existed for her except the climax hanging so tantalizingly close and her words were incredibly vehement, he sprang to his feet and snatched the scarves away from her wrists. He yanked her out of the chair and tumbled her to the floor, rolling to cushion her from the fall, then pin her under him.

"Now," he growled. "Now, dammit."

His fingers bit into her hips. He plunged himself into her, sheathing himself to the hilt with the first stroke. She was stuffed full of him, stretched beyond endurance between his cock and the toy in her backside.

He twitched, and her clit throbbed hard at the slight change in pressure. Viola shuddered.

He slid his hands under her and gripped her derrière, shifting the dildo inside her. She keened her pleasure and he repeated the movement again. She was completely under his command, from her nose, which breathed his scent, to her legs wrapped around him, yet she felt more alive than ever before.

He pulled out and thrust hard, and thrust again. And again. Viola howled and climaxed, her body arching and shuddering as waves rippled up her spine.

He bellowed his own rapture, his body shaking as he spent himself inside her.

Viola was grateful when he simply took her to bed afterwards and she could fall asleep. Her reaction to this man, whether in the bedroom or elsewhere, was not something she wished to ponder.

Chapter Eleven

"When do you think the cavalry will arrive to escort you to Fort McMillan, Mr. Evans?" Viola asked, and promptly wished she hadn't spoken. William and Evans guarded her as closely as they had the day before, perhaps more so after the scene with Lennox. If she went onto a public street, both of them escorted her with one walking on each side of her.

But the cavalry's arrival would mean the departure of Evans and most of William's men, to haul supplies for the new fort. Given Lennox's anger, it was far safer for William and herself when all the teamsters were in Rio Piedras.

"Two days or perhaps a little longer, Mrs. Ross," Evans answered equably, as polite as ever. Even the haughtiest arbiter of society would never guess by his manner that he spoke to his employer's mistress. "We're ready to depart now."

"Leaving Sarah's cooking far behind," William quipped. "No more omelets for you."

Viola nodded amiably at Evans's answering badinage and leaned on William's arm a little more for comfort. At least he would be staying in town to prepare for the second supply caravan. She would hate to lose his company, although he might be safer facing Apaches than Lennox. She had seen and heard too much of Lennox's viciousness toward employees he thought insufficiently dedicated. She shuddered at what he might do to William.

Glass shattered a block ahead and a chair sailed through the Oriental's window and into the street. Instantly, William and Evans pressed her against a building behind a wall of their big bodies. They faced the street with guns drawn, ready to take instant action. Viola's heart skipped a beat.

"Stay back, Viola," William ordered. She hadn't known he could draw a gun so quickly. Not as fast as Evans, who was famous for his speed, but definitely faster than most men.

"Goddammit, McBride!" a man shouted from the saloon just ahead. "Where the hell did you get four aces from? You show me, here an' now, there ain't nothin' else up your sleeve."

"Or else what?" another man sneered.

"Thought you told Lowell to stay out of the Oriental if McBride was around," William remarked, holstering his gun.

"I did. And fined him five dollars to make sure he heard me," Evans agreed. "That just about covered the damage from the last fight."

Viola peered around them just in time to see two men erupt from the Oriental, fists flying. Thomas McBride, the miner, was having yet another fight with Lowell. Even Mrs. Chambers, the minister's wife, had been known to wager on exactly how many men would be involved in the subsequent brawl.

"Fistfight, boys!" someone shouted inside the Oriental.

"Morgan, do you think both of McBride's brothers are in the Oriental at this moment?" William asked.

Viola winced as Lowell knocked McBride into the horse trough. McBride erupted out of it with a shout, shaking water from his face, and charged Lowell to restart the fight.

"They all work the same shift at the mine," Evans said thoughtfully. "But only one of them frequents the saloons as much as he does. The other is probably close by, though."

"And here come the lads from the depot to help Lowell," Evans added as a dozen teamsters ran up the street toward them.

A stocky miner rushed out of the Oriental and leaped onto Lowell's back. More miners crowded out of the Oriental onto the boardwalk, a few steps away from joining the fight. A trio of Mrs. Smith's girls in their best finery, led by the beautiful and curvaceous Sally, paused to watch.

"Two bits on the Irishmen, boys!" someone shouted.

"Done!" shouted another. Viola could see others eagerly gambling on the fight's outcome.

William snorted. "Please stay with Evans, Mrs. Ross. I'll deal with this."

Lennox, followed by his three thugs, emerged from the mine offices a few blocks uphill from the Oriental. The crowd silently parted for them until they could watch every move, standing as icily as a judge at a hanging.

Viola went cold. She managed to nod but could not force a single word past the lump in her throat. Hopefully, having so many teamsters would stop Lennox and his thugs from doing anything to hurt William. But Lennox's viciousness should not be underestimated. And if anything happened to William . . .

She whirled on Evans. "Aren't you going to help him?"

Evans snorted. "If he needs it, which he won't. Just watch, Mrs. Ross."

William ran into the street and stopped several paces away from the fight, drawing his big bullwhip. He shook it lightly once to loosen it. Then he abruptly cracked it less than a yard away from Lowell.

The throng immediately stopped talking.

Viola gulped. She'd seen William win Lowell's bet but this was different. He was taking command of a crowd, holding their attention, simply by using his whip.

Something sensual deep inside her came alert at the sound and whispered, *I like this man when he fights like this.* Her nipples firmed even as her mouth went dry.

Lowell froze at the whip's sound, clearly recognizing the danger. The other teamsters stopped their noisy rush up the street and waited. Mrs. Smith's girls oohed and shivered.

Thomas McBride drew back his fist to land another punch. William cracked the whip barely a foot away from McBride's ear.

McBride jumped but kept his fists up. If the miner would simply stay in one spot, he'd be safe.

Viola shivered.

"Stand still, you fool," hissed Sally.

William repeatedly snapped the whip on each side of Mc-Bride, fencing him in leather.

The man flinched, hands flying up over his ears, but his feet finally took root in one place.

Gossip said William's bullwhip was custom-made, with buckshot braided into the tip. If so, it was a lethal weapon. But in his hands, it was as graceful as an arpeggio dancing through a concert hall's hushed silence.

And as capable as any Chopin ballade at exciting Viola's blood. Her womb clenched convulsively in a spurt of pure lust. She bit her lip until she drew blood, fingernails digging into her palms.

The other McBride brother started to kick Lowell. William's whip abruptly wrapped around his ankle and yanked him to the ground. He landed with a loud grunt as air was driven from his lungs. He was utterly motionless except for his head turning frantically to watch William.

The whip freed itself silently and returned to swirl at William's side.

Sally moaned, "Oh, Mr. Donovan."

Viola took a deep, shuddering breath, shaken by the strength and grace of the weapon and the warrior. Dew trickled down her thigh.

McBride helped his brother up and the three combatants faced William together. He, on the other hand, seemed as relaxed as if he were in his office.

"Gentlemen, may I suggest you resolve your differences and shake hands? Thank you," William said, with no apparent sense of superiority, as the three men warily exchanged nods and grips in a semblance of cordiality. "Mr. McBride, do you have anything to say? No? Good day then. I hope to see you again soon in a more relaxed setting."

The two McBride brothers backed away until they reached the boardwalk. Joined by their friends, they filtered back into the Oriental. Evans quietly handed some coins to the Oriental's saloonkeeper, who returned to work with a smile.

Sally and the other soiled doves lingered to cast lascivious glances at William.

Viola hissed softly at the plump blonde, and her fingers formed into claws. She had William now, not those hussies. By the Almighty, she'd teach them a lesson if those *nymphs du pave* came too close to him.

Finally, the beruffled sluts turned to Mrs. Smith's house. Viola slowly relaxed, then wondered why she'd been so angry with them. Women like that would be his companions again in three months, after she left for San Francisco. Something twisted deep inside her at the thought.

She was barely aware of Lennox's departure, as he and his thugs talked quietly amongst themselves.

Lowell started to walk toward the depot.

"Lowell." William's level voice halted the teamster.

"Yes, sir?" Lowell turned to face his boss.

"Ten-dollar fine for misunderstanding Evans' orders, Lowell. Also, Carson needs some help in the forge. You'll probably be there until midnight, maybe later. And if I catch you in the Oriental again at any time, you're fired."

Lowell's Adam's apple bobbed as he swallowed. "Yes, sir. And thank you, sir."

"My pleasure, lad." William had his bullwhip coiled and returned to his weapons belt by the time he rejoined Viola and Evans. He offered her his arm as if the interruption had been no more than a slight social inconvenience. She accepted, still shaking a little as she tried to reconcile her carnal reaction to his masterfulness and her jealousy of the other women.

*   *   *

William glanced down at Viola. He frowned slightly at how she trembled, but said nothing. It wasn't surprising a woman would find a streetside scuffle distressing, although he'd heard she'd kept a cool head when she'd seen Indian fighting.

She studied a reflection in the bank's window as they passed by. Curious, William caught the same reflection and frowned. Why would Viola Ross glare at Mrs. Smith's girls? Could one of them have said or done something to offend her? If so, he'd make sure she'd be on the next stage out of town. He could do nothing to protect Viola from censure by the town's few respectable women, but he could silence the working girls, especially if he added a cash incentive for holding their tongues.

He'd worry about that later. For now, it was enough to be walking with the most beautiful woman in the world and know he'd spend the evening in her arms. She seemed content to live with him, especially after she first played the piano.

He'd been so pleased the other day when she'd asked him about his business.

He hadn't worried much about Viola's happiness in the beginning, being too caught up in visions of her in his bed. But now the first frantic rush to sate himself was past, he could consider her well-being more. Talking about freighting and railroads meant she was willing to share something of her thoughts with him. Perhaps she was healing from her past vicissitudes. Saints willing, she'd be able to remarry and live happily again.

William touched his hat in response to the watchtower sentry's greeting as they approached the compound. Morgan had done a good job of rebuilding it as a base of operations, the result reminding William of a hill fort in ancient Ireland. The fountain had been broken when William first saw it, leaving the spring to spill its life-giving waters over the courtyard's cracked bricks. Now tidy plumbing guided the water to the fountain, the baths, and the kitchen. Combined with the stout walls, the compound was nearly impregnable against attack from Apaches or white men.

But this wasn't the world Viola belonged in. She should be in New York City, the wife of a wealthy aristocrat who could enhance her status in the world.

He could see her now, enjoying the delights of such a life: the long dinner table covered with white damask and set with the finest Limoges china and Sheffield cutlery, goblets sparkling in the light from the immense crystal chandeliers above. She'd sit at one end of the table, tightly corseted in her fashionable Parisian gown, politely listening to the self-important politician next to her.

He knew what Viola's future husband would look like, with his expanding girth and patriarch's beard. With a pedigree as long as any in the Bible, he'd never suffer an Irishman at his dinner table to meet his wife.

William gritted his teeth at the thought.

Morgan excused himself as soon as they entered the courtyard, and headed for the stables to check Tennessee, the recovering lead mule. Viola greeted Abraham politely, made her excuses to William, and disappeared into the bedroom.

William traded his hat for a cup of tea from Abraham and leaned against a column, listening to his faerie maiden in her bath. She was humming a melody, one he'd heard sung at Lyonsgate. Lady Irene had called it a German art song, something about lost love.

Married to a man like that, Viola would never suffer the dangers of poverty. Her children would never be homeless and starving. She'd never give birth in a ditch during a rainstorm . . .

Suddenly William hurled his cup across the courtyard. It shattered loudly against the mud-brick wall, causing the chickens to fly up and the goats to bleat in panic. The dumb animals calmed quickly, sooner than William's heart did.

*   *   *

Abraham bowed himself out of the sitting room with the last dinner dishes, leaving William and Viola alone. Silence covered the room before William started to crack a walnut, his long fingers graceful and sure.

Viola swirled the lemonade in her glass, still thinking about the beautiful girls from Mrs. Smith's. How much time had he spent with them? Had he learned all his carnal skills from women like them? Would he eagerly visit such sluts again?

It shouldn't matter, not when Viola planned to depart for San Francisco in three months. And yet she kept wondering where he'd learned, while her pussy throbbed at the images of a younger William leaning over a woman who sobbed with passion.

"William?"

"Yes, sweetheart?"

"Where did you learn to, uh . . ." Her voice trailed off as she tried to find words. Sometimes the subjects she discussed with William Donovan were so unusual that the polite conversational phrases of a Cincinnati drawing room simply didn't apply.

An elegant black eyebrow lifted. "Where did I learn what, sweetheart?"

"To pleasure women," Viola managed. "To lead them on with your voice, then command them with your hands and mouth until . . ."

She stopped, swallowed. William's face conveyed only courtesy as he waited for her.

She finished in a rush. "Nothing matters except the ecstasy of obeying you and reaching the peak. Was it here in America or in Ireland?"

"Ireland, sweetheart."

She frowned. Could he have afforded prostitutes there? He'd been young, but he must have been just as beautiful then as he was now. "Who taught you?"

He tilted his head quizzically but answered steadily. "An English lady, the daughter and widow of earls."

Another woman? An unexpected pang shot through Viola.

"She and her husband are my good friends now," William continued. "They provided the funds to start me in business in California."

Relief flooded Viola, as hard and fast as her earlier pain when he'd mentioned the English aristocrat. The woman was married, so William couldn't have formed an emotional entanglement with her. "Ah." She sipped her tea.

He began to coax the nut's meat from its shell.

Another thought crept into Viola's brain. She voiced it before she considered the implications. "What else did she teach you?"

William started to smile.

He glanced sideways at Viola while he wondered how much to tell her. She was a passionate and trusting filly, who'd blatantly enjoyed whatever he'd asked of her so far. He could tell her a little, so long as he was careful not to distress her.

"A great many things, sweetheart," William answered her. "Positions learned from the great books of the Arabs, the Indians, and the Chinese. The use of ropes to bind and adorn one's lover."

Her eyes were huge as she hung on his words. But she didn't flinch. Instead, she licked her lips. Encouraged, he went on.

"How to employ a flogger or whip to excite. And other trinkets, with a wealth of purposes," he drawled, remembering some memorable fantasies he'd enacted there.

"Trinkets? Do you mean jewelry, like a bracelet or pin? How could you use jewelry for carnal effect?"

William's cock stirred happily at her curiosity. He forced his voice to remain casual. "Remember the ivory dildo that filled your backside yesterday? That was a trinket."

"Truly?" She blushed as her tongue crept out to touch her lip. "It was very exciting. It made me so aware of everything your hands and cock"—she turned an even deeper shape of red—"did to my pussy."

The last words were little more than a whisper but she hadn't changed the subject or run from him.

"That's what trinkets are for, sweetheart: to enhance one's pleasure. Would you care to see some others?"

She nodded eagerly. "Yes, please."

"Come with me to the bedroom then." He rose and held out his hand. She took it and accompanied him like an eager student.

He retrieved his chest of trinkets, a farewell gift from Mr. Fitzgerald. It had once been a money chest, and its iron bands and multiple locks still ensured the safety and privacy of anything William placed in it.

"Your chest reminds me of pirate's treasure," Viola breathed, staring at the sturdy wooden box as she hovered next to his elbow.

William smiled and kissed her lightly on the forehead. "Some trinkets can be considered treasure, sweetheart. I have heard the Chinese emperor collects dildos, for example."

"The emperor collects dildos?" Viola gasped. "Why, in heaven's name, would anyone want to have very many of those?"

William chuckled softly as he opened the chest and removed a few rolls of trinkets. Each was carefully wrapped in colored silk, sometimes padded, and always tied with colored ribbons. The variety of sizes and colors represented meant he could quickly find what he wanted.

"A dildo's size and shape can be greatly varied, as can the material, every combination creating a different sensation in the wearer," he remarked, unrolling the first set and removing the carvings. "Or a dildo can be educational, to teach an inexperienced concubine details of what she'll soon experience in the flesh. It can also be a work of art, as beautiful as any sculptured bronze."

"But not something you'd expect to see in an exhibit hall. I can hardly imagine the good ladies of Cincinnati, for example, lining up to see an ivory dildo as an example of their city's preeminence in the arts."

"Not in public perhaps, where discretion rules. But many more things are possible in the bedroom."

He produced the first carving, a dark green dildo. Viola gasped and her hand flew to her mouth as she stared. William saw her nipples harden under her tunic's soft blue silk. He smiled privately; he looked forward to discovering how far her curiosity would take them both.

"Jade? And in so many colors, too. How lovely," Viola breathed. Truly the half dozen dildos were beautiful as they gleamed against the silk in the lamplight. Two were ivory, the other four of jade ranging in color from deep green to a delicate pink. All of them appeared remarkably lifelike, even if noticeably smaller than William's enticing cock. "May I touch them?"

"Of course." William handed her the elegant green dildo.

She held it up to the light, fascinated by how the darker veins in the stone mimicked a man's throbbing veins. She caressed it, exploring the smooth texture. Her hand easily fell into the same movement she used on William's heated cock.

He choked. Viola glanced at him and caught sight of a very impressive bulge behind his fly. Her mouth twitched while her blood beat a little faster.

"You mentioned different sizes, but all of these appear to share the same dimensions," she remarked demurely.

William unrolled two more cases from the chest. Viola gasped. "Dear heavens, what could anyone hope to use one of these for? They're immense."

He handed her the largest, exchanging it for the one she'd held. She explored it delicately, enjoying how its cold surface quickly warmed in her hand. She squeezed it experimentally but couldn't wrap her fingers around it. It was, after all, slightly larger than William's cock when fully erect. "And an experienced concubine can take all of this into her channel," she mused.

"If you'd like to see something other than dildos," William suggested with a faint rasp in his voice, "you might examine one of these."

"Thank you." His tone made her eyes widen briefly. She accepted a string of five jade beads, all the size of large marbles and spaced well apart on a stout linen cord. The cord had a long tail before ending in a wide braided ring. "What is it? Not a bracelet, surely."

"Not designed for that, although you could wear them that way if you wished. They're more often slipped inside a lover's backside, to tease and stretch the senses."

Viola considered the beads dubiously. "As you used the little ivory dildo? But that mimicked your cock, while these have no such stiffness. They'd be more likely to dance inside one."

She glimpsed his face as she toyed with his beads. The hunger blazing from his eyes answered her question and ignited an answering heat deep in her core. What would it feel like to be his plaything, excited beyond endurance by the trinkets he could no doubt wield with fiendish skill? Ecstasy surely, especially when he studied her so closely, like a pianist considering his instrument before a concert.

Viola swallowed, her breasts firm and aching under the soft silk. For the first time, she was glad of how quickly the Chinese costume could be removed.

"What if a woman is bound by ropes?" she whispered, voicing her oldest fantasy. "Can she still be pleasured?"

"Sweet singing Jesus, of course she can be."

"Perhaps we can try such a thing one evening."

He chuckled, a soft rumble evocative of masculine anticipation. "Tonight, little temptress."

Viola's eyes met his. She blushed but didn't look away from his lust. "Yes, please."

William scooped her up in his arms and kissed her, a long sweet dance of lips and teeth and tongues that set her pulse racing. She swayed when he set her down, giddy and barely able to stand erect. He kissed her again, then steadied her.

She forced her eyes open to watch him when he turned to the bed. He returned with a thick coil of soft cotton rope, like a magician would use. Her eyes widened at the amount.

"Relax, sweetheart," he soothed. "It's very soft, with just enough roughness to hold a knot. It won't hurt your skin."

"I'm not afraid of that," Viola denied promptly. "I'm certain you would never harm me. But what could you possibly need so much rope for?"

He grinned. "To dress you in, sweetheart, like an exotic sacrifice to a man's hunger."

Her fascinated pussy immediately throbbed. Viola gulped, unable to find words.

William kissed the top of her head, nuzzling her hair. "But for your first time, we'll just use this single length of rope to bind your wrists."

She bit back her disappointment and nodded obediently. He was always very concerned that she trust him, no matter what he did. Tying up more than her wrists might be frightening for some women, if they had no prior experience of how a man treated them while bound.

Viola longed for more than just a single bond, to be utterly helpless to resist his wicked hands and mouth. Her breasts ached at the thought of being entirely at his mercy. If not tonight, then surely they could do so on another night.

He dropped the rope onto the chair and set about undressing her. She couldn't have moved if she'd wanted to, not while his hands turned the release of every frog of her tunic into an opportunity to caress more of her skin, both over and under the silk. He licked her neck and nibbled her ear until she was nearly dizzy from excitement.

Finally William cupped her face in his hands. "Sweetheart," he drawled.

A stray thought wished he'd just once use that lovely Irish accent of his throughout an evening, instead of his western drawl. Viola still managed to answer him. "Yes, William?"

"Place your hands behind your back, wrists overlapping each other."

She glanced down to see where her hands were and squeaked in surprise at her dishabille. She didn't have a stitch on and her breasts jutted strongly.

"Sweetheart," William reminded, a faint thread of laughter softening his deep voice.

"Sorry," she murmured, and quickly put her hands where he'd ordered. The posture made her flushed nipples even more prominent. She closed her eyes and shivered.

"Sure you want to do this?"

"Yes," Viola growled. She might not be entirely certain of everything involved but she knew quite well when she was aroused. As she was now.

He kissed her shoulder. "Little spitfire." He wrapped a couple of loops around her wrist and tied a knot. "Comfortable so far?"

She tested the result. The rope was close to her skin but not nearly as tight as Hal's efforts when they were growing up. He'd practiced every sailor's knot on her wrists and ankles, striving to find a combination she couldn't slip free of. "Quite comfortable," she answered honestly.

"Good." His voice had deepened, which her pussy thought was a splendid omen. Blood mounted to her skin and heat built deep in her core.

"Sweetheart," he said softly, "will the rope hold you?"

Viola blinked at him. "Do you want me to test it?"

"Yes, of course, sweetheart. Be thorough."

She obeyed him. The ropes around her wrists definitely had more play in them than she'd expected. Still, she couldn't reach the rope ends to untie herself.

"A dozen roses if you can free yourself, sweetheart."

"You don't think I can."

"No, sweetheart, I don't. But you must be certain the bond will hold before we can explore its possibilities."

She tugged gently. Force wouldn't free her.

"Are you sure yet you can't slip free? Try again, sweetheart."

Viola frowned. Perhaps she could reach the rope ends if she twisted and arched her back at the same time. She'd been very flexible during her tomboy childhood and adolescence. Plus, she'd worked long and hard in Edward's various failed mines, burrowing through the rocks and earth. Perhaps some of those moves would help her here.

William choked softly. She glanced up at him, keeping her body in the same position. He seemed fascinated and startled, close to Hal's expression the first time he watched her wriggle free.

"Do you want me to stop?" she asked softly.

"Oh no, sweetheart, please continue. You simply surprised me, that's all."

She considered him dubiously for a moment. He nodded encouragingly at her and she returned her attention to the knot.

Rope brushed the heel of her hand but she couldn't quite grab it. Encouraged, she tried again.

This time, Viola also rolled her shoulder, bowing herself into close contact with the soft rope. An end fell into her hand. She caught it and slid her finger into the loop. A few seconds of intense effort later, she pulled the knot free and brought her hands around in front.

She looked back triumphantly at William.

"Bloody hell." His jaw dropped. He looked utterly dumbfounded and quite frustrated. His trousers no longer sported a spectacular bulge behind the fly.

Viola gulped as she realized she'd bested him. Outmaneuvering Edward had always brought swift, and unpleasant, retribution. Casting her eyes down, she tried to think of an apology.

Then William started to chuckle. She smiled demurely, hopefully.

He threw his head back and laughed. Viola looked up at him through her eyelashes and smirked. He caught her up into his arms and sat down on the bed, roaring with glee. "You brazen little filly, you took me at my word. You escaped my harness."

Viola laughed, chin high in triumph. For the first time, she felt like his trusted friend as she shared his laughter. It emboldened her enough to tease him. "Where's my dozen roses, oh expert ropesman?"

He laughed again. "In the garden, oh lady of a thousand surprises. They shall be spread before you in moments, after your humble servant recovers."

They laughed together at his tomfoolery, savoring the moment.

William chuckled again. By the saints, Viola had been sweeter than sweet when she freed herself from his rope. And when she smiled, with all that demure mischief in her gaze, like a filly who'd escaped from the paddock and was now happily munching her way through the kitchen garden, joy had bubbled through his veins like champagne.

William controlled himself finally and lifted his eyebrow at her. "Well, sweetheart, shall we try again? After you're tied, I'll fetch your roses."

Viola's eyes twinkled and she dropped a demure curtsy. "As you wish, sir."

William tied her again, making very sure she couldn't escape. The dance excited her even more this time until she was flushed and panting, with dew sliding over her pussy, when she lay fully bound on the bed.

To his delight, she was even more responsive when bound. She couldn't touch him when she was tied like this. All she could do was what he permitted. And he wished her to think solely of the pleasures found in her own body.

He nuzzled and licked her pussy, feasting on her dew for a few minutes, before he reluctantly went into the rose garden.

She turned her head to watch the door and smiled when he returned. She was blushing, but she didn't ask to be released.

"Your reward, sweetheart." He offered the roses with a sweeping bow, and she laughed.

Then he tickled her with her dozen roses until her giggles became gasps of arousal. Viola moaned and bucked as he urged her excitement higher and higher until she shattered, sobbing her rapture. "William, oh William, thank you."

His heart stopped beating and triumph surged through his veins. He'd taught her something new about pleasure.

Then and only then did he finally take her. He lay down on the bed and draped her over him like living silk as his cock slid home. He stayed still for long minutes, enjoying how her pussy held him. By all the saints, he'd pleasure her well before he released her.

In this position, she had to focus solely on his movements. Given her liking for cock, this should be the ultimate reward for a woman who also enjoyed being bound.

She shuddered slightly but didn't try to escape. A soft moan escaped her lips.

Then he kissed her and fondled her back in all the ways she liked, while his cock slowly teased her inner muscles. He rebuilt her arousal slowly, until carnal fires burned fierce and bright in both of them.

William groaned as he climaxed, feeling her sharp teeth bite his shoulder as rapture rocked her. Triumph bubbled through his veins.

Afterwards, William carefully untied Viola's wrists and slid her under the covers. She always slept so very soundly after lovemaking.

Paradise, here in this room. In an isolated town, circled by hostile Apaches as dangerous as any castle's moat. For now, he could forget about the outside world where no amount of wealth could make men forget his Irish parentage.

He needed to be careful not to believe too much in the warmth of her embrace. Fantasies were greatly enjoyable, and they could lay bare the heart as nothing else he'd ever done. But society would exact its tolls when one left the bedroom's sanctuary.

He'd learned that lesson in San Francisco years ago, when he'd first been flush with his share of the Comstock. Marriage had seemed a good idea at the time, since it would give him the home and family that he longed for. He'd been a member of San Francisco's leading fantasy club by then, a place where willing men and women met discreetly to explore the darker side of their carnal imaginations. Lady Irene had sponsored him years ago to London and Dublin's best fantasy clubs. His acceptance there, combined with an extremely large sum, had gained him membership in San Francisco's version.

His favorite filly at the San Francisco fantasy club had been Belinda Carlyle, a widow from a respectable eastern family. Given their carnal compatibility, he'd decided to ask her to go driving with him, a respectable activity that could lead to a relationship outside the club. Possibly even marriage.

He'd arrived early on his next visit to the club and looked for her in the parlor outside the women's retiring room, the usual place for masters and fillies to meet. To his surprise, he'd found himself alone in the overheated room, with its red damask wallpaper, fussy little chairs, and explicit paintings.

In the hush, he'd heard Belinda talking to her best friend from inside the dressing room. "Donovan? Don't be absurd—I'd never let myself be seen with him in public. He's good enough for a fantasy or two, but nothing more. No matter how much money he may have, he's still Irish."

Those few sentences had destroyed his half-formed dreams of a wife who'd also be a true companion in the bedchamber.

He'd never enacted another fantasy with Belinda, of course. Now he reminded himself, yet again, that an affaire was not marriage. A woman could enjoy one without tolerating the other.

Chapter Twelve

The waltz stuttered to a stop. Viola sat perfectly still, fingers resting lightly on the keys, as she tried to regain her concentration. But she couldn't remember the passage, even though she'd first memorized it at age ten. All she could think of were Mrs. Smith's girls.

Would William's next mistress be one of them? She'd overheard tales of how gentlemen selected a companion for the evening in a brothel. She could see the scene now: a dozen simpering women, each preening and posing to catch his eye, while he studied them from the doorway. They'd throw their chests forward to better display their abundant bosoms, and they'd lick their lips at the chance to gain his affections.

Sluts, every one of them. At least a parlor house's madame would choose a suitable companion after conferring with the gentleman, thus removing any chance for the trollops to thrust themselves upon his notice.

She cursed softly, using a phrase that would have shocked Edward. She tried to play again, this time an exercise so fundamental that she'd first learned it under her grandmother's watchful gaze.

Grandmother. Family was so important to Grandmother Lindsay. Three sons, nine grandsons, and two granddaughters. She'd always teased her husband, the Commodore, that he provided for the sons so it was her joy to look after the girls.

Sons. Donovan & Sons. One day, William would marry to gain those sons.

Unbidden, a vision of his wife rose up between Viola and the piano. She'd be tall and richly curved, the picture of fertility as she carried a baby in her arms, while a little boy clung to her skirts. The lad would be the image of his father, with raven black hair and bright blue eyes.

Viola's fingers curled into claws. Even the security of wearing European clothing, instead of the Chinese silks William preferred when they were alone, didn't make her happier.

The stamp mill's beat swept through the room, muffled somewhat by distance.

Viola swept her hands across the keyboard and slammed the lid shut, repudiating the vision. It was none of her business whom William married. Besides, he was so intent on building a fortune, he'd likely have little attention to spare for his family.

She pushed the bench back and stood up. William had encouraged her to stay in the compound this afternoon, instead of working in his office. She'd planned to play the piano, but now she'd have to think of something else to do until he returned.

The courtyard outside was silent, except for the stamp mill's steady beat and a few desultory clucks from the chickens. Abraham stood still as a bronze statue by the shrine, listening to something beyond the compound. No billiard balls clacking, no pans banging in the kitchen, no sentries whistling as they watched for Apaches.

Viola looked up at the watchtowers to see what they were studying. Both telescopes were focused on the depot below, not sweeping steadily across the landscape beyond Rio Piedras.

A distant roar came from the depot, composed of thuds and men's voices saying nothing understandable. The hair pricked on the back of her neck.

Picking up her skirts, she ran up the stairs of the closest watchtower.

The sentry jerked back from the telescope and reached for a rifle when she burst in. He was unknown to her, probably one of the teamsters William had brought from San Francisco.

"Let me see," she demanded fiercely, made nervous by his tension.

He hesitated. "Mrs. Ross, you shouldn't. It'll overset your nerves."

Viola raised an eyebrow. "Apaches?"

"No, ma'am."

"Of course there aren't. You'd have raised the alarm if there were, wouldn't you? And anything else can be dealt with. So stand aside." She tapped her toe impatiently.

He looked down at the telescope, then slowly moved away with a final, plaintive, "Mrs. Ross, it's really not a sight for ladies."

She ignored him as she pounced on the instrument. A moment later, she stared at a brawl that seemed to involve most of the town's male population. Miners fought teamsters hand to hand, kicking and biting and gouging when fists weren't enough. She could hear no gunfire, but every other weapon and fighting technique imaginable was being employed.

Where was William? What if this riot had been staged by Lennox to crush him?

She scanned the riot in a desperate search for her lover. Her breath stopped when she found him, fighting for his life against three of Lennox's thugs who were armed with knives and cudgels. The thugs were obviously accustomed to working together, coordinating their attacks well enough to threaten William from all sides.

Then she found Lennox, standing aside as he eagerly watched. His expression wasn't aloof and remote; instead it reeked of hunger and carnal excitement.

She turned to the sentry to demand intervention.

He shook his head, reading her mind. "Sorry, ma'am. My duty is here, against the 'Paches. If one of them shows up, I can shoot. If someone fires a gun down there, I can shoot. But I can't fire a shot otherwise unless someone gets killed."

"That could happen any minute."

"But it hasn't yet. Sorry. Believe me, if anything happens to the boss, I'll kill the fellow responsible."

"Damn." Viola whirled and ran back down the stairs. No use in looking for the sheriff. He was probably pouring whisky down his throat while waiting for Lennox to tell him whom to arrest.

Abraham still stood guard in the courtyard.

"Can you stop that brawl?" Viola demanded.

"No, madam, I can't leave you. I swore I'd guard you, no matter what."

"Mr. Donovan could be killed."

Abraham flinched slightly, the first sign of emotion she'd seen in him. Then he shrugged. "I would be very sorry to see that happen, madam."

"So I must be the one to do something."

"Mrs. Ross . . ."

"I promise you I will not go within reach of anyone's fists. Is that good enough?"

"Yes, madam."

"Then bring an incense censer from the shrine and come along."

His eyes widened, but he obeyed without further discussion.

Viola snatched a loaded shotgun from the armory. Then she ran down Main Street to the general store, glad she'd chosen to keep William's coins and their comforting jingle in her pocket at all times.

The shopkeeper stood on the boardwalk in front, watching the fight a few blocks away, as did other businessmen. Even Mrs. Smith was watching, with all of her girls beside her. Unlike yesterday's scuffle, no one was wagering on the brawl's outcome, which spoke volumes about its ugly atmosphere. And with Lennox involved, they'd be risking their leases and their livelihoods if they tried to intervene.

The prematurely gray proprietor turned as she came up. "Good afternoon, Mrs. Ross."

No time now to ask about his wife's health, although Viola had visited her daily before Maggie's departure. "A half dozen quarter sticks of dynamite and a box of your special shells, Mr. Graham. The ones loaded with rock salt."

His jaw dropped. "Are you sure about that, Mrs. Ross?"

A man cried out from the depot, the long chilling scream of someone shocked by pain. Viola's jaw set. "Now, Mr. Graham," she ordered coldly.

He had the wisdom to hold his tongue. She followed him into his store, Abraham beside her like a faithful shadow. Dynamite and a small wooden box quickly appeared on the counter.

"Thank you, Mr. Graham." Viola handed the dynamite to Abraham and put down one of Donovan's gold pieces. She quickly reloaded the shotgun, pocketing the original shells, and ran for the door.

"Good luck, Mrs. Ross," Graham called after her.

She simply nodded and picked up her skirts for extra speed.

The riot was worse now, with men limping or rolling on the ground. Mules bugled their distinctive alarm call.

Evans punched one miner in the jaw, then ducked to avoid another's blow.

William was still on his feet, but there was blood on his arm as he faced the three thugs. One of the thugs was limping but held a knife ready. Lennox watched avidly from a few steps away, one hand fondling his groin while the other twirled his sword stick.

Viola took up position across the street from the depot, which placed her only a few yards from the edge of town. "Ready, Abraham?"

"Yes, madam." He sounded curious, but she had no time to consider his thoughts.

She took a quarter stick of dynamite, lit it from the incense censer, and tossed it into the desert. The resulting explosion was loud but brief, sending a brief swirl of dust into the air.

Mules and horses screamed. Hooves beat against a mud-brick wall. Men froze, then cautiously turned to look for the cause of the explosion.

William's eyes caught hers, widened, and returned to the thugs. One of them started to swing his cudgel again.

Viola cocked the shotgun. The sound carried clearly in a break between the stamp mill's booms. Abraham stood beside her, holding the dynamite in plain sight. The two of them could mow down any, or all, of the rioters in seconds.

"Gentlemen, your shindig is delaying my supper. Please shake hands and call it a day," Viola shouted.

A man took a step toward her, no one she recognized. Viola took aim at the fool where he stood next to the depot's bell. "Now, mister, this shotgun is loaded and I will use it," she warned him.

"I ain't taking no orders from no damn woman," he complained, and took another step. She shot the bell beside him, which erupted into furious clanging. The fool dropped to the ground and curled into a ball.

As she reloaded, she sent up a silent thank you to Edward for his insistence on shooting lessons. She was merely passable with rifle or revolver, but quite comfortable with a shotgun. None of which prevented a bruised shoulder, as she would have later.

The other men glanced around, then dropped their weapons. The fool cautiously lifted his head.

"Thank you, gentlemen." She lowered the shotgun and swallowed hard.

Lennox glared at her and started to say something, but fell silent. She'd have trusted him more if he'd cursed her.

The fool sat up slowly, then stood up to dust himself off. Handshakes were exchanged as miners and teamsters complimented each other on a good fight. Viola rolled her eyes at masculine thinking.

Sheriff Lloyd finally arrived, reeking of whisky and panting hard after propelling his bulk forward at an awkward trot. "What happened here? Don't stand around, folks. Off with you all, now, and be quick about it."

Graham snorted and turned for his store, along with the other businesspeople.

"Gentlemen, the infirmary is open," Doc Hughes announced. He was a successful horse doctor for Donovan & Sons, and he treated people as successfully as most medical doctors would. Men murmured and a few followed him to his office in the depot.

Miners departed quickly, many pausing to shake hands with Viola. Teamsters dispersed to clean themselves up or return to their chores. Thankfully, no one remained in the dust, too injured to move.

The three thugs nodded at William and left the depot, following Lennox back up the street. Viola's blood ran cold at the look in Lennox's eyes when he passed her. Merciful heavens, what would happen when the cavalry came and most of the teamsters left for the new fort?

She shivered as William crossed the street and kissed her hand. "Many thanks, Mrs. Ross."

"My pleasure, Mr. Donovan. How did this function begin? Did Mr. McBride arrive, with a few of his friends, to speak to Mr. Lowell?" Her voice quavered a bit.

"Exactly so, Mrs. Ross." His eyes searched her, then he offered his arm. "Shall we proceed to the depot? I believe there are horses and mules in need of soothing."

She handed the shotgun to Abraham and accompanied William to the stables. Abraham separated from them with a polite bow and walked toward the magazine, carefully holding the dynamite and incense censer very far apart.

Her knees wobbled as she entered the friendly darkness. The horses in here were much calmer than the mules outside. She could already hear their restless movements slowing down.

William wrapped both arms around her in a comforting hug. She clutched him, letting his strength seep into her. His heart was beating hard and fast under his respectable wool suit.

"Your arm needs to be seen to," Viola murmured, her cheek resting against his chest.

"Merely a scratch. It's already stopped bleeding." He kissed the top of her head and kept his grip close. His voice was entirely Irish. "Ah, Viola sweetheart, my heart stopped beating entirely when I saw you standing there. Give me a few minutes to catch my breath, will you?"

Viola nodded, making no other movement. If she'd lost him to those hoodlums . . .

Saladin poked his big gray head over a door to study them curiously. Two doors further down, another horse placidly chewed straw as she watched. What was Lennox's new mare doing at Donovan's depot? Then his voice recalled her.

"You're a beautiful woman, Viola. Aye, you're as brave as a lion," William crooned, then added in a husky whisper. "But your beautiful body can make my heart skip a beat, as well."

Viola was too emotionally tired to tolerate pretty speeches. "I am not beautiful. I'm short, scrawny, and pallid."

"Is that how you think of yourself?" William pulled back to stare at her. "Do you not feel how my body reacts to you? You're lovely beyond compare, sweetheart."

Viola opened her mouth to deny it again, but stopped when a ray of sunlight illuminated his face. His expression was entirely open to her for the first time outside the bedroom. William was telling the truth.

"But I have no curves," she stammered.

"I can hold your breast in my mouth. Your hips cradle me

and take me to the heights. What need is there for more? Your hair has moon magic woven through it and your eyes are the color of the dawn sky. And your mouth. Ah, sweetheart, do you want me to describe in detail all the ways your mouth has roused me to ecstasy?"

Viola shook her head, blushing as she tried to smile. Her eyes blurred with moisture.

"Look at yourself through my eyes, sweetheart. You're a beautiful woman in every way—mind, heart, and body."

His conviction took root in her heart. Her smile grew as she, too, believed in her own beauty for the first time. "Thank you, William."

She leaned up to him. His lips met hers in a long, sweet kiss that melded their breath as much as their lips and tongues. She couldn't have said how long the moment lasted as she savored the hard strength of his muscular body behind layers of clothing.

She slipped her arms around his neck and simply enjoyed the kiss. He seemed content to do the same, holding her close and safe and gently stroking her back.

Undemanding companionship seeped into Viola from his touch. He wasn't demanding carnal fulfillment, simply offering his affection. A knot around her heart slipped loose.

Perhaps William might be someone to ride the river with, someone she could trust to stand with her no matter what the odds against them.

William Donovan possessed few of the virtues her mother had deemed essential for a husband. He had money but little else Desdemona Lindsay valued. To begin with, he didn't belong to the right church or the right clubs. He couldn't claim ancestors who'd fought in the Revolution. He lacked family, especially kinfolk who could pull strings in business or politics.

Viola knew the pampered life her parents had planned for their daughters: the dinner parties for the right people, the balls with the right people, summers at Saratoga Springs. A

Paris wardrobe, of course, with magnificent jewels. And an elegant piano in every house for her amusement.

The husband would be carefully selected for his bloodlines and wealth. He'd probably be fat, pompous, and disinclined to seek her company for sensual amusements after he'd bred a few children on her.

He'd lie to her whenever he pleased, cheat his social inferiors whenever possible, and hunt power at all times with the obsessive energy of a rabid wolf.

In short, he'd be everything she should want.

Viola leaned her head back against William's shoulder. She had three months remaining with him before the bargain demanded her departure. It had to be enough for her heart.

Paul Lennox strode into his office and tossed his sword stick down on the desk. The O'Flaherty brothers silently followed him in. The youngest, favoring his right leg, closed the door behind them.

Paul unlocked the ornate cabinet against the wall and pulled a decanter of Napoleon brandy and a single snifter out of it. He poured the snifter full and drank it down, favoring his wounded hand. It warmed his insides, but not as much as a good killing.

Revenge for today's debacle would be very sweet, when he finally had Donovan in his clutches. And when Viola had paid in blood for wounding him like this.

He smiled, considering the possibilities, and twirled the crystal goblet.

Then he filled the snifter again, capped the decanter, and settled into his chair. The O'Flahertys had doffed their caps and remained standing, as befitted their inferior social status.

They'd served his family for a long time, ever since they arrived in New York as young men in 1850. He'd heard whispers their father had been a bitterly unpopular land agent in County Cork, eventually ambushed and killed by "unknown assailants." Paul cared little about their background, except for how it had developed their instincts and skills as the most feared thugs in Five Points.

"What next?" he demanded of the senior O'Flaherty. "Staging a brawl won't work twice."

Conall shrugged slightly. "Simplest way would be to wait for the cavalry to come. We strike hard when they take that big wagon train and most of the teamsters up to the new fort."

"We can't wait that long. If Lindsay comes straight through from Colorado, he could be here in two days. I must have Mrs. Ross before then."

"Her mother was quite the one for shopping, remember, Conall? Buying those rifles we had to deliver to Richmond for her. Maybe this girl likes to shop, too, and we could snatch her off the street," the youngest brother offered.

"Richmond? You delivered rifles to Richmond during the recent unpleasantness for Desdemona Lindsay?" Paul's head spun. A naval officer's wife committing treason?

"Yes, sir, we did," Conall agreed.

"And you'd swear to it in court?"

"Of course, sir. God's own truth, for once."

Paul smiled slowly, stroking his muttonchops. Viola Ross would either marry him or he'd destroy her mother, and her family's reputation.

"Very well then," he said briskly. "Snatching her from a shop should work. Afterwards, you'll escape into the mine tunnels below Main Street before Donovan can come to her rescue. There's an abandoned mine where we can hold her until she turns biddable. Yes, that should definitely work."

"Donovan'd probably come hunting her," Conall mused, a feral battle light glowing in his eyes. He enjoyed killing as much as Paul enjoyed watching. They'd spent more than one delightful evening together in Five Points, indulging their mutual appetites.

Paul stirred reluctantly. The only other bids he'd ever received for freighting goods into this godforsaken hole demanded half again as much as Donovan & Sons. He couldn't afford to lose Donovan & Sons a day earlier than necessary, especially since he planned to keep the Golconda. Nick might want to sell it and focus on railroads but Paul found the hunt for silver too exciting to give up. "Might be better if he didn't. Perhaps I can bribe him."

With money? That hadn't worked before. There must be something else he could offer, something Donovan couldn't obtain any other way and would be properly grateful for.

Perhaps an invitation to join the Pericles Club. Yes, that might do very well. He'd seen how Donovan's eyes widened with hunger when he mentioned his own acceptance. He'd ensure the Board of Governors voted Donovan down, of course. A quick note to Nick should do the job.

Nick had coaxed the governors into admitting Paul into Pericles Club, despite all the ridiculous gossip about Paul's war record. He was well-spoken, accounted handsome by the ladies, and a skilled blackmailer who worshipped his older brother. Yes, Nick should be able to easily block Donovan's admission.

"Yes, plan to kidnap her Friday morning before the stage arrives. That will give you time to clear the entrance to that old mine so we can keep her there," Paul ordered. "I can send her a note while Donovan's at the depot, purporting to come from that fool Graham, which should fetch her immediately. You'll have to eliminate the Chinaman, of course."

"Of course, sir. We've fought his type before and won. Paddy will dispatch him in a trice."

"Try not to use a gun. I don't want any untoward attention."

"Very well, sir."

"Anything else? You're hesitating."

"Donovan looks a bit familiar, that's all."

"Common name in the old country," Conall's youngest brother suggested. "Especially in southwest Cork."

"Maybe that's it. But I swear I've seen his eyes before.

Never mind my fancies, sir. We'll snatch the woman for you."

"Fetch some mules from the mine's stables and return here in an hour. You can start work on clearing the rubble from the abandoned mine tonight."

"Yes, sir," the O'Flahertys chorused.

Paul walked them out to the street, planning to stop by his house next. A plume of dust in the distance caught his attention. He shielded his eyes against the sun's glare and squinted. Then he chuckled, a sound he'd taught Virginia civilians to know and hate during the war.

"Gentlemen, the cavalry will be here by nightfall. The supply train should depart in the morning, taking Donovan's men with it."

"Are you sure about that, sir?" Conall questioned. "It's coming from a long way off."

Paul's humor was too buoyant to be offended by any challenge to his judgment. "Learned my dust clouds in the recent unpleasantness, O'Flaherty. That dust is loose and fluffy, thrown up by horses' hooves, not heavy wagons. Cavalry, nothing else. The prize will be ours come Friday."

Chapter Thirteen

Viola took another spoonful of snow pudding as she watched William sip his tea and stare into space. Sarah had outdone herself with this rich dessert but it meant little when compared to tomorrow's dangers. Viola set aside her spoon and began to nervously crumble lemon biscuits into the creamy white sweet.

The cavalry had come a day earlier than expected, damn them. Evans and most of William's teamsters would leave tomorrow for at least a week. They wouldn't have the usual overwhelming complement, since William and some other teamsters were staying behind in Rio Piedras to guard Viola. Apaches could kill them all in a single attack.

William had to be concerned about his men's survival. If only she could do something to distract him.

"Tea?" William offered, lifting the pot.

"Yes, thank you," Viola replied automatically. The hot drink flowing into her cup raised different questions. Perhaps she could use them to divert him.

"William, have you ever indulged in strong liquors?"

He shook his head as he filled his own cup. "Never. I saw too much of how they could destroy a man when I was twelve. I took an oath then never to imbibe, except for the Sacrament at Mass, of course."

"Of course," Viola nodded. He attended Mass every week here in Rio Piedras. She'd attended Mass almost a dozen times with Molly and Brigid O'Byrne. It had seemed an exotic but comforting ritual to her eyes, and she respected its appeal.

"Did you take any oaths as a child not to engage in an adult activity, Viola?"

She cocked her head as she considered. "When I was eighteen and the war broke out, I swore I'd never join a political party. But women will never get the vote so it's not much of an oath, is it?"

"You'd keep the vow, if it came to pass, wouldn't you?"

"Certainly."

"Then it's a true oath. But why that one?"

Viola hesitated: how much could she tell him? But the war had ended six years ago and she could surely speak freely of at least a few matters. If nothing else, the story might distract him from worrying about Evans. "My father and brother served in the Mississippi Squadron of the Union Navy during the late conflict. My mother's family, including her brothers and nephews, served in the Confederate Army."

She snapped another lemon biscuit in two, remembering the anger and fear that had drenched her home. William patted her hand, comforting and undemanding.

"Did your mother sympathize with the Southern cause?"

Viola laughed bitterly. "Indeed so. Very strongly, in fact. She fought verbal duels with my father on the subject, which lasted for hours, both before he enlisted and afterwards, as well. I would run from the house and ride my horse for miles, or play the piano with the doors shut, trying not to hear them." Especially the time when Father backhanded Mother across the face . . .

She thrust the memory back and went on. "I swore I'd have no part of politics, if that's what it did to families."

She snorted as she remembered some of the slogans

shouted then. "Mother called herself 'a true daughter of the South,' who would fight for what she considered right when her own flesh and blood would not."

Viola laced her fingers with his for strength. "Mother held parties at our house, where she'd flirt and flatter Union soldiers into telling her confidential matters. I watched her as closely as I could and diverted the conversation whenever possible." Viola shivered as the old knots tightened in her stomach. "But I'm afraid some secrets were leaked to her, only to be passed to other Southern sympathizers. I grew to dread afternoon socials and dinner parties, even church bazaars. People called me such an attentive daughter for staying so close to my mother at all times. But all I desired was to stop Mother from harming anyone."

"Ah, my poor darling," William crooned and kissed her hand.

She closed her eyes as a tremor swept through her. His lips were firm and warm, reminding her of today's joys rather than yesterday's pain. This room was so far away from Cincinnati that the old agonies seemed a distant memory, something to be aired out then put away like laundry.

She opened her eyes slowly as she tried to regain her balance. William's eyes were intent on hers, compassionate and patient. Perhaps she could say a little more. If nothing else, she was diverting him from worrying about Evans' departure.

"Mother acted on her beliefs, too," Viola said carefully. *Don't say too much even now; just speak of things Mother wouldn't be tried for.* "A captured Confederate general escaped one Christmas, thanks to Mother's help. She, who was the wife and mother of Union sailors, helped return a man to battle, a soldier who'd surely kill her menfolk if they crossed him."

William's eyes flashed. His fingers tightened on hers, then slowly loosened.

"Mother showed no remorse, ever, for risking her family's lives," Viola finished. Who was William angry at? Could he be disgusted by her, since she hadn't stopped Mother?

"The bitch. The stupid bitch to risk her son's life." William uttered a string of what must have been curses in a foreign language, his face blazing with anger.

Viola stared at him. She'd carried the burden of her mother's treason alone for so long that it was burned into her soul. Sharing the knowledge with someone else, someone who understood her bone-deep anger and disgust with her own mother, was an emotional release that left her shaken.

A knot deep in her heart fell away and her eyes blurred with tears of relief. She patted his cheek. "It's over now, William. The war has ended and my father and brother survived. No harm was done."

"No thanks to her." He added a few more words, all of them heated.

The conversation obviously needed a new direction, since she hadn't intended to make him angry. Her nerves were still unsettled but perhaps his past would be more relaxing. "Are you speaking Irish?" Viola asked softly, blinking away salt tears.

William opened his mouth, then smiled sheepishly. "My apologies for using profanity, sweetheart."

"Where do you come from in Ireland?" Viola shrugged off his apology. She'd never heard a word about his life prior to 1855, when he'd started his freighting company.

"I was born near Bantry Bay in County Cork, on the estate of Lord Charles Mitchell."

"Did your family have a farm there?" Viola's ever-present curiosity bubbled into full life.

William hesitated for a moment, his eyes searching hers. She smiled at him encouragingly, hoping to hear a good story.

"My parents were servants at the great house before Lord

Charles turned them off to save money in '45. My father had a wee farm after that, and a few good horses for trading."

Viola did some calculations in her head. She'd been born in 1843 but she'd still heard talk of Ireland. "The first year of the famine."

"Aye." Old agony echoed in his voice.

"But your family," Viola sighed and fell silent, thinking of the stories that had been told and retold in Cincinnati. Molly and Brigid had said only that they were too young to remember much. Their grim expressions had discouraged any additional questions.

"We were evicted from our farm in '47," William answered her. "My two little sisters, my mother who was eight months gone with child, my father, and myself. They burned our home and they left us penniless and starving in the rain."

Viola was horrified. How could anyone leave a pregnant woman and three children without shelter in the rain? "The callous sons of bitches," she cursed, entirely forgetting propriety. "Wasn't there someplace for you to go? The workhouse, perhaps?"

"We took shelter in an abandoned cottage. But my mother went into labor the same night."

Viola stood up and hugged him fiercely, as her eyes blurred. "Dear God."

William froze, then leaned against her, as if seeking shelter from that night's cold rain.

"The labor was difficult, with the babe turned in the womb and not helping. My father did his best to help her, while I tried to comfort my sisters. They tried to be brave but, Blessed Virgin, how they cried."

He stopped, his face engraved with anguish. He must have looked the same way on that wet Irish night so long ago. Viola stroked his shoulder tentatively, afraid to speak.

"My father sent me for help. The storm was fierce and it seemed to take forever before I found the midwife. I wished with every step that I could do more. Put a strong house around them, food on the table to give her strength, anything."

Tears blinded her but she hung on William's every word.

"My brother Séamus came into this world that night, although he never drew breath here. My mother died before dawn, too worn from hunger to survive the long labor. I swore on their graves that no wife or child of mine would ever suffer as they had."

"Oh, my poor darling," Viola gasped as she fought to breathe past the sorrow that choked her. She'd longed for a child of her own but she'd never felt a babe quicken in her womb. William's loss made her emptiness deeper and stronger until she could scarcely think. She trembled, but kept her arms around him.

"Typhus claimed my sisters within the month," William rasped as he stared straight ahead, one hand gently patting her. "Da took me to Cobh after that, where he earned a living as a forger. He partook of gin, deeply and often, to escape the memories. I swore I wouldn't do the same, since that would be deliberately forgetting the lost ones."

Sobbing, Viola buried her face against his hair, but his last words cut into her heart.

"And I swore I'd gain money any way I could. If we'd had cash, my family would still be alive."

Merciful heavens, no wonder he sought money and power so fiercely.

Abruptly, William wrenched her onto his lap and locked his arms around her in a bruising grip. Great shudders ran through his body. She buried her face against him and wept enough for both of them.

It seemed hours before she stirred. Her head hurt from crying so hard, her nose was running, and her eyes and throat felt like sandpaper. His shoulder was sopping wet from her tears. She undoubtedly looked a fright, but William simply handed her his big bandanna.

Viola wiped her cheeks and blew her nose. How had he survived that much pain?

He turned her in his arms and settled her against his other shoulder. Exhaustion marked his face and his eyes were red.

She nestled as she considered how best to comfort him. Viola caressed his cheek. "Darling William," she murmured, and leaned up to him.

Their mouths slid over each other as if relearning the shape, then settled into a gentle kiss. Viola caressed his head and enjoyed the simple renewal. But all too soon William lifted his head and closed his eyes, one hand warm on her back.

He needed more easing.

Viola untied his neat silk cravat and unbuttoned his stiff white collar. William cocked an eyebrow but said nothing when she carefully removed both cravat and collar.

She paused for a moment to consider her next move. His legs' strength was as hot and solid under her silk-clad derrière as the desert floor on a summer day. She could see the pulse beating in his throat and feel the steady rise and fall of his chest as he breathed. He was so vitally alive, unlike his lost family. She needed to celebrate his survival.

Viola unbuttoned his shirt's top button, then another and another. William sighed as the soft collarband loosened its grip around his throat. She pressed a kiss to the small scab there. He rumbled soft approval but didn't open his eyes.

She opened his shirt and the cotton undershirt. She slid her hand inside and briefly glided her fingers over his nipples. He shuddered as a soft gasp escaped him.

Even in dishabille like this, his western clothing was so much more respectable than her Chinese tunic and pants. But the Chinese clothing could be removed so much faster. She smiled to herself.

"Lean forward please, William. Let me take off your jacket."

"We should go to the bedroom," he murmured, and started to straighten up.

Viola settled herself more firmly on his legs. "No."

"Are you refusing me?" He blinked at her and her heart twisted at how tired his eyes were. Had he ever spoken of his loss before? Probably not, or he'd have learned to be less drained by the telling.

She tilted her chin at him in mock hauteur. "Me? Refuse you? Certainly not. But I do believe you could remove some of your clothing without doing harm."

He chuckled and some of the light returned to his face. "Teasing me, are you? Very well."

He shifted in the chair as she'd requested, and she quickly removed his jacket. She slid his braces off his shoulders and down his arms, then peeled his shirt off and stood up.

He lifted his hips to free his shirttails, his expression quizzical. "You seem very determined tonight, sweetheart. Must I be polite lest you blast me with shells full of rock salt?"

Viola giggled at his gentle banter. "I am certain, sir, that a true gentleman like you would never need to be rebuked with salt," she answered demurely. Then, more briskly, "Your undershirt next, William."

"As you wish, sweetheart." He peeled the intruding garment off while remaining in the chair, leaving only the crucifix and medals around his neck.

She sighed at the picture he presented. She'd learned enough of the masculine physique, thanks to him, to recognize its sensual temptations.

She'd always thought him beautiful, and now she feasted her eyes on him, anticipating the evening's frolics. The broad shoulders, strong arms, deft hands with their long, nimble fingers. The strong chest, with its muscles and neat pelt of black hair above the clean ridges of his abdomen. His skin was milk-white except where the sun had kissed his throat, forearms, and hands.

Her breasts tightened at the sight.

Viola removed his clothing to the piano, then stood over him, arms akimbo as she pondered her next move. "You need to be rid of those boots," she decided, and stooped down.

"As you wish, sweetheart." He aided her as much as he could while remaining in the chair. Soon the offending footwear, including his wool socks, departed his feet.

She stood up to place his elegant Wellington boots alongside his other attire and caught a glimpse of the solid ridge behind his fly. He was breathing harder now and a faint sheen of sweat clung to his chest.

Viola choked as a blaze of lust scorched her. Her nipples were hard and urgent, and her pussy tightened, as if to embrace him. Dew slipped down her thigh in welcome for this man.

But he didn't move. He didn't pounce on her. "Sweetheart, do you mean to stand for hours with my boots in your hand?" he drawled, his voice rich with carnal undercurrents. He must be enjoying her attentions.

"Of course not." She brought herself back under control and took his socks and boots away. "Kneel on the floor please, before the piano."

He came to his feet with the easy grace of a prowling mountain lion and strolled to the spot designated. Dear heavens, his back was magnificent with the smooth sweep of his spine bisecting those magnificent muscles.

"Kneel, sweetheart?" he questioned.

"On all fours, if you would, after you unbutton your fly."

"You are a constant surprise, sweetheart. Very well." He unbuttoned his trousers very slowly until she trembled with hunger. She could see the hard length of his cock, and watched it stretch and fill with every movement as he deliberately teased her. She did so enjoy the sight of him.

She bit her lip until she drew blood, and somehow managed not to lunge at him. The silk was very damp between her legs.

He lowered himself easily to the floor, then looked up at her over his shoulder. "Now what?"

"You're obviously overdressed for the occasion," Viola observed huskily. She ran her fingers lightly down his spine, as if playing an arpeggio. He shuddered and arched into her touch.

She smiled more confidently and skimmed her hand over his shoulders in the lightest possible touch. "You are so beautiful, William."

Her hand slipped inside his trousers. He gasped and lifted his hips toward her. Another tremor slid through him, and she knelt down beside him.

She fondled his hips and derrière, enjoying the contrast between soft skin and hard muscle, the hard line of his spine and the solid curve of his buttocks, his flat stomach and the rearing heat of his cock when it brushed her fingers.

She leaned closer to him and rubbed herself over him, savoring how her tunic's silk barely shielded her skin from his shape and textures. She straddled his leg and rubbed her eager mound against his thigh. She pressed her nipples into his back and he jerked, rumbling a stream of Irish words as she teased him.

His thick black hair fell forward around his face. The golden lamplight caressed his skin until he seemed a god. His hands clenched into fists but he obeyed her requests.

Nothing in the world existed except this man and herself.

"Bloody hell," he moaned, "now she starts enticing me of her own will. Sweet singing Jesus, how can I protest?"

"Then don't, silly man." She dropped a kiss on his shoulder as she cupped his balls, his crisp hairs tickling her fingers. "Just let me remove your pants. And drawers, too, of course."

"Of course." His voice was husky, almost rasping.

She drew the intruding cloth over his thighs, baring him to her avid gaze. She nuzzled his hip and licked him. "You have such a beautiful ass."

"Dammit, woman," he growled, his hips twisting and shifting.

"Did I use the wrong term for this portion of your anatomy, William?" Viola asked, straight-faced, then swept her tongue over him again.

He moaned again, louder, then choked out, "You used the correct word, sweetheart."

"Excellent. On your stomach now, please." She backed away slightly, reluctantly.

"What?" His head shot around to stare at her.

She lifted an eyebrow. "How long do you plan to delay?"

"Wretch," he grumbled, but laughter sparked in his eyes. He obeyed, muttering something in Irish as he settled flat on the floor.

"Splendid," Viola approved. Magnificent, in fact, or at least her pussy thought so, judging by how it wept in eagerness for him. An opinion seconded by her womb, which clenched hungrily for him, and her breasts, which throbbed as if they hadn't felt his touch for weeks instead of the few hours since morning.

He turned his head to watch her but said nothing, his gaze fevered and intent upon her.

She sighed and reached up to undo her hair, closing her eyes against the distraction he offered. A few practiced movements later, her pale hair fell over her shoulders. She shook her head until her hair swirled around her.

William groaned something. She glanced at him, startled by his reaction since she hadn't touched him. He closed his eyes, trembling, and his hips pulsed.

He liked her *hair* that much?

Viola trailed it over his back lightly. The lamplight reflected on the strands until her hair seemed part of the light.

He groaned again.

She could excite him with something as simple as brushing him with her hair. For the first time in her life, her body seemed an asset to catching a man's attention.

She purred and repeated the caress, pouring her hair over every line and fold of him, enjoying how the lamplight blazing from it highlighted his powerful body.

He shuddered and moaned her name. His hands tightened on the rug. His hips began to rock rhythmically.

She kissed his spine and licked his shoulder, fanning her fingers over his arms to gather his heat into every pore of her body. Her skin burned for him until she thought she might explode.

"Bloody hell, Viola, do you mean to burn away my wits with excitement?" His rough, broken voice stoked the fire deep in her core. She was flushed, aching with excitement.

She rolled away and fumbled to remove her clothing. Undoing the tunic's frogs would take far too long, so she concentrated on the pants' drawstring. Finally, they came untied and she stood up to strip off the offending silk.

She was attired only in the silk tunic now, with her bare legs gleaming below and her hair streaming over her shoulders. She was available for anything, in heady contrast to the tunic's rich cloth, and too excited to be embarrassed by her dishabille.

"Dear God in heaven."

She stopped and looked back down at him. William had rolled over and lay at her feet, outlined against the rich oriental rug like an exotic delicacy. His brilliant blue eyes blazed as bright as a smelter's fires, his skin was gilded by the lamplight, and his cock was fiercely crimson in its rearing impatience, its color deepened by the delicate film of his seed slipping over it.

He closed his eyes as another tremor racked him. "Viola, sweetheart, fetch me a condom from the sideboard before I forget myself and grab you."

Viola threw her pants onto the pile of his clothes and did as he bid. He remained on the floor and slipped it on quickly, tying it with clumsy fingers.

She crouched beside him and unconsciously licked her lips as she watched. Those thin sheaths that prevented pregnancy seemed a waste of precious time, compared to her urgency to claim him.

He laid his head back and closed his eyes, as his hands fell away to his sides. "Do you mean to do something other than watch, sweetheart?" he asked softly.

"Do you know how beautiful you are?" Viola whispered. She reached out to run a delicate finger over his hip. He was magical like this, a creature of earthly strength and carnal fires that made her very bones melt.

He shivered and arched, fingers clawing at the rug.

Compelled by an instinct older than time, Viola swung her leg over his hip, seized his cock, and mounted him. She sank home, her pussy welcoming him like a violin coming alive for its bow. His hips bucked to meet her.

"Yes, oh yes, William," she moaned.

She shifted slightly, delighting in how her intimate folds nestled against his balls. She purred as she arched her back and discovered new places deep inside where his cock could delight her.

"Bloody hell, Viola, you will make me lose my mind." He caressed her sides and played with her nipples in just the way she liked. She leaned forward to encourage him.

"Ride me like your favorite horse, sweetheart," he bit out, and arched under her.

Instinctively, she rocked her hips. She moved on him more and more, in response to his hands' clever urging of her breasts and his hips' steady motion. Soon she was plunging up and down on his cock, riding him like the reckless horsewoman she'd once been.

She threw back her head and trembled with the sheer delight of life. An eager beat built in her loins and spine, reached out into her blood. His gasps and groans were pure counterpoint, a fugue building to a crescendo.

Fire built with every motion, every wet slap of skin against skin, every gasp and shudder. Soon she could no longer remember why she waited, only that this man was wonderful beyond all others. His rough finger slipped between them and pressed her throbbing clit.

Viola sobbed aloud as rapture burst through her veins. She came again and again, shattering into pieces in a world where the only thing of importance was William's explosive climax.

She collapsed on him afterwards, too spent to do more than cuddle as she slid into sleep.

William's face was calm as he dressed in the predawn darkness by a single candle. Viola watched him as she brushed her hair, desperately aware that Lennox could attack as soon as the supply train left. He should be warned.

"Lennox arranged the riot yesterday at the depot," she said abruptly.

"I know, sweetheart."

"How?"

He shrugged. "Probably the same way you do: he was entirely too smug when he watched me fight the O'Flahertys."

Viola nodded agreement. But William needed to know everything possible of Lennox's villainy, so he could be fully prepared. "He killed Edward personally. He ran him through with that sword stick of his."

"Good God." He came to her and gently took her by the shoulders. "Are you certain? For a man to court a woman whose husband he killed is unbelievable, even for Lennox."

She nodded. "He told me so himself."

"The murdering bastard." William's face was taut with suppressed violence before he calmed himself. He leaned down to kiss her and the Colt belted at his hip nudged her elbow.

"I'm sorry you had to face that loss alone, sweetheart."

She clutched his shoulders, feeling his warm life flow into her cold fingers.

He nuzzled her forehead. "Steady now, sweetheart. That

villain will not catch me by surprise nor harm you, I swear."
He straightened up and slid a long slender knife into the
sheath on his right wrist, then buttoned his cuffs. He seemed
a warrior angel, ready for battle at any time. He deserved so
much more than she could give him.

"I should go to Lennox and tell him I'll marry him."

William suddenly spun away from the dresser and dragged
her up against him. She stared up at him, her heart racing at
the look on his face.

"No. Hell, no," he snarled. "You promised me three
months and I swore to protect you. By Mary and all the
saints, you'll not leave me until that time is up."

"It's not worth seeing you killed." Her throat was so tight
she had difficulty getting the words out.

William shrugged impatiently. "He tried to shoot Morgan
the other day but failed. There'll be no peace in this town
until one of us is dead, no matter whose house you live in. So
you'll stay with me, where you're safe, even if I have to lock
you in."

"You wouldn't do that," she protested.

He lifted an eyebrow. "Don't be silly, sweetheart. Of course,
I would."

Viola searched his face in the flickering light, all shadows
and occasional flashes of insight. His expression was calm
and inflexible. She sighed and yielded. If Lennox had attacked Evans, then there truly would be fighting even if she
went to Lennox. "Very well, I'll stay with you." *And I'll
pray,* she added silently.

"Good girl." He kissed her quickly, then turned away to
shrug into his coat.

She wished she could help him somehow, do something to
ease him. Perhaps something carnal.

"William."

"Yes, sweetheart?"

"Can we do whatever you want tonight?"

He turned to stare at her. Primal hunger and intimate masculine knowledge flickered there for a moment before his thick eyelashes swept down to conceal his thoughts. Something in her melted and surged toward him.

"I thought we always did what I want," he drawled.

Viola blushed scarlet but pursued her goal. "You're always so very kind and considerate toward me. Are there activities you'd enjoy if you didn't need to worry about me?"

His face froze, shifted. He seemed to consider infinite possibilities. Then he shook his head. "No, don't think about that, sweetheart. We do very well as we are."

"There are other games to play, aren't there?" Viola persisted. "Games with a rope, or a little whip, or maybe something else."

She stopped at the look on his face.

His eyes blazed brilliant blue. Her pussy clenched, anticipating the pleasures his expression promised.

"What are you asking me for, sweetheart?" He tilted a finger under her chin. She met his fierce gaze openly. They were so close together she could feel his chest rising and falling under his proper suit.

"To play the games you dream of, without worrying about me." She gulped, then bravely finished with the truth. "I'm certain we'll both enjoy them."

William swallowed hard, his cock a hot ridge against her belly. "Oh, sweetheart," he growled, "tonight I will show you such fantasies as would make your head spin. I promise you'll forget about everything else in the world."

Viola gulped. If they could both forget Evans' departure, taking so many teamsters, and Lennox prowling outside like a ravaging beast hunting for an opening . . .

William kissed her, long and hard, certain of his welcome. She threw herself into her response, eager to distract herself from the coming danger.

William double-checked the powder wagon one last time, ensuring the knots would hold during the long journey ahead. The other wagons stood waiting on the desert just beyond, ready to leave for Fort McMillan with their cavalry escort. Most of his men would depart with them. He'd prayed for them that morning during his usual devotions at the Blessed Virgin's shrine in the compound.

He'd remain behind to prepare for the next supply train from Fort Yuma and to protect Viola from Lennox. He had few worries for his own fate but mountains for Viola's future.

His eyes lifted to find her, watching from the colonnade outside the office, an island of feminine calm in the depot's hubbub. She smiled at him and he touched his hat to her, then returned to the knots.

He wondered, not for the first time, why Lennox sought her so fiercely. Hurt pride from her repeated refusals? Maybe; heaven knows he had pride enough for a thousand men so he'd likely take poorly to being publicly crossed. But why did he want her to begin with? She was the only woman in this town from a fine family, but Lennox could hunt for a wife in other towns.

Viola deserved better than Lennox's cruelty.

For a moment, William imagined Viola as his wife, not Lennox's. They'd attend Sunday Mass together, dressed in their finest, and the bishop would give her a fond greeting afterwards. He'd take her home in a magnificent carriage, the matched team trotting fast enough to ruffle the feathers in her hat. She'd laugh and cling to his arm, eyes dancing as she anticipated the embrace he'd give her when they reached their house. The hours of passion afterwards would pass quickly as he showed her marriage was just a beginning, not an end, to their love.

Bloody hell, William snarled silently, and wrenched himself away from that foolish dream. No daughter of America's finest families would ever tolerate an Irishman as a husband, or the Catholic religion. No, Viola would leave in three months and he must make the most of the time remaining.

By all the saints, he'd do his best to ensure she remembered this Irishman whenever she was with another man.

"Ready, Donovan?" Morgan's rich tenor interrupted William's thoughts.

"Ready." He turned to face his friend.

Morgan was dressed in his usual attire for the trail: well-worn flannel shirt and canvas trousers, a broad-brimmed battered slouch hat pulled well down on his forehead, and pistol belt close to his waist with a Colt on each side, butts forward in the cavalry style. Leather chaps rose above high-heeled boots and Mexican spurs. His rifle was balanced Arizona-fashion on his saddle's pommel and an old Navajo blanket rested at the cantle. His Indian pony could outlast almost any other horse in Arizona, and still be capable of a sprint at day's end.

Locals said Morgan could ride and track as well as any Apache. This morning, his appearance matched every bit of his reputation and more.

Viola appeared beside him. "Please take care of yourself, Mr. Evans. I will pray nightly for your well-being."

Morgan's face softened. "Thank you, Mrs. Ross. I promise you we'll return as quickly as possible. A week, maybe less."

Viola nodded, her smile a bit tremulous. "Sarah has a splendid supper planned for your return."

She slipped her hand into the crook of William's arm. He patted it reassuringly.

"Take good care of her, Donovan. Otherwise, I'll just have to look after her myself."

"The hell you will," William retorted. Morgan laughed, and the tense moment was over.

Morgan touched his hat to Viola, then wheeled and rode out of the depot, while William and Viola followed him on foot.

In the street outside, Morgan waved his hat to the cavalry lieutenant. An instant later, a bugle sounded, setting the blue-clad horsemen into motion. The great wagon train uncoiled itself from the open plain and lumbered onto the trail. William and Viola, with the townsfolk and remaining teamsters, waved good-bye.

Seven nights, at best, would pass before his men would return. Until then, he, Abraham, and his few remaining men would protect Viola from that scum Lennox.

Chapter Fourteen

Hal Lindsay climbed down from the stagecoach's roof, grateful for escape from this particular form of torture, as Holbrook steadied the horses for the passengers to disembark. Its height and width of little more than four feet were not designed to hold his big frame in comfort, even if he'd been the only passenger.

That hadn't been the case, of course, so he'd escaped to the roof as often as possible. And from there, he'd been privileged to help fight off more than one Apache attack.

The headache gained in the Santa Fe attack had finally disappeared a few days ago, although he still wore the doctor's carefully wound bandage. He badly needed a barber to restore his goatee's usual tidiness. He was also both filthy and hungry, conditions he never tolerated while piloting.

"Thanks for the help, Lindsay," Holbrook called down to him, his gray eyes vivid in his weathered face. "We sure had our hands full during that last attack, 'til you cut loose with your Henry rifle."

"My pleasure," Hal answered as he tucked the repeating rifle comfortably against his side. He'd bought it from another traveler just before Apache Pass and thanked God for it during every Apache attack since.

He accepted his carpetbag from the station agent, a sturdy man with watchful eyes. He glanced toward the west and frowned at the setting sun. The last Apache attack had cost more time than he'd hoped. He stood little chance of reaching Rio Piedras today, if it was as far as men said.

"Where can I buy a horse to ride to Rio Piedras?" Hal asked.

Holbrook laughed as he, too, finally jumped off the stagecoach. "You ride out of Tucson alone and you'll be dead before sundown, thanks to the Apaches. Waste of a good horse, if you don't mind me saying so. No, you're better off catching tomorrow's stage."

"When does it leave?"

"Pulls out of here at dawn and reaches Rio Piedras after noon. Makes a quick turnaround there so it can be back here before midnight. We run two stages on that route for safety."

"Thanks." Hal surveyed the neighborhood around the depot and frowned. He'd heard stories of Tucson, especially as a den of villains. But this looked worse than he'd expected. "Any advice on where I can stay?"

"Two hotels in town, and you'll want the one at the end of this block. It has a good bathhouse and barber," Holbrook added. "Spend some time there and they'll get you fixed up right. Good food and beds, too. Don't waste your money on any other place."

Hal nodded and started to turn.

"One more thing." Holbrook spoke confidentially. "You might want to exchange that bowler of yours for something better suited to keeping off the sun. Strange things happen when a fellow wears narrow-brimmed hats."

Hal raised an eyebrow. "Really?"

"Fact. Those Rio Piedras fellows like to make sure no eastern headgear is seen in their town. All in fun, of course."

"A tough place."

"Makes Tucson look like a Sunday school, especially when those miners and teamsters start a brawl." Holbrook's tone held a wealth of warning.

"Thanks for the warning, friend."

"Pleasure's all mine."

The two men exchanged nods of perfect understanding before Hal proceeded down the block, carpetbag and rifle in hand. He kept his distance from other pedestrians, as he had first learned in Natchez Under-the-Hill at fourteen. That way, he could see anyone who wanted to attack him—and there seemed to be many interested in doing so. If this was a Sunday school, then what was Rio Piedras like? What kind of situation had Viola found herself in?

The recommended hotel was a tidier establishment than any other on that block, with a few respectably dressed men and women lounging on its porch.

Hal stopped when he saw the gold mourning brooch adorning one of the women. The brunette wore flashy attire otherwise, typical of a respectable woman throwing good money after bad taste.

Hal's mother and his sister Juliet would have laughed at her. Viola would have tried to interest the woman in other choices.

He approached her eagerly, heedless of their audience. "Excuse me, ma'am, but can you tell me where you obtained your brooch?"

The woman's face paled, and she looked around as if seeking rescue. Her eyes fixed on a man a few feet away, but he remained engrossed in his conversation with another. Every instinct honed in Hal's sixteen years as a pilot sprang to attention.

She returned her attention to Hal and visibly gulped before answering. "It's a family piece. I inherited it from my grandmother."

Hal frowned at the blatant lie and pulled out his watch. "Ma'am, that brooch is an exact match for my watch, down to the monogram and the ship. Only two such brooches were made, one for my sister in New York and one for my other sister who left Colorado a year ago. Did you obtain it from my sister Viola?"

Everyone on the porch was now openly listening. The brunette fell back a step, glancing nervously at his rifle. He was immediately grateful for his villainous appearance, if it would force the truth out of her.

"No. I mean, yes, she sold it to me," the woman stammered. The man was finally coming toward her, his homely face alive with concern as his hand slipped to the Colt on his hip.

"When? Is she still alive?" Hal demanded, dropping the carpetbag to the porch's floor but keeping the rifle in his hand. His voice cut the silence like a knife. The watchers on the porch murmured but didn't move, while passersby gathered on the street to stare.

"Viola Ross is quite well, mister," the man interjected.

Hal's attention swung to him. "Where is she?"

"In Rio Piedras."

"Living with Donovan," the woman added. "In sin," she added spitefully, sidling behind the homely man.

Hal stiffened. Calm flowed into him, the same ice he'd once felt while running the blockade past Confederate forts on the Mississippi. "What did you say?"

The brunette shrank back at his tone, leaving the man to answer. His fingers hung barely an inch above his revolver's butt as he spoke. "My wife meant nothing disrespectful to your sister."

Hal stared at them both for a long moment until the woman dropped her eyes sullenly. Their audience was motionless. "Here's twenty dollars for the brooch. I'll return it to my sister."

He thumbed out gold pieces, watching the two closely.

She hesitated, hissing under her breath, then unpinned the golden token and tossed it to him. The pair scuttled down the street a moment later, clutching the money.

Tomorrow's stage couldn't reach Rio Piedras too soon for his taste.

*   *   *

Viola sat at the piano and tried her best to concentrate on the Chopin nocturne. William had made his excuses just after supper, murmuring something about seeing to the horses. But other things kept distracting her, like Lennox's surprising inactivity.

She'd not seen Lennox since he'd watched, with the rest of Rio Piedras's residents, the supply train leave for Fort McMillan. She'd spent a few hours at the depot afterwards to finish up the paperwork, then returned to the compound via the private stairs. She worried what that blackguard would do next.

Better to think about her clothing instead.

She was attired in a simple blue silk dinner dress, cut modestly enough for dinner at her grandmother's house. Her silk stockings were equally respectable, as were her black kid dancing slippers. She had no idea where William had found such items in Rio Piedras since they were far too demure for a parlor house, even Mrs. Smith's upscale establishment.

No, the true problem was what lay underneath, or what wasn't underneath. She wore a white silk chemise, as tissue-thin as an evening scarf and embroidered with white roses at the neck and hem. It could have been invisible, for all it concealed of her body. She wore nothing else, neither drawers or corset.

The weather was unseasonably warm and rather humid for the desert, including a brief thunderstorm just before supper. She was sweating lightly and the two layers of silk clung to her. The chemise in particular showed a strong disposition to hug her breasts.

Her breath caught at the carnal images evoked by that thought and her hands stilled on the keys.

Viola lowered her head and took a deep breath. She tried to play the nocturne from where she'd left off but fumbled to a stop after a few measures, distracted by thoughts of what William would do to her naked pussy. She quivered.

After she had herself back under control, she performed a set of those carnal exercises he'd prescribed. A week of doing so, whenever she stopped playing, had strengthened the muscles he'd so wickedly introduced her to. She began the nocturne again, but from the beginning.

It flowed smoothly this time, singing of the night and the magic therein. She escaped into its world more easily, forgetting the clothes and William's possible plans.

Suddenly, a light silk cloth floated over her head. Viola stiffened in shock. Then two strong arms wrapped around her and pulled her back against a broad chest.

"Ah, my faerie queen, I've captured you now," William purred in her ear. "Will you fight me with your hands and feet and teeth? Or will you try to spin another spell, like the web your music weaves?"

Viola blinked. He'd spoken before of fantasies, of escaping into a pretense of being someone else and enjoying the carnal delights of their world. They'd enacted a small fantasy at his office. But to become a faerie queen? She was an ordinary person, not an exotic, powerful being.

"I've hunted you for years, faerie queen," William continued. "You will be *my* lover now."

Viola's breath caught at the possessive note in his voice. She made up her mind quickly. If he wanted her to be a faerie queen, then she'd do so. If nothing else, it would be so very different from her everyday life, she could forget everything else.

What might Spenser's faerie queen have said? She tried a phrase and an experimental wiggle, as if struggling to break free. "Foolish mortal, you forget yourself. Unhand me immediately," she snapped.

"Never!" William responded, tightening his grip on her. "And you'll not call me a fool tomorrow, after you've learned the delights of my bed. You may do your best to break free, but you're mine for tonight."

So he wanted her to fight a bit? Very well. She began to struggle more vigorously, lifting her elbows and trying to slide out from under his embrace. "Wretched brute!"

"Not quite as easy as you thought, eh?" William laughed and picked her up. A quick twist, then he tossed her over his shoulder.

He strode out of the room purposefully, but the silk prevented her from seeing exactly where they were. She was certain he hadn't taken her out onto the colonnade and into the courtyard, but she could guess little more. Judging by the direction and number of steps, he'd bypassed their bedroom.

Viola continued to try to break free but his iron strength kept her close. She kicked and pummeled his back, calling him the worst names she could think of as she demanded to be released. The longer she fought, the more she felt like an abducted queen.

But he simply laughed softly and kept moving.

He entered a room new to her, whose door closed with a solid thud behind them. William stood her on the floor and lifted her arms over her head.

Viola tried to shake the cloth from her head but couldn't. She ordered angrily, "I demand you release me, clumsy lout!"

Her only answer was a soft chuckle. He quickly wrapped a soft rope around her left wrist and tied it to something else, an anchor that kept it in nearly the same position, no matter how hard she tried to move it. Her right hand received the same treatment. Then her left foot, and finally her right.

"Importunate peasant," she tried to snarl, but her breath broke on the last word. Merciful heavens, her situation was so close to her old fantasy of being a captive maiden. Heat burned deep inside, from her breasts to her pussy. She could barely breathe for anticipation.

"Indeed. And you'll soon be grateful for my persistence." William whipped the silk away from her head and tossed it aside.

Viola blinked in the brilliant lamplight, but her eyes

quickly adjusted. She stood on a carpeted platform in a large room, probably a storage room once but now empty and immaculately clean. The ceiling's exposed beams hosted strong iron hooks, from which a series of ropes descended. Persian rugs covered the floor, while a curious hammock hung in one corner.

But she had no time to consider the hammock now. Not when each of her limbs had three ropes attached—one from the front, another from the rear, and the third arriving from the side. Her hands and feet could each move a few inches in any direction, enough for comfort but not to fight him.

"What say you, my faerie queen? Do I hold you fast now?"

He had changed from the polite suit of suppertime into work clothes. A rough linen shirt covered his broad shoulders above coarse woolen britches and high leather boots. His fists were propped on his hips, a riding crop dangling casually from one. A peasant's costume indeed, and he couldn't have looked more magnificent. The platform raised her high enough to almost look him in the eye.

And her core considered him a very fine prospect indeed, given how dew gathered between her legs. But a faerie queen's arrogance still ruled her tongue. "As soon as I'm free, you'll regret this treatment," Viola sniffed. "I'll turn you into the toad you already are."

William's eyes danced. "You must learn to keep a civil tongue in your head, sweetheart. Calling your host a toad is hardly proper language."

"Toad is only one of your relatives! You are closer to a . . . uh . . ."

His mouth closed over hers. Viola choked, gasped, then melted. He was such an expert kisser, it was hardly fair to expect her to fight. She blinked like a drunken fool when he finally lifted his head and she realized his big, callused hand was fondling her breast. Quite boldly, in fact.

Her breath caught as small darts of heat danced from his

fingers and into her veins, totally unhindered by her clothing. "Wretch," she announced with deep sincerity as she closed her eyes, to better savor the feeling. How the devil could she even pretend to fight him if he insisted on handling her in such a fashion?

"Foolish faerie," he chuckled softly, then kissed her again. Long minutes later, he released her mouth and drew a knife from its sheath at his waist.

Viola quivered, feeling a shocking burst of dew slide down her leg. He looked so magnificent and completely male.

William set the sharp blade to the shoulder of her dress, blunt edge to her skin. "I'd never harm you, sweetheart," he insisted, blue eyes intent on hers. Merciful heavens, when he looked at her like that, it was all she could do not to tell him he could do anything he wanted to her.

"I know you wouldn't. But you should release me so I can return to my kingdom," she answered, slipping back into character.

"Don't be absurd, sweetheart." He sliced open her dress without so much as scratching her skin. One shoulder of the dress fell forward, exposing the thin chemise and the quivering flesh underneath.

"You peasant, you," Viola moaned at the controlled violence. Her heart thudded and her bosom rose and fell rapidly, flushed with passion.

Aroused and impatient, she watched as a second cut destroyed the dress' other shoulder, while a third cut down the front left the blue silk pooled around her ankles. Her hips pressed forwards toward him, but he simply swatted her derrière lightly, in a clear demand for patience.

He paced around her, leisurely studying every facet of her body. "Perfect," he pronounced. His pretense of indifference would have been more effective if he hadn't sported such a strong ridge behind his trousers' fly.

Then William set his lips and tongue to work on her nipple. He suckled her hard and deep, drawing her needy flesh into the heated depths of his mouth as if she wore nothing. The chemise could have been in New York for all the protection it offered.

"Dear heavens, William," Viola moaned and writhed, wishing she could hold him. Yet the sensations he evoked were somehow stronger because she had only them to focus on, not the eternally distracting feel of his hair or skin.

She gasped and jerked in her bonds at one particularly deep pull. He repeated the caress again and again, making her arch toward him in the same rhythm. It caught deep in her bones and ran down to her core, where the tempo evoked a flood of dew down her thighs. Her pulse pounded stronger and stronger. Her head fell back in agony as orgasm hung so close, and yet so terribly far away.

Then his teeth closed around her nipple and delicately bit her. The sudden sharp sensation flashed through her veins and burst into her core. He bit her again and she fell, gasping, into rapture.

She struggled slowly back to awareness and found him nuzzling her shoulder.

"Are you awake yet?" he asked, seemingly more interested in her collarbone than her answer.

"Ah, yes, I believe so." Why was he asking?

"Good. Time to attend to your other breast then."

"What?!"

William lavished exactly the same attentions on her other breast and once more launched her into rapture.

Viola sagged afterwards. Her body seemed boneless now, sustained only by her grip on his ropes.

"You are so beautiful like this, a perfect expression of passion waiting to be unleashed. Your mouth red and full, your breasts hard and crowned with ripe nipples, and your mound outlined by thin silk," William mused. "The only question is how shall I enjoy you first?"

He kissed the nape of her neck and licked it. He lightly nipped the sensitive point where neck and shoulder come together. She shuddered and tried to regain her scattered wits when he stepped away for a moment.

Viola blinked, then gasped when a round fullness pressed against her asshole. "William, uh, mortal man, what are you dealing to your faerie queen?"

The fullness slipped in easily, her flesh now pliant to his every whim. She whimpered, then moaned as it shifted inside her, sending a wave of pleasure into her pussy. "What the devil have you done?"

A second fullness nudged her in the same place. "I am filling you with beads, sweetheart, that your every dimension may be awakened to my will," William purred, his voice a dark velvet rumble against her ear.

The second bead eased inside. It felt enormous, yet her flesh seemed made to hold it. Viola moaned again as her pussy clenched in sheer delight. "Oh, William . . ."

"That's my sweet filly." His own breathing harsh, William slipped a third, then fourth, and finally a fifth bead into her asshole. She was stuffed with delight, the pressure reaching up through her spine to her breasts and triggering lances of sweet sensation into her nipples.

"Good girl. You're doing well. Just relax, sweetheart, and enjoy yourself," he crooned, and steadied her with gentle hands on her hips as her body slowly adapted.

Viola shuddered and arched and groaned his name again as unknown muscles clenched and rippled and hummed in pleasure. An orgasm flowed through her gently.

She stood still afterwards, shuddering for breath. If she moved too abruptly—and almost any movement felt like a possible trigger—the beads caressed her insides and sent wave after wave into her pussy. She was quite convinced any incautious jerk would send rapture bursting over her again.

"Now, sweetheart, you must come alive to my music," William said softly.

She blinked at him. He stood directly in front of her, a

small many-tailed whip lying across his hand. It looked soft and harmless, even with a knot at each tail's end, compared to his big bullwhip. Her pussy remembered its interest in his skill with a whip, and quivered happily.

"Oh yes," Viola purred. "Oh yes."

She felt the softest leather imaginable trail over her shoulder. The little knots rippled over her skin like the opening notes of a sonata.

Viola whispered William's name in gratitude and hunger. How had he known she longed for this?

He ran the little whip over every inch of her, interspersing that caress with others by his hands and mouth. Her sweat and his mouth dampened the chemise's silk until it clung to her and almost vanished.

Viola shuddered and moaned. She twisted and arched her body to follow his touch, whether given by his skin or the leather that was an extension of him.

William's touch changed slightly. Subtly the whip's caress became sharper, like a sonata moving from andante into allegro. The changed rhythm echoed through her body, raising fine tremors in her muscles and her pussy. The beads easily transferred the whip's rhythm to her core, until she didn't know whether the beat came from outside her skin or inside.

His hands and mouth dwelt on her, building her anticipation through the kisses and caresses she most loved. She couldn't have said which touch was his hand or the whip— both came from him and both excited her to the bone.

Viola moaned with pleasure as the whip danced over her body now, like Chopin's great "Fantasie Impromptu," in which no note ever fell where expected yet each one was perfect. Every stroke drew a response from all the cells in her body, as the rhythm beat into her muscles and bones and fired through her veins. Her deep inner muscles clenched again and again around the beads, building waves that echoed in her pussy.

She was on fire now, her skin hard put to contain her passion. Her blood raced hot and fast, and every inch of her was exquisitely sensitive to his slightest touch.

"Sweetheart," he groaned. "Beautiful lady."

William began to rub his body against hers, his arm or his hip, then his shoulder. The rough cloth excited her and his scent became part of her.

Reality narrowed to him, not the ropes nor the platform nor the lamplight. Only her big Irishman.

He peeled off his shirt and rubbed himself against her again, sliding over her easily, thanks to sweat. And still the whip danced over her flesh and through her pulse. The chemise might as well have not been there, for any protection it offered.

"Do you want me? Do you want this?" He wrapped his arms around her from behind, nestling her derrière against his cock. The beads rippled deep inside, and Viola sobbed, throwing her head back against his shoulder.

"Or do you need something stronger?" His hand cupped her mound and his fingers rubbed her chemise's silk against her pussy. The little whip thudded against her hip as he tugged her clit.

Rapture shattered Viola's senses as it ripped out of her clit and up to her breasts and sent her spinning into unconsciousness.

The feel of his teeth on her breast drew her back to reality. She reached instinctively for his head but a rope prevented her. She slowly realized she was on her back, in a nest of ropes. A slowly swaying nest of ropes.

Her eyes flew open.

She was lying on that unusual hammock, shaped somewhat like a star. Her body was woven into it by coil after coil of silken rope, which held her limbs and her torso. Her legs were higher than her head, and spread wide. She was utterly available to the predator who watched her with brilliant blue eyes. She licked her lips hungrily.

"Do you approve of my web, sweetheart? Is it magic enough to match your music?" William purred as he stepped back from the hammock to watch her.

He had shed his clothes, and his masculine strength was revealed in all its glory under a fine sheen of sweat. His cock stood hard and proud, jerking with eagerness for her, and his balls were high and tight.

Viola fumbled for words. "Yes, it's magnificent," she managed, and groaned as the damn beads shifted inside her.

Her body hummed with desire, existing only to feel this man in any manner he permitted. She closed her eyes and moaned at the possibilities.

"Beautiful queen." He stepped up between her legs and caressed the delicate skin of her thighs. His rough fingers reminded her of the contrast between his strength and her fragility. Her pussy throbbed in eagerness for more.

"Watch me, sweetheart. See how large my cock is?"

She nodded, and didn't speak of her disappointment that it now wore a condom.

"You'll be a snug fit, sweetheart, with the beads stretching your ass. My cock will rub against the beads with every stroke, so you'll feel me taking both your vagina and your ass. Do you understand?"

"Yes. Just, please, hurry," she implored, and closed her eyes.

"Greedy wench," he chuckled, a harsh broken sound. Then he gripped her hips and began to enter her. His cock stretched her folds taut, more agonizing than the first night when her pussy had memorized the feel of his cock.

Only the thinnest of membranes seemed to separate those beads and his cock. The beads rolled and shifted and twisted, sending shafts of fire through her body. Viola groaned and gasped for breath as her body slowly adapted to his cock.

"Viola, sweetheart." William shuddered against her when he was finally sheathed, a tremor she felt as if it were her own. Then he began to withdraw slowly. Distressed at losing him, her muscles clamped down hard around him, using the strength he'd insisted she learn. Viola panted for breath.

He grunted in surprise and stopped. "Ah, sweetheart, you're killin' me here," he whispered. "We'll fly together, you and I, if you'll just let me take you there. So ease up, you impatient filly."

Viola moaned as her body released its tight grip.

"Ah, sweetheart, that's better. You're finding the knack of it now," he growled, and slid further out of her, the beads rippling in his wake.

He shuddered and groaned something in Irish. Somewhere, in what little remained of her brain, she realized the beads must be caressing him, too.

Then he thrust back into her, quick and strong. Viola sobbed William's name as the hammock swung in response, the beads danced, and her pussy flowed around him. The net seemed part of her now, a safe vessel set in midair.

"And now we're going to ride."

He fucked her hard and surprisingly long, every movement overwhelming her with sensation. She had no connection to gravity, only to his heat and strength. The beads rolled and pounded inside her body, sending shockwaves up through her spine until thinking became impossible. His hands plucked her nipples until she writhed and arched, supported and encouraged by the hammock.

All she was, all the pleasure she could ever hope for, came from being the woman he enjoyed.

An orgasm burst through her. Her muscles started to relax in the aftermath.

"Not yet," he growled, and kept driving into her, preventing her from losing arousal's high pitch.

Viola gasped as hunger rose in her again. Her hands clutched the ropes, as if for courage.

And still he rode her, faster and stronger. Another orgasm built inside her. She welcomed it, sought it eagerly, but hungered to share it with him.

Viola groaned his name.

Suddenly William threw back his head and howled. His cock pulsed inside her as his climax erupted.

He yanked the beads out of her and wild waves of ecstasy exploded inside her, like a dance of life. Viola burst into rapture, flying into a world where nothing existed but pleasure and this man.

Chapter Fifteen

Hal kept his rifle trained on the rocky outcrop where he'd last seen an Apache as the stage jolted through the pass. Anderson, the driver, had warned this was the last place likely to experience an attack. But since he had encountered even more Apaches on this journey than the trip to Tucson, Hal had no intention of relaxing any time soon.

Anderson shouted back to him, "There's Rio Piedras up ahead."

Hal eagerly turned to look, hoping to see a neat metropolis rising five or ten miles away. Surely the Apaches would stay at least that far from a prosperous company town, however rough its manners. Instead he sighted a hamlet on a pile of rocks, rising from the desert floor a few miles away.

Rio Piedras was a singularly uninspiring town as it straggled over the long spine of a rocky ridge, like a lizard shedding its skin. The highest point of the ridge was crowned with a large mud-brick compound, boasting two watchtowers like ears on the lizard. Behind it, in the lower saddle of the ridge, clung the wide roofs of a large factory, probably the mine. Further back stood a truly ugly wooden house, which must have cost a fortune to build in this treeless country.

A wide street linked the factory to the compound before dropping down to the desert. A Catholic church, with its curved belltower, stood across the street and slightly lower than the compound. A Protestant church's single pointed steeple stood isolated a few blocks further away, perched on the lizard's shoulder. The town's other buildings clustered around the street and below the compound, as if seeking shelter. A small stream trickled into the desert, only to fade rapidly into the sand.

Nothing about this place reminded Hal of Cincinnati. None of the buildings, except the big compound or the churches, looked fit to house his horses, let alone his little sister.

The two stagecoaches swung past a big depot at the ridge's base, overtopped by the compound on its rocky cliff. From his perch atop the stage, Hal glimpsed several mud-brick huts straggling along the dying stream beyond the depot.

Thunderclouds built over the mountains and the scent of water touched him. There'd be rain, and plenty of it, soon, judging by how fast the clouds were moving. Possibly enough to bring that stream to roaring life.

The stages climbed steadily up the street, passing a cluster of hovels on a side street, even more villainous than those beside the stream. A few slatterns waved and posed hopefully before the hovels. Whores, no doubt.

Hal caught himself looking for Viola's bright hair amongst them and snapped his head away. Surely she would never be that desperate. He was grateful when the stagecoaches halted barely a block further, and he disembarked quickly.

Hal turned to the guard who'd admitted he knew where Viola had gone to live after Ross's death. Hopefully, she'd still be there, as an independent widow rather than a fallen woman. "Which way is my sister's house?"

"Just past the depot, down by the stream. Can't miss it: she's got yellow roses by the door."

Flowers sounded like Viola. "Thanks. Good luck on your journey back."

"Same to you, pardner. I'll give your carpetbag to the station agent to hold for your return."

Hal strode rapidly down the street, taking in the scene as

he went. A pair of filthy miners lolled outside a saloon, talking to an overeager gambler. A whore swung her hips at Hal and started to speak, but fell silent at his glare. He shuddered at the reek of sweat, and worse, rising from her.

He spared a single, fulminating stare at the big freight depot and its appellation of "Donovan & Sons."

Later, he promised himself. Later. If that teamster had ruined Viola, his depot would be in ashes before nightfall.

The mud-brick hovels revealed themselves as a pitiful group, with ill-fitting doors and crumbling bricks. Hal's gaze alighted on the sole hut adorned with roses, obviously the one dwelling whose occupants had made an effort. Stray dogs and children dropped from his notice as he forged ahead.

He reached the place in minutes and halted outside. This hut was smaller than the others and its only window was broken. The ragged curtains fluttered gently in the rising breeze.

Hal swallowed, his collar suddenly too tight. He was all too conscious of the bullet holes in his duster, courtesy of the Apaches on the road to Rio Piedras. Even his new broad-brimmed slouch hat had a couple of bullet holes, making him look more like a road agent or river pirate than a river pilot. It was not the sort of attire he'd have chosen to coax a much-loved sister into forgiving her repentant older brother.

"Viola?" He tapped on the door lightly. To his shock, it gave under his touch and swung sluggishly back into the hut. His heart skipped a beat.

"Viola?" he queried again, and stepped forward. A patch of sunshine in the far corner lightened the gloom inside. No one was there.

"Viola, it's your brother." He cautiously entered the tiny hut. Mud-brick walls were totally covered by peeling pages from magazines and catalogues, forming a poor man's wallpaper. The roof was a canvas tarpaulin, split open over one corner. A pool of water underneath the rip showed the stormy cause of the roof's failure. A pair of mice skittered away over the hard-packed dirt floor, and into the gloom.

Hal's stomach plummeted into his boots at the utter contrast to the last place he'd seen Viola.

She'd faced him from her bedroom's center, clad in an elegant dark blue morning dress from M. Worth of Paris. The room had been flooded with light from a great bay window. Chinese Chippendale furniture, passed down from Grandmother Lindsay's mother, and a priceless Axminster carpet, which the Commodore had won at cards, had filled the spacious room. The walls had been alive with hand-painted wallpaper from China, while silk brocade had hung at the windows.

Everything there was as it had been on that April morning in 1865. The Captain had ordered it kept that way for her return, one of his few orders that Hal agreed with.

"Jesus Christ." Hal had run away from home at fourteen to work as a deckhand on the Missouri River. He'd lived a hard life there in the beginning, scraping out survival on the edge of the river. He'd fought pirates and visited gambling saloons and bawdy houses in some of the worst places west of the Mississippi.

His throat tightened. He'd rarely seen anything that reeked of bare survival as strongly as this deserted hut. And to think his beloved little sister had lived here . . .

A broken whisky bottle, with a handful of dried yellow roses scattered nearby, lay by the window. Its sharp edges were covered in dried blood.

"Dear God, Viola." Hal's knees gave out and he sank to the floor by that damning bottle. He touched the bottle's razor-sharp edge with a single, trembling finger and fought back tears.

Marrying that drunken malingerer had brought his sister to this, a tiny hut not fit for a donkey on the edge of civilization.

If he'd shown more brotherly concern, if he hadn't fought with her, if he'd bought off Ross as the asshole had hinted, she'd be safe now.

Hal's shoulders shook. The rose petals fluttered in the strengthening breeze, reminding him of the garden that should have been Viola's. A sob fought to make its way out of his heart.

His eyes welled up and he shuddered. He couldn't fight the next tear, or the next. Then the tears became a stream, and a flood. Soon he was crying like a child, as he hadn't since the night he ran away from home.

Viola leaned back from the piano and stretched her arms over her head. She bent first to the left then to the right, starting the series of exercises she'd first learned while studying the piano in Cincinnati. She'd practiced them later as a miner's wife, helping her recover from prospecting. The exercises had the admirable fringe benefit of easing many of the aftereffects of a night in William's bed.

The inner muscles surrounding her channel, as he called the passage to her womb, complained only slightly. They'd already been pampered by a long, hot bath that morning and were ready to welcome William at any time.

She tilted her head, smiling at the thought. He'd promised her she'd fly and she certainly had, better than any bird. He'd also enjoyed himself as much as she had. In fact, he'd arisen from bed so late he'd simply shaved before departing, rather than bathe as well.

Thunder rumbled in the distance as Viola purred at her success in distracting him. She'd have to think of something else for them to do that evening. Perhaps he could read poetry to her before they turned in; there was a volume of Elizabeth Barrett Browning's sonnets in the sitting room. Or perhaps he'd introduce her to the other contents of his small ironbound chest, the one he'd returned the little whip to.

"Mrs. Ross? A boy just brought this note for you." Abraham stood at the door, steady as always in his respectable black.

"From Mr. Donovan?" Viola took the note eagerly.

"No, ma'am. This was brought by one of the local children, not one of Mr. Donovan's men."

Viola frowned at the handwriting, a very ornate style she didn't recognize. Shrugging, she opened the missive and quickly deciphered its meaning. "Dear me, Mrs. Graham has taken a turn for the worse and asks me to attend her immediately."

"I'll accompany you, Mrs. Ross."

She cast a wary eye at the sky. It was almost pitch black to the west, promising a big storm. If they moved quickly, they could reach the Grahams before the rain started.

"Yes, of course." She smiled at him. "I'll fetch my new bonnet and we can be on our way." Her attire today was extremely respectable, in marked contrast to the previous night's: a pale blue walking dress of sturdy linen and a matching bonnet, both neatly trimmed in white and blue ribbon. Her underthings were also very conventional, of fine cambric with elegant blue ribbons and embroidery. Even Juliet would have been impressed.

Viola and Abraham hurried down the main street and into the general store. Mr. and Mrs. Graham lived above the store, and expected callers to confirm their welcome with Mr. Graham before proceeding upstairs.

The store was surprisingly quiet, without the usual leisurely shoppers or discussion of the latest betting craze. The walls were lined with shelves of bottled and canned goods. Display cases full of more expensive items like guns stood a few feet in front of the walls, intermixed with heavier worktables, with their storage space underneath.

There was no evidence of its proprietor at all, unless he was hiding under one of the worktables.

Viola revolved slowly, scanning the room, then spoke to Abraham. "Will you glance outside to see if you can see Mr. Graham? I'll look around in here a bit more."

"Very well, but stay within sight, Mrs. Ross."

"Of course." She turned to survey the side door, wondering what could have happened, as she brushed against a heavy worktable.

Suddenly a big hand clapped a wad of sickly sweet-smelling cloth over her nose and mouth, while simultaneously yanking her back against a stout body.

Dizzy from the overwhelming scent, Viola still drove her elbow back into the brute's belly. He grunted sharply but kept the cloth over her nose.

"Mrs. Ross!" Abraham shouted. Something crashed.

Viola felt her muscles waver and slacken as her vision blurred. Her attacker picked her up just as everything went black.

Viola awoke to an intense headache. Men's voices spoke over her head. She swallowed hard, fighting back nausea, and tried to guess where she was. She lay on a rocky floor, her hands tightly bound behind her back with coarse rope. Water trickled over the ground near her feet, which mercifully weren't tied.

She opened one eye cautiously, but shut it quickly when her head immediately protested.

"You two go back into the tunnel and keep watch for anyone coming this way," Lennox ordered. "Don't be too clever. Just make sure to warn me."

Lennox. Damn. It had to be him.

"Yes, sir." Footsteps thudded against the rock before fading away.

"Wake up, Mrs. Ross. We didn't use much chloroform, so I know you're alive."

Viola opened both eyes and stared stonily at her enemy. Her stomach objected but not as emphatically as before. "Mr. Lennox," she acknowledged.

"Welcome to the Mueller gold mine, Mrs. Ross," Lennox said jovially, stroking his muttonchops with his bandaged hand. "Magnificent, isn't it? I'll mine it after we're done here, of course."

"Indeed. How did you find it?" Viola slowly pulled herself into a sitting position and moved away from the water, especially where it disappeared into the floor. She refused to grovel on the floor like an earthworm in front of Lennox. She'd lost her bonnet at some point, but her clothes remained respectable, albeit sadly torn, rumpled, and smeared with dirt. At least they hadn't raped her while she was unconscious.

A more marked contrast to last night's delights with William could not have been imagined.

Lennox sat down on a rock facing her, with his lantern at his right, and rested his Colt on his thigh. He did not offer her any help as she sat up, but watched her coldly.

"The boys found an unknown old tunnel last week," he answered. "It had some odd quartz chips in the wall, almost like signs. They objected to exploring it, saying the rock was unstable, so I sent the O'Flahertys down. They found this cavern."

Viola sat down near the rock wall and forced her breathing to remain even. Lennox's lantern and a half dozen candles around the chamber provided more than adequate light to assess her situation. The cavern was shaped like an oval, with a deeper and darker pocket a few paces to her right. It was a very spacious cavern as these places went, probably hollowed out primarily by water. It was certainly a good deal larger than any underground space she'd worked while mining with Edward.

Some thick blue veins showed in the rock behind Lennox, making this a likely place to mine as long one was careful to avoid cave-ins.

Water oozed from the wall just to Lennox's left, and trickled across the floor between them before disappearing into a hollow by the wall to her left. It probably signaled instability in the rock. Unfortunately, the walls of this old mine weren't shored up with modern square sets, such as she knew the Golconda used.

Something scuttled at the edge of the light. Cave rats, no doubt. She'd spent enough time mining to know them as friends, albeit friends she preferred to keep at a distance.

Lennox lifted his Colt and casually fired a shot into the darkness. The sound reverberated through the rock.

Viola flinched and frantically looked for cover. Dear God, the fool could bring the cavern down around them with his shooting.

A small squeal, a very soft thud, and a dead cave rat rolled into the light just as a few rocks and dust dropped around Lennox.

"Hate those little bastards," Lennox mused as he cast an uneasy glance at the roof and shifted his seat closer to the lantern. "And there's not enough light in here to be rid of them."

Swallowing hard, she asked another question to buy time. "How did you know it was Mueller's?"

Lennox laughed. "Who else could it belong to, except the crazy German who was swept away by a flood? Besides, his camp is over there, about five feet to your right."

Viola peered more carefully into the pocket and repressed a shudder. Sleeping bag, fire pit with kettle hanging above—everything looked as if the owner had just stepped out.

Fire pit? She looked more closely at the candles. The one between her and Mueller's old camp was flickering erratically, unlike the one closest to Lennox. Boulders obscured that portion of wall, hiding any exits.

The original passage must be near that candle, given the breeze disturbing it. Perhaps she could make her way out, after she somehow got these ropes off her wrists.

She needed to escape quickly. The coming thunderstorm would be a bad one, possibly as big as what Mueller had died in.

This chamber could collapse at any time, especially if water burst through or if Lennox fired his revolver again. The confined space would amplify the effects of the gunshot, shaking the rock and possibly causing a cave-in.

"Have you recovered from the chloroform yet, my dear?" Lennox asked, in a neat mixture of solicitude and superiority. "In either event, let's discuss your situation."

Viola raised an eyebrow and waited, her fingers seeking the ropes around her wrists. Her stomach flopped again.

"You have two choices—marry me or die. Either one makes very little difference to me. If you die, I'll simply forge a wedding license and claim your money. But you'd be more comfortable if you lived."

"I am not rich," Viola objected. Dear God, he was willing to kill her? Ice washed over her.

Mercifully, the ropes weren't so tight as to stop all circulation in her hands. Her hands twisted faster, careful not to make any movements that would betray her to Lennox.

"Your grandmother left you a quarter of a million dollars."

"Dear heavens." Grandmother Lindsay dead? Sorrow flashed bright, only to be ruthlessly repressed for the moment. She'd mourn her favorite grandmother later.

Lennox must be speaking of Grandmother Lindsay's egg money, her famous store of small change to do whatever she wished with. Her sons had joked more than once that their mother knew more about the China Trade than any man.

"It should build me a very impressive mansion, don't you think?" Lennox smirked.

Something in Viola snapped at his continued assumption that she'd be a docile female. She'd been raised to meet that standard and her married life had centered around it. Only William enjoyed her unconventional side.

"No, I think it won't build you a mansion at all," Viola spat. "Now why don't you untie me and we'll forget about this little conversation?"

His eyes flashed. "Before you refuse me so quickly, Mrs. Ross," he snarled, "consider something else—your mother's activities during the recent unpleasantness."

Viola froze, terrified. Cold washed over her skin and she stopped plucking at the unyielding rope.

"Oh, Mrs. Ross, if you could see your face!" Lennox laughed triumphantly. "Yes, I know all about your mother's thousand rifles and how they went to Richmond."

He lingered over the last word. Viola shuddered but defiantly kept her eyes on him. A single rope end brushed her wrist.

"Richmond, the capitol of the late rebellion. A hanging offense, if there ever was one," he purred.

"No one will convict a woman of treason now, six years after the war's end," Viola asserted, angling her hands to catch the rope.

Lennox clucked his tongue. "The courts are too clumsy and slow for a matter like this, Mrs. Ross. No, I believe your mother's activities should first be discussed with her husband. After all, a man is responsible for his wife's behavior, is he not? I cannot imagine Captain Lindsay will take kindly to this news. And Hal Lindsay should also be informed, as the representative of the family's next generation," Lennox added.

Viola's stomach twisted into knots as the old nightmare reawakened. Dear God, she'd married once to hide Mother's treason; must she do so again?

The trickle across the floor had strengthened, causing a foot-wide stream to run across the cavern floor and disappear into the hollow, which was now a small pool. Water dripped from the ceiling.

"No," she managed as she wiggled away from the water. She would not yield to blackmail again. "No. Your choices are nonsense, sir, since Mr. Donovan will soon come for me."

"Ah, now that's where you truly misunderstand the situation. I have offered to sponsor Donovan's membership in the

Pericles Club, if he accepts our wedding. I see you understand how much he covets that social plum."

She knew precisely how much William hungered for society's acceptance. He needed his family to dine richly and in comfort at a great club, to guarantee they would never starve and die in a gale, as his mother and brother had.

She could see his plump wife now, with rubies gleaming around her throat, as he escorted her to dinner at the Pericles Club, while their four sons watched from his mansion's window.

Viola gritted her teeth.

But she had to believe in William. He'd given his word to her and he'd keep it. He had to.

Viola shook her head slowly. "He promised me he would protect me. He will come for me."

Chapter Sixteen

William whistled softly as he worked through his correspondence, preparing to send it off on the afternoon stage. It was bloody hard to think about stockpiles of axles in Santa Fe, though, when his body was still purring contentedly from last night. Viola had been so exquisitely beautiful in her abandonment to passion. He was damn proud he was the one who'd brought that expression to her face, that sated relaxation to every muscle in her body.

Perhaps they'd spend a quiet evening tonight and savor the trust built between them. Perhaps some music or poetry. Or perhaps he'd simply take her to bed.

He glanced up at the polite knock. "Enter."

"Letter for you, boss," Lowell announced. "Lennox's clerk just brought it. Shall I tell him to wait?"

William's eyebrow lifted. "Does he expect a reply?"

"Says it's up to you."

He turned the letter over in his hands, appreciating the envelope's high quality. It had the look of a formal invitation, something he'd rarely seen directed to him. "No, he can go," he answered absently.

He slit the envelope open with his penknife.

> *My very dear Mr. Donovan,*
> *I find myself lost in admiration for your high*

principles. I believe the Pericles Club would be honored by your membership and have taken the liberty of submitting your name for their consideration. Viola Ross is now my guest and I need hardly say that I'm certain you will wish us every success in our marriage.

Your humble servant,
Paul Lennox

Paul Lennox offered him membership in the Pericles Club if he would give up any claim to Viola?

William read the letter again without changing its meaning.

Viola Ross is now my guest, Lennox had said. Bloody damn, Lennox held Viola, and she must be terrified. If Paul Lennox was alive for another five minutes, it would be four minutes too long.

William dropped the letter on his desk, doused the lamp, and headed for the gun rack.

The door slammed open and a harsh voice interrupted his grab for a rifle. A big, blond Viking with dark blue eyes and a neatly trimmed goatee, in a black suit and duster, filled the doorway.

"You Donovan?"

"Aye."

The big Viking threw a punch with a ham-sized fist. William blocked it and the struggle began. William found himself fighting a man whose size and strength equaled his.

Normally he would have enjoyed a good fistfight but this was not the time for delay. He needed to reach Viola now. Crampton's table collapsed when he slammed the other man against it. The lamp and bottle of ink shattered when they hit the floor. A cloud of papers scattered across the room.

"Where's my sister, you bastard?" the Viking bellowed as he aimed a kick toward William's balls.

William dodged and kicked the other man in the shin, making him back off momentarily. Viola's brother.

"She's not here." He needed to end this.

"You're hiding her." The Viking charged him again.

William dodged, spun, and slotted his shoulder into his opponent's armpit, as his arm went around Lindsay's neck while his other hand slipped up the chest. With a sudden surge, William locked his hands together in a three-quarter nelson and flipped Lindsay onto the floor.

The big armchair crashed against the wall. An instant later, William landed on top of Lindsay. "Lennox has her."

To give him his due, the Viking simply snarled and tried to keep fighting.

William settled his full weight on Lindsay.

The Viking grunted, "Damn you."

"Listen to me, you fool," William gritted. "Lennox kidnapped Viola and I need to rescue her. We can fight later."

The big body stilled. "Lennox?"

"Letter's on the desk."

"If you're lying, I'll kill you."

"Fair enough." He released Viola's brother and backed away. The other gasped for air as he read the invitation.

Suddenly, the big alarm bell began to ring from his compound above.

William ran for the door, snatching up a rifle from the wall rack. He brushed past Lindsay without apology, but the man followed him quickly, picking up a Henry rifle that had been leaning against the wall outside.

Every man in the depot joined them in the yard, all armed and ready to fight. The sentries on the roofs facing the desert seemed bewildered as they looked in all directions. But the sentry facing the main street let out a long whistle.

"What is it?" William demanded.

"Abraham's fighting Lennox's thug just outside the general store, sir. There's no sign of Mrs. Ross."

"Jesus, Mary, and Joseph." William headed for the gate, Lindsay at his side and his men behind.

He reached the street in time to see a spectacular display of whirling kicks and blows as Abraham and the youngest O'Flaherty fought. Then Abraham kicked a gun out of O'Flaherty's hand. The weapon spun into the air and the young fool tried to catch it. It went off in his hands, sending a bullet through the thug's head. He collapsed into the street.

Abraham swayed, then grabbed a hitching post to steady himself as he stood on one foot. "Mr. Lennox and his men stole Mrs. Ross from Graham's store, sir. They took her back up the street but I didn't see their destination. I am deeply ashamed."

"You did very well for being outnumbered," William reassured him. "You okay?"

"Only a sprain, sir."

Still the alarm bell continued to ring, loud and clear above the stamp mill's din. Bloody hell, not an Indian attack, too.

People swarmed into the streets and boardwalks until they were full. Every man was armed, and most of their women, as well. The McBride brothers appeared together, guns ready. Even Mrs. Smith came running with a shotgun, followed by Lily Mae with a cleaver and the other girls with a startling assortment of firearms.

The bell stopped and its attendant sentry came to the watchtower's window nearest the street.

"What's the problem? Apaches?" William shouted. If it was, he'd have to go after Viola alone and leave his men to defend Rio Piedras.

"No, sir, no Indians. But Lennox and two of his thugs ran up the street from Graham's store into the Oriental's back room. One of them was carrying a woman with her head wrapped in a sack. Looked like Mrs. Ross's dress, from what I could see."

The crowd muttered and stirred.

"Kidnapping?" a woman gasped. "Mr. Lennox abducted Mrs. Ross?"

"Hanging's too good for the likes of him," a man snarled, and a chorus rose in agreement. Kidnapping a white woman was an unforgivable sin on this rough frontier.

Too icily calm to speak, William nodded at one of his teamsters, who promptly helped Abraham back to the compound. Another teamster headed for Graham's store.

Then he headed for the Oriental, Lindsay still close by his side. The townsfolk parted to let them pass, then fell in behind, guns at the ready.

Lightning cracked in the ominous skies above. The coming storm looked to be a gully-washer.

"He must be heading for the mine," the eldest McBride said suddenly, from just beyond Lindsay.

"What do you mean?" William asked without breaking stride.

"There's an old entrance there, from when the ore was closer to the surface."

"Can you guide me?"

"My pleasure."

They reached the Oriental just as the skies opened in a blinding torrent of rain.

William handed his rifle to one of his teamsters, wary of taking a long gun into a mine's confined spaces. "Take some men up to the Golconda's offices and make sure he doesn't slip out that way."

The normally quiet, ex-Union cavalryman nodded. "Glad to. Lennox has needed killing for a long time."

By unspoken agreement, all of the women headed for the mine's offices. William didn't envy any man who tried to stop them.

He glanced over at Lindsay. "Any problems with small spaces?" he asked the big man.

Lindsay shook his head as he checked his Henry rifle. "I served four years on Mississippi gunboats. Reckon a mine's a mite more spacious than they were."

William's mouth quirked. "Reckon it might be. Come on."

They burst into the Oriental's back room behind McBride, followed by his brothers and more men, and found a pair of solid wooden doors gracing the back wall beyond a large table.

McBride wrenched the doors open, grabbed a lamp from the table, and disappeared into the darkness beyond barely a step ahead of William.

The doors opened to a hole in the ground with a ladder disappearing into it. William climbed down it quickly and soon found himself in a small chamber, pitch-black except for McBride's lamp. He ducked to avoid a beam and stepped out of Lindsay's way as other men crowded in. His back rubbed against plank walls.

"Which way?" he asked McBride.

"Could have gone either direction. Most likely is to the right, toward the hoisting shaft and the offices. But . . ."

"You'd have gone to the left."

"Yes, sir. There's an abandoned tunnel we just found. If I was to hide anywhere, that's where I'd go."

"Then we'll go left with you. The others can split up to cover both directions."

Lindsay growled his agreement, hunching his big frame to fit between the heavy uprights. William smiled sympathetically, well aware he was doing the same thing. He'd been in many mines since he'd arrived in California but he'd never learned to enjoy them.

"Good idea. My brothers can lead the other party," the eldest McBride added.

A single clap of thunder sounded overhead, followed by heavy drops of rain.

"Lowell, you and the other teamsters stay with the miners and follow their lead. If they start running, you run, too, understand?" William said quietly.

Lowell looked around and caught sight of water trickling

between the planks beside him. He blanched and nodded. "Yes, sir."

"And don't use a gun. The sound alone could bring down the roof."

Lowell grimaced and holstered his revolver. "Yes, sir."

William clapped him on the arm, then followed McBride, with Lindsay a short step behind him, and then a dozen miners. The tunnel was level and almost straight here, with plank flooring underneath. The plank walls occasionally gave way to bare rock.

"Any suggestions for me?" Lindsay asked quietly. His rifle was now under his duster.

William glanced back at him, surprised.

Lindsay shrugged. "You're the local, not me. I'll learn from anyone."

"Ever been in a silver mine before?"

"Nope."

"The wooden timbers are called square sets. Six feet long, fourteen inches wide, mortise and tenon joints at both ends. Set them together and you have a fairly stable honeycomb to hold back the rock. Plank flooring underneath if there's another level below."

"What if it's not strong enough?" Lindsay questioned, quickly spotting the weakness.

"See the plank walls? That's where the rock is too unstable to be restrained by a single beam."

Lindsay grunted. "Most of the walls here are planks."

"Very unstable rock around here, especially when water's involved."

"Any advice?"

"Hear the rats? Some call them a miner's best friend because they hear the ground moving first. You hear them run, you run, too, as if the devil's at your heels."

"Aye aye, sir." Lindsay gave him a fast salute.

William's mouth quirked as he returned the gesture.

They moved cautiously through the tunnel for almost half an hour without encountering anyone else. The weight of the rock above seemed to press down on William, but he shook off the fancy.

Small streams and waterfalls flowed out of the walls in some places, raising William's hackles. Water could make rock slide like a child's sled on a snowy hill.

He stopped cold when they reached one chamber, staring at the ceiling. Wood creaked close by and small red eyes gleamed from the darkness. A foot-wide stream of water ran across the rocky floor.

McBride chuckled humorlessly when he followed William's eyes. "Aye, this is the new digging. You can tell by how few timbers that greedy bastard lets us use. Tregarron oversaw the work where we entered and it'll stand 'til Gabriel blows his horn. But this shoring?" He spat. The other miners murmured agreement.

William nodded. He'd never seen such light shoring to support a chamber this large. "Are we close to that abandoned tunnel?"

"That way, maybe twenty feet." He nodded toward an unsupported stretch of tunnel, clumsily hacked from the living rock. "Looks like someone's been down here in the last day or so, digging it out. Inexperienced, too, since they paid no heed to the lode."

"Then let's go."

Suddenly a dozen rats dashed between their feet and raced back down the tunnel toward the Oriental.

"Cave-in," said McBride softly. Miners shuffled their feet but stayed.

William snatched the lamp out of the man's hand. "You head back. I'll go on."

"Sure?"

Another rush of rats went past them. Miners started fading back toward the tunnel's stronger section.

"Run, boyo!"

"May all the saints be with you, Donovan!" And McBride left, running toward safety.

Carrying the single lamp, William and Lindsay sprinted toward the unsupported tunnel like men possessed.

Rock creaked and groaned. Water spilled out of the ceiling around them. Something snapped. A boulder rolled free from the wall, followed by another and another.

With a roar, the chamber collapsed on itself. Rocks tumbled from the ceiling behind William and Lindsay, spurring them to greater speed.

The cave-in stopped as suddenly as it had started. A small rock rolled into the tunnel and the dust settled sullenly, quickly turning into mud.

William turned a corner and slowed to a halt. He leaned against the wall, panting for breath. Lindsay followed his example in the turned house, where the tunnel made a sudden change in direction.

William said a silent prayer for the miners and crossed himself.

"Can we get back through there?" Lindsay asked, nodding toward the chamber behind them.

William shrugged and checked the tin of matches in his pocket. Still dry, so they'd have light as long as the lamp's oil lasted. "Maybe. It was a small cave-in, as they go. So if the rock didn't fill the chamber, you could reach the main tunnel."

"Have long have you known mines?"

"Sixteen years, since I came to California in '55."

Lindsay's eyes narrowed. "One of the vigilantes?"

"I helped clean up San Francisco, yes. More to the point, I helped Hearst haul the first load of silver ore out of the Comstock and over the Sierras to be assayed."

Lindsay grunted but asked nothing more.

The tunnel here was narrower and taller than an average mine tunnel, comfortable for a man to walk in but not a good match for square sets. William frowned and looked at the wall more closely. He ran his fingers along its face and then rubbed them together, testing the rock's consistency.

"What is it?"

"The tunnel before the turn was cut very recently, say, within the last week. But this side is much older, maybe ten years old, and it avoids the muck."

"Muck?"

William chuckled. "Silver ore can be hard rock or soft, in almost any color. It often appears as a clay that gums up your tools. We had worse names than muck for it, in the Sierras."

"What are you thinking?"

"There was a German named Mueller out here before the war, prospecting for gold. He was caught in a flash flood and drowned. But nobody ever found his camp."

"And?" Lindsay prompted.

"Suspicion was Mueller camped in a cave below ground, where it's cooler. This tunnel avoids the silver ore, like the blue muck here, so it might be his. Heard he was about my height, so this would be a comfortable tunnel for him."

"Viola could be in the cave."

"Yes."

"Let's go."

"Just remember—the more muck you see, the more unstable the rock is." William made one final test of the old family dirk up his sleeve.

"Bloody hell," Lindsay said with feeling, as he checked his own Bowie knife.

"Exactly."

Then the two men set off down the tunnel, moving as quietly as possible.

The tunnel's walls and floor were very uneven as it made frequent turns. Pockets sometimes opened on either side, while the ceiling would occasionally sweep up over their heads.

Echoes of a distant gunshot floated down the tunnel toward them. The two men froze and listened intently.

No further sound came.

The two men glanced at each other but there was no need to say anything. They moved ahead more quickly after that.

Rats faded away before them, moving leisurely and without fear.

William stopped abruptly at a different sound coming from ahead. A man shouting, and what seemed to be a woman's softer voice. A dim glow lit the tunnel.

"Viola," Lindsay whispered.

"And Lennox," William agreed, and doused the lamp. He freed his crucifix, kissed it, then tucked it back inside his shirt.

They traveled faster, while trying to stay as quiet as possible.

The wall opened up to the left, under William's fingers, and he followed it instinctively. The voices were stronger now. A breeze touched his face and shoulders, then a rush of air from above.

He flung himself forward just as a man dropped on him from a ledge. A knife sliced his jacket and skimmed his ribs. He twisted aside, driving back with his elbow. A grunt answered him, and his attacker moved away slightly before rushing him again.

He met the blow with his own knife, guided only by sound and instinct. It was a brutal, vicious fight there in the bowels of the earth.

Grunts and thuds came from behind them, then a hiss of pain. Lindsay must be fighting the other O'Flaherty.

William drove a knee into his opponent's belly. The man gasped and fled, his silhouette soon clear against the light.

Conall O'Flaherty.

William sprang for him.

Chapter Seventeen

Viola glared stonily back at Lennox. William would come for her. Somehow, someway, he'd keep his word.

The trickle had become a waterfall as it rushed down the wall between Lennox and Mueller's camp. The torrent raced across the floor to vanish in what was now a whirlpool, only a yard away from her feet. The water's noise drowned out any trace of the world beyond, including whatever the O'Flahertys might be doing.

Mueller's stool tilted and fell over, then was swept away. His sleeping roll began to slide. Water showered from the ceiling near the camp.

"So, Mrs. Ross, are you going to marry me or am I going to kill you?" Lennox growled, and aimed his gun at her.

"Fire that Colt again and you'll bring the roof down on both of us," Viola pointed out, keeping her chin high. She had a finger under the rope now. If she could make it slip down to the narrow part of her wrists, she should be able to free herself.

She arched her back slightly and pressed her elbows closer together to encourage the rope's movement. It would be easier if she could hunch her shoulders, but that was risky with Lennox watching her.

Suddenly a knot of fighting men tumbled into the cavern

from the tunnel beyond. Their struggle carried them to the torrent's brink.

Lennox sprang to his feet, spewing a long stream of vicious curses.

"William!" Viola shouted gladly and tried to rise.

William Donovan was fighting an O'Flaherty.

William had come for her, as he had promised.

Viola's heart soared. She rolled her shoulders and coaxed the stubborn ropes. If she could just break free, she could hit Lennox with a rock.

She didn't care whether she bashed him over the head with one or simply threw it at him. If she could play fetch with Mrs. Smith's guard dog, she'd kept enough of her childhood games to be effective.

Mueller's sleeping roll disappeared into the whirlpool. The muddy water ripped a boulder out of the wall and swallowed it in an instant. Water poured from the ceiling closer and closer to Lennox.

The whirlpool's edge brushed Viola's boot. She ignored it as she finally untied the first knot.

The two fighters broke free for a moment, with O'Flaherty on the torrent's edge. William was magnificent, all strong masculinity with his heaving chest and a long knife in his hand. His jacket's waist was stained a darker shade, but he didn't seem to be slowed by any injury.

Lennox's Colt remained steady on William. He cast an uneasy eye at the ceiling, but didn't fire.

"You're Donovan's brat, from County Cork, aren't you?" O'Flaherty spat, a heavy knife in his hand. "I remember those sniveling women and burning your pitiful cottage."

Viola hissed as she worked the ropes, pulling her feet back from the whirlpool. She couldn't take time now to move away from the water. O'Flaherty must be the blackguard who'd sent William's mother and family into the storm. She'd gut him herself if she had the chance.

The first loop slipped over her hands.

"And you'll die here for that, gombeen man," William spat.

O'Flaherty's face went white as he growled. The two men surged together like enraged bears.

"Damn you, O'Flaherty, kill him now!" Lennox screamed.

The ropes fell free from her wrists just as water lapped around her boots. Viola came to her feet and grabbed the nearest piece of silver ore that would fit her hand. A larger chunk crashed down where she'd been sitting and she moved closer to Mueller's camp.

The two fighters strained against each other.

Suddenly O'Flaherty stiffened.

"For my brother, who never drew breath," William spat as his knife hand twisted and shoved.

Shock, then comprehension, slid over O'Flaherty's face.

William wrenched his knife free and spun toward Lennox.

O'Flaherty crumpled to the ground and lay still, eyes staring vacantly at Lennox. The water swirled around his head and shoulders, then the corpse began to slide toward the whirlpool.

"You'll die for this, Donovan," Lennox roared.

Just then, another big man, bloody and filthy with a bandaged head, charged into the cavern from the tunnel and faced Lennox. His hair was blond where the water had washed some of the mud away, and he looked somehow familiar. He chuckled mirthlessly. "Remember me, Lennox? Or did you think you stopped me in Santa Fe?"

Lennox froze, eyes shifting uneasily between the two big men. "Are you going to let him attack me, Donovan? Only I can give you membership in the Pericles Club."

"Go to hell, gobshite," William snarled, and stepped forward. The newcomer chuckled, his big knife gleaming with blood, and did likewise.

Lennox's finger tightened on the trigger.

Viola threw her rock. It struck Lennox's shoulder just as he fired and sent him staggering into the waterfall behind him.

The gunshot was deafening in the small space. Echoes pounded the air, almost drowning out the water's noise.

For a moment, everyone stood still.

Then a chunk of silver ore crashed down on Lennox. He screamed and threw up his hands to protect himself. He caught a chunk of blue rock in both hands, straining to keep it away. Suddenly his wounded hand failed and the boulder crashed down on his head.

"No!" Lennox screamed, and crumpled to the floor. Another chunk and another, then a rain of silver ore covered his body. A candle sputtered briefly as it fell into the water, then went out.

"Viola!" William shoved his knife up his sleeve, then leaped the flood between them. He snatched her up in his arms and turned toward the tunnel that had brought him.

Viola clung to his shoulders as he cradled her in his arms, loving the feel of his strength and life around her.

A boulder rocked beside William, then slowly rolled toward the whirlpool, accompanied by two smaller brethren. Thunder called from the gap, where a candle had once flickered, as water began to rush in. A horde of rats rushed toward the new opening, clearly the shortest route to safety.

Viola's eyes met William's in perfect comprehension. Mueller's exit was reopening.

"Come with us!" William shouted.

Still carrying her, William followed the rats. Viola glanced over his shoulder and saw the other man charging after them, barely dodging the rocks falling all around him.

William surged up the incline and Viola gasped when he slipped in the running water. Boulders and rocks crumbled away on either side to roll into the cavern below. The noise of falling rock and thunder was deafening.

"I love you, William," Viola shouted into his ear.

He froze for a moment, then continued his fight to reach the outside. "Love you too, Viola," he panted. "If anything happens, I'll always love only you."

She gulped and kissed his shoulder in mute agreement. God would not be so cruel as to part them now.

As if their words were a passport, William's head and shoulders broke into the open. Moments later, he was running down the ridgeline toward Rio Piedras, dodging rocks and cactus as rain poured from the sky and lightning sparked the mountaintops.

The stranger caught up to them within a few steps. "Viola," he panted. "Thank God you're alive."

"Hal?" She stared in disbelief, then began to grin. The big nose, the pale blond hair, the blue eyes so like hers. It was her beloved brother.

"Dear brother, I'm so glad to see you again." She smiled at him but made no effort to leave William's arms. Staying with him was much more important than greeting even a long-lost sibling.

She looked back to see the ground shudder and heave. A shallow depression appeared where the cavern had once been.

"You could set me down," she suggested to William a few steps further.

"Hell no. Sweet Jesus, Viola, when I saw Lennox holding a gun on you . . ." He shuddered. "Just let me hold you for a while longer so I can believe you're alive."

Viola caressed his face reassuringly. "I'm fine, darling. He didn't hurt me."

He kissed her fingertips as he slowed to a more measured pace.

The rain stopped as suddenly as it had begun. Wisps of steam rose up from the ground and their clothing as they began to dry. The air held the sweet fragrance of freshly washed greenery.

William finally set her down as they entered Rio Piedras at

the upper end of Main Street. They walked into town hand in hand, with Hal on her other side.

Teamsters and miners rushed up to meet them. Townsfolk applauded. Lily Mae and Mrs. Smith, backed by her girls, cheered.

"Thank God you're safe," Lowell blurted.

"Ah, didn't I tell you, boyo, that St. Bridget looks after all Irish boys?" McBride chortled.

"Or the devil does," Lowell retorted, and everyone laughed.

Viola leaned against William and laughed with the rest of them.

"What happened?" Sally asked as she pushed through the crowd.

"Cave-in took out Mueller's old camp and Lennox, too. We escaped through the old exit, which reopened in the flash flood," William answered briefly, his eyes never leaving Viola.

Her clothes were muddy and damp and torn. Her hair hung in bedraggled tendrils around her face. But she'd never felt more beautiful in her life than when William grinned down at her.

She caught his face in her hands. "Mr. Donovan, will you marry me?"

He stared at her, his mouth open. Didn't he want to be with her?

Silence spread across the crowd. Even Sally was quiet as she strained to listen.

Viola started to stammer, "Of course, if there's somebody else . . ."

"Hell yes, I'll marry you!" William roared. He wrapped his arms around her and kissed her breathless.

When he finally lifted his head and she regained her wits, she found the crowd cheering. She blushed, but nodded and smiled.

"Viola," Hal hissed. She glanced at William, then followed

her brother to the boardwalk, away from the commotion in the middle of the street.

Hal took her hands in his big paws.

"You don't have to do this, Viola. You can come home. I swear I'll never tell the family what happened here."

"Hal, I don't care what they think. I hope you'll accept me as your sister. But even if you don't, I'll stay with William, where my heart is."

"If it's money . . ." Hal hesitated.

"It's not that—I know about Grandmother Lindsay's money. Please understand. I love him."

Hal nodded slowly. "He risked his life down there, so maybe he's worthy of you. But if he ever hurts you, you just let me know. I'll be glad to take care of him."

Viola threw her head back and laughed. Then she kissed her surprised brother on the cheek.

"Viola?" William asked from behind her.

"William." She turned. Thanks to the boardwalk, she nearly reached his shoulder. She walked her fingers up his chest and he watched her hands with a very bemused expression.

"Mr. Donovan, what would you say to a church wedding? Padre Francisco could marry us after the men return from Fort McMillan."

"A Catholic wedding? Do you understand what that means? There's no need for you to do that."

"Your sons need to be as Catholic as you are, Mr. Donovan." She drew out the syllables of his surname. "I intend to do my best to be a good mother to them, which means being part of your church."

William hugged her, shaking.

Chapter Eighteen

Viola waited patiently in the courtyard as Sarah fussed over her dress, while Abraham watched the time. It was a magnificent creation and she had no idea how the Chinese tailors had finished it so quickly. The gown was extremely fashionable, with its tight bodice and bustle above a sweeping skirt. More to the point, its white silk brocade and her crown and bouquet of yellow and white roses were the perfect reminder of William's faerie queen, as she'd requested.

She could hardly wait to see his reaction.

Church bells rang steadily from the Catholic church across the street, summoning the faithful. They'd invited everyone in Rio Piedras to the wedding, of course. Most of them wouldn't fit in the tiny building, but it should be a well-attended ceremony.

Lennox had been buried yesterday, after his body was finally uncovered. She hoped he found some peace in the afterlife.

Hal ran a finger around his collar yet again. Viola smiled privately. He'd been shocked at how well Abraham and his helpers had done his laundry and cleaned his effects. He'd even gone so far as to say he couldn't find better service in New York. Now he looked every inch the first-class riverboat pilot setting out to impress the world.

He'd restored to her the mourning brooch for the Commodore, which was now pinned at her waist. Around her throat hung the pearls he'd recovered in Colorado.

She wasn't optimistic enough to think Father and Mother would accept her marriage so easily. But frankly, she didn't much care what they thought, given how they'd hurt Hal. Mother's treason had risked Hal's life more than once. And she needed no contact with any man who'd caned his son as hard and as often as Father had.

Today, and for always, William was more important. She prayed again she'd be a good wife to him. Padre Francisco had been a great help during the past week, explaining in his careful English the details of marrying and raising a family in William's faith.

"Just think, Hal," she teased. "One day, you may be dressing for your own wedding."

He grimaced. "Never. There are more than enough Lindsays now, without my contributions. Father will simply have to look to his nephews for the next generation."

Viola raised an eyebrow. Sarah stopped straightening folds in the wedding dress's silk.

Hal had kept his aversion to doing anything that Father planned? Even children? "You might fall in love with someone and want to spend the rest of your life with her," she suggested mildly.

Hal snorted. "I'll never give Father the satisfaction of seeing me leg-shackled and breeding grandsons for him. Nothing's worth that."

"Be careful what you say. You might have to eat crow."

He shook his head. "No, not a chance."

"It's time, Mrs. Ross," Abraham announced, snapping his pocket watch shut. A rush of joy welled up in Viola's veins.

Sarah moved away from Viola and smiled at her. "Good luck, Mrs. Ross."

"Thank you, Sarah." She hugged her friend, then took Hal's arm. "Ready?"

"I've been ready for hours," Hal growled, and marched her off.

She smiled contentedly when they reached the little church, aglow with candles and roses now like an island of happiness. Our Lady of Guadalupe and St. Francis of Assisi seemed to smile from their niches. The Mexican band's trumpets, violins, and guitars struck up an excellent rendition of Mendelssohn's "Wedding March" as she started forward.

Every pew was filled to capacity, with guests standing along the walls and in the back. Mr. and Mrs. Graham watched from the first pew, while Mrs. Smith's best hat bobbed in the back beside Lily Mae's bonnet. Carson and Lowell sat next to the McBride brothers, and cavalry officers made a brave show in their blue uniforms. William's men had returned earlier than expected from Fort McMillan, without the loss of a single man or mule. Still more people gathered outside.

She saw William the moment she entered, gorgeous in a superb black suit, not withstanding his fading black eye. His eyes blazed and he smiled at her tenderly.

She had never bothered to ask either Hal or William where they had each gained those black eyes. It was enough that they respected each other. And what a relief for William to have Evans standing by his side.

Abraham and Sarah slipped in from the side door, Abraham moving better and better on his sprained ankle.

This wedding was so utterly different from her first, conducted by a justice of the peace—and drinking buddy of Edward's—in his front parlor.

Her heart lit with joy at the sight of William. She tugged Hal down the aisle, moving faster and faster until she was almost running by the time she reached her lover. Soft laughter rippled across the church and even Padre Francisco seemed amused. She didn't care what they thought, not if William was happy.

Hal gave her hand to William after a single exchange of very masculine glances. She'd eavesdropped on their conversation the night before about what Hal would and would not tolerate in Viola's husband. Since William intended to fulfill all of his expectations, and more, the two men had actually found themselves in agreement, something that was occurring more and more often.

She was quite content the two men had settled their differences themselves, without her involvement. She might have been driven to mention how much fun she and William shared in private, especially since she'd flatly refused William's nonsensical suggestion that they sleep apart before the wedding.

William accepted Viola's hand and turned to face the altar. Padre Francisco began the ceremony as William and Viola sank to their knees. Viola said a quick prayer privately, of thanks for finding William and hope she'd be a good wife to him.

The Latin words wrapped their magic around both of them. Viola tried hard to follow along, grateful for sharing Hal's Latin lessons long ago.

They both made their responses loudly, William's voice a little hoarse but steady as his blue eyes glowed. Viola's voice was loud and clear and her eyes only a little blurred by tears of joy.

Her happiness burned through every cell in her body when he placed the heavy gold band on her finger. In sheer joy, she caressed his fingers quickly after sliding the matching ring on his hand. He caught her hand in a quick, loving grip and they smiled at each other.

Padre Francisco said a few more words, and William kissed her reverently as she lightly caressed his shoulder.

Finally the nuptial mass ended with Padre Francisco's benediction, using the Irish blessing William had requested. They rose to face their friends and neighbors, both of them grinning like idiots.

Lowell shouted, "Isn't somebody going to really kiss the bride?"

Viola laughed and turned to William. He tilted her chin up

and kissed her sweetly, which seemed a fair start for their life together. She threw her arms up around his neck and melted against him. He immediately crushed her close and kissed the breath out of her, his cock swelling against her in promise.

She was flushed and sparkling when he finally released her. She could have flown like one of the angels over the altar, now that she was married to him. Their audience filled the air with whoops and cheers as he ran her down the aisle and outside.

They made their way down to the depot, followed by their guests, and settled in for a huge celebration. William had provided all the food and drink, plus the excellent local Mexican band. He'd offered up a season's supplies for the depot, including some popular—and rare—hams, plus all of the Oriental's wines and liquors.

Teamsters and miners, shopkeepers and Mexicans mixed freely as they celebrated. Sheriff Lloyd, of course, ate and drank a great deal. But Carson and the McBride brothers had formed a corps of "honorary sheriffs" to keep the peace tonight.

William and Viola confined themselves to drinking lemonade, while the others enjoyed champagne and beer. Viola blinked when she saw two full tables of teamsters drinking lemonade. "William, did your men take a temperance pledge?"

He followed her gaze and chuckled. "No, not them. They haven't done their time as sentries yet. They'll make up for lost time after they've done their two-hour tour."

"Good. I want *everyone* to have fun tonight."

William growled softly at her words, eyes alight with carnal intent. He tilted her chin up with a single finger and kissed her, heedless of their audience.

She grinned like a fool when he stopped and rested her hand on his thigh, enjoying his heat and strength.

She wasn't bold enough to caress his cock at a public gathering, even under the table. Perhaps someday, after they'd been married for a few years.

As the light began to fade, Chinese lanterns were lit. Ah Lum and his friends performed a lion dance, accompanied by the loud clanging of drums, cymbals, and gongs.

Then the Mexican band appeared and European-style dancing began. William led Viola out for their first dance together, a waltz. He gazed down at her as if she were a goddess to be mounted on a pedestal.

"Don't look at me like that," she whispered, "or I'll beg you to take me home, just to show you I'm not made of glass."

"Wait fifteen minutes, until after the fireworks."

China Mary had promised a magnificent display as her present. It was every bit of that and more, but still far too long for Viola's taste.

She was more than eager by the time they slipped up the stairs to the compound an hour later. The central courtyard was quiet now except for the fountain's murmur and some sleepy clucking by the hens.

Viola wrapped her arms around William and hugged him. He kissed the top of her head and she clung closer, savoring the feel of him in her arms. Her man, her lover, her husband.

"Let's go to bed, Mrs. Donovan," he murmured.

"Oh yes, please."

He swept her up in his arms and kissed her patiently, then kicked open the door to their bedroom. William stopped cold, just shy of crossing the threshold.

"What the devil? This is not what I ordered," he growled.

She blinked at the condition of his bedroom. It now contained only a small iron bed, Evans's bed, most likely. No chair, no chest, no rug, just the one bed. It could probably accommodate William, but hardly the two of them together.

Then a strange noise caught her attention from the street beyond the compound: shouting, whistles, and discordant banging. "What the hell?" he murmured, and turned toward the door.

A shivaree? Viola listened for a moment longer and heard Hal's deep voice mixed with the others. Oh yes, definitely a community gathering. She whooped softly, happily, and pulled free of William's arms to run into the bedroom. She bounced onto the bed, still fully dressed and holding her bouquet.

William stared at her, speechless for once.

"They're giving us a true shivaree, William. Quick, get in the bed. Oh, William, I always wanted a big celebration for my wedding. And a shivaree will be wonderful."

William shook his head to clear it from shock. Then he sat down and wrapped his arm around her. He'd seen shivarees but never thought to be the subject of one, since the match had to be so well accepted by the townsfolk. It was one thing to eat and drink what he had provided, but something totally different for his neighbors to publicly display their affection and approval.

Sure enough, the noise grew and focused on the compound. It streamed into the courtyard until William could barely hear himself think. Old kettles were banged, while the band's trumpets bellowed loudly in an attempt at "The Yellow Rose of Texas."

Then Morgan and Hal appeared at the door, with Carson and Lowell behind them. Remarkably steady despite the champagne he'd consumed, Hal bowed low and announced, "My dear brother and sister, you must come out to greet your friends."

Viola giggled and put her hand over her mouth. William laughed and hugged her closer. "Brothers, do your worst."

Each man took a corner of the bed. Hal chanted, "One, two, three, and up!"

And the bed rose off the ground with only the slightest jerk. The four men somehow moved it outdoors where others crowded around, lifting the bed onto their shoulders like a maharaja's palanquin. Cheers rose, and the music, if one could call it that, started again.

They were carried onto Main Street while the crowd sang "She'll Be Coming 'Round the Mountain." The townsfolk happily paraded them up the street to the mine, then back down to the depot, all the while singing and banging on a strange mélange of instruments. Kettles, shovels, tongs, and spoons all played a part. Somewhere in the background, Mexican trumpets blared and Chinese whistles wailed.

There were so many willing helpers that the bed usually seemed more of a flying carpet than an iron contraption. The greatest danger to Viola was being bounced off, as friends jostled each other in their eagerness to help.

Hal and Morgan were gradually edged out, but returned with kettles to join the serenade.

And Viola leaned against her husband and chuckled happily. William held her close, lest one of the bearers slip, and enjoyed his neighbors' approval. He also glared at any man foolish enough to try to touch her.

The mob finally returned them to the compound's entrance and hesitated, wavering a bit.

"Dear friends," Viola shouted. "What shall I do with these flowers?"

"Throw them!" "Here!" "To me!" "Over yonder!" were some of the cries that went up in response.

The bed lurched, and William tightened his grip on his wife as some men tried to point to where they thought her bouquet should go. By general agreement, the bed was placed on the ground and the bearers moved away to see the toss.

"Help me up, please," Viola hissed.

William's eyebrow lifted in surprise, then he helped her stand up on the bed. She measured the crowd around them while still more suggestions arose. Then she threw the bouquet down the street, straight at the furthest unmarried woman.

A roar went up. "Who's going to marry her, boys?" someone shouted.

"You lads can settle that. Who wants to dance?" Morgan shouted in answer.

The crowd shouted its approval and surged toward the depot. William jumped off the bed, snatched Viola into his arms, and escaped into the compound before anyone could change their minds about resuming the shivaree. Much as they'd both enjoyed that foolishness, he needed to be someplace private with his wife.

A few laggards hooted their approval as he kicked his front door shut.

Viola giggled and laid her head against his shoulder, the roses tickling his cheek. "Don't you want to invite them?" she teased.

"No, they can find their own women. Enough is enough, wife. Society's approval is all well and good but, dammit, not always necessary."

He captured her mouth in a hard kiss. She sighed her agreement, her nipples urgent buds as she shifted to move closer.

He shouldered his bedroom door open, a little uncertain as to what he might find. But this time the setting was perfect. His furniture stood where it should and candles blazed from every surface. The bed was covered in rose petals, with more scattered over the Persian rugs. Sheaves of corn decorated each post, in echo of the old Irish fertility custom.

"Oh, William, it's beautiful," Viola breathed.

"A bower for my beloved faerie queen. I swear I'll do my utmost to make you happy."

"Just love me always, as I'll love you, *mo mhùirnìn,*" Viola whispered.

William's heart stopped beating. She'd even reached out beyond the bounds of English for him. "You speak Gaelic now?"

"Just a little. McBride translated a few words for me, such as darling." She flushed adorably, her deep blue eyes enormous. "I enjoy hearing you speak that language and I hope you'll say more if I encourage you. Perhaps one day we can share it with our sons."

"*Mo bhean,* my wife, you are too good for me." He kissed her forehead gently, shaking a little. "I love you."

She caressed his cheek gently and traced his jawline. Her fingers slipped lower and stroked his throat, just above his stiff white collar. "*Mo cridhe.* You truly are my heart."

He kissed her again and set her down on the bed. He leaned over her and traced her face below her silver-gilt hair and crown of roses. Her enormous indigo-blue eyes, features as clear and pure as a faerie maiden's, supple lips that so eagerly welcomed his mouth, or any other portion of his anatomy.

He explored her with his lips, worshipping her wordlessly. He kissed and laved her ear, then the sensitive spot just below on her neck. He lingered there, awakening her senses in the fashion she enjoyed so well. A little scrape of his teeth over her pulse caused her to moan his name as her arms came up to welcome him.

His hand curved over her breasts as he returned to her ear. She shuddered and shifted under him, lifting up to meet his caresses. Her breasts firmed and her nipples hardened under the rich cloth.

His breathing became harsher as his own nipples stiffened in response. "*Mo mhùirnìn,*" he growled as his rough finger slipped under her dress to find her skin's silk.

"William," she gasped. Her fingers threaded into his hair as her breathing became ragged.

He shivered and returned to her mouth. Long moments passed before his fingers returned to her clothing. Then he undressed her with all the expertise he'd gained in a lifetime without her, the skills that would now be bent toward her alone. He removed her garments smoothly, far more interested in the woman he explored and pleasured than the outer shell demanded by society.

She groaned, her little cries telling him how much she enjoyed his attentions. Rich blood colored her breasts, speaking clearly of her carnal excitement.

His mouth lingered there for a long while, tracing every muscle and vein. Her nipples bloomed for him and he rewarded them, licking and nibbling. Finally he suckled her, using the deep pulls she so loved.

She arched off the bed convulsively and sobbed his name. He repeated the caress over and over again, his hand fondling her other breast in the same rhythm. He switched sides, making sure he incited both equally. She shuddered and moaned, then found a peak of rapture.

William smiled quietly, triumphantly. He'd be happy to feed her delight for years to come. Sarah could be correct, that Viola only needed to add a few pounds in order to gain the strength to conceive children. But he was in no hurry to see that happen. He'd rather have her than risk her life for a houseful of sons or daughters.

He eased her wedding dress off and tossed it carelessly onto the chair.

Viola murmured something, likely an objection.

He nuzzled her sweet shoulder, then asked, "Did you say something, sweetheart?"

"Nothing of importance," she sighed and ran her hands down his back. "Except, perhaps, you seem to be over-dressed for this occasion."

He rumbled his appreciation of her hint and stood up to discard his clothes as rapidly as possible. A small hand fondled his ass when he bent to step out of his trousers.

William looked over his shoulder at her quizzically. "Yes, wife?"

She blushed and smiled, the image of demureness except for her fingers' boldness. "Just inspecting my new property, husband. It's remarkably fine."

He threw back his head and laughed. "I'm glad to hear it receives your approval, sweetheart."

Seconds later, he faced her without a stitch on. "Still satisfactory, wife?"

"Very much so. Very much indeed." She rested her hand on his belly, then delicately slid her fingers up the thin line of hair to his chest.

His cock, already erect, jerked and grew still more. A single drop glistened on its tip, then slid down toward his aching balls. He sucked in his breath.

She purred and kissed his hip. "Beautiful."

"Temptress," he retorted, and automatically started to reach for a condom.

Then he froze, shocked by a new idea: he had no need for any of those tonight. For the first time in his life, his cock would feel a woman's pussy and not a man-made contraption designed to prevent pregnancy and disease.

"What is it?" Viola whispered. "Why did you stop?"

"I don't need a condom." His voice was rough and his hands shook slightly.

She frowned. "I don't understand."

"My cock has never touched a woman's pussy before. There's always been a condom over it."

"I'm your first?"

He nodded. "Perhaps I'm the virgin tonight."

She blinked, then smiled slowly. Female triumph lit her eyes. "Oh, *mo mhùirnìn,* tonight is the beginning of both our lives. And you are taking entirely too much time."

He chuckled hoarsely as he rejoined her on the bed. He moved faster this time to remove her clothes until she could meet him, bare skin to bare skin. Their mouths fused as his hand delved between her legs.

She was rich with dew, her sweet folds gliding over his fingers. Her clit stood proudly free of its hood, and ripe for carnal fulfillment as her musk scented the air. He tested her opening with one finger, then two, then three.

His balls were heavy, aching for her warmth. His skin was hot and tight, as if desperate to burst.

Viola shuddered with eagerness as her channel quivered. The hard peaks of her nipples stabbed his chest.

He took his cock in a shaking hand and brought it to her. He growled as her wetness flowed over him and seeped into his pores. Words utterly failed him.

He rubbed himself over her pussy, as his most sensitive flesh discovered every contour and texture of her. His cock swelled and his balls tightened further until he thought the feel of her would drive him insane.

She moaned and her head fell back. Her body writhed as her hips circled, seeking to bring him closer.

He entered her slowly, shuddering as he fought for discipline. Some distant corner of his brain suggested he should take his time and explore every nuance of her sweet pussy. But the pulse building at the base of his spine and in his cock was more urgent and demanding.

"William, ah, dear heart," she groaned.

"Dear God, Viola," he growled at the needy sound of her voice. His control snapped and he roared his intense pleasure as his cock surged into her. He lay still for a short moment, with every fraction of his cock tightly embraced by her hot channel, and a few shudders rising up his body from where they were joined. He'd never felt the kiss of a woman's pussy hair against his balls like this, without a ribbon or condom between them.

"*Mo cheannsa,*" he groaned, a statement of possession and love for all eternity.

Then his hips began to move.

He rode her with the passion of a lifetime, driving in and out of her like a madman. Blood pounded through him as its beat echoed in bone and sinew.

She wrapped herself around him with her legs snug around her hips. She sobbed and gasped and arched into his every movement. Her pussy stretched to hold him as it overflowed with dew in welcome. The muscles he'd trained tightened around his cock on every thrust. Wet slaps echoed through the room as their bodies worked together.

Viola clawed his back as she surged up against him. She keened her pleasure as rapture burst through her. Her pussy rippled and convulsed around him.

Her ecstasy ripped him free of his last tie to earth.

Orgasm shot through his cock and up his spine, shaking him until he went blind from wonder. He howled in ecstasy as he poured his seed into her.

Sometime later, he woke enough to pull a sheet over them both. She muttered and buried her face against his chest, rejecting any reminder of the outside world.

He kissed the top of her head. "Love you, wife."

"Love you, too, husband."

Author's Note

Fort McMillan, the Golconda Mine in Arizona, and the town of Rio Piedras are entirely fictional creations, although I have tried to be as accurate as possible. All errors are strictly my doing.

A list of textual sources is available on my website at www.dianewhiteside.com.

We don't think you will want to miss Lori Foster's
JUST A HINT—CLINT,
coming in September 2004 from Brava.
Here's a sneak peek.

A bead of sweat took a slow path down his throat and into the neckline of his dark T-shirt. Pushed by a hot, insubstantial breeze, a weed brushed his cheek.

Clint never moved.

Through the shifting shadows of the pulled blinds, he could detect activity in the small cabin. The low drone of voices filtered out of the screen door, but Clint couldn't make out any of the slurred conversation.

Next to him, Red stirred. In little more than a breath of sound, he said, "Fuck, I hate waiting."

Wary of a trap, Clint wanted the entire area checked. Mojo chose that moment to slip silently into the grass beside them. He'd done a surveillance of the cabin, the surrounding grounds, and had probably gotten a good peek in the back window. Mojo could be invisible and eerily silent when he chose.

"All's clear."

Something tightened inside Clint. "She in there?"

"Alive but pissed off and real scared." Mojo's obsidian eyes narrowed. "Four men. They've got her tied up."

Clint silently worked his jaw, fighting for his famed icy control. The entire situation was bizarre. How was it Asa knew where to find the men, yet they didn't appear to expect an interruption? Had Robert deliberately fed the info to Asa, to embroil him in a trap, so Clint would kill him? And why would Robert want Asa dead?

Somehow, both he and Julie Rose were pawns. But for what purpose?

Clint's rage grew, clawing to be freed, making his stomach pitch with the violent need to act. "They're armed?"

Mojo nodded with evil delight. "And on their way out."

Given that a small bonfire lit the clearing in front of the cabin, Clint wasn't surprised that they would venture outside. The hunting cabin was deep into the hills, mostly surrounded by thick woods. Obviously, the kidnappers felt confident in their seclusion.

He'd have found them eventually, Clint thought, but Asa's tip had proved invaluable. And a bit too fucking timely.

So far, nothing added up, and that made him more cautious than anything else could have.

He'd work it out as they went along. The drive had cost them two hours, with another hour crawling through the woods. But now he had them.

He had *her*.

The cabin door opened and two men stumbled out under the glare of a yellow bug light. One wore jeans and an unbuttoned shirt, the other was shirtless, showing off a variety of tattoos on his skinny chest. They looked youngish and drunk and stupid. They looked cruel.

Raucous laughter echoed around the small clearing, disturbed only by a feminine voice, shrill with fear and anger, as two other men dragged Julie Rose outside.

She wasn't crying.

No sir. Julie Rose was complaining.

Her torn school dress hung off her right shoulder nearly to her waist, displaying one small pale breast. She struggled against hard hands and deliberate roughness until she was shoved, landing on her right hip in the barren area in front of the house. With her hands tied behind her back, she had no way to brace herself. She fell flat, but quickly struggled into a sitting position.

The glow of the bonfire reflected on her bruised, dirty face—and in her furious eyes. She was frightened, but she was also livid.

"I think we should finish stripping her," one of the men said.

Julie's bare feet peddled against the uneven ground as she tried to move farther away.

The men laughed some more and the one who'd spoken went onto his haunches in front of her. He caught her bare ankle, immobilizing her.

"Not too much longer, bitch. Morning'll be here before you know it." He stroked her leg, up to her knee, higher. "I bet you're getting anxious, huh?"

Her chest heaved, her lips quivered.

She spit on him.

Clint was on his feet in an instant, striding into the clearing before Mojo's or Red's hissed curses could register. The four men, standing in a cluster, turned to look at him with various expressions of astonishment, confusion and horror. They were slow to react, and Clint realized they were more than a little drunk. Idiots.

One of the young fools reached behind his back.

"*You.*" Clint stabbed him with a fast lethal look while keeping his long, ground-eating pace to Julie. "Touch that weapon and I'll break your leg."

The guy blanched—and promptly dropped his hands.

Clint didn't think of anything other than his need to get between Julie and the most immediate threat. But without giving it conscious thought, he knew that Mojo and Red would back him up. If any guns were drawn, theirs would fire first.

The man who'd been abusing Julie snorted in disdain at the interference. He took a step forward, saying, "Just who the hell do you think you—"

Reflexes on automatic, Clint pivoted slightly to the side

and kicked out hard and fast. The force of his boot heel caught the man on the chin with sickening impact. He sprawled flat with a raw groan that dwindled into blackness. He didn't move.

Another man leaped forward. Clint stepped to the side, and like clockwork, kicked out a knee. The obscene sounds of breaking bone and cartilage and the accompanying scream of pain split the night, sending nocturnal creatures to scurry through the leaves.

Clint glanced at Julie's white face, saw she was frozen in shock and headed toward the two remaining men. Eyes wide, they started to back up, and Clint curled his mouth into the semblance of a smile. "I don't think so."

A gun was finally drawn, but not in time to be fired. Clint grabbed the man's wrist and twisted up and back. Still holding him, Clint pulled him forward and into a solid punch to the stomach. Without breath, the painful shouts ended real quick. The second Clint released him, the man turned to hobble into the woods. Clint didn't want to, but he let him go.

Robert Burns had said not to bring anyone in. He couldn't see committing random murder, and that's what it'd be if he started breaking heads now. But in an effort to protect Julie Rose and her apparently already tattered reputation, he wouldn't turn them over to the law either.

Just letting them go stuck in his craw, and Clint, fed up, ready to end it, turned to the fourth man. He threw a punch to the throat and jaw, then watched the guy crumble to his knees, then to his face, wheezing for breath.

Behind Clint, Red's dry tone intruded. "Well, that was efficient."

Clint struggled with himself for only an instant before realizing there was no one left to fight. He turned, saw Julie Rose held in wide-eyed horror, and he jerked. Mojo stepped back out of the way, and Clint lurched to the bushes.

Anger turned to acid in his gut.

Typically, at least for Clint Evans and his weak-ass stomach, he puked.

Please turn the page for an exciting
preview of Erin McCarthy's
HOUSTON, WE HAVE A PROBLEM.
Also available in September 2004 from Brava.

Josie Adkins had to stop waving her hot little ass in Houston's face, or he was going to have to slide his hands across it and squeeze.

Which would fall squarely under the heading of sexual harassment. He could see the headline. *State of Florida vs. Dr. Houston Hayes. Surgeon fondles resident and loses license.*

Sweet little Josie had no idea he was plotting ways to lick her like a cat does cream. She wasn't tempting him with her curvy behind on purpose, so he couldn't really blame her for the detour his thoughts had been taking on a regular basis.

But just how in the hell an orthopedic surgeon could be so damn clumsy was beyond him. And Jesus, was Josie clumsy.

So clumsy that at least six times a day he was subjected to the sight of her bent full over at the waist retrieving something from the floor she had dropped. Today was even worse.

They were alone in a semi-dark alcove, for the purpose of looking at a patient's X-ray, only Josie had done her usual butter-finger bit.

The film Jose had been holding had slipped out of her hand, hit the floor, and disappeared under the desk next to her. She was now on her hands and knees, wiggling around searching for it.

God help him.

No one with a body that lush and womanly should be wiggling on her hands and knees unless she was naked and it was part of foreplay.

"Whoops. It just jumped right out of my hand, Dr. Hayes," she said, in a cheerful voice.

Houston counted from one to ten and back again until he was in control of himself and his bodily urges. He didn't know what it was about her that had him hiding hard-ons left and right and sweating through three pairs of surgical scrubs a day.

She wasn't his type at all. She was on the short side, with an odd haircut that made her light brown hair flip around at gravity defying angles. When she smiled, twin dimples appeared and she looked about twenty years old. She talked constantly. He had heard other staff members affectionately refer to her as a dingbat.

Yet here he was, unable to look away, all too aware that her scrubs were worn thin in strategic places.

"It has to be here somewhere." She chattered on, her head half under the desk.

"What the . . . ?"

As she pulled her hand back, Houston saw she was holding a crust of moldy bread.

"Gross." She flung it down.

Time to leave a note for housekeeping.

Josie disappeared back under the desk, at least the front half.

The back half was still in full view.

He could see her underwear.

The thin scrubs hid nothing, and the position she was in on her knees pulled them taut, giving him a clear view of her panties. They were riding up just a little, sliding into the crevice between her cheeks, fitting close and tight. There was a little red lip print stamped on each side of her panties, and he wondered what she would do if he leaned forward and laced his own mouth right on one of those lip prints.

And bit her.

He was fascinated by the full curviness of her behind, and ached all over from the desire to taste her, to cup his hand between her legs and feel her heat pulsing through his fingers.

He wanted to know if there was a matching lip print on the front of her panties. So that if he kissed it he would feel her soft dewy mound give a little beneath his mouth.

It seriously annoyed him, this edgy uncontrollable desire.

Houston had never had a problem maintaining his professional distance with both patients and coworkers. If anything he had been accused of being too reserved. Now this one woman, this tiny tornado of smiles and klutziness, had successfully breeched his aloofness.

Impatient with his thoughts, he glanced at his watch. How long had she been on the floor? It felt like hours.

"Do I need to come back, Dr. Adkins, when you can make your X-ray films behave?" Visions of making her behave with his hand on her soft bottom flitted through his mind, playing like a porno video. He had meant it to sound like a cool rebuke, but came out sounding suggestive.

Either of which seemed too subtle for Josie. She laughed from under the desk, like he was simply teasing her, then gave a little cough.

"Yuck, I think I inhaled a dust bunny."

Her head reemerged long enough to smile at him in reassurance. "Just give me a sec. I'll get it."

"Really, we can do this later." Since he had learned just about nothing could hurry her up.

Of course, he could brush her aside and get the damn thing himself. But he didn't want to hurt her feelings. Josie always tried so hard to gloss over her gaffes. Plus he was a total masochist who didn't want to deny himself the glorious view of her backside, even though he knew he couldn't, shouldn't, *wouldn't* act on his lust.

So Houston resented the distraction and cursed himself, but still couldn't tear his eyes away from her, not even long enough to pick up the X-ray himself.

"Almost got it." She gave him another blinding smile, head cocked to the right as she stretched her hand a little farther.

He put his hands on his hips and reminded himself, again, that getting involved with a resident would be a complete nightmare, no matter how freaking adorable she was.

"I need one of those rubber arms, like Stretch Armstrong, that real weird doll my cousin had when we were kids. Remember that?" she asked him.

He shook his head. Rubber dolls were the least of his problems right now.

"Well, it was kind of cool, in a bizarre sort of way, kind of like molded silly putty. What did you play with?"

Her eyes widened a little, and Houston fought the urge to moan. Josie managed to mix innocence with that lush body, all tossed alongside her brains and her quirky personality. It was an unusual combination he was finding damn hard to resist.

Especially in this room that wasn't really a room, but a very small, very crowded alcove cut out of a corner in the hallway. Where Josie was just inches away from him.

"When you were a kid, I mean, what did you play with?" She kept feeling around on the floor. "Risk? World domination seems like your thing."

Should he be offended? "No."

"So what then? Nerf football? Twister? Chess club?"

He folded his arms and rubbed his chin. He'd forgotten to shave that morning and the stubble was irritating and itchy. He was well aware that if another coworker had engaged in this ridiculous conversation with him he would have walked away.

"I played doctor." Let her figure out exactly what he meant by that. Except that Josie seemed immune to sexual innuendos.

"Here it is!" She pulled the film out and handed it to him.